GW01458064

BIG GAME HUNTING AND COLLECTING IN EAST AFRICA

A YOUNG RHINO, TWO DAYS AFTER CAPTURE

Frontispiece.

BIG GAME HUNTING AND COLLECTING IN EAST AFRICA

1903-1926

BY

KÁLMÁN KITTENBERGER

WITH 200 ILLUSTRATIONS

FROM PETER CAPSTICK'S LIBRARY

ST. MARTIN'S PRESS

NEW YORK

To the Reader:

The editors and publishers of the Peter Capstick Adventure Library faced significant responsibilities in the faithful reprinting of Africa's great hunting books of long ago. Essentially, they saw the need for each text to reflect to the letter the original work, nothing having been added or expunged, if it was to give the reader an authentic view of another age and another world.

In deciding that historical veracity and honesty were the first considerations, they realized that it meant retaining many distasteful racial and ethnic terms to be found in these old classics. The firm of St. Martin's Press, Inc., therefore wishes to make it very clear that it disassociates itself and its employees from the abhorrent racial-ethnic attitudes of the past which may be found in these books.

History is the often unpleasant record of the way things actually were, not the way they should have been. Despite the fact that we have no sympathy with the prejudices of decades past, we feel it better—and indeed, our collective responsibility—not to change the unfortunate facts that were.

—Peter Hathaway Capstick

Translated from Hungarian

BIG GAME HUNTING AND COLLECTING IN EAST AFRICA, 1903-1926. Copyright © 1989 by Peter Hathaway Capstick. All rights reserved. Printed in the United States of America. No part of this book may be used or reproduced in any manner whatsoever without written permission except in the case of brief quotations embodied in critical articles or reviews. For information, address St. Martin's Press, 175 Fifth Avenue, New York, N.Y. 10010.

Library of Congress Cataloging-in-Publication Data

Kittenberger, Kálmán.
    Big game hunting and collecting in East Africa, 1903–1926 / Kálmán
Kittenberger.
          p.   cm.
    ISBN 0-312-03294-3
    1. Big game hunting—Africa, East—History. 2. Wild animal
collecting—Africa, East—History. I. Title.
SK255.E27K57 1989
799.2'6'09676—dc20   89-30424
                                                CIP

First U.S. Edition

10 9 8 7 6 5 4 3 2 1

EDITOR'S NOTE TO
THE REPRINT EDITION

IT was a lovely morning on the slopes of Mt. Kilima Njaro, the early equatorial sun of German East Africa catching the dew on the long lion grass and beading it with rare gems of liquid light.

The bright, pulsing spray of arterial blood from the small man's arm added a gleaming, ruby brilliance as he staggered to his feet, inches from the body of the dead lion. Lurching away in a wide swathe of gore, he thoughtfully fumbled his handkerchief in a rough knot above the ripped flesh. The man tucked his tooth-torn 7 mm rifle—purchased from the famous German sportsman, C. G. Schillings—under his armpit and, staggering, tried to walk back to camp.

Afraid to call for help from his safari of two men and a boy, in fear they would bolt from the bleeding apparition, he noted with detached interest that the bright dawn was darkening. With relief, he saw his men approaching and collapsed from shock and loss of blood. In his ringing ears was the loudest sound he had ever heard: the dull, dead, metallic click of the firing pin on a dud cartridge as the lion had charged. It echoed through his numbed brain as his men carried him to his tent. Regaining consciousness, another interesting thought struck him: He had just bartered his medical outfit for a bit of food and some native artifacts for the Hungarian Museum, as he was due to return home in a few days after nineteen months in the Pori. There were only a few more birds he needed for the Budapest collection ... surely no risk of serious injury.

He took stock. There was only some cheap cotton cloth, so he washed out his wounds with boiled water. With the dreamy detachment of the badly injured, he noticed that the middle finger of his right hand was hanging by a few scraps of lion-bitten flesh. Calling for a skinning knife, he amputated it before the shock of the mauling wore off and called for a small bottle of preservative. With the care he took with all his scientific specimens, he dropped the amputed finger into the bottle, sealed it and added it to his collection for shipment to the Museum at Budapest. Smiling tightly, he felt the first horror of pain. The shock was beginning to wear off.

EDITOR'S NOTE

That gesture of the greatest grit-toothed humor is the best synopsis of the life and personality of Kálmán Kittenberger....

The next day, he was carried to Moshi, lower down the great Kilima Njaro slopes on a rough litter, completely convinced of the revelations personally learned by the late Dr. Livingstone: That the wounds gotten of a lion did not hurt until a few hours had passed. After that, agony. Africa also treated him to a special bout of malaria over the terrible five-day trip and, at one point, he was carried over the Daryama River by teetering bearers walking across a fallen tree. Crocodiles waited below in numbers—Hungarians being a rare, imported delicacy.

The trip, an experience of unmedicated hell, was highlighted by the fact that no water was available on the fourth night for the fever-wracked, fang-shredded hunter. A herd of highly antisocial elephants kept his men from drawing water at the Rau River and his tortures were compounded by thirst to near insanity.

But, at last, Moshi and help! Here, Kittenberger knew there was a surgeon and proper medical attention.

Only, there wasn't.

The District Surgeon had come down with an ulcerous liver—no wonder, considering the conditions under which he must have lived in 1904—and Kittenberger had to wait the night with only a native orderly for the rather dour comments and treatments of a missionary doctor who thought that the world could stand the loss of one more hunter.

But despite his lion wounds and his inability to resist his constant bouts of accumulated malaria, Kálmán Kittenberger walked away after three months of careful nursing. Good thing he did, or we would never have been able to read one of the greatest literary treats that the joys and terror of Africa have to offer—*Big Game Hunting and Collecting in East Africa.*

To exemplify my point, only Kittenberger, the diminutive, perceptive and humorous hunter-collector, could have written of the lion mauling and his shipped finger: "...the Museum...noticed the marks of arsenic poisoning under the nail and perceived how busy I had been collecting birds and preparing them for despatch." Kittenberger used arsenic compounds for the preservation of specimens against insect damage.

If his words don't show pluck, show me where I may find better.

Every now and then, an editor and writer runs into somebody special in the fascinating field of African hunting. Kittenberger is just such an example.

EDITOR'S NOTE

The reader will better understand Kittenberger's appeal when it is realized that the "classics" of African hunting which have become campfire titles are almost exclusively written by English-speakers. Our legacy of the great deeds of African hunting and exploration were from a pretty well-closed shop in favor of the British and, many years later, the Americans. The Boers of South Africa were mostly uneducated people. They did not write at all, being far too busy fighting off extremely inhospitable local spearmen and dodging assegais and arrows to jot down any notes. The works of those who spoke more familiar European tongues have survived such as the French hunter-explorer, Foà, the Portuguese hunter-explorer, Das Neves, and the Austro-Hungarian, Von Höhnel. An occasional "exotic" hunting book such as that of the Polish nobleman, Count Potocki, has been translated into English, as has that of fellow nobleman, Hungarian Count Széchenyi.

Still—thank *nkulunkulu*—a few of the finest of the great African adventure books written in tongues other than English have been translated and enrich every moment beside a low fire and a wet dog.

Among the best is Kittenberger.

I found the copy from which this reprint has been reproduced some ten years ago through the courtesy of a dealer friend who insisted that I buy it. I was not familiar with the name, and the price was failry steep. But I took his advice and have never made a better friend than Kálmán Kittenberger.

As you will soon see, Kittenberger's style has an appealing quality that immediately makes the reader like him. An affinity is established, as with Selous and Bell, Kittenberger's book seeming more like a personal letter, meant especially for you. I have tried to analyze his work and have concluded that the secret lies in his writing without any pomposity, despite his being one of the best educated and observant hunters I have ever read. His adventures are the best of reading, yet he never pounds his chest or shows the slightest concern for the hairiest escapade. Not many writers can or have accomplished this in print.

Kittenberger certainly was a phantom with reference to his background. I have been unable to discover his lineage or even his education, let alone his birthplace. This could be on account of my Hungarian being a mite rusty. Still, he was obviously a very well educated man to have been sent off by the Hungarian National Museum for so many years to the infant East Africa where he represented the Museum for the accumulation of their displays on African game, birds, and wildlife. The problem was that they didn't pay him enough money for a steak dinner. The lure of Africa, however, was enough. Kittenberger, as you will see, lived mostly from his personal collection of trophies which he sold to dealers while he did his duty for the Museum in Budapest.

Possibly the most delicate task of an editor is to tell the reader about the author without ruining any of the fine adventures that make up the work itself. A short chronology of Kittenberger is therefore in order. It is, in any case, my perception of the gentlemanly aspect of the man himself which makes him so charming in print.

Kittenberger started off his first African trip in December 1902, sanctioned by the National Museum of Hungary, so we know that he was not only well educated but that he was especially steeped in what was then known of African wildlife and, in particular, birds. He spent three-and-a-half years in Africa, a pauper because of his low pay, returning to Budapest in the European summer of 1906, most likely suffering from a fresh bout of malaria, amoebic dysentery, or one of the other easy dividends of bush living. He returned for another collecting expedition in the Danakil country and spent almost two years there before he was called up by the army at home and became an officer. This took a bit over a year and he finally started on his third expedition to German East Africa (a political ally of Hungary) at the end of 1908. He spent another three-and-a-half years in his real home, the bush, but only the photographs and diaries of this third trip had survived by this point, the rest having been lost or destroyed. Worse was in store.

Kittenberger was prevented from starting out on his fourth trip when the First Balkan War broke out. He only got away in May 1913. Perhaps it would have been better had he stayed at home.

His greatest wish from boyhood had been to get into the Ituri Forest of the Belgian Congo. While he was in the Bugoma Forest of Uganda in 1914, he received a polite note to please report to the administrative *boma* at Hoima. Unaware of the outbreak of The Great War, Kittenberger was arrested and became a prisoner of war and was shipped off to India where he was held for the entire duration of the war. Broke and in rags, he did not get home until amost 1920. Poor bastard! Kittenberger felt his career had been ruined. It was six more years before he had the chance to safari back to the Africa that had so artfully out-maneuvered him, courtesy of a wealthy, fellow Hungarian hunter who knew of Kálmán's exploits. This book is largely about that trip but contains much on his earlier adventures of collecting and hunting to live.

EDITOR'S NOTE

Perhaps the greatest mark of Kittenberger's integrity lies in his attitude to the British who lured him to captivity and who very nearly ruined his life. Yes, he was an officer, enemy of the crown, and was thus fair game for capture or a bullet. Despite his broken heart at being taken from his wild Africa, Kittenberger never seemed to hold anything against the British. Perhaps this was because of the time he had spent in their African territories of Kenya and Uganda and we presume that he spoke English reasonably well.

Further evidence of this lack of bitterness is seen in Kittenberger's choice of a British officer to write his Foreword—none other than Major Gerald Burrard, D.S.O, a very fine sportsman in his own right who wrote the "plum" chapter, "Rifles for Big Game," for the still-prestigious volume of the Lonsdale Library on Big Game Shooting in Africa (Volume XIV). Take the time to read Burrard's Foreword. He knew his big game and its writers.

Having read *Big Game Hunting and Collecting in East Africa* at least six times, I have to tap it as one of my favorites. Among the things that make it so are such observations by Kittenberger as to the ridiculousness of the legend that lions kill big game such as Cape buffalo with a paw stroke. He agrees with Selous, as do I, that a lion's claws are made to grip and to hold, most certainly not to swat dead animals which have necks the size and texture of tree trunks. Lions kill by biting and, without doubt, their paw grip on the front of an animal's face may cause it to break its own neck when falling over. But I believe that this is by accident rather than by design.

This aspect of Kittenberger's writing where he tells the truth as he observed it during his years in the bush points up his absolute veracity. Remember, he was writing in the era of sensationalism in African hunting, when amateur hunters had dangerous game doing all kinds of nutsy things to the greater glory of their own achievements. Not Kittenberger. That the great "Samaki" Salmon, legendary game warden and elephant control officer in Uganda, was his close friend shows that a man may be counted by the company he keeps. The reader should tattoo his field notes on stalking on the back of his hand. They are true. He even goes so far, without any known corroboration from W. D. M. "Karamojo" Bell, to substantiate Bell's information as to the origin of the biggest elephant tusks in the world having been taken by a Chagga slave of Shundi, the slaver. Kittenberger was in Shundi's same area of Uganda not long after Bell.

Bearing in mind that this book was written long before most of the "modern" revelations of animal behavior and the hunting of dangerous game,

EDITOR'S NOTE

you will find that Kittenberger tolls as true as a platinum bell. There are no "sea stories" here, as an old pal of mine, a Congressional Medal of Honor winner, was inclined to call savory deviations from fact. The finest fiction, if I may paraphrase The Bard, never could stand up in the face of the truth. Kittenberger tells the truth. Enjoy it and treasure it.

Perhaps if Kittenberger, through the fickleness of kismet, were tapping out an Editor's Note on one of my books, he would have appreciated the following observation so that his credibility would not be questioned: in the printing of his book, the plates following pages 264 and 321 both erroneously term the animal to be an "aardwolf" whereas they are actually aardvarks. It was simply a "printer's devil" as the correct captions appear in the List of Illustrations.

Kálmán, you owe me one!

—PETER HATHAWAY CAPSTICK

AUTHOR'S PREFACE

I STARTED for my first African trip in December, 1902, sent by the Hungarian National Museum to collect zoological and especially ornithological material in German East Africa, round Kilimanjaro. The primitive nature of my outfit and my lack of ammunition were great hindrances, though I was treading on virgin soil and could have achieved splendid results with a good outfit. The Hungarian National Museum's payment for the collected skins came to very little, and I had to help myself out by selling my trophies.

In the summer of 1906 I had to return to Europe on account of my health, but started off again in December of the same year to continue collecting on behalf of the Hungarian National Museum. The work at first was very difficult, in the country of the fanatic Danakils, and when conditions had begun to improve, in autumn 1907, I had to return home, as I had been called up by the military authorities. After having taken the officers' examination, I started for my third trip in December, 1908, to German East Africa, on the eastern shores of Victoria Nyanza. I took most of my photographs and observations during this expedition, and these I managed to keep in safety, whereas the photographs and diaries of my first, second and fourth trips were partly or wholly lost.

I returned from Africa in May, 1912, bringing with me not only my museum specimens but also a large number of live animals for our new Zoo. During the expedition I had made a very valuable collection of East African great mammals, which could not be procured nowadays for a very large sum. Unfortunately this material has been lost owing to after-war conditions.

The outbreak of the first Balkan War prevented my starting on my fourth expedition, on behalf of the Hungarian National Museum until late in May, 1913. I headed for English territory

—Uganda—intending to cross to Eastern Congo, where I should find new collecting fields.

To this expedition I attached great hopes. I felt entitled to do so from all the painfully acquired experience and the much-improved outfit which were the results of my three previous trips.

I shall always think with the greatest sorrow of those painful days when my hopes were destroyed. Forests of Congo! Fairy-land of my dreams! How many unknown specimens are still hidden in the darkness of your thickets in that damp gloom where the sun can never penetrate! How often I dreamt that there, in the home of anthropoids, I might be able to learn some more of nature's secrets, to understand her mysterious language. I was confident that my spirits would not be affected by the heavy atmosphere of those dark forests, which have killed so many white men or compelled them to a swift return. I wanted to spend years there, and felt immune enough against tropical diseases. Time should not count. I meant to devote my youth, my whole life to those forests, and I should then have obtained results that would have been the real expression of my African work.

The Great War swept away all my dreams. While I was in the Bugoma Forest in Uganda, I was suddenly summoned to Hoima, little realizing that the summons was to be the prelude to more than five years of captivity, most of which were spent in India. The loss of freedom and of the collections I had acquired with so much labour made those years a nightmare. I shall never forget the terrible feeling of uncertainty, the doubt as to how we should emerge from this madness, and the awful loneliness.

My African career seemed finished, and it was not until the end of 1919 that I returned home poor as a beggar. As our transport came through the Red Sea the sight of the sunlit African shore brought me painful memories. When should I see these lands again?

Six years later the chance came! One autumn evening in 1925 Mr. Eugene Horthy de Nagybánya, the great sportsman and big game hunter, said to me in his characteristic, laconic way: "Shall we go?" "Yes!" I answered before recovering from my stupefaction. And in November we started indeed. Count

Seilern, for whom this was a first trip to Africa, joined us in Vienna.

To tell the truth, Mr. Horthy had no need of me on this African trip at all, for he was quite at home in Africa, as the splendid results of his two previous visits clearly prove. But he found it a pleasure to help an old African hunter again. The chief results of this expedition, and a survey of the changed situation I found in East Africa, are included in this volume.

The illustrations are from my own photographs unless otherwise acknowledged.

KÁLMÁN KITTENBERGER.

FOREWORD

By MAJOR GERALD BURRARD, D.S.O.

IT is now getting on for half a century since East Africa began
to be opened up as the most prolific of all fields for the Hunter
of Big Game, and during the last thirty years books describing
the experiences of sportsmen in that part of the world have been
appearing with persistent regularity. As is but natural, these
books vary greatly in interest and quality: a few will always live
because of the adventurous glamour of their pages: others can
be reckoned as standard works on the subject with which they
deal. But the great majority are read but once—possibly twice—
for the sake of the enjoyment which they give a reader whose
tastes are kindred to those of the author.

Those which earn the distinction of a place in the "standard
work class" must obviously be of exceptional merit; and equally
obviously few can gain such a position. For to become a standard
work a book must be written by a man who possesses much experience; great powers both of making observations and interpreting
them when made; a certain scientific grounding; a gift of description and exposition; and finally, I think, a sense of humour. This
last may not be so essential in a book dealing with some abstruse
theory, but I do regard it as essential in any work which describes,
even indirectly, travel and life in a country inhabited chiefly by
wild game and untutored savages; for it is impossible to deal
successfully with the latter without unlimited patience backed up
by a keen sense of humour.

When I first began to glance through the manuscript of Mr.
Kittenberger's *Big Game Hunting and Collecting*, there were two things
which struck me immediately about the author: the almost pedantic
care with which he studied wild life, and his amazing pluck. These
qualities cannot but appeal to all who are ever likely to turn over the

following pages: they certainly encouraged me to begin to read
the manuscript through with the closest attention; and once I began
I could not stop.

For first and foremost Mr. Kittenberger is obviously a very
gallant and generous-hearted sportsman.

His account of his mauling by a lion describes a magnificent
stand and fight to the finish; he belittles his own hurts and mentions
the dressing of his wounds almost with nonchalance.

And sportsmanship? Well, we find Kittenberger's unveiled
contempt for sitting up for lions over a kill, while he explains that
when he used a heavy cordite rifle on lion it did not seem quite
fair. I will follow up this line no further.

But however taking sportsmanship and gallantry may be, they
are not in themselves sufficient to enable anyone to write a standard
work. Kittenberger, however, can reinforce these qualities with
an obviously long experience, and the fact that he is first and foremost an ardent naturalist. The main purpose of all his expeditions
was to obtain specimens for the Hungarian Natural History
Museum at Buda Pest, and later to capture young animals alive
for the Hungarian Zoo. Further, no one who had not altogether
exceptional knowledge and training could have cured the entire
skin of a white rhinoceros as he did: and I have never heard of
any other man who has performed a Cæsarian operation successfully on a cow rhinoceros!

In view of his experience and powers of observation I personally found Kittenberger's comments on the comparative danger
to be anticipated from the hunting of various game animals of
exceptional interest. This is a subject to which there can never
be any finality as so much must depend on circumstances, but
Kittenberger very clearly brings out the point that the restriction
in numbers of any species to be shot must make a difference,
because, in elephant hunting for example, the sportsman will be
bound to make his way into the middle of a herd in order to make
certain of getting a bull with good tusks; while if he could shoot
an unlimited number he might not be so particular. Such re-
strictions were unknown in olden days and consequently the opinions
of hunters of a past generation are no longer applicable to present-
day conditions.

As an Englishman I felt most gratified at reading the author's constant eulogistic references to the efficiency of the game laws and administration in British Territory, as well as to the courteous kindness which he invariably received from British Officials, all of which is frankly acknowledged, even though the author did first hear of the outbreak of the War while he was after elephant in Uganda and was interned for "the duration."

It is hard to say which I liked best in this book: the almost boyish excitement of the hunt; the reasoned argument in support of, or against, some suggestion; the complete absence of any dictatorial views; or the equally complete observations on wild life. And it is because all these appeal to me so much that I shall be surprised if this lucid and detailed book by a Hungarian hunter-naturalist does not join the select band of "standard works" both by reason of the spirit in which it is written and the information which it contains.

CONTENTS

xi

CONTENTS

CONTENTS

LIST OF ILLUSTRATIONS

BIG GAME HUNTING AND COLLECTING IN EAST AFRICA

CHAPTER I

The Lion

FOR a sportsman East Africa is a land of vast possibilities. The strange continent with the new surroundings, its unknown game, the unfamiliar way of hunting it, its native tribes still living in prehistoric conditions, all may have great charm, but it is the shooting of big and dangerous game that really gives Africa its enormous attraction. Even in days of modern high-velocity rifles the shooting of big game involves certain dangers, and it is this that makes it so fascinating.

Experienced hunters distinguish five kinds of dangerous game, namely, lion, elephant, buffalo, leopard, and rhino. We may call them "dangerous," because hunting them can be, and often is, more or less dangerous. The chief wish of anybody going to East Africa for the first time is probably to sight a lion, but even stronger is the hope to get a chance of shooting one of these princely cats. It is a most natural desire, for even the very idea of lion hunting brings back many long-forgotten childhood dreams.

All animals which interfere with the spread of human civilization will have to confine themselves within ever-narrowing limits or they will soon be entirely extinct. The domain of the lion is already greatly restricted in Africa, and I need hardly mention that lions have not been known in Europe during historic times, while even in Asia the only likely place to find one would be in the Gir forests of Kathiawar. Unfortunately I know very little about the occurrence of the lion in Persia and Mesopotamia, but I presume their practical extinction in those regions took place at an early date, although there are rumours of lions having been seen in Mesopotamia and on the western slopes of the Zangros Mountains.

1

Lions are common in the savannas of East Africa, by which I mean the territories of Kenya (British East Africa), Tanganyika (formerly German East Africa), Somaliland and Portuguese East Africa, where there are still vast herds of game to be found. And it is not even rare for lions to be shot close to the ports of East Africa. A few years ago the British Government in Kenya limited to four the number of lions to be shot by any individual sportsman in a year, but this must not be regarded as an indication that lions were approaching extinction, for the regulation has since been cancelled, so that to-day no limit is imposed on the number of lions a sportsman can shoot.

Different types of lion have been observed in East Africa. In the north the Somali lion is smaller than the southern lion of Tanganyika, while the big lion of the Equatorial coast carries but little mane.

Of all the cat tribe the male lion alone is maned, and the mane is regarded as highly by the lion hunter as are the antlers of a stag by the deer-stalker. The thicker the mane, the greater its value in the eyes of the sportsman. But the finest trophy is the black-maned lion. Incidentally it may here be stated that the manes of lions living in a wild state are never as thick as those of their brothers kept in captivity.

There are several theories about the development of the lion's mane. Many, for example, maintain that lions living in bushy tracts have but a feeble growth of mane, as nearly every tree or bush in East Africa is of thorny nature and the lion's mane gets tangled and torn, whereas those living in the plains have long and thick manes. They are finer still on lions living in the colder regions of the highlands.

This seems to be a logical conclusion, but it happens to be false. I have shot beautifully maned lions in the densest bush, while I have shot male lions without any manes whatever which inhabited the open plains. Further, I have seen and shot lions both with and without manes out of one single troop, some of which had dense black and some scanty fair manes. I have reached but one conclusion, namely, that the short-legged, stocky, heavy-bodied type always has a finer mane than the taller lanky lion, and that the former eventually grow black manes. One can always be certain that lions bearing big manes are old animals.

The finest black-maned lions I ever saw were to the east of Victoria Nyanza, on the river side plains of the Ruvana, a country which was surely the very best lion-preserve of German East Africa in pre-war days.

Years ago, when my knowledge of lions was derived from picture books, I always imagined them as dwelling in the desert, because in the books they were always depicted there, usually with the Pyramids in the background and underneath some such legend as "King of the Desert." It would, however, be useless to search for lions in the desert, as such country could not provide food for them. But it is also true that the large, dark rain-forests are not likely places for lions either, because of the comparatively small amount of prey obtainable there. I had never seen tracks of lions in these vast, dark jungles, and so I was greatly surprised at finding the tracks of a large lion in the Baamba forest west of the Ruwenzori Mountains during my last trip to Uganda. The natives told me that lions had recently appeared in these parts, especially after the rainy season. They seem to have followed the giant hog. A few months later I heard the same story in the Bugoma forest east of Lake Albert, although in 1914 I had never, during my stay of a few months, noticed any lions there, and at that time the natives never even mentioned them. It is probable that the rinderpest, which had made great ravages among the hogs, accounted for these lions visiting the forest after easy prey. It is also possible that certain lions, finding giant hogs especially tasty, acquired the habit of feeding on them and that it is only these individuals which have been seen in such unusual places.

The real domain of the lion comprises the plains and the bushy woods of the savannas, where vast herds of different varieties of game live together in great masses. Reed-banks in such localities will almost certainly prove to be the lair of lions, and it is here that hunters will probably get the best chances of sport.

Close to the Uganda railway track, near Stony-Athi station, a cane-break may be seen through the windows of your train. Old Africans will be pleased to tell their companions, that since the Uganda Railway has been opened many more than a hundred lions have been shot in this small island of reeds.

The Athi Plains were also splendid for lion-shooting, and the number of lions which have been bagged there is simply incredible. Lions are still numerous there and it is very easy to find them, which explains why every sportsman tries to get his first in this neighbourhood.

Of all those districts which I visited, the best for lions was the country between Victoria Nyanza and the Great Rift Valley, which are uninhabited regions. The Ruvana Plains I have already mentioned and south-east of the Serengeti are the richest hunting-grounds. The Ruvana Plain has recently been visited by innumerable big-game hunters and I have heard that they obtained great results. Unfortunately the recently built motor-car road—of course I mean "road" in the African sense of the word, being a track upon which motor-cars may be able to travel—has made it possible for record-hunters to flood these parts of the country. During my expedition to Uganda I met an American who had killed twenty-six lions in but two weeks—if I remember rightly—and this on "my" Ruvana Plain! He told me himself that he actually bagged but twenty of these lions, the remaining six escaping severely wounded into thick scrub. These he never even tried to follow up—more unsportsmanlike behaviour I cannot imagine,—and so I conclude that the others were most probably half-grown animals! Unfortunately there are many who, trying to make records, shoot at anything that can be called a lion, even if it is still a tiny cub. What pleasure the killer can derive from such records is more than I can understand.

On the Ruvana Plain I saw the biggest troop of lions I have ever seen. I counted twenty-six of them. Before that I had only seen smaller troops of five or six lions. In the big troop there were, of course, cubs and half-grown animals hardly bigger than a large sheep-dog. I must mention that I did not kill a single one out of this unusually big troop. They had seen me in time and took to flight. I followed them at full speed, running and firing a few times at a splendid black-maned lion, who stopped and turned on me from time to time. I had the faint hope of stopping them by my shots, but, when at last I had gained ground and my bullets seemed to get nearer them, my lion leaped into the thicket, where the others had already disappeared. Similar collections of lions can be observed in times of drought, near the rare water-holes you find in arid countries, to which naturally all game crowd in from afar to drink. Of course, big numbers of lions can only exist where zebras and antelopes live in thousands.

With the exception of full-grown elephants, rhinos and perhaps hippopotami, the lion will attack every East African animal. Even the buffalo, who can well defend himself, and the enormous bull giraffe, whose kick would be enough to break his bones, will usually be felled by a lion. Lions seldom hunt alone if their prey is of a dangerous nature. Unfortunately I never had the chance of seeing such a fight, although I have often come on the remains of killed buffaloes; but I am sure that lions only attack buffaloes and giraffes if they cannot find easier prey.

Vultures soaring in the skies, and then suddenly closing their wings and letting themselves fall down like a stone, often showed me where to find the remains of animals killed by lions. And my experience shows that lions mostly kill zebras after heavy rains, when the deep retentive soil retards the escape of hoofed animals. On the Ruvana Plains the wildebeest is often killed by lions, and we took advantage of this by collecting the tails of the gnus and exchanging them later on for cows, for the warriors of the Masai and Wagaya tribes who live on the eastern shores of Victoria Nyanza value them greatly and use them as ornaments, fifteen tails being worth a cow.

Old books written on natural history state that the lion only feeds on his own kill and will never touch carrion. This is not true, because in times of scarcity lions, like all other rapacious animals, eat carrion. That old, toothless animals live on it is all the more natural.

Aged and disabled lions living in countries which are densely populated, but lacking in game, become man-eaters. On the coast of former German East Africa man-eaters sometimes compel the terror-stricken population to desert their homes; but in the whole history of East Africa the most notorious man-eaters were those which took to eating the men building the Uganda Railway.

Major Patterson, who was lucky enough to kill the leader of

the murderous gang, was worshipped like a hero.   It is marvellous how deliberately the lions hatched out schemes and how shrewdly they went to work, when they were hunting man.   No wonder that the natives, and still more the superstitious coolies imported from India, believed that supernatural forces were at work and thought the lions were devils in disguise.   These man-eaters of Tsavo were in the prime of youth and strength.

When searching for an explanation why these lions got into the habit of killing men, I can only presume that when the troops of workmen arrived, all the game fled from this disturbed and unsafe country, and the lions lacking food, were forced to attack human beings.   Contagious diseases decimated the unfortunate coolies and the dead were often left unburied, the corpses lying around in the brushwood.

I still remember the deep impression made on me when standing by the grave of the engineer O'Hara, who had been dragged out of his tent by a lion.   It was one of my first impressions, for I had been but a few days in Africa.

The following story would be a curious hunting episode, even if it had not ended so tragically.   Hoping to make a comfortable ambush, three men lay in wait for the man-eating lions in a railway car which was left standing on the railway track.   They kept watch in turns, but finally the one on duty was overcome by sleep.   Some people said that too much whisky had been drunk and that this was the cause of the disaster.   The door of the car was left open because of the suffocating heat, and the lion jumped through the open door, snatched up one of the men, and as the door had slammed behind him after his entrance, left the car through the window.   I afterwards made the acquaintance of the two survivors.

I have never had any personal experience with man-eaters, and in the countries I camped in I never even heard rumours of them, but on account of the objects of my expeditions I mostly kept far from habitations in the regions where game existed in vast numbers, and it would be very rare to find man-eaters there. Nevertheless, even in these parts lions will assault the villages of the natives and wreak great havoc among their cattle.   The revenge of the herdmen never fails, for the East Africans, armed with poisonous spears, defy lions and fight to protect or to avenge their herds.

That famous hunter, Captain C. H. Stigand, who was killed in the Sudan, wrote in his book *Hunting the Elephant in Africa*, that, according to what the Somalis say, the lion frightens man three times. First, when his roar is heard for the first time either by night or day; of course when it is very dark, it is still more alarming. The second time, when his track is first found; even if you have been searching for it, you get a sudden feeling of sickness when you come upon it. The third and final feeling of fear comes when you actually see the lion. According to the Somalis the bravest man must experience these three pangs of fear; but after getting over the third, you are never afraid any more.

Although I cannot regard myself as one of those happy creatures who know no fear, I have not been alarmed three times as mentioned above. When I first saw the track of "Simba" ("lion" in Swahili, it was the first word of that language I learned) I was unarmed. That same night I heard a lion's roar for the first time. I had only been in Africa a fortnight, and the impression the lion made on me was somewhat mitigated by the fever I had caught in Voi, as I was overcome by it that same day.

The first lion I saw I succeeded in killing, the details of which will be given in a following chapter. But nothing, not even my first lion, impressed me as much as the lion-concert I once heard later on at very close quarters. Many an evening, and hundreds of times, have I listened with a soul full of reverence to those grand sounds and most wonderful music of the African plains. However, this music can also give thrills of terror, if you are awakened by it coming from a few yards outside your tent. The aspect of the "safari" (caravan) at rest suddenly changes, and the most humorous scenes follow. The smouldering camp-fires suddenly blaze up, as natives are wonderfully quick at kindling fires. But after heavy rains, when the downpour has put out the fire and the night is pitch-dark, in their alarm they simply dash head over heels into the tent of the white man.

I remember a night in the papyrus swamps near the river Mara (later it was called Ngare Dowash). I was hunting elephant and my tent was pitched fifteen minutes' walk from the bomas of the natives. Suddenly the roaring of some lions thundered through the night. To keep the lions at a distance the natives began to beat their tom-toms and blow their horns (made out of the horns of antelopes). They made a terrific noise, but, as I heard next morning, without the desired result, for the lions were very bold at night, and killed a cow.

The full-breasted roar of the lion is not half as impressive as that deep, rattling growl he gives when he is taken by surprise, or when he charges.

The reason why lions roar at night has been discussed in hundreds of books. There are ever so many theories, but my own idea is that those who declare that the lion's roar is not only a call to their companions, but a very important expedient of their nightly hunts, are nearest to truth. Lions usually hunt together, and while some of them do nothing but roar in chorus or separately, in order to draw the attention of their victims in a different direction, the others creep up to their prey and kill without a sound. Their object may also be to drive their prey into the jaws of those that are lying in wait.

I have read descriptions in old and recent books of how all animals, domestic and wild, begin to shiver when they hear the lion's roar. I have never seen these scenes of panic, but what I did see was enough to convince me that these descriptions are only figments of the writer's imagination and cannot be regarded as true.

I have often noticed that in the early morning and late afternoon grazing game never take notice of noisy lions. Perhaps they can tell exactly when their roar means danger and when it does not. For example, lions feeding on their kill always roar, although they are surely not then dangerous.

Even the sight of lions makes very little impression on herds of game. Once, for instance, I shot a zebra for bait and watched a lion, who was dragging it through a large opening into a cover. Five snorting and astonished topi antelopes (*Damaliscus jimela*) followed the lion at a distance of about 30 yards; further on, 70 yards away, a small troop of zebras was grazing, and only the leading stallion turned his head towards the enemy.

LARGE BAOBAB TREE IN FLOWER AT MOMBASA

A VIEW OF MOMBASA

NATIVE BAZAAR, MOMBASA

SOMALI COFFEE-HOUSE, MOMBASA

EUPHORBIA CANDELABRUM

SINGING ACACIA WITH STARLING NESTS

Kongoni herds on the high plateau

Suspicious Zebras

I was late that morning and, because day had already broken, I could no longer approach the ambush I had selected near that bait. I had, accordingly, to content myself with watching this unusual scene from a distance of 350 yards and was so taken aback by it, that I quite forgot to use my rifle.

Captain Stigand gives us a charming description in his book:

"I think I have never seen anything funnier than two belated lions I met near the Ndurugu, British East Africa, returning home with their stomachs dragging on the ground. A herd of kongoni was following them and running after them to look at them. I never saw anything look so sheepish and ashamed as those two lions. Both were much too full to be comfortable, and were subject to the stare of a whole inquisitive herd in broad daylight. They looked intensely deprecating and self-conscious, as if they wished to say, 'It was not us at all that killed one of you last night, we are just taking a walk and wouldn't do any harm to anyone. I wish you wouldn't stare so, it makes us feel uncomfortable.' " [1]

I have never actually seen a lion kill. Very often did I come on the remains and a few times I have even found lions still in the act of feeding on their kill. On these occasions I shot a few; but although I found quite fresh kills, I could not possibly give an accurate reconstruction of the moment the victim was brought down. Mostly I found the neck torn open by the powerful fangs of the lion, and once I found a zebra with a broken neck.

When lions hunt together it is usually the lioness which leads them. This I gather from the wonderful flashlight snapshots in Professor C. G. Schillings' *Mit Blitzlicht und Büchse.*

Carcases of buffaloes and giraffes have been found lying beside the carcase of a lion, proving that the buffalo and giraffe can kill lions. If such a fight takes place, it very often ends in death on both sides, leaving the two victims lying close together. But even smaller animals have caused the death of lions. For example, lions have been pierced to death by the pointed horns of the plucky oryx; and when I shot a young lion whose fangs were missing or broken, my men always joked, saying that he had been kicked by a zebra.

Whenever I had the chance of observing lions eating, I noticed that they always began feeding on the umbles of their victim

[1] *Hunting the Elephant in Africa.* By C. H. Stigand. (Macmillan & Co., 1913.)

and after having eaten plentifully of it, buried the rest in the ground. Then they proceeded to taste the haunch and parts of the neck and dragged the rest under cover, trying to hide it from vultures. Then, after drinking, they returned to their kill and lie up by it. Animals of the size of zebra are devoured on the spot in no time by a troop of lions.

News of two lions sighted behind a bush was once brought to me by one of my trackers. When I arrived at the spot, the companion the man had left behind pointed out the bush, but I only saw masses of vultures standing around. From time to time these vultures tried to approach the bush, clumsily hopping towards it, but suddenly a lioness darted out from behind it with a fierce growl, frightening the impudent birds away.

Both were females and they were keeping watch by the carcase of a zebra. In the hopes of getting a good photograph I advanced, but the vultures flew up, inducing the two lions to trot away. I did not shoot, because I only rarely shot lionesses during my later expeditions.

Once in the early afternoon we saw a hyena casting towards the protruding parts of a covert, where it stopped just as a pointer would. It seemed undecided what to do and having made a few steps forward, it cautiously backed again. Its mouth was half-open, its nose twitching about catching the scent and it seemed to be saying: "What a sublime odour of carrion is streaming towards me, but the same wind also brings another terrifying scent, and I have not got the courage to take the risk of getting close to this gorgeous repast lying so near."

We were only a few yards away, but my camera was not at hand, and while my gunbearer was coming up and unfastening it, the hyena became aware of our presence and bolted.

Near that bush we found the remains of a roan antelope, and all round it traces of a lioness. Advancing a few steps we were startled by a short "uff," and she flashed away. Now I knew the reason of the hyena's seeming timidity. It would have been quite easy to get the lioness, and if it had been a lion, I certainly would have tried. I should only have had to send my men back to the camp, instructing them to make a noise all the way, while I myself lay in wait till the lioness returned to her kill.

Lions, according to my experience, are polygamous. I have often seen one male accompanied by several full-grown lionesses, but old beasts lead a lonesome life.

In the rutting season one can see troops of lions following a lioness and the males fight each other. These times of love and war are exceedingly noisy and lively. On the Ruvana Plains I had the chance of hearing and seeing this exciting spectacle, and in one case I was even attacked by one of the favoured males. I will tell of this later. Even in the same country the season of pairing is not at the same time. For instance, the first I saw was on August 10th, 1910, the second on November 2nd, 1911. In both cases I killed the best lion of the troop.

The lioness usually has two to four cubs at a time and carries them 108 days. She generally gives birth to the litter in a bed she has previously prepared in a thick bush and I never have seen a lioness in this condition hide in rocky caves. It is curious that the cubs are very often speckled and scarcely to be distinguished from leopard cubs, but in time the spots usually disappear, although sometimes you can still find them on a grown lion, especially on females.

I now much regret that I never took measurements of my lions. Of course there was no possibility of weighing them, but I am sure that my big Ruvana lion was heavier than the one mentioned as a record in Rowland Ward's *Records of Big Game*, which weighed 516 lbs. This book was only able to give a few particulars regarding weights, because it seldom happens that hunters have got the means of weighing lions in the wilderness. In these days of the motor-car it should be different.

I think I am not much mistaken if I say that a full-grown, well-fed male lion must weigh from 450 to 500 lbs. The lioness is smaller and weighs not more than 250 to 300 lbs. According to Rowland Ward, the length of the African male lion from nose to tail is 10 feet 7 inches, the Indian lion being 10 feet 4 inches long, so there is no great difference between them.

CHAPTER II

The Lion (*continued*)

ALMOST anyone can shoot a lion, provided there are some in the district, if he can make a stay of a few weeks and does not mind roughing it, but of course a good deal depends on luck. I have no intention of giving details as to how chance brings hunters and game together, but will venture to offer a little advice regarding some available methods of hunting lion.

The sportsman must be up very early when the lions have been roaring during the night and before dawn. I always got up two hours before sunrise, that is at four o'clock (nights and days being of exactly the same length on the equator). Fully prepared to start, I sat in front of my tent, my escort crouching round the camp-fire, and we waited for dawn to break. The moment the sky in the east began to brighten we started in the direction of the last sound heard. On moonlit nights we did not even wait so long. Sometimes we had to march for a long time, but the lion's roar was always a reliable guide.

In unfrequented localities, where lions have been undisturbed, they usually go on roaring after daybreak and then you can be sure of finding them. As an almost invariable rule, lions roar more and for longer periods in the rainy season than they do when the weather is dry and fine.

If they stopped roaring at dawn, we had to follow the last sounds heard in the night. My men who were keeping watch used to lay long rods on the ground pointing in the directions of the sounds, the one indicating the last roar being specially marked.

This is a simple method, but it has led to good results. In the Ngurumini Mountains (eastwards of Victoria Nyanza and south of the Ngare Dowash River) I was twice rewarded for getting up early and braving the icy dampness of the dewy high grass, by bringing the hides of two wonderfully maned lions back to camp.

When I shot the first of these lions I was out with another object in view and disregarded the chorus of roars emitted by lions during the whole night, for I was following up a rhinoceros. Having been told by the local natives that a cow with her calf had been seen in a thicket some way off, I thought of capturing the calf.

We had been marching towards this thicket for a long time and the sun already stood high in the sky when a lion roared quite near us. Naturally this induced me to give up my original plan and I turned my attention to the lion. After we had been following the sound for half an hour, one of the men behind me spotted the lion and pointed it out to me. It was facing us and had already seen us through the high grass. My first bullet got him in the shoulder. He reared, spun round and dashed away, but a second shot in the neck made him turn a somersault, and he fell dead. In any case, he would not have gone far, as he was mortally hit by my first bullet. This was the first time that I had used my heavy ·470 cordite Express and my pleasure was somewhat mitigated as it seemed unsporting to use such a heavy rifle to kill a lion.

There were still about fifteen lions hidden in the high grass, but they fled after my shots. I could not catch sight of any of them, but I knew the direction they had taken by the swaying of the grass. My men, who were all much taller than I, were pointing at them, shouting at me, showing me which to shoot, for there seem to have been several half-grown lions among the troop.

It would have been quite simple to follow their traces in the dewy grass, but I had not enough skinners with me, so I gave up further pursuit. Next day I was amply justified in having chosen to follow the lion instead of continuing the attempt to capture the rhino calf, for, visiting the thicket, I found the female rhino, but the baby was a half-grown youngster, whose capture would have been a fruitless task. Naturally I went away without disturbing them.

Two and a half months later, on June 19th, 1911, we pitched

camp in exactly the same place and again started in the direction
of the roars at dawn. The sun was well up in the sky above the
Ngurumini Mountains, when we suddenly heard a roar, and realized
we were quite near the lion we had been following. It was just
in time, because we had already begun to discuss which direction
to take, and I had sent two of my ablest men to look for tracks.
Soon one of them, my best tracker, Kikombe, ran back, making
signs for us to hurry, as he had already viewed the lion. When
I got there, I had to step on the trunk of a tree that had been
struck and burned by lightning, so as to be able to see something
in the high grass. First I only caught sight of the lion's ears,
but as he sat up, he also became aware of my presence. This
cannot have pleased him very much, because he put back his
ears, ruffled up his mane and lashed his flanks with his tail. I
took aim at his head, but as the distance of 80 yards seemed too
great to take any risks, I changed my mind and shot him in the
chest. Giving an angry roar, he leapt up and disappeared in
the grass.

We found no blood on the very visible track he had left in
the dewy grass, but a little farther on the blood began to stream
from his wound, and after following very cautiously for 250 yards
we found him lying dead beside a small shrub. He was a fine
old lion, covered with the scars of former combats and half his
lower jaw was torn off. His mane, although well developed, was
not as good as that of my first Ngurumini lion.

So the plan of following the last morning roar had again
proved successful. We invariably either caught sight of the
animal itself or found the fresh tracks, and following these could
tell exactly where it had entered the jungle, so that when we
started a drive we could be nearly sure of getting our beast. If
we failed it was owing to unfavourable conditions or mostly to
my own awkwardness. But often I did not shoot because the
beast we had run down was a lioness and during my third journey
to Africa I gave up shooting them because the preparation of their
hides was not worth my while, as I had better work to do.

To be able to hunt with sufficient results requires great knowledge of the "pori" (East African wilderness) and of the lives
and habits of all animals. This knowledge is far more helpful

to the sportsman than mere luck, and without it he may miss his best chance. He must possess far more than an ordinary know-ledge of lions: must understand every sound and every movement of the jungle and draw his own conclusions in regard to the habits of lions. Everything he sees and hears must carry its own mean-ing and warn him of the slightest change in the situation. He should know the habits of all animals, especially anything that concerns the biggest of all beasts of prey, the lion. For a hunter, whose eyes are open and senses alert, it is far more easy to under-stand and learn than to try to describe what his experiences have been.

The signs Nature gives are so varied and change so rapidly according to circumstances, that one can only give a few general hints, without being able to put into words all the minute differences and variations of details which convey their message to the experi-enced hunter. For instance, if a herd of game has taken notice of us, but nevertheless continues to look in the opposite direction, and other herds, following this example, all turn to look in the same direction, we can be certain that they have sighted a lion or some other big beast of prey.

In case of danger all animals give warning to each other, no matter whether of the same species or not. Anybody can prove this at home, for has not a magpie or a thrush spoiled your stalk, or did not a squirrel or owl betray you, when lying motionless?

It is a well-known fact, that big flocks of vultures live in districts where lions are common because these winged scavengers live mostly on what the lions leave. In the early mornings we always watched the flight of the vultures, for it generally had something to tell us and often revealed tragedies of the past night. We saw them swooping down on the spot and if we got there in time, before the vultures had scratched away spoor, we could tell, not only what the victim was, but also what kind of animal had killed it.

Vultures betray a lot by their behaviour. If they precipitate themselves successively with closed wings, you can be sure that there is no dangerous enemy feeding on the carcase, for jackals, which are sure to be there, do not count. These are content to get away with a bone or a piece of flesh without being too badly pecked or beaten by the wings of the big birds. But vultures behave quite differently if a lion or some other big beast is near the kill. Both they and marabous then make big circles in the air and come down slowly to perch on trees near by. If they sight men occupied with the remains, they are even more cautious and will soar very high and, after circling, settle down on trees farther off. If whole flocks of birds of prey suddenly rise, it means that some big animal, or man, is approaching. In the first case they will just fly up and alight again, but if men come to disturb their feast, they do not come near again for a while, but sit around in a big circle perched on trees and watch their opportunity. Other birds, also, often tell of the presence of lions. The noisy and treacherous crowned plover (*Stephanibyx coronatus*), which is a nuisance to every East African hunter, has twice given me warning that a lion was in a thicket. Another time I was tracking a wounded lion amongst the bushes and thorny shrub of the bed of the river Tirina on the Ruvana Plains, when a pair of chattering warblers, sitting on a bunch of reeds, warned me of the wounded lion hiding in the bushes. And only just in time, for all our caution could not have saved us from a charge at close quarters.

All members of the cat tribe are clever at hiding and take advantage of the smallest cover to conceal themselves from their enemy, and it is certainly surprising that an animal weighing about 450 lbs. can hide in a place hardly fit for a fox. An old joke of the Nairobi bar-room is that if you put a matchbox on a billiard table a lion could disappear behind it.

Intending lion hunters will do well to mark these jesting words, because they may some day benefit by them. When following up a lion it often happens that it suddenly disappears mysteriously and then the hunter will do well to be careful and not disregard the smallest shrub, for each may hide a crouching lion.

In connection with this I will give an account of what happened to me on the Ngare Dowash River. Tracking a buffalo and a rhino with her young, we suddenly came upon three lions, and immediately took to following them. Some granite blocks lay to the left of our path and some way off was the forest of Ngare Dowash. The grass had all been burned down, excepting that round the small granite clump a kind of border of grass was left, knee-high, absolutely stiff and dry and in many places trodden down by game. The three lions stopped before this border and I took my eyes off them for a moment, and when I looked again they were gone. Of course I thought that they had leapt over the stone blocks and I climbed up on them as quickly as possible, in the hopes of getting a shot. But when I had reached the top, and still panting badly, lifted my glasses, I could see nothing but an expanse of flat land parched to the roots by the prairie fire. In vain did I and my men gaze in all directions; there was nothing which could have hidden the lions from us.

My gunbearer and I were turning round when we suddenly broke out in exclamations of utter surprise, for there were the three lions just where they had been! They had flattened down next to the grass-border and did not stir even when seven of us passed by within a few yards. One was a male in the prime of life, but poorly maned, and the others grown lionesses. I had not wiped the oil out of my Mannlicher-Schönauer rifle that morning and while I took my aim I thought of this and in view of past experience in such circumstances, I took a much lower aim than I would have done normally, but my bullet still went too high, passing just over the lion. When he rushed off, my second shot, delivered at random, stopped him just as he was on the point of entering the forest.

The lionesses stopped by his side and turned on me in a threatening manner. I was still perched in my rocky fortress, quite prepared for them to charge, but to my relief they did not. For a time they stood round their fallen lord, seemingly angry and growling, but then they thought better of it and took to the forest.

Lions can be driven easily, especially in countries where this has not been done often. If it is known that there are lions in a thicket, one can very easily ascertain where they have entered it by finding their spoor, or by watching them enter in the early morning. If the wind is favourable it is better to stand up on that side. The hunters and beaters must take their places as quietly as possible, but when everybody is placed, a few moments of loud "shauri" (discussion) is a good scheme to make the lions leave their hiding-place.   In the heat of the day, however, it is extremely unlikely that they will break covert.

Although it would certainly be much more successful, it is impossible to get the natives to beat without noise.   They must give vent to their excitement, fear and joy by frantic yells and howls, and it would be impossible to keep them quiet.

I have always found that the lioness is easier to drive than the lion, because the latter will very often crouch down and let the beaters pass him and then slip back unnoticed, and I have afterwards found his tracks, showing how he had fooled us.

If there are several lions in the drive, the lioness is usually the first to dart out with an angry snarl and go ahead of the beaters, while the lion is very prudent in using every scrap of cover available and tries to get away noiselessly.

If a lion is wounded and springs back into the beat, the sportsman must give a previously arranged signal, so as to warn all the beaters that there is danger, and to be ready to hide behind or in trees.   Of course the beat must be stopped at once, and the beaters ordered to join the gun.

In the chapter in which I propose to give some of my personal experiences in lion-shooting, will be found accounts of some more drives.   Now I will only mention one more adventure, the memory of which still vexes me.   In a thicket of the Tirina, which we had driven a few times, I had already put out a zebra for bait, because we had seen a very fine lion pass into it on the previous evening. We knew the place thoroughly and remembering a little slope in the ground, I was convinced the lion would be hiding there. Ten to twelve yards in front of this slope was a thick bush, giving the best cover imaginable.   For a while I watched the thicket and then I returned to camp, leaving three men sitting on trees round about.   At noon I wanted to begin the drive.   I had made up my mind to get a good photograph of this lion and after he came out I intended first to use my camera and later my rifle. My men were experienced beaters and enthusiastic about my plan and I was in high spirits when I took my stand, leant my rifle against the bush to have it handy when wanted, focused my camera to the distance anticipated, and waited.

The drive had begun.   Then the lion stepped out just where

I thought he would. He came out so slowly, that I had every chance of taking a picture from about 10 yards. The click of the shutter stopped him short and he looked in the direction of the beaters. This was my undoing. I thought I would take another picture, and in my excitement, when changing the plates, I forgot to pull up the cover over the exposed plate, so the light came in and spoiled the best plate I have ever taken in Africa!

I got so upset about it, that I was too late with my rifle as well, sending a futile shot after him as he sprang away.

The names I called myself on my march back to camp are not fit for print!

Lions are also shot over a bait. Game shot on the previous day must be put on a spot which can be easily approached and the following morning the hunter is sure to find one or two lions feeding on it. If he arrives too late the lions will have dragged the bait away, or finished feeding and left the spot, but even then it will be easy to follow up their fresh spoor. If this spoor should lead into a reed-bank or some other thick cover, it will be better to drive it out.

Although the number of animals allowed to be shot is limited, there will always be enough for bait. In Kenya shooting of zebras is unlimited, and twenty kongoni are allowed on the licence. Until night falls one must always leave one or two men to watch the bait in order to scare away the birds, for if this were not done, nothing would be left of a zebra in half an hour. The attention of all beasts of prey is attracted to the bait by the vultures circling overhead and so shortly after one's departure lions may very likely come to the bait. One of the men left behind will then be able to bring the news to camp, while the other can stay to watch the lions.

If one has the chance of shooting a rhino, it will always serve as an excellent bait, but if it were left skinned in an open place, the vultures would devour it in a few hours. If these birds are kept away, the huge bodies of elephant, giraffe and rhino will last several days, for the lion does not mind his meat high.

Vultures are very useful as advertisers of the bait in luring lions and leopards to it, but very often they entice the company of the unwanted hyena; and usually out of ten nightly visitors, nine will be hyenas.

Shooting lions on a bait will only be effective so long as it is not overdone; for they, more than any other big beast of prey, are quick to learn the ways of men.

An easier way to get a lion is to keep watch at night over the bait, and although East Africans look down very much on this method, many lions have been shot in this way. Naturally it is poor sport, but a beginner may do well to spend a few nights sitting up in a thorn-blind or on a high platform near a bait. A night-watch near a water-hole is of particular interest and most useful, as a hunter can learn much about wild animal life during his vigils. I only got one lion this way, for it did not appeal to me.

For a night-watch a high platform is preferable to a "boma" as there is less chance of the lions getting the hunter's scent. But there are occasions when trees are not to be found near by, or when a tree is covered with ants, when a "boma" is better. This "boma" should be of very strong construction, otherwise it may prove a fatal trap for the hunter hiding in it. Lions are very audacious at night and the coastal lions especially are usually dangerous. Coastal lions live mostly on the bush-pigs they find in the plantations, where these animals do a lot of harm, and for this reason the settlers do not appreciate lion-hunters. They only change their minds when pig-eating lions become man-eaters and dangerous to the men working in the plantations.

Hunting the lion on horseback must be the finest sport of any, but I never got a chance to try it, as we could keep no horses on account of the tsetse fly. In my time this sport was hardly known in German East Africa, because horses could only be kept in the higher regions of the Kilimanjaro. In Kenya this thrilling sport is more common. After the lion has been run down by the mounted hunter it will suddenly turn on the pursuer, so it is essential to maintain the right distance. The moment the lion stops, the rider must be out of his saddle and prepared to shoot. Although the lion is not capable of overtaking a horse stretched at full speed over easy ground, experts say that, given a standing start, there is no horse to which a lion could not give a handicap of 25 yards in 100.

During my stay in Africa I could not keep dogs either, on account of the tsetse fly, and so I could never try hunting lions with hounds, as is sometimes done. Mr. P. Rainey, an American sportsman, brought his pack of puma hounds to Africa, but in any case I should say that a lion run to bay, standing in the middle of the yelping pack, must be very easy to shoot. In Kenya hunting lions with hounds is prohibited.

During my last African expedition I heard about a sportsman who shot lions with a bow and arrow. In Nairobi I saw a photograph of him standing by a fine lion with an arrow sticking out of its side. This must be thrilling sport, but even if others follow his example, there need be no cause to be afraid of their shooting too many lions! The motor-car hunter is far more deadly. Motor-cars crossing the plains of Africa at night attract lions into the beams of their head-lights, when they fall a very easy prey to the motoring highway hunter, who would otherwise never have dreamed of shooting a lion. It is impossible to say how many lions perish miserably from the S.S.G. of the guns of half-breed and Goanese chauffeurs, but they certainly outnumber those killed by the rifles of true sportsmen.

There can be no doubt that as a sport our way of hunting the lion cannot compare with the method adopted by the natives, who kill them with spears. We must here differentiate between the tribes who kill the king of the savannas with poisoned arrows and those who chase the lion till he turns on them and charges, fighting him only with their spears. Although the Ruvana country was often visited by the young warriors of the Majita Peninsula of the Lake Victoria Nyanza and our plain was the scene of these big lion-hunts, I could never get the chance of seeing one. My envoys often negotiated with them, asking permission for me to take part in, or at least to watch, their hunts. I even promised not to use my rifle, but my hopes of seeing these thrilling combats between man and beast of prey were never realized, and I heard afterwards that my camera was the reason of their suspicion.

This kind of lion-hunt always results in a few hunters being killed and wounded; but as the natives laconically say: "This is men's business."

I have often talked to Majies, who told me that accidents only occur if one of the hunters, when they have closed round the lion in a ring, loses courage and retreats or, even worse, takes to flight.   For if the lion charges and the man stands his ground covering himself with his shield, there is always time enough for the others to pierce the lion to death with their spears.   The native spears are made of soft iron and so can easily be bent by a lion's teeth.   There are always great festivities at the court of the Chief in honour of the successful hunters returning to their homes, and even the badly wounded take their part in them.

The missionaries of the sect of the Adventists, who had settled on the Majita Peninsula, asked for a ban on the hunting on Saturdays (being their Sundays) because their flock had given up going to church in order to join in the lion hunts; but their request was not granted.

Men of the nomadic tribes, especially the Masai, will attack a lion single-handed, if their cattle are in danger.

I once had as a guide a Masai boy, or "laiun," of sixteen, who had killed two lions single-handed, and his companions did not even acknowledge him as a hero, saying it was quite natural for a Masai to risk his life for his cattle even if he was young.   I am afraid that the Masai of to-day have changed very much for the worse since they have "advanced" with civilization.

Shooting lions with arrows needs less courage than killing them with spears.   Natives use poisoned arrows and shoot from an ambush.   It is certainly dangerous to follow up a lion which has been wounded by an arrow and very often accidents occur because the native gets excited and eager and follows before the poison has had time to work.   A zebra will travel a long way after being hit by a poisoned arrow, but a lion succumbs quickly.

CHAPTER III

The Lion (*continued*)

THE game-ranger, Mr. A. Blayney Percival, is very well known in Kenya as one of the ablest of sportsmen and one who knew East African animal life thoroughly. Every beginner ought to read his book, which contains much good advice. He is of the opinion that it is dangerous for a man to have too much luck with lions at first, as it will make him underrate them, when he may come upon bad trouble. Some writers of to-day like to class big game hunting, and particularly the pursuit of the lion, amongst non-dangerous pastimes, and this is especially the case with those who have rarely met a lion face to face. They often seem to want to add a little spice to their own experiences by stating that the lion they shot was—curious so say—in the act of charging them; but the lions other people shoot never think of doing such a thing, being very harmless animals! As a contrast, writers of yesterday—especially those of the Latin races—exaggerated the dangers of lion-hunting. But we must not forget that in those days, when weapons were far less perfect than they are to-day, the danger was certainly greater.

Theodore Roosevelt is right when he states in his book that those who have shot but twelve to twenty specimens of the five dangerous kinds of African animals, must be very cautious before generalizing. Even those who have shot hundreds, and are reliable observers as well, hold very different opinions about the dangers of big game hunting. Some say this, others say that animal is dangerous, but as everybody hunts under different circumstances and in different surroundings, it seems quite natural that their experiences should also be different. Even individual animals living in the same district differ in character. Some may be naturally aggressive and likely to charge, while others will not charge even when wounded. Amongst animals living in herds—for instance, the elephant—some whole herds earn a bad reputation, but this is generally the result of their having been disturbed too frequently. The same may be said about lions, for instance, the coast lions are more dangerous than those of other regions.

The lion is certainly a very serious antagonist, for even great authorities like F. C. Selous, who was equally as famous as an accurate observer and as a great hunter, declares that the lion is the most dangerous animal to hunt in Africa.

Even so, it can be accepted as a rule that in districts where lions are not often hunted they will never attack or turn on one, even when wounded.

In a dense reed-bank, where rushes and sedges grow in tangled masses, or in the impenetrable high grass, where the pursued has the advantages of the situation, it is always dangerous to follow a wounded lion. Still it may happen, as it has often happened to me, that on hearing his pursuers approaching, the lion, hiding in the grass, will only growl and try to escape, without even thinking of charging. Very often the wounded lion is made to move on again and again, until at last he gets annoyed, and attacks at the most unexpected moment. So one can never be sufficiently careful when following up a wounded lion.

Some declare that if the pursuers advance in mass formation a lion will not charge, because the sight of a crowd is too much for a lion's courage. This may be partly true, yet when the natives hunt lion and finish by closing round one, it will always try to get away by charging.

One thing you must make a rule of, and that is always to take your time when aiming, and you must aim with precision and try to disable him by smashing one or more of the big bones.

The lion hunted on foot without dogs will always be a very dangerous opponent, and inscriptions on the tombstones of the Nairobi cemetery will tell you why lion-hunting is such a thrilling sport.

That most successful elephant hunter, W. D. M. Bell, in his book *The Wanderings of an Elephant Hunter*, states that amongst the forty sportsmen who hunted lions seriously in Kenya in one

MY SECOND LION, ENTIRELY MANELESS. SHOT ON LETEMA MTS. 1904

YELLOW-MANED LION, SHOT ON RUVANA PLAINS

COLLECTING-CAMP AT LETEMA

THE SKULL OF MY FIRST LION

SKINNING MY LAST RUVANA LION

PANDASARO AND MY FIRST RUVANA LION

CHEETAH-KILLING "HEROES" IN THE CAMP OF SULTANI KUDUTU

year, twenty were injured and ten died from their wounds. Mr. Bell explains this by the fact that even the most cool-headed sportsman who wants to shoot a lion has a tendency to become hasty and imprudent, and my own idea is that he is right. I myself behaved like this at Semliki in January, 1926. When the opportunity of shooting an Uganda lion had at last come, I was too excited to shoot carefully, as I will recount in another chapter.

When a lion is in the act of charging, he first puts his ears back, and the males bristle their manes up into a kind of hood, and his tail, stiff as a rod, is lifted vertically. When attacking from close quarters he is very quick in all his movements; but if he is farther off he will approach first at a trot, his gaze fixed on you; then he will break into a fast gallop when about 80 or 100 yards off. It is a magnificent, fearfully wonderful spectacle—it electrifies your nerves and will live in your memory for ever! But I don't want any more of it; I don't like the charging lion!

The lion is not tough—far less so than any of the larger antelopes—and yet when he charges it is hard to kill him outright, even if your nerves are steady and your rifle held straight. Hunting on horseback has the advantage that you need not wait for the charging lion: you can jump into saddle and take to flight. On foot, however, you can only rely upon your rifle, for it would be fatal to run away. Sometimes it may be advisable to climb a tree, if one is at hand and if the natives have not occupied every attainable place, which they certainly will have done ninety-nine times in a hundred, before the hunter has even thought of it!

I have heard and read how the well-aimed bullet of the dauntless hunter struck the lion in the act of making its murderous leap on his foe. When I was a child I read such stories with a certain reverence and thrill; but when I grew up I realized that these stories are mostly told when sitting up with a bottle of whisky. For I have been told by others and learned from own experience that the charging lion does not spring at his enemy. Often have I seen lions attacking; and twice have I seen a lion actually hit a man down. The second victim was Najsebwa—my old *munyampara*—but long before that, during my first trip to Africa, I myself was badly mauled by a lion.

It was June 11th, 1904, and the combination of my imprudence and a misfire was the cause of the accident. A lion had visited during the night the bait which I had put out near camp. It was easy to follow his track in the dewy grass and I soon sighted a maneless lion, although all I could see of him was his head and neck, for the grass was very high. The distance being hardly 40 yards it would have been easy to shoot him in the head, but as I did not want to shatter his skull, I shot him in the neck, and he rolled over with a gurgling sound. My entire escort consisted of a Mtchaga boy, who carried my shotgun and a basket, because I was in fact out solely for the purpose of collecting birds. After my lion had lain quiet for a time, I shouted to my boy, for he had kept well behind, to bring my kodak and assistance from camp. Incidentally I may say that my whole safari at that time comprised but three men, one of whom was little more than a child.

My lad ran off, and I, wanting to see more of the lion, advanced a few steps towards where he lay hidden in the long grass.

But a fierce growl made me stop short with my rifle at the ready. I did not have to wait long—the lion charged me. I aimed at his head and pressed the trigger, but a click was the only result and the next moment the lion stood before me and pawed at me just as a cat would do when fighting a dog. He struck my thigh and knocked me over. I lay sprawling on the ground, with the lion standing over me, and I held my rifle cross-wise in both hands and tried to keep his head away by pushing the rifle into his open mouth. The marks made by the lion's teeth on my 7-mm. Mauser, which I had bought from the famous German sportsman C. G. Schillings, are still visible. Somehow or other I managed to reload and fired without aiming or even lifting the rifle to my shoulder, and by wonderful luck hit the lion's eye, shattering his brains and killing him on the spot. During the short scuffle I was on my back all the time, and when I stood up I must have been a nasty sight, for my clothes were in rags and I was covered with blood. At first I thought I was very badly mauled,-but then I saw that most of the blood, which was smeared all over me, came from the lion.

But above my right wrist the blood shot out in a thin spray, so I bound my handkerchief around it and, using my rifle as a stick, I began moving towards camp. I did not call for assistance, as I knew well that the natives would not come as long as they were not certain that the lion was dead.

I noticed that I was leaving a broad blood spoor behind me, then everything became dark and I had to sit down. When I got up again I could hardly move, but my men suddenly turned up from behind a bush. On seeing my torn and blood-stained condition they were on the point of running away, and it was only after I had reassured them that they carried me back to camp.

As I had intended to leave for good in a few days, I had just exchanged my medical outfit for victuals and objects of ethnographical value, so I had hardly anything with which to dress my wounds. I made my men tear long strips of the cheap cotton cambric I had got in exchange and washed my wounds with boiled water. I then cut off a joint of my right middle finger, as it was only just hanging on.

I put this amputated finger-joint into alcohol and sent it home to the Museum with the rest of my specimens, and there they noticed the marks of arsenic poisoning under the nail and perceived how busy I had been collecting birds and preparing them for despatch.

I agree with Dr. Livingstone, who said that wounds inflicted by a lion are painless at first, but all the more painful later on, and the days following this lion affair were disagreeable for other reasons also.

The Chief of Arusha-Chini, who fortunately had lately been rendered tractable by a punitive expedition, sent some men the next day to transport me on an improvised litter to Moshi, near the foot of Kilimanjaro. We only arrived there on the fifth day. It was a terrible journey, as my wounds were very painful and fever and malaria tormented me.

The start was really the worst, because we had to cross the flooded Daryama River, and what the two sturdy natives did, in carrying me over a tree-trunk that had fallen across the river, would have done credit to any professional rope-walker. The slightest stagger and we should have been prey for the crocodiles.

During the last night of the journey I could not even get

drinking water, for the men who went for it to the river Rau were frightened away by a herd of elephants, and it was only then that I learned how simple man's desires can be. Second only to my craving for a glass of water, was my longing to lie on an operating table under the hands of an able surgeon.

But misfortunes never come singly. On arriving at Moshi, I learned that the surgeon who was stationed there had had to be taken to a coastal town because of ulcers in the liver which needed an immediate operation, and so I was only tended by a native hospital assistant.

Next day the doctor of the Protestant Mission from Marangu, the dear old Dr. Plötze, arrived, having been summoned by an express messenger. He looked very gloomily at my badly neglected wounds, but in three months I had quite recovered, thanks to the careful nursing I received. I also had a bad attack of malaria, but I was really very lucky, as blood-poisoning is a common result of a mauling by a lion. Every sportsman ought to have a good syringe in his outfit, so as to be able to squirt a wound with a strong antiseptic solution.

As I am on the subject I may as well continue. When my *munyampara* was mauled by a lion it had not been wounded. The accident occurred on February 5th, 1911, near our camp on the Ruvana Plain, at a place called Makori, where there were several water-holes surrounded by masses of tangled bush and grass, which afforded the lions a wonderful hiding-place, and which I never allowed to be set on fire.

The day before the accident happened I had shot two zebras for bait. When I crept up to one in the early morning, I saw that a big lion had fed on it and had then carried off the remains into a neighbouring thicket. On the other bait, which was hidden in rather high grass, I noticed a number of animals moving and through my field-glass I made them out to be lions. One was a big, heavily-maned beast; there was another smaller one and nine lionesses. The distance was quite 400 yards, yet the brutes had already seen me, as there was no cover to hide me from their view. They took to flight and from time to time stopped to look back at me, and on this occasion as on others, I noted that lions have very long sight but poor powers of scent. I had left my gun-bearers in camp because there was heaps of work to be done and I had brought one of the porters to carry my double-barrelled cordite rifle, while I myself had my 8-mm. Mannlicher-Schönauer. As we approached the bait the man suddenly caught me by the shoulder, pointing towards it, and there I saw an old lioness which had evidently not left with the others, crouching on it and growling at us. Her attitude was very menacing, for she threw up her tail several times in an angry way, so I had to fire from a distance of 70 yards to keep her from charging. I aimed at her head and she dropped out of sight without a sound.

Paying no more attention to her we ran after the big troop of lions which was making for the Makori thicket, and we afterwards found this old, toothless lioness had dropped dead on the spot with a shot in her forehead.

The black-maned lion we were now following, stopped at the edge of the thicket to take a last look at us, and turned his whole side towards me. But I was well aware that if I advanced another step he would disappear into the thicket, so I had to recover my breath, sit down, and then risk a shot at long range (400 yards). I heard the bullet strike and saw the lion collapse, but as we approached he partially recovered and, dragging his hindquarters, vanished into the cover before I had another chance of a shot. On arrival at the spot where he had disappeared, I spotted a lioness on the other side of the thicket and gave her a round which knocked her over, and then finished her with another shot. Then I began to examine the place where the maned lion had been first hit, but a low growl made me look back to where I had just shot the lioness. Once more a lioness was standing on the very spot where I had, as I thought, killed one, and presumed that she had got up again, so I fired at this one also, knocking her down with the bullet in her shoulder; but she recovered immediately and made off. I then sent another bullet after her, breaking her forelegs, and as she sat down she got my third bullet in the chest. Had it not been for her broken leg she would probably have charged, but as it was she drew back into the grass and hid in a slight hollow in the ground. This was a great relief, for had she charged I should have been helpless, for a bullet had got stuck in the barrel during the process of reloading from the magazine, and my man with the heavy rifle was far behind. It was a common occurrence with Austrian cartridges for a bullet to be separated from the case and get stuck in the bore.

Going over to the other side of the cover we found the second lioness dead where she had collapsed and then we tracked the blood-spoor of the third. As a matter of fact we could have followed merely by the scent, as the wretched beast kept on vomiting up the very high breakfast she had just eaten. We found her a hundred yards away from where she had been wounded, lying low under a tree, growling fiercely, but a merciful bullet soon ended her career.

Meanwhile the rest of my men had arrived from camp, attracted by the numerous shots they had heard. At their head, magnificently attired in feathers and skins, was my unfortunate boy Najsebwa. He felt very important every time a lion was killed, for he was the one who cut him open and superintended the skinning operations, and so on all such occasions he put on all the finery he could collect.

My men persuaded me to leave the skinning of the three lionesses for the moment and to try to drive the fourth wounded male out of the thicket into which it had escaped. So I took my stand on the other side, where he had entered the bush, and soon the drumming and shouting began, accompanied by heavy thuds of falling stones. Suddenly I heard a menacing snarl and instantly told my men to leave off and retire behind trees, but, trusting in the success they had had up till then, they continued drumming under the leadership of my gunbearer Magambo, as they thought that the wounded lion would break covert on my side. This in fact did happen the next moment, but it was not the wounded lion that leapt right into our midst, but an unwounded and savage lioness. My men panicked and dispersed in all directions, running for their lives, which rather hindered my shooting. However, I fired, but with the certain knowledge that I had aimed too far back. After I had fired I saw the lioness overtake Najsebwa, then stand on her hind legs and hit him on the head, tearing his shoulder and felling him to the ground. Although I was quite close, I could not fire again without hitting one of the men as well as the lioness. With a shot at point-blank range

I could have saved the situation, but a water-hole separated me from the scene of the catastrophe.

Forgetting that I had seen a big crocodile in it a few days ago, I plunged into the breast-deep water and when I crawled out between the reeds on the opposite bank, I saw our giant gunbearer, Magambo, dashing to the rescue of his chief. By this time the lioness had left her victim, for startled by the splash I made when entering the pool, she had sprung back into the thicket.

When poor Najsebwa stood up he was a ghastly sight. We carried him back to camp on a litter and our return journey was very different from the triumphant procession he had led when coming out. I dressed his wounds with a strong solution of corrosive sublimate, which I squirted into his wounds with a big syringe I used for the preparation of snakes to be preserved in spirits, but before using it on Najsebwa I boiled it in water. This syringe had served me through three African expeditions. Poor Najsebwa was very brave during the proceedings and encouraged me all the time to do it thoroughly, because natives believe that if a hair of the lion remains in the wound it is sure to be mortal. I don't know which helped most to relieve his pains— the maximum dose of morphine he got or the cow and calf I presented him with as balm for his hurts.

I then sent him to Uteghi, which was a few days' march away, and put him under the care of Dr. Breuer, surgeon in charge of the sleeping sickness hospital. He entirely recovered in two months.

I came to hear of a curious native superstition as we carried the wounded man back to camp. Noticing that two of the elder men kept apart and refused to help, I gave vent to my great indignation by swearing at them and scolding them; but Najsebwa himself begged me not to force them to help, as it might be fatal to all of them. All three had had intimate relations with a married woman, and in such a case, if one of them comes to grief through a lion or leopard and the other touches him, the wounded man is sure to die, while the other will also be killed by a lion. According to this belief, the big cats of the wilderness are guardians of men's morals!

It may be of interest to state that when I met Dr. Breuer a few weeks later and asked how Najsebwa was getting on, and mentioned the wounds on his head, which had given me such trouble in trying to shave his thick hair round the edges. The doctor looked surprised and wished to know which wounds I was speaking about. Apparently Najsebwa had not thought it necessary to mention them to the "Nganga Kubwa" (big doctor) as they had fairly healed during the six days' march! The calf of his leg, that had been torn off by a stroke of the lioness' hind leg as she turned to leave her victim, took the longest time to heal.

On account of this accident I could not follow the wounded maned lion that same day, but looking for him on the next we came upon his carcase, which had already been found and partly devoured by hyenas. The three lionesses had been skinned to my entire satisfaction and their hides prepared by my men without any superintendence.

The attack of a lion is usually so determined that nothing but a mortal shot can stop him in time, and yet I have seen a case when a lion only feinted. It was two months after Najsebwa's misfortune and I was out collecting near my camp. Some time before we had found a crested crane's nest and I now perceived from a distance a yellow spot moving near it. I was completely at a loss to make out what it could be, as my Goertz field-glasses had been ruined when I made my Makori plunge. I presumed that it must be the young crested cranes walking about, so, without taking any precautions, I headed towards it. When I arrived at the spot, an infuriated lioness suddenly came charging out at me. I fired almost at random and she spun round and disappeared in the high grass. I could find no blood and no hair, so I can say for certain that I missed her. I think this lioness feigned attack only to mislead us while her cubs were escaping.

Some experienced hunters declare that if you come upon a number of lions together, you should always shoot the lioness first, because she is more apt to attack. This may be good advice, but it is hard to follow, especially if one of the males has a wonderful black mane. I—at least—am sure that I should not lose much time in thinking about which to shoot.

I think I have mentioned already that a lion is not very tough

MY FIRST BLACK-MANED RUVANA LION

HE LAY DOWN, NEVER TO RISE AGAIN

CARRYING HOME THE CHAMPION

and that a modern high-velocity small-bore rifle is quite sufficiently powerful. Percival advises a large-bore rifle for a sportsman on foot and a lighter one for the mounted hunter. I recommend the small-bore because on account of its light weight one can carry it himself. One should always carry one's weapon; those who do not will often repent and I have missed many a good chance through my laziness. The gunbearer is usually not near enough and by the time he comes up to you the animal sighted for a moment will have gone. However hard it may seem to the parched and weary hunter in the extreme heat, he must have sufficient energy to carry his rifle himself.

In regard to ammunition, the soft-nosed bullet is best for a small-bore, while more readily expanding bullets should be used in a large-bore rifle. Many, for example Percival and Bell, advise a solid bullet for use in a small-bore.

CHAPTER IV

Some Lion Hunts

TOWARDS the end of the year 1903 I had pitched camp on the bank of the Daryama River, east of Kilimanjaro, at the foot of the Letema Mountains. It was the first independent collecting station I built, and although the little hut was only made out of dry banana leaves, it served.

I was particularly pleased with the surroundings of my camp as until then I had never camped in a spot where game was so abundant. It was here that I first saw in Kilimanjaro territory that most interesting member of the gazelle tribe, the Gerenuk, which is something between a dwarf giraffe and the beautiful lesser kudu. It was here also that I shot my first leopard and my first lion, but I shall tell of that later.

But the vicinity of my camp was even more abundant in birds of all kinds, and was a perfect El Dorado for an ornithologist. Accordingly I had high hopes of my expedition proving a success, especially as other zoologists had not as yet been collecting in those parts. But in those days I fear the hunter in me got the better of the collector.

On December 24th I went out on the slope of a hill towards the evening to shoot something for the pot. This hill-side was covered with umbrella acacia forest, mimosa and thorny scrub and was the haunt of the lesser kudu. I had had my first glimpse of one of these animals a few days before as it flashed by between the bushes. Having only a shot-gun in my hand I could do nothing until the man carrying my rifle had come up, by when the lesser kudu had vanished, and although we gave up collecting for the day, we followed it in vain.

On this occasion I hoped again to come across some rare kind of game, but we had no success, and only saw a female gerenuk as it dashed past us, although we wandered all over the hill-side for many hours. I began to regret having spent all our time in the woods when I could have shot either Grant's gazelle or impala for food in the open country, so, as night was approaching, we hurried to the Daryama River, in the hopes of getting the chance of shooting a waterbuck as it came out of the jungle to drink.

We found a track used by the nomadic tribe of the Wandor-obos and just before we came to a flat stretch two dik-dik jumped up before us, one of them stopping short in the middle of the path. A quick snap-shot brought it down and my porter, a Manyema who had embraced the Mohammedan religion, ran up and cut the still struggling antelope's throat. He then threw the little beast over his shoulder and we continued our way.

When we reached the river, just as the sun was setting, we saw five waterbuck grazing in a small clearing. The conditions being very favourable I was able to get to close quarters and hit one in the shoulder. He stood motionless for a moment and then stumbled forwards and collapsed only 50 yards further on. The four younger bucks went on grazing and paid no attention to our approach, only leaving the spot when my men almost walked on them.

We were forced by darkness to leave the buck without skin-ning it or cutting him up, or even building a boma round it to keep off hyenas. But my men left camp early next morning to bring it back, in the hopes of being on the spot before the vultures, if the hyenas had not devoured it already.

I had just finished breakfast, and as it was Christmas Day I had determined not to do any work but to stay in camp, when one of the porters arrived out of breath and greatly excited, saying that the waterbuck had been dragged away by a lion. The others soon arrived too, when I inquired closely into their story.

They were all agreed that the lion had followed our track—perhaps he had scented the blood dropping from the dik-dik my man was carrying—and then he had dragged the carcase of the waterbuck away through a thorn thicket into a dense bit of jungle. My men followed his spoor, thinking the lion had left the carcase, but they were frightened by a sudden fierce snarl at very close quarters. "He is as big as an ox and very vicious" was the report they gave. I did not wait further, but shouldering the 7-mm. Mauser I had bought from Professor C. G. Schillings, I headed towards the place indicated.

We picked up the track at the spot from which the bait had been dragged away and followed it up prepared for any eventuality. I now saw for the first time in my life evidence of the terrible strength of the king of the African wilderness. The waterbuck must have weighed 500 lbs., while his horns catching in the dense foliage and thick creepers must have added to the task, yet the lion had lifted and carried him through thickets through which human beings could hardly have forced their way.

We arrived at the place where the lion had scared my men away, but the waterbuck was no longer there, and we only found parts of the entrails, pieces of bone, and gore. It was no hard task to follow the spoor and we soon found the whole carcase, which had been practically disembowelled, while only part of one haunch and some of the neck were missing.

At that time I lacked experience, but still I knew that if a lion was not satiated he would not leave his prey for good. So I followed his trail until I lost it. Then, for several hours on end, we described varying circles round the carcase, but in vain. All the time I was certain that we must have brushed past the lion's lair without rousing him.

Finally, seeing no other way, I decided to sit up and wait. My men seemed enchanted at being sent back to camp, as they were well aware of the risk of the situation and they left me keeping up a loud conversation.

I returned to the carcase with the Masai boy and the porter to build some kind of a suitable hiding-place, but as we approached a warning growl informed us that the lion had returned to his booty. For a second I was taken aback, but all hesitation left me the moment I saw the lion's head. Taking a hasty aim I pressed the trigger and my first lion dropped dead.

The Masai boy, standing behind me with a drawn sword, ran forward before I could stop him and then shouted to me, that the lion was dead.

As I stood beside the dead lion I felt the excitement of the hunt returning and was filled with exultation, when I was suddenly brought back to earth by the Masai boy's remark: "It is easy to get a lion with a rifle, but the real manly way to kill him is with the spear, as our *elmorans* do it."

In the meantime the porters, who had vanished, began to come up and I sent him after the others to call them back. They had heard the report of my rifle, and had stopped on their way waiting for news.

As I stood contemplating my first lion, I lived through again all the emotions which this wonderful hunt had given me. The bullet had entered the eye and, without touching the brain, had shattered the neck, causing instant death, and I doubted whether a better Christmas gift could possibly be given to any beginner in African hunting.

But something usually happens to take the gilt off the ginger-bread, and my joy was soon spoiled. I told my men to make a litter and carry the lion back to camp, as I naturally wanted to take a photograph of it, and then attend to the skinning in person; I hurried on in advance so as to have time to make the necessary preparations.

Hours passed and my men did not turn up. Finally, towards evening, one of my boys came, saying that being unable to carry the lion they had put it down and they now wanted food for the night. I sent them what they wanted and my best wishes as well!

By daybreak I was on my way to meet them and when I did reach them I was welcomed by a pitiful sight, for my wonderful black-maned lion was now blown up into a shapeless mass, looking more like a hippopotamus than a lion. My desperation only increased after we had skinned it, for the hide began to slip and big bunches of hair came out. We did everything possible to stop this, rubbing alum and salts into it and stretching it out in the sun to dry. This procedure showed how ignorant I then was, and the skin was completely ruined. However, I comforted myself with the reflection that even if I had succeeded in keeping my first lion's skin, I should very soon have been forced to sell it in order to raise money for pushing further afield, for in those days the Hungarian scientific institutions were very poor and their envoys poorer still. Anyhow, the skin of my first lion was never for sale and I could at least keep the skull myself.

Hardly had I taken up my quarters on the banks of the Tirina on the Ruvana Plains in 1910, than I was bowled over by a bad go of fever, which on the following day turned out to be "blackwater fever" (*Febris biliosa hæmoglobinurica*).

I was decidedly perturbed when I first saw the signs of this terrible disease, but as the fever increased, a certain lethargy stole over me. It was useless to rebel against Fate and the end seemed imminent. For two days my constitution fought a bitter fight against the disease, on the third my strength seemed to revive and joy of life began to awake once more while my brain began to work out plans for the future and only my body was weak and tired. For a time I just hung round camp and had no energy for work, but at last on June the 4th I felt strong enough to go for a half-day's excursion to collect some birds, which was always my favourite occupation.

The sun had not as yet appeared above the mountains of Ikoma when we left camp, and rain that had fallen recently had made the trees burst into leaf and the grass green again, while the sweet scent of the tiny white mimosa blossoms was wafted on the early morning breeze. How wonderful it seemed to be alive after being so ill!

I was walking ahead of my men with the slow and rather unsteady gait of the convalescent, when I noticed a flock of sand grouse chattering softly, cleaning their plumage and basking in the morning sun. As I took out my camera my gunbearer touched my back whispering the word which always sent a thrill through me, "Simba."

I had not seen a lion on the Ruvana Plains this trip, although I had been there over two months. On previous occasions I had seen many, but thanks to my own stupidity I had failed to bag one, so my present excitement was easily explained. I remember I had hoped not to meet a rhino or a lion before starting out, as I still felt too weak to face such doughty antagonists.

The lion was about 450 yards away and was trotting through sword-like sansevieria bushes. My men obeyed my signal and threw themselves on the ground and lay quiet, while my gun-bearer and I, running from bush to bush, tried to get ahead of the lion before he could reach the Tirina jungle. Running in a bent position took my breath away and after 200 yards I was trembling all over. I rested for a few moments behind a small mound of earth and tried to steady my trembling hand, but my heart was going too fast to let me take a steady aim. I did not want my men to think that I was afraid, so I crawled from behind my good cover.

The fine maned lion was standing broadside on 180 yards away, and in ordinary circumstances it would have been easy to kill him, but my hand shook so, that I was quite unable to steady the bead on the lion's shoulder.

Again and again, furious at my own helplessness, I raised my rifle, and at last the lion saw me and trotted away, growling all the time. "It doesn't matter now," I thought, and sent two bullets after him.

I had long got over the beginner's wish to see a lion charge, for by now I knew but too well that the best hunter's chances are poor if a lion charges him.

But now I did almost wish the lion to turn back and charge, because in my desperation I thought that the feeling of danger would make my former strength return. As a matter of fact I doubt if a charge would have had the desired effect and escape would have been out of the question.

The lion went into the thicket, and as following him was out of question, I only marked the spot and continued collecting birds, and the pleasure I derived from this work made me forget my chagrin at the morning's fiasco.

Towards noon I turned back entirely exhausted and sat down in the shade of a mimosa bush, just by the spot where the lion had entered the thicket. As I felt that I must spend some time there in order to regain my strength, I sent back to camp for more men, for I decided on driving the jungle. My second headman, the quick-footed Pandasaro, who a few months later was trampled on and crippled for life by a buffalo, ran to camp, returning with all the men with brass kettles, antelope horns, pikes and all manner of noise-giving instruments. I enjoyed a refreshing sleep while waiting for my men and awoke in the best of spirits, determined to make up for the morning's failure. I gave orders as to how to drive the thicket and hid behind a small bush just where the lion had gone in.

I had hardly taken my stand when I heard a funny growling, whistling and rattling noise. I was told by an experienced old African hunter that he had heard the snoring of a lion taking his midday nap, and I could only presume that the sounds I heard were made by the sleeping lion.

I had to wait a long time while the beaters were making a big circle before they could begin the drive. My men had not had much practice at driving yet, so they made a terrific noise, drumming, piping and clashing tin and brass tools together.

Some Coucal (*centropus*), the most honourable of the cuckoo family because it builds its own nest and hatches its own eggs, flew up heavily out of the grass and on the approach of the beaters a bright yellow old reedbuck darted out and rushed past me.

Nothing more stirred before the line of beaters as they approached. Then "Svaini we" yelled the Usukuma Mareni, who had spent three years in chains for cattle stealing and murder and had had opportunity enough to learn a few German expressions. A clatter made me raise my rifle and a herd of waterbuck, led by a hind, not unlike our European stag in shape and carriage, rushed towards me, while a stately bull brought up the rear.

The beaters were not 40 yards away, and I felt sure that the lion had crept back through their line, and was on the point of stopping the drive when a sudden roar crashed through the cover. My men raised a shout and I stood with rifle raised and breath held, ready to shoot.

The next instant the reeds were divided and a large lioness thundered down on me. I cannot say if she was charging or not, for I fired when she was 8 or 9 yards off and hit her in the nape of the neck, when she turned head over heels and lay dead.

The lion seemed to have outwitted us and did not show himself, and in view of my men's weariness and my own health I gave up the drive. But it gave me immense satisfaction to have bagged this first lion of the Ruvana Plains, especially in view

SECOND MANED LION OF NGURUMINI

Standing (From left to right) Kigombe, Magambo, the Author, Magombe

TWO INSTEAD OF ONE

MY FIRST MANED LION OF NGURUMINI

Hunting-dog

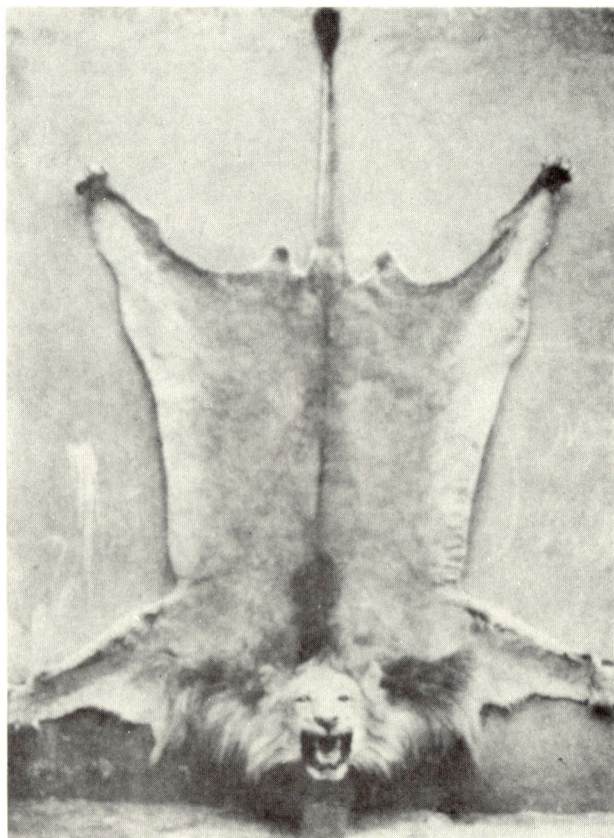

Skin of the lion marked down by hunting-dogs

of the fact that I shot her on the first day of my restoration to health.

A litter was quickly made and my men carried the lioness back to camp with shouts and cheers, and my old headman, Najsebwa, presented me with the two "lucky bones" (the rudimentary clavicles of the lion). I soon had a fine collection of these bones, but enjoyed no great luck—probably because "*Amri ya mungu*," "Allah ordered it differently."

The hunt which I will now describe also took place on the Ruvana Plains, close to my collecting camp. In few parts of German East Africa could as many lions be found as on these plains and all kinds of game were very numerous.

It would be hard to give an exact picture of the thousands of antelope, wildebeest, hartebeest, impala, Grant and Thomson gazelles, zebra, and ostrich grazing in large herds. The reader who has not travelled for months in these uninhabited regions of East Africa, cannot imagine them, and may scarcely believe me. As a natural consequence of this abundance of game, big beasts of prey, especially lions, were extremely numerous.

Towards the end of July, 1910, I heard awesome, yet wonderful serenades during the nights. Sometimes five or six lions roared only a few yards outside my rickety hut, and the worm-eaten rafters of the airy grass building vibrated with the tremendous volume of sound. After heavy showers, and on dark, stormy nights, the lords of the plains were particularly restive and noisy. Their time for hunting had come, because the hoofed animals sunk knee-deep into the soft ground and were easily overtaken. Zebras comprised the principal quarry, for the lions seemed to be just as fond of the zebra's fat, sweet meat as were the men of our safari.

During such nights I often heard the bark-like neigh of the leading stallion, followed by the thundering of hundreds of startled zebras, galloping past, and sometimes through, our camp.

On June 19th we awoke to see a glorious dawn after a dark and stormy night. Before we began our usual daily work I sent two of my trackers in the direction from which we had heard the last of the lions' roaring during the night. The trackers were armed with only a spear and knife each, yet they set off gladly and without fear. There was, in fact, less danger than might be supposed. The trackers were familiar with the wild life of the plains, knew the habits of all the animals and belonged to a race which has eyes like falcon's and muscles of iron. If they found a lion's spoor they would follow it till they sighted it or knew exactly where it was. One of them would then run back for me, while the other climbed a tree, from which he kept watch, and would observe every movement of the "simba" until I came. Generally the spoor would lead into a reed thicket, where it was impossible to follow, so we had to drive it out or burn it down.

If the drive was a success, I gave the caravan plenty of "pompe" (native beer), while the trackers were presented with generous baksheesh, and hailed in the presence of the whole caravan as " wewe manamume kabisha," or " whole men."

After my trackers received their orders they started in the direction pointed out to them and I joined the men who were at work thinning the hide of an eland, which I had shot two days before. The uninitiated will not be able fully to appreciate the difficulties of preserving the skin of a large animal, weighing far over 1,000 lbs., in the wilds. It must be worked up thoroughly and put into such a condition that a skilled taxidermist can afterwards make the animal seem alive again. My men had had plenty of practice at that time, and I was not obliged to stay with them; so having handed out the necessary amount of alum, salt mixtures and arsenic solution with full instructions, putting my headman in charge of the whole work (he was my chief skinner), and leaving one of my gunbearers to help and superintend generally, my other gunbearer and I went to try our luck in the opposite direction to that which the trackers had taken.

When we started the sun was high up in the sky and the lions had stopped roaring and retired to their hiding-places. A pair or two of overfed jackals could still be seen, sneaking off between the herds of gazelles. The graceful little animals took no notice of them, for they knew that these scavengers could do them no harm. The refreshing rain following the fires of previous days had brought out fresh grass, and enormous numbers of game could be seen all over this wonderful green pasture.

As we advanced cautiously, watching the flight of the vultures and observing spoors, my gunbearer, who was in front, suddenly started and the next instant fell head foremost over something which darted out of a hole in the ground with a vicious snarl. It was an aardvark, and unfortunately my bullet smashed this rare animal's skull to pieces. It is quite harmless and because of its under-developed teeth feeds only on insects. As I looked regretfully at the damage I had done, its mate burst out of another hole. This time I took very careful aim and succeeded so well that both my bullets pierced only the ground of the Ruvana Plains!

I sent my man back to camp with the aardvark in the hopes that it could still be saved for my collection, and continued alone, following the dry bed of the rivulet which ran along the border of a jungle, in the hopes of meeting a rhino cow and calf. Wandering about aimlessly, yet continually observing all the wild life I could, I found myself a long way from camp and only began to think about returning at noon. As I had a lot of work awaiting me, I retraced my steps and took as many short cuts as possible Suddenly a peculiar sound caught my ear, just as if some beast of prey were throttling an animal. I looked through my field-glasses in the direction of the sound and was surprised to see my tracker blowing into the bugle he had made out of a roan antelope's horn, for we had agreed definitely that he was only to blow it if he wanted to attract my attention in the event of his sighting a lion. Accordingly I lost no time in joining him, which was just as well, for my trackers had found the spoor of the lions and had followed them until they had entered a patch of very high grass, from which they had not emerged.

I quickly returned to camp to get some lunch, while my tracker gave full details of what he had seen.

All my men being wanted badly in camp, I could only take the two trackers with me for the hunt. This was contrary to my usual custom, but I armed one of them with a shot-gun, loaded with buckshot, which is not a very sportsmanlike thing to do, although a gun can sometimes be very useful in thick and high grass; but I am thankful to say that we didn't have to use it.

The spoor led us to the spot where the lions had entered the grass, which was very high and partly green where it grew on swampy soil, and consequently it had not been scorched by the fires. We made a round of the grass and as no spoor going out could be found, we were sure the lions must be lying up in the middle of the patch where the grass was highest. But how could we induce them to leave their safe resting-place ? On the opposite side to where they had entered, stood a straggling, half-dead mimosa tree. One of my trackers, the skilful Sindano (who had to leave my service a few months later because I noticed he had developed symptoms of leprosy), climbed to the top of this tree, taking a bagful of stones with him. After he was comfortably perched in the branches I made a big detour and returned to the place where the lions had gone in. My second headman, Pandasaro, stood behind me with the shot-gun. We were both partially hidden by a sickly little mimosa bush about as high as a man. Sindano then began to throw his stones into the grass patch, talking loudly all the time, probably in order to encourage himself, and kept mocking the cowardly lions which would not show themselves.

At last one of the stones must have gone very near, or perhaps even have hit the lioness, for she jumped out with an angry snarl. I missed, but immediately reloaded my Mannlicher-Schönauer, when suddenly two heads appeared, gazing at me stupidly, to the right and left of the lioness. As the lioness was the most serious adversary, I gave her another shot, which this time sped true, for I heard a roar of pain and a second later her death rattle. But by then I was already aiming at the bigger head of the two lions, for at times like this one works the magazine with astonishing rapidity. With ears set back and growling hideously he turned on me after my shot. Later I discovered that as I pulled the trigger he lifted his head, so that the first bullet grazed his jaw. My second stopped his charge and the third was only an act of mercy which killed him a few paces away.

The third lion—a maneless one—frightened by the shots, ran a little distance off, and then suddenly turned straight on us. "*Piga, bana, piga!*" stammered the man behind me. At that instant I fired. After a second's hesitation on he came again, but my next shot in the neck killed him on the spot. But he was not more than six yards away. My first shot had broken his left upper eye tooth, for his mouth was wide open as he charged me.

All three lions were breathing their last as I turned to see my man's terrified, ashen countenance, with eyes dilated in horror. I have never seen fright so visible on a human face. But the moment the rattle of the dying lions ceased his colour returned and his features relaxed. He put out his hand to me which I shook cordially. Then we went to fetch Sindano, who had by now crawled off the tree.

While Pandasaro ran back to camp for men and the camera, Sindano over and over again gave me lively illustrations of what had happened, as from his uncomfortable, but absolutely safe, retreat he had been an onlooker at a rare scene.

Soon the men arrived with great shouts of joy.

Next day we were occupied with the preserving of the skins, and it was not until late in the afternoon that I could visit the carcases. Perched on all the trees round about were hundreds of overfed vultures and marabous squatting stupidly, while on the ground round the carcases were the signs of the terrible combats these greedy birds had fought. The earth was fairly ploughed up and nothing was left of the three bodies but bones strewn about.

It was a nasty sight and made me think of human society. How often will those who should have every reason for gratitude, be the first to profit by the misfortunes of others.

How often had those winged gravediggers of the savannas fed on the morsels left from the feasts of their fallen lords !

On turning over the pages of my diary I think it is worth while giving an account of what happened on August 10th.

I was anxiously waiting for day to break, to hear how the latest recruit to our camp, a rhino calf, was feeling.

A short time before two mission boys, who were employed in the building works of the Adventists' mission house in Ikissu, had gone into the jungle at the foot of the Tyamriho Hills in search of timber and had been charged and badly mauled by rhinos. On August 8th, I got the bull, and while my men were still working on the enormous hide, I followed up the cow, shot her, and captured the young calf alive.

Next day the little pachyderm was already on friendly terms and followed me about like a dog, crying softly for a sucking bottle when it felt hungry.

With his little tail on end he trotted after his attendant all over the camp, took his four bottles of milk at a time and then retired, led again by his attendant to the bed prepared for him under a shady bush.

The usual camp life was in progress. Most of the men of the safari were occupied in scraping the rhino skin, which is tedious work, and sometimes takes nearly a week.

During my absence the white ants had badly damaged my grass hut and I spent the morning cleaning and tidying it up; but as I hated this occupation I soon gave it up and, shouldering my rifle, went for a stroll.

Before leaving camp I looked at my rhino calf. The little animal seemed fond of me, came to meet me, and sucked my naked knees with great pleasure, because the tropical sun, the sharp grasses and thorny bushes of the savannas had made the skin something like an old rhino's hide.

I was deep in thought when I left camp. The last two days had been so eventful, as more had happened in them than usually occurs in several months. I planned schemes for the future and rehearsed in my thoughts the adventures of the last few days. On the day on which I had caught the rhino calf I had received an order by special messenger, that I, as an ensign in the reserve, had to present myself at my regimental headquarters on April 10th (it was then August 8th). To be frank, I must admit that I did not worry very much.

What I wanted was to get to a part of the Tirina jungle where the bed of the Tirina broadened into a small lake, filled with water all the year round. It is here that I liked to be, when times were hard, as I could really enjoy the wonders of my nomadic life in such exquisite spots, being well content with an occasional slice of luck.

It was glorious to be undisturbed and to observe the lives of the various denizens of the small lake. Swarms of water-fowl, chattering in subdued tones, swam about between the large lotus leaves, and the splendid crested cranes displayed their finery as they stepped their wedding dances. When I heard the loud conversation of monkeys up in the trees I could tell just what it was all about; whether they were giving vent to their curiosity, or abusing a cowardly crocodile, or were scared by the sight of a leopard. There are thousands of signs which only those who are true lovers of forests, plains, swamps and hills can understand.

On a barren waste outside the Tirina jungle a large herd of topis stood sunning themselves, and close to them a gang of baboons was rummaging about. Of course each group of animals had their outposts on duty. Those of the baboons were perched on the highest trees, while the outposts of the topis stood on the tops of ant-hills.

I was just thinking that the lions I had heard in the night must have gone very far away because these vigilant creatures seemed so peaceful and completely at ease, when suddenly a terrible growling, snarling, roaring and yelling broke out of the reed thicket behind my back. As quickly as possible, I put five cartridges into my Mannlicher-Schönauer, for my rifle was not even loaded, and then I tried to see through my field-glass what the noise was all about.

It was a little way off but still I could see the reeds swaying to and fro and then they suddenly parted to let a wonderful, powerful, black-maned lion dash out. I had never yet seen his equal, and close on his heels came another in pursuit; not so fine, nor so large, but taller and in better condition. And then, like lightning, the slim body of a lioness flashed past, coming and going through the reeds. So I knew that a fight for the possession of the female was in progress, which explained why they were so noisy and wideawake after nine o'clock in the morning.

The black-maned lion went straight in the direction of the camp, while the other one followed the lioness and soon disappeared in the reeds.

I was afraid that the vanquished lion might do some harm in camp, and was particularly worried on account of the rhino calf, for the black-maned "Lord" seemed in the worst of tempers. Accordingly I hurried after him, but had hardly gone 50 yards before the other two lions came dashing out of the reeds towards me, never ceasing their angry snarls. I went down on my knee to aim, but was panting so hard that I missed, and both lions went back into the reed clump.

I reloaded and without giving them another thought ran after my black-maned beauty. But I had hardly covered more than a few yards before his rival burst out of the thicket again. On seeing me he stopped for an instant, stared at me and then, for some quite incomprehensible reason—for he was 150 to 160 yards off—he put his ears back and dashed at me in a frantic gallop.

I was in a dangerous predicament, for on the flat plain there was no cover whatever, and I was so out of breath that I could not hold my rifle steady. When I first pulled the trigger I knew that I was going to miss, but I thought that perhaps my shot would frighten and stop him. However, he paid no heed to it, but continued coming at me.

In the meantime four other lions came out of the reeds, but seemed so impressed by the report of my rifle that they backed into cover again.

I fully realized my danger and my hand became steady, when my second shot stopped him definitely.

The bullet made a curious sound as (it happened for the second time in my life) I had struck a tooth in his open mouth. Later I found a splinter of the bullet entangled in his mane.

My third shot got him in the shoulder, inflicting a mortal wound. Slowly he turned away as if he realized that the distance was too great for him in his wounded state, and made for a sansevieria bush.

I sent three bullets after him from a distance of 100 to 120 yards. He acknowledged each shot with a lift of his tail, and then, very slowly and majestically, continued moving towards the bush, but on the way lay down quietly to die.

The death of this lion, the description of which I have here given in plain illiterate words, made a very deep impression on me; I understood now why ancient writers called the lion king of the beasts.

On hearing my shots the black-maned lion, which was not 50 yards from camp, turned away and disappeared.

Naturally my men had all fled up trees like a troop of baboons.

Our baby Rhino

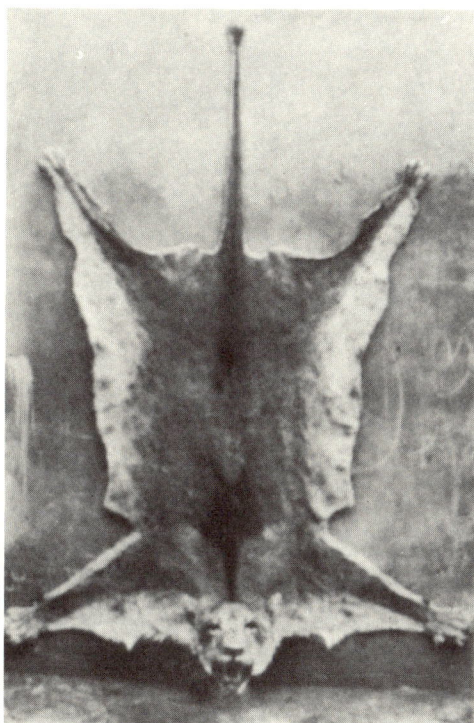

Skin of Ndassekera lioness

My two munyamparas, however, Najsebwa and Pandasaro, gave proof of great personal courage and devotion. After my second shot I saw them running towards me, one with my shotgun and the other brandishing a spear.

Meanwhile two more lions appeared and I was again so overcome by excitement that I missed them.

On my arrival in camp I was received with shouts of joy and I praised my munyamparas before the whole safari.

We then returned to the fallen hero and were witnesses of an unusual sight. A Thomson's gazelle had come up within 20 yards of the carcase and stood there—the personification of curiosity—lifting first one foot and then the other, turning its head in all directions and seeming to want an explanation of all that had just occurred.

We watched it for a good while and even my men, who were generally unmoved by such things, smiled and continued to talk about the "swala nazimu" (mad gazelle) in the evening round the fire.

The lion was carried back to camp amidst shouts of triumph.

I then pitched my tent near the Ruvana, some four miles away from our main camp, as this spot seemed most suitable both for capturing and collecting animals. But I had a disagreeable adventure during my last night in this flying camp. At about eleven o'clock I dreamed that I was shut up in a burning hut and that the flames were already parching my skin. I woke up with a start and actually feeling the heat, leapt out of bed and dashed out as quickly as possible. Driver ants, the "siafus," had invaded me. Their bite is very painful, itches like the sting of a nettle, and by brushing them off, the body only is removed, while the heads stay in the skin like those of ticks, itching and burning continuously.

I ran to the camp-fire and my men got rid of the nasty insects and I then had my bed put up outside and tried to sleep but could not, for the men had been stung while they tried to help me and kept dancing about in their pain. Afterwards they could not tell enough anecdotes and stories about the siafu ants.

In the very early dawn, while there was still moonlight, we packed up to join our main camp.

Half-way home we met Najsebwa with the news that I should hurry on to shoot a lioness which had got caught in the leopard trap the previous night.

It was an easier thing to say than to do, for the lioness had dragged the trap along and taken refuge in a dense thicket into which it was impossible to follow her. For a time I heard her angry growls, but then they ceased and I climbed a tree in the hopes of catching sight of her. I had to look for a long time before I could make out the trap; but the lioness was gone. She had pulled her leg out.

I quickly got off the tree and ran to examine the spot. The trap was covered with blood and hair, and after a careful examination I found a claw which had been torn off one of the lioness' hind paws.

I saw by the spoor that the lioness had left slowly, for she must have been exhausted by pain and fright; but as I, too, was tired and had a lot of work in store for me, I did not follow. Besides, shooting a lioness gave me little pleasure.

I put the claw I had found away in my collection of similar trophies—lucky bones, splinters of bullets, and points of arrows found in bodies of shot game. Of course I never thought of meeting my lioness again.

Three months later, when out on the banks of the Tirina, I was stopped by the chirping of some "rhino birds."

These starlings always accompany herds of game, as they sit on their backs and feed on the vermin they find on them. As we had seen a few rhino there recently I sent my two gunbearers by a roundabout way to the other bank in case the rhino birds meant a herd of rhinos. The wind was favourable, so I continued stalking in the direction of the sounds, thinking what wonderful luck it would be if my men reported that a rhino cow and calf had drawn into the jungle. It could not be so dense, thought I, that I could not get through it. But these were vain hopes, for suddenly I came upon a little clearing in the jungle, where fifteen to sixteen water-buck were grazing and the rhino birds were perched on their backs.

Meanwhile one of my gunbearers came rushing up making signs. What could have happened? What had they seen? I asked by signs for the reason of their hurry, but one of them, only half turning towards me, repeated the signal that I was to join them.

After I had joined him and as we ran on together, he told me that Sindano had seen a lioness drinking and if we were quick we might probably still find her there. I had hoped for something better, but this was not too bad.

We met Sindano coming towards us and I knew by this that the lioness had left. He reported that after she had quenched her thirst, she had seen him and with a leap sideways had disappeared in the jungle.

Meanwhile, the men carrying the net, who were following at a distance of 200 to 300 yards so as not to disturb us, had come up. "Hallo," said I, "we are going to drive that lioness out!" They had by now become so accustomed to driving that they liked the idea, and quickly laid their burden down and picked as many stones as their rags could hold and then climbed up trees. I took my stand at the spot where the lioness had entered and as there was nothing to hide me, I cut a few branches off a bush, and laying them down knelt behind them.

Very soon my men began throwing stones and yelling. One of my porters—Maremi—got so excited that he gave away his European culture by yelling "Swaini we" and "Saukerli du!"

Another Usukuma, the thick-necked Kedja, showed off his English, by saying all the time, now very appropriately, "Ondoka, you nigger!"

The drive lasted long and was without result. My men came down from the trees from time to time and collected stones. When they had got enough, they ran forwards and climbed up other trees, from which they continued bombarding the centre of the thicket. But after a while they got tired of the fun. Pandasaro, who was always full of jokes, had come to the end of his vocabulary, although the other porters acknowledged every one of his words with peals of laughter.

I had a strong feeling of uneasiness all the time, as if a pair of eyes was watching me, and began to look in all directions without seeing anything, until at last, just opposite me, I noticed something out of the ordinary.   It took me long to make out the contours of half a lion's head and a small part of its neck.

Very cautiously I lifted my rifle, but as the lion would not stir, I had to wait in that position for a long while.

I did not want to take a risky shot, but if I waited much longer I might hit a beater as they were already coming up.   So I made up my mind quickly and pulled the trigger.   After the report the roar of a wounded beast told me that the bullet had gone home.   The lioness, for it was a female, rolled over, but the next moment got up again and disappeared, so I called to my men to stop and to join me.

When they had all come up I made them stand back, because our assembling in an open space seemed unnecessarily foolhardy.

At that moment one of the porters named Sungura (Sungura means hare, for in the natives' animal stories the hare plays the same rôle as does the fox in ours) began to shout: "Huju!   Huju!" ("There!   There!").   On this the wounded lioness darted up with a roar, but my bullet knocked her over.

I said that we would start looking for the wounded lioness in half an hour and gave Sungura a scolding for his stupidity, as it would have been enough just to point at what he saw, without howling like a jackal.

When we had waited half an hour we cautiously went up to the spot where the lioness had lain down, and to see better we climbed trees round about from which we peered into the high grass, but without result.   Stones were also thrown, but in vain.

We looked for spoor in the thickest jungle, for I did not give up thoughts of tracking, when at last one of the men, who was perched on a tree, thought he saw something yellow and I climbed up to join him, only to confirm his belief.   Also an unusual piping sound caught my ear.

I took my rifle and fired, but this turned out to be unnecessary, for the lioness was dead.

She lay entangled in the creepers of the thicket and we had to cut her out with our bush knives.

My first shot got her in the chest and had broken her shoulder, which explained why she had not charged us when Sungura began shouting.   My second shot had gone through the liver.

I left a few men to skin her while we continued our excursion with the object of catching wildebeest, and did not return to camp until late in the evening. Najsebwa received us with a beaming countenance and told me excitedly that the lioness I had shot in the morning, and whose hide he had been working at all day, was "our lioness," for one claw was missing off her hind leg. So we had got the hide to complete the claw!

At the time when the following episode occurred I was more of a catcher of live animals than a collector of specimens.

One morning I perceived a lonely zebra foal, whose mother had probably been killed by a lion or perhaps only chased away by wild dogs.

Wanting to protect this poor orphan (perhaps it is unnecessary to mention that our wish was not wholly altruistic!) we hastened to lay out our net.

When we had finished doing this and the beaters had taken their places to begin the encircling drive, a large herd of zebras appeared. Hearing the plaintive neigh of the forsaken colt, the leading stallion separated from the herd and coaxing the little one tried to lead it back to the others. Swearing was of little use, so we picked up our net and began to follow them.

The herd went on ahead while the stallion and colt walked after them a long way behind. As I wanted to capture the foal I had to kill the stallion. It seemed a heartless thing to do but zebras swarmed on my plains and not much harm would be done by shooting one stallion. Further, I was in need of meat for the men and beasts of prey I had already captured. Unfortunately I only wounded it badly and it left the plain for a bush-clad range of hills, closely followed by the foal.

I went forwards with my gunbearers to look out a suitable place for putting out the nets, never letting the wounded animal with the foal out of sight, although they were quite 350 to 400 yards ahead of us. Suddenly the stallion began to sway and totter about and then collapsed. But in a few moments he got up again and went on very slowly.

Then a large-headed animal stepped out of a thicket which hid a water-hole and approached it. It was a lioness, and I signed to my men to lie flat, while I cautiously advanced from bush to bush.   I got as near as 180 yards to her when a nearer approach would only have meant being seen and she would have vanished from sight in a moment.   So, taking a quick aim, I fired.   The lioness leaped an incredible height up in the air and then spun round and disappeared in the thicket.   Although I felt as I pulled the trigger that I had shot a little too far back, I was sure I had heard the bullet strike, while I had seen the effect it had had on her.   We approached the spot cautiously but found no blood trail, and then we circled the thicket but found no spoor leading out of it, so the wounded lioness could not have left it.   To penetrate into the dense thicket would have been foolhardiness, so we were forced to try to force the wounded lioness out of the place, which was suitable for a drive, as there were high trees along the edges.   My men climbed up these trees with sufficient supplies of stones and I stood up on the opposite side behind a scanty bunch of grass, and after the usual signal had been given the bombardment began.   As the lioness was wounded I had expressly told my men not to leave their trees until ordered to do so.

In a few moments I heard the thudding noise of a heavy gallop and something yellow flashed by like lightning and vanished into the neighbouring water-hole.   I had no time to worry as to whether this was the wounded animal or not, for again I heard a thudding coming in my direction.   Yes!   This time it was the wounded lioness and she was charging me!   I aimed at her head but then realized that she had not even noticed me.   Consequently I let her pass at a distance of five yards and then sent a bullet after her which killed her on the spot.   I instinctively reloaded and aimed my rifle at her again, but this proved to be unnecessary.

I beckoned my men to come down, when we approached cautiously and on examining her closely were greatly surprised to find only one shot in her shoulder.   And yet it seemed impossible for me to have missed her.   We were trying to find an explanation when Sungura came up yelling and gesticulating in a frantic way.   He then told us that he had gone into the thicket in search of poles to carry the lioness on and was suddenly "blown at" by a lion!   So the previously wounded lioness must still be in the bush but apparently in a weak condition, or else Sungura would never have had a chance of bringing us the news! Very cautiously we approached the spot and the wounded lioness "blew" at us also, but at the next moment a merciful shot had put an end to her pain.

So, instead of bringing home a live zebra foal, we carried back two dead lionesses on a litter, while the little orphan had left its dead protector and rejoined the herd.

A very interesting variety of wild hunting dog inhabits these African plains.

Packs of from five to twenty-five of these animals hunt together and chase their prey with tenacious perseverance for many miles until it succumbs to their worrying.

The scientific name of these coloured wild dogs is *Lycaon pictus*, and neither the large eland, the shrewd leopard nor the powerful lion is safe from them, so the natives declare.

Two lion skins hang on the walls of my study. One is not very large, but black-maned, while the other is of an unusually big lioness.

I will now describe how the lion was shown me by these wild dogs.

For a week we had been trying to catch a young giraffe, and time after time we had searched the plains covered with mimosa bushes in bloom, but without result. We had caught a topi and then an impala calf, but giraffes were hard to get, because the calves were already big and difficult to take alive.

At last we came upon a troop with two young ones in it, so we put up our nets and began our drive. Through the awkwardness of two of my men the animals, which I thought were already mine, broke out of the drive, and our work proved fruitless. My gunbearer and I tried to bar the way of the fugitives but without success, although if we had been but a few yards ahead we might have returned as triumphant captors of a giraffe calf.

Tired to death, I sat down with my two gunbearers on the edge of a rock on the crest of the hill, and having nothing better to do, I had my lunch.

My men were picking up the nets on the other side of the

hill; they were also very tired, but still had enough energy left in them to beat the two poor wretches who had spoiled our catch and with it the promised feast! My gunbearers were munching at pieces of roast meat and I was breaking the shell of a hard-boiled egg against the heel of my boot, when I heard a wilde-beest bull's startled bellow and then I saw two of them, tails lifted and floating behind them like little flags, dashing along at full gallop.

Then some wild dogs emerged out of a little fluting acacia bush,—one—two—three—seven of them. I thought I under-stood the reason of the wild flight of the grotesque wildebeests, but suddenly saw something else which made me change my opinion. The wild dogs took no notice of the wildebeests, but sidled back again in single file, while the last of them—apparently the leader—turned in the direction from which one or two vultures with heavily flapping wings had risen, and barked in whining tones.

I began to suspect that the wild dogs had given way to lions, and at any other time I should have hurried down the hill, but, tired as I was, I continued drinking tea and kept an eye on the spot.

One of my men, Matiko, just then joined us. As he was one of the most ambitious members of the safari, I had given him titular "munyamparaship," of which he was proud. I was very fond of this wild nigger. He had an immense mouth and made me think of American cartoons. He was left-handed, and if I signed to him to box the ears of an impertinent or stupid "black gentleman"—Matiko took such orders too seriously—the victim guarded his left cheek, but got a quite unexpected smack on the right one. This was so funny, that even the delinquent used to laugh.

So when Matiko appeared I signed to him to find out why the wild dogs were in such a bad temper. I could see plainly through my field-glasses his expression of utter satisfaction as he went off because of the flattering confidence I had placed in him. Then he stole towards the acacia bush which I have already mentioned. In a few minutes he reappeared and beckoned with his spear and hands, by which I understood that we ought to join him.

As I jumped up, I knocked over my thermos flask, but never worried over the accident as by this time my passion for hunting had again got the better of me. I snatched the heavy cordite rifle out of my giant gunbearer's hands and while running on, took the solid bullets out of it and changed them for soft-nosed ones. These are much more effective for use on lions, because when they strike bones they mushroom and make a large and mortal wound, whereas the solid bullets just pass through the body. Matiko waited calmly for us to join him and then told us in a whisper that he had found a lion and a lioness, which got up and growled at him, but then had left separately in different directions and had gone into the scrub jungle of the plain.

I had followed the tracks of the lion for 200 to 300 yards, when I saw him hardly 40 yards off, standing broadside on in a clearing in all his yellow-maned glory. I did not want to shoot him in the head, for that would mean a great loss in value—and a poor Hungarian collector must think of these trifles—nor in the neck, for on account of his dense mane it was hard to see the right spot (in moments like this floods of thoughts flash through one's mind), so I determined to shoot him in the shoulder.

Slowly I lifted my rifle, but somehow or other the sling got caught in my field-glasses and I could not aim. I disentangled the strap as quickly as possible, but was too slow, for with a growl the lion sprang into the bush. I sent a risky shot after him, but of course missed. I ran to cut him off at the next clearing where he was bound to pass, but an angry snarl from a neighbouring bush brought me to a sudden standstill.

I saw something dark coming in my direction through the bushes and thought it was the lioness charging me and wished her with the devil, but as it changed its direction I realized that a black-maned lion was bursting out of a thicket 80 yards away from me.

He crossed a clearing, which was hardly 20 yards in width, at a heavy gallop, but when he was only half-way over he got my bullet and turned a somersault like a rabbit shot in the head. While we were skinning him a few marabous came along, with the usual flock of vultures, and one of them sat upon a tree near by and I picked him off with my little Winchester. It was lucky, because this marabou had the finest feathers I have ever seen.

Matiko was duly rewarded and what was more, got the lion's fat, which is known by the natives of Africa as well as of India as a miraculous remedy against many ills.

But my good Matiko did not know how to make the most of this treasure like others of his race, who sell it and make a fortune. His comrades soon found him out and, pandering to his vanity, called him "munyampara." He would then give away his valuable property for the pleasure of getting a title.

I left the Ruvana Plains with a small safari in September, 1911, and crossing the vast, uninhabited Wandorobo wilderness, headed towards the steep walls of the East African Rift Valley for the purpose of catching rhino. Rhino were said to be numerous in the jungles covering the mountains of Oliondo and Ndassekera, but we had to return without the baby rhino of my dreams because I had too few porters for my continually expanding collection and some of them fell ill from lack of vegetable foods. Yet I shall never forget this trip through East Africa's most wonderful wilderness.

I had pitched camp by a clear, fresh mountain spring—what a treat after the thick, yellowish puddles of the Ruvana Plains, full of frogs' spawn!—and hid our tents in the Wandorobo hunter's fashion. As I had my best men with me, our camp was very quiet, and all spoke in subdued voices, never raising them above a whisper, because they realized that human voices would be even more disturbing in this quiet solitude than the report of a rifle. Game would take the latter for thunder or the crash of a falling tree; but the sound of voices would frighten them right away.

Moreover, the unaccustomed scenery had greatly impressed my men. They came from the plains, and had never seen hills, while a passing cloud would suddenly envelop us in a dense fog, and every night clouds heavy with rain settled down like the Masai parrots which came to roost in the woods.

It was after I had stayed here a few days that an incident befell which few hunters can have experienced. An extract from my diary will be the shortest means of describing it, as well as the most reliable, for I wrote it down at the time for my own private benefit.

September 26th. It was very chilly in the morning, and I hated getting out from under my ragged blankets, but we started at an early hour while the sun was still sleeping somewhere near the Natron Lake. We had literally to wade through the ice-cold dewy grass which reached to our shoulders, and went as fast as we could.

The birds were singing everywhere. The noisy Touraco (*Turacus*), clown of the jungle, is the first to welcome the breaking dawn; then follow the Masai parrots and the Nectarinias with their cheerful greetings.

We were climbing towards the spot where two years ago the well-known Hungarian hunter, Balint Fernbach, got his first buffalo bull, and were just crossing a jungle path when the chirrup of a rhino bird and the sudden start of Magambo—who is now my favourite gunbearer—warned me that something was near. I took my cordite rifle and at the same instant I saw a big greyish mass.

I thought it was the record bull, which snorted, turned and charged, but I then saw that it was a "faru" (rhinoceros). My bullet knocked it down at once. Hardly had I regained my balance, from which I had been pushed by the heavy recoil of the elephant gun, when a second rhino came puffing at me, and the bullet from the left barrel killed it also.

Prepared for all possibilities, I went up to investigate my quarry. First the bigger one—which, to my dismay, I saw was a cow about to calve. Fortunately she had fallen on her back with her four legs sticking up, but even in this position it was hard work to make the Cæsarean section and cut open the thick hide. The solid bullet propelled by the 75 grains of cordite proved a very effective anæsthetic both during the operation and even after! At last we got the calf out. Magambo's knife had cut it slightly under the eye and by the ear. During the operation it showed no signs of life, but its heart was beating feebly. After its entry into this world it opened its mouth and began to breathe. We cut the umbilical cord, bandaged its wounds, and began to give it the necessary massage, just as a skilled maternity nurse would have done. Magambo, true to the Washashi traditions to be followed with a calving cow, blew into the baby rhino's nostrils and ears, so as to blow a soul into its body. The tiny "amuny" (the Masai name for the rhino) began breathing more strongly, and then, after about half an hour, tried to stand up, and at last began to squeal after the fashion of young rhinos. For a good while he continued squealing in this peculiar way; then, noticing the bad company in which he found himself, he snorted at us just like a grown "faru." I tried vainly to console him, but at last he fell asleep. The men had returned to camp to fetch a large canvas sheet to serve as litter and he awoke only when we put him down before my tent, when he even drank a bottle of milk. But unfortunately, so it turned out afterwards, I fed him too soon and this was the cause of his early death which befell six days later.

October 2nd. We saw a rhino on the other side of the brook on an open grassy hill-slope, but when I got there it had gone, so we continued our way. Vultures in big flocks had settled on all the trees near where the remains of the two rhinos were still lying, but I was so engrossed in my thoughts that I took no notice of this hint which ought to have warned me, but approached the carcases with nothing but a stick in my hand. When 5 or 6 yards away from them I was stopped abruptly by a furious snarl, and at the same instant a lioness whisked back into the jungle.

October 3rd. We started long before dawn. When we approached the rhinos' carcase, I heard the roar of two lions and then saw a lioness swinging round and away like a flash. I fired, although in the morning mist I could see but very badly, but Magambo was sure he had seen her collapse at the shot, and I thought so too.

As everything—trees, bushes, gullies and the valley of the stream—was lost in drifting mist, I could not investigate the spoor at the spot where the beast I had shot at had been standing. We waited for the sun or wind to disperse the fog but all in vain, so we gave it up for the time being, and only returned to the spot a few hours later. Meanwhile we had the unusual luck of seeing a pair of rhinos engaged in intercourse, a sight which few Europeans can have seen.

On our return I felt very uneasy about my lioness. Should I find her? Was she dead? Two of us thought we had seen her roll over, but Matiko said he had seen her gliding into the forest. I had a vague feeling that I had aimed too high and later I saw with a pang, that my rifle sights had been raised for 300 yards—possibly by a branch in the thicket—while she had been very close. So my hopes sank to zero.

We found nothing on the spot where she had been standing. Neither her, nor her blood spoor; but we heard a purring growl emanate from the dense jungle, into which it would have been hopeless to follow.

October 5th. Last night I was debating whether I should stay or leave this place and at last I let Fate decide. Matiko played the part of Fate and spun a coin. I was told to stay.

I did not like rising early next day, although at the time I did not feel the rheumatic pains which caught me half an hour later.

We started fully equipped, that is with a small tent, blankets and victuals. Elephant hunters or would-be rhino-catchers must always go provided for a few days, because following up an animal may lead them far afield.

I again made for the place where the two rhino carcases were lying. Although it had been quite fine a few hours before, mist was now hanging over the valley in which the stream ran. I had fortunately exchanged the solid bullet for a soft-nosed one, little thinking that I would meet another lion, as I was sure that the lioness must have had enough of yesterday's intrusion and gone for good. Besides, there was hardly anything left of the carcases beyond pieces of the skin and two hind legs.

On approaching the remains of the two *farus* I could not make them out on account of the dense fog.

I was but a few steps away from them; vultures flew with lazily flapping wings up into the neighbouring trees; a hungry hyena, scenting carrion, howled in the jungle. Then a fierce growl! But my eyes, trying to pierce the fog, could see nothing. Suddenly Magambo—just recovered from pneumonia—clutched hold of my shoulder and pointed to the lioness which was evidently in the act of charging us,—with mouth wide open. I fired and she stopped; and as the fog lifted we stood over the body of an unusually large and powerful lioness. My bullet had smashed her skull to pieces, luckily without damaging the skin.

CHAPTER V

Sitting up over Kills

ALL day long I was doing the thing I liked least—writing letters. Only when the sun was sinking westwards and not more than an hour or two remained before the dark equatorial night would suddenly sink on us, did I start for a short collecting stroll near the camp.

The boys whom I had called away from their day's work assembled before my grass hut and their leader distributed the necessary things—rifles, shotgun, camera and the collecting glasses. Then the little safari marched swiftly away in single file.

Just before we left camp my headman, who had been laying out traps, returned, reporting that he had seen a solitary old bull giraffe crossing the savanna in the direction of an acacia forest. "He is there still," he observed, and then asked me to shoot something, because meat had given out and my boys wanted food.

Soon I, too, spotted the giraffe, and for a good while watched the grotesque gait of this animated tower striding across the plain. It was a common sight, for we could see herds of from thirty to forty giraffe every day. Rhinos and lions also came within sight of the camp and on a few occasions we were even able to watch wild dogs hunt in full daylight. I never derived any pleasure from shooting giraffes, and only fired unwillingly at these harmless antediluvian creatures. In many parts of Africa they no longer exist. In the South human greed has exterminated them entirely, because the long whips which Boers use to drive their spans of oxen were made out of giraffe hides and worth several shillings each.

At the time, however, I wanted a giraffe's skull for the Hungarian National Museum, so I decided on stalking him, especially as killing a solitary bull means doing no harm to the stock.

We soon reached the place where the giraffe had entered the brushwood, and I became very cautious in my advance, as I was sure that the old fellow would be grazing off the tops of the trees not far away.

The giraffe's powers of scent are not very good, but their eyesight is marvellous and can be compared only to that of vultures, so that from his height of 18 feet he will see anybody crawling up to him. Further he has great horror of modern rifles as well as of the poisoned arrows of the natives; and, though this may seem curious, it is very hard to spot a motionless giraffe standing amongst mimosa bushes, as the variegated speckles of his hide merge completely into the surroundings.

On this occasion he saw us first, and crossed a clearing 120 yards away in his comical, heavy, swaying canter. After the sharp report of my 8-mm. Mannlicher-Schönauer he changed direction, and this fact, in addition to my distinctly hearing the sound of the bullet strike, as well as the twist of his tail, made me certain that he was hit. My second shot got him again and I saw him tottering along through the bushes of the savanna, his speed diminishing rapidly, until at last he became exhausted from loss of blood and stopped.

Swaying from side to side, knees bending under him, he still tried to keep erect, but down he went with a terrific crash and my third bullet finished him and closed for ever those big, wonderful, melancholy eyes mentioned often in Arab poetry.

We set about skinning him and found a few terrible scars which gave us an idea of the horrors of the "lion's ride." After we had finished and my men had packed away the better parts of the meat we returned home in the feeble light of the crescent moon, and left the enormous carcase to the beasts of prey of the night.

Arriving home, I made my nightly round to see that everything was in order. I visited my small zoo (for I was then already catching animals), heard the report of the keepers, then superintended the sharing out the due "posho" (victuals) to the boys by my headman, and with this my day's work was over—except for the writing of a few more letters.

Next day I made an early start in the direction of the giraffe's carcase, hoping to get a shot at a lion or a leopard on it. For these noble beasts of prey are well known to visit carrion, contrary to what old books on natural history tell us, declaring that lions feed on nothing else but their own kills.

Darkness slowly gave way to dawn as we were approaching the carcase of the giraffe and found the spoor of an unusually large herd of eland, which must have passed half an hour before. We then came upon an eland calf which had strayed from the others and got left behind, so we lost no time in putting down all unnecessary impediments and tried to close round the calf, using every bush for cover. But it was quicker than we gave it credit for and becoming aware of our presence it dashed away. Some boys ran after it, but this was mere waste of time, for the eland calf was well grown and could not be overtaken so easily.

Dropping vultures and marabous coming down in small circles with legs stretched out told me that no lions had been attracted by the giraffe's carcase, for had lions or leopards come to feast there the vultures and marabous would have settled on the surrounding trees and awaited their turn.

When we arrived, all the birds rose with heavy, noisy flight and half a dozen jackals slunk away. Little enough would be left for these animals once the big birds of prey had become masters of the situation.

We hurried up to the bait to see what could be made of the spoors of the visitors who had been feeding there during the night, for shortly all the tracks would be trampled out by the birds. From these tracks we saw that a large lion had come and fed on the bait voraciously, and after examining the surroundings my gunbearer presented me with a long black hair which he had found caught on a thorné-bush close by and whispered, "Bwana Mzé" ("The old Master").

We already knew this old, black-maned lion quite well, for my boys had often seen him quite close, while I myself had also seen him once or twice, although never at close range. So I sent two of my men back to camp to call Najsebwa, my old head-man, and a few others, to bring hatchets and bush-knives, for I wanted them to build a platform over the carcase, in which I thought I would spend the night.

Tent pitched on a timbered plain

Trophies being transported

FICUS CAMP

I left one man to keep the birds of prey away while we started on the spoor of the "Old Master."

We knew that a well-fed lion is lazy and would not go far from where he has had his repast, but would be lying up somewhere near. Tracking on the dry and stony ground was difficult and we soon lost the trail, so continued to range the jungle at random. Most probably we passed the lion several times, but as he did not stir we returned to our bait without having found out anything. My men were already waiting for me to give instructions for the building of the hiding-place.

In East Africa, where horses and dogs cannot be kept, lion-hunting is mostly a matter of luck. This is the reason why there are many old African hunters, such as the well-known German explorer, Major v. Wissmann, who have never shot a lion.

Plenty of lions have been shot from hides, and sometimes this is the only possible way unless one has the chance of walking up a lion. Sitting up over a bait is not a really sporting method and I never liked doing it, although one can never get a better opportunity for making interesting and useful observations. But shooting from a fairly safe platform, or thorny "boma," at an unsuspecting animal feeding a few yards away, never appealed to me, and I can congratulate myself on the fact that I have only shot one lion in this way.

This time I had decided to sit up, but only because I wanted to be quite certain of getting the old black-mane and partly because I wanted to enjoy thoroughly this, my last night, the night of the savanna which is so full of wonders. For I had to leave for a few weeks because the most precious treasure of my zoo—the baby rhino—had to be delivered to its new owner.

Choosing a site for a platform is always a difficult matter. None of the acacias which surrounded the small clearing in which the giraffe had fallen were suitable because red ants were swarming up and down every trunk, and woe to a hunter who would spend a night in a tree covered with ants! So, in place of anything better, I chose a strong bush which looked something like our hawthorn.

On top of this bush we built our nest out of creepers, grass and reeds matted together, the whole being supported on poles, so that it was strong and safe, but not really high enough and very uncomfortable, as it was too small for the two of us. But what would a hunter not endure for a chance at a fine black-maned lion?

When we had finished we carefully tidied everything up, for the material scattered about would be sufficient to warn wild animals of human presence, and then, leaving a man to keep the vultures off the bait, we returned to camp.

By 5 p.m. I was on my way back, accompanied by my gun-bearer, Sindano. We had hardly reached it when we met the boy, who had stayed there to scare away the birds, just starting for camp. Without the slightest concern he told us that he had seen a lioness bolting away and calmly pointed to the right, to where she could still be seen making off about 250 yards away. I might have risked a shot, but as there was a chance of the "Old Master" my interest in the lioness was slight.

After sundown we crawled up to our hiding-place and tried to make it more comfortable with the blankets we had brought for the purpose. It was dark and looked like rain: the moon was hidden behind clouds and only a little light still shone from the western sky. Silence reigned; for the noisy guinea-fowl had already gone to roost, while the birds of the night had not yet begun to chatter.

The tops of the trees, by now mere vague shadows, were melting slowly into a single dark mass. Shrubs and bushes put on fantastic shapes, and when they quivered in the breeze, I imagined I could see animals moving about until my field-glasses dispelled such illusions.

The carcase of the giraffe showed up as a big black mass, bulging out of the luminous white quartz dust which was strewn over the ground, and was alive with red-headed blue dung-flies buzzing up and then settling down again. Flocks of bats and night-jars fluttered over the decaying body, and one of the latter perched on a branch above us and gave us a melancholy tune.

But the mosquitoes—worst of all nightly musicians—had already found us. One or two were buzzing round our heads and I was just about to squash one of the nasty pests on my unshaven cheek, when Sindano, sitting on my left, shoved me gently.

Noiselessly, like a ghost, a curiously-shaped figure approached the bait. What on earth was it? Like some well-known character from a fairy-tale—a dwarf with long beard and bow legs—it comes jogging towards us. A few seconds later I made out through my glasses the mighty form of the "Old Master." His black mane and short front legs were plainly visible against the white background, while the rest of his body, being of a lighter hue, melted into it. This was why I could not make out the apparition at once.

I was so intent on watching the movements of "Bwana Mzé" through the field-glasses, that I quite forget the rifle lying across my knees. He strides slowly round the bait, looking twice in our direction; but as we are well concealed he suspects nothing. Then, purring quietly, he begins his repast. Crouching down, he tugs the enormous carcase suddenly and vigorously, when thousands of carrion-flies flit up, buzzing like a swarm of bees.

Now I can hardly see him, for he is on the other side of the big carcase. From time to time I can only hear bones cracking, for he is gnawing at the ribs.

As we have to keep motionless and cannot think of defending ourselves, the bloodthirsty mosquitoes are taking full advantage of our plight. Bats flitting over our heads do their best to thin their ranks, and sometimes they pass so close that we can feel the soft touch of their wings on our faces, just as if some small velvety hand had caressed us.

The moon is trying her best to look through the dissolving clouds, and cautiously I exchange field-glasses for rifle. Sindano touches me slightly. A second lion is approaching just as noiselessly, and from the same direction, as the "Old Master." He, too, is a powerful lion, as large and as well-maned, but fair. He stops broadside towards us before touching the carcase and that instant the moon breaks through the clouds. I might now use my rifle, but I am spellbound by the wonderful sight and wait to see what will happen. Besides, my first shot is being kept for the black-maned "Old Master."

The light-maned lion stands motionless for a long while, turning his head away from us towards his growling companion and then back again.   Then he leaves as noiselessly as he had come.

Who can tell if he had been scared away by a stronger opponent, or if he had somehow become aware of our presence?

Anxiety makes me hold my breath.   Will he return?   Has the subject of my dreams also scented us?   No, he continues to crack bones and tear flesh with undiminished appetite.

I had just decided to fire when a cloud passed over the moon and darkness again fell.   Westwards, just opposite, somewhere near the Victoria Nyanza, flashes of lightning illuminated the sky. Taking advantage of this light I tried to aim, but it was impossible, and I did not on any account want to take a risky shot.

Then came minutes of suspense.   I was afraid that my lion would get satiated and then go.   But once more a little moonlight burst forth and with sudden decision my finger pressed the trigger. A tongue of fire flashed out and the thunderous report was followed by a short, muffled roar which told me that my bullet had gone home.   I fired a second shot, but this was unnecessary, for an examination when it was light showed that the nape of the neck had been shattered.

Through my field-glasses I feasted my eyes on the glory of my trophy.   At last I had got "Bwana Mzé."   But I missed the indescribable feeling of pleasure a hunter enjoys when he has killed a lion he meets face to face.

After the report of my rifle the birds flew up and fluttered about, but gradually settled down again, and the heavy beating of wings and subdued cries told us how they were fighting for their former places.   Sometimes a dry branch, on which they shove and knock each other about, would break under them and come down with a crash.

But all this noise dies away slowly.   Silence reigns again.   A constant soft, ringing sound, like the chiming of a thousand tiny glass bells coming from under the earth, fills the sleepy wilderness. To European ears this sound is unknown.   It is the croak of many thousands of tiny frogs and the chirp of as many crickets which inhabit the reed bed.

Now two shadows—jackals—glide out of the dark and fall upon the bait with incredible greed.

But what has happened? They suddenly stop gorging and, turning to the left, sneak sulkily away. My rifle is already covering the spot from which another noble guest must be approaching the bait.

With slow, noiseless strides the yellow-maned lion is again approaching. Before touching the carcase he stops for an instant, giving me the chance of a shot. At the report the lion rolls over, roaring; but to my disappointment, after a few kicks he recovers and, spinning round like a flash, disappears into the bush. I sent another bullet after him, but this missed.

It was a hurried shot and I knew that I should not find the lion anywhere, for it seemed clear that I must have grazed his spine, as collapsing and then dashing away without ever being recovered are characteristic of such a shot.

I was, I admit, annoyed, but soon felt consoled by the wonderful sight the black-maned lion presented through my glasses.

Again the sky became overcast and the loathsome howl of hyenas could be heard from afar, but, scenting lion, they dared not approach.

My boy had fallen asleep, and I myself began to feel drowsy, as the long strain of watching had exhausted me. I went on dreaming with eyes wide open. Scenes from my life of wandering, hours of pain and happiness, came back to me, like pictures in a cinema. . . .

A cold blast passes through the wilderness. I feel an oppressive weight resting on my soul, and shivering, raise my eyes in the direction where I suppose the constellation of the Great Bear should be shining. My imagination spreads its wings, flying north, over seas. . . .

At last! at last the roar of lions comes to me through the African night! A wayward breeze carries these grand sounds from afar, from the Ruvana, many miles away. Only the beginning of the roar, that full thunderous rolling sound, can be heard distinctly; the finale continues to quiver and die away in my imagination.

A barn owl shrieks and makes me feel at home, for there is no difference between the call of our barn owl and the African, the plumage alone giving slight variations to a trained ornithologist.

Meanwhile the sky becomes overcast again and rain begins to fall.   I wrap myself in my waterproof and doze away, as the mosquitoes have also been swept away by the rain.

The cry of a lemur wakes me and the clouds begin to lift. Gradually the stars disappear.

Jackals investigate the carcase again, but my cautiously raised ·22 Winchester cracks and one of the jackals is stretched out in death, while the other saves his life by a quick retreat.

Stars are getting fewer and one or two birds begin to sing. The blurred mass of the trees dissolves, and they separate out in the growing light in different shapes and colours.   I can discern near objects without my field-glasses.

Morning dawns.   We crawl out of our blind and, having stretched our stiff limbs, run to investigate our quarry.

For a trophy such as this it is well worth giving up a night's rest to feed mosquitoes.   No words can describe my joy at the beautiful black mane, which is like pure gold on the head and turns jet-black, like silk drenched in ink, on the shoulders.

Najsebwa, smiling all over, had come out of camp to greet me.

We dragged the big body away from the giraffe's high bait, which was already alive with the grubs of flies, and began to skin him.   My short hunting knife, as sharp as a razor and well used to such work, glided straight as an arrow through the "Old Master's" skin.

CHAPTER VI

My Last Days in the Semliki Valley

THE last day of the year 1925 was a lucky one. Before descending the cliffs of the Great Rift Valley we had camped on the banks of the Nyabarogo. After we had pitched our tents I started for a little scouting expedition and found many old buffalo and still older elephant spoors everywhere. While I was examining them, my guide suddenly said in the most casual way, "Pembe!" (Horn or tusk; in this case it meant elephant).

And, truly! just underneath us in the small valley of the brook, covered with elephant grass, I saw first one enormous head and then another; then a third elephant's ears and then elephant backs showed wherever the grass was not quite so high. I made a thorough examination of them and also later of another herd consisting of eight more elephants. But there was not one out of the whole lot that would have been worth shooting, although one or two had very long tusks.

I must mention that the elephants of the Semliki are generally known as "bad elephants." Their tusks are long, thin, and of hard ivory, which means that they are light in weight and of little value. A hunter must be very careful, because long and extremely white tusks will easily deceive him and induce him to shoot one under weight, which means, at the very least, the confiscation of the ivory.

The first morning of the new year was not so lucky, as, when sitting at breakfast, a tsetse fly of the most virulent kind (*Glossina palpalis*) bit my bare knee. We were in a district which had just been isolated on account of the sleeping sickness that is disseminated through the bites of these flies.

On the afternoon of New Year's Day, just six weeks after we

71

had started from Budapest, we arrived at the Semliki River and had at last reached the real hunting-grounds. In the Semliki district game is plentiful in comparison with other parts of Uganda, but few varieties can be found there.

At first we camped on the river bank and saw elephants our first day, but they were not shootable. Buffalo were also plentiful, but there were no good heads. I intend later on to devote a special chapter to the Semliki buffalo.

The waterbuck, on the contrary, in this district were very fine compared to those of other parts. The horns of these water-buck can be said to bear the same proportion to those of other parts, as do the antlers of stags in the Hungarian Carpathians to stags in the Alps. On the sandbanks of the river numerous crocodiles were sunning themselves. To shoot these sleeping monsters and render them harmless for ever gives peculiar pleasure to the African sportsman, who has had opportunities enough of hearing about the atrocities committed by the armoured reptiles. I do not like to shoot anything but elephants in elephant country, yet here I shot eight enormous crocs. The natives on the Congo side must have been delighted, for they eat crocodile flesh as well as any other meat.

At first we camped, as already stated, near the river and went out hunting from there. Our first camp was pestered by mosquitoes; the second was even worse, as there was no protection whatever from the rays of the burning sun. So we decided on leaving the Semliki and going east. The Wahima guides were not greatly pleased by this, as they lived in the neighbourhood and could make use of every morsel of game killed. First they said that it was already included in the Game Reserve, but we then explained to them (they knew it just as well as we did) that the Reserve lay far more to the east and began at the Vasa River (the so-called Toro Game Reserve). Then they pretended that the Duke of York, who had passed through this country a year ago and had shot a good tusker, had forbidden hunting in those parts. But when, at last, they saw that we stuck to our plan and could not be dissuaded, they agreed to guide us, a decision which was really settled by the meat question. When we left the land of the Semliki, covered with elephant grass, we crossed through large

THE DEAD LIONESS AND HER KILL

ONLY A SKELETON

A Camp on the last expedition

Pushing the Ford along

Relli Rest Camp

Rest-house built of elephant grass (Ruwenzori)

COUNT SEILERN WITH MASURAMKE, ON AN ANTHILL

MIMOSA TREE BROKEN DOWN BY ELEPHANTS

coppices of borassus palm-trees and the habitations of the Wahimas. On these beautiful pastures we saw very little game, but when we left the plains and began to ascend slowly, we very soon noticed that our new hunting-grounds were the home of numerous buffaloes. Even at eleven o'clock in the morning an enormous herd passed us, grazing on the new grass, which was already sprouting on the recently burned plains. This "after-grass" will always serve as a favourite pasture for game.

The number of buffaloes, as well as of other game, induced us to pitch our camp and we very soon found a good spot on the banks of an intermittent stream, called Nakabiso, under the shade of an enormous ficus, which had served for years as the resting-place for elephants. We made but one mistake about it. It was the season of wild figs and the flying foxes came in swarms during the night. Camping underneath them was disagreeable, and our tents were dirtied by the shower of filth falling from above, and mine is still speckled like a cheetah's hide. On January 10th we began to be dissatisfied with the situation of our camp. There were elephant tracks all over the place, but they were made by unshootable beasts and so, on the next day, we decided that we would make one final attempt and then go north. We headed towards Albert Nyanza and our plan of following tracks towards the lake, or else moving south-west into the Ituri Forest in Uganda, would depend upon what we learnt from the spoor.

Some porters bringing food for my men in the evening declared they had seen about ten elephants from a distance, amongst which they thought there were two good tuskers. That night we heard the trumpeting of elephants from the direction they had indicated, so we changed our original plan, and Eugene Horthy went south after the elephant, while I continued to go north.

I was trudging along after my Wahima guide in a very bad temper, for I had dosed myself with quinine and this makes one feel cross. Hardly had we reached the top of the hills encircling Nakabiso when I made out a large herd of buffaloes calmly grazing on the opposite slope. A careful scrutiny through my glasses showed that there was not a big bull amongst them, although many were of a reddish colour.

So we went on. I had to keep on telling my guide all the

time to go slowly, for Andrea was quick-footed and sometimes seemed to bolt, while I could hardly follow.

Game was everywhere plentiful, even if not quite to the same extent as in some other parts of East Africa. At times a reedbuck would start up with tremendous bounds; then a sounder of "giri" (wart-hogs) seen; or a cautious Jackson's hartebeest would be watching us from afar. Suddenly one of the guides stopped and pointed out a large herd of buffalo moving towards us, grazing calmly. We were standing amongst some bushes, so I could watch them at leisure. My calmness seemed to influence my men as well, for they usually get very excited if buffaloes are near. My gunbearer, however, got a bit nervous as the herd approached, for not very long ago a wounded buffalo had broken his arm, and so his respect for the animal was natural.

"Johanna!"

"Ya sa!" (Yes, sir).

"Tell the Wahimas to herd these cows to your house. I give them to you as a backshish!" said I, jokingly.

Johanna's "kiboko" (hippopotamus) mouth opened in a wide grin and he seemed reassured.

We continued our advance and reached an open patch. Now the herd noticed us and I was curious to see what effect our presence made on them. They lifted their heads, left off grazing, seemed astonished and curious and slowly began moving towards us.

"Do you see, Johanna, they don't want herding; they just follow you home," I said.

On reaching our spoor, they stopped, and then slowly turned away towards the direction of their resting-place. I regret I had no camera, or even better a cinematograph, for I could have made some wonderful pictures of buffalo, and am certain that no better spot could be found for photographing them than the surroundings of the Ficus Camp.

A little further on I spotted a lot of Sunu, or Uganda kob (*Kobus Thomasi*); then another herd of these animals calmly grazing and later again two old "sunu" bucks which were gazing inexplicably in a direction opposite to where we were. Andrea, pointing in that direction, said: "*Nyama namna gani?*" (What animals are those?) I recognized them instantly to be lions moving in the high grass ahead of us, and as they are very rare in Uganda my luck was great.

I whispered: "Mpologoma" (Luganda for lion) to Johanna and tore my Mannlicher-Schönauer out of his hand as I ran towards the lions. They spotted me at once and began to move about uneasily, while the two younger ones took to flight.

I went down on my knee and examined them through my glasses, but unfortunately could not see one with a good mane. A large lioness was sitting as a dog would, with her back turned towards us, and seemed to take no notice of my approach. I aimed and fired and heard the bullet strike. The other lions sprang away in all directions, so I could not tell if she had collapsed, or had fled with the rest. The grass was not very high in comparison to most Uganda grass, yet high enough to hide a wounded lion.

I hoped that after my shot a fine-maned lion might suddenly turn up, but this was not to be, so, seeing that one was very much larger than the others, I fired at him, thinking he must be a maneless male. But he turned round just as I pressed the trigger, and I distinctly saw my bullet hit the ground. This apparently annoyed him as he turned with a fierce growl, standing broadside on to me. After waiting a few seconds to collect myself, I gave him a second shot, to which he responded with a loud roar and high spring, when I saw that one of his forelegs was broken. Better and still better chances for another shot kept presenting themselves as the lions made off in single file, but they all seemed too young and so I let them go. And then, suddenly, I thought I saw the wounded one, and fired two rapid shots, which missed —one high and one low.

In the hope of cutting off their retreat, I sped after them, while Johanna ranged up by my side handing me cartridges, and then called my attention to the lioness I had shot at first and whose backbone was broken. She was lying not far off and growling at a vulture which had settled down near her. Poor beast! Even as helpless as she was, she was still defending her legal property; for I now saw that the troop of lions had been feeding on the carcase of a Uganda kob.

I approached her and gave her two more shots which put her out of all her pain.

Here I must mention that this second bullet, although it was a solid one, did not go through the lioness, but stopped right under her skin on the other side. The steel jacket was split and the lead expanded and flattened. This was neither a good advertisement for the reliability of Austrian Mannlicher-Schönauer cartridges, nor very reassuring in regard to my anticipated elephant shooting, as only solid bullets should be used on elephants.

Hurriedly I cut the lioness open, leaving the skinning to my men and went after the other wounded lion, but with no success, for, neither I, nor my men, could find anything, not even blood spoor. However, I feel sure that we passed him several times in the high grass. This aggravated me much, as I hate to leave such noble beasts to decay and also this would have been my thirty-third lion. I had shot miserably on this occasion, for the lions were not more than 200 yards away. There was little excuse beyond that I was feeling the effects of quinine and was over-anxious at the chance of getting a Uganda lion.

One of the Wahima guides begged for the lion's flesh. "Take along as much as you can carry," said I. With this he cut off a couple of joints and went back to camp. When I asked him if he was going to eat the lion's meat, he said indignantly that he would surely not. He was going to dry it, take it to the Baambas, and exchange it for vegetables.[1] When I returned from my hunt after the other wounded lion, I found only the bare bones lying next to the remains of the Uganda kob.

It would have been quite useless to search longer, so I turned homewards. Our path led through a wonderful country. Scorched prairie-land savannas covered with fresh green lawns, were dotted with large, spreading trees and coppices. One could see by the spoor that elephants had used these cool and shady coverts as places of retreat during the rainy season. Now they were the home of buffaloes.

Two wart-hogs started out of one of these "elephant hotels." One was small, but the other seemed to carry fine tusks, so I rolled it over and discovered that although I was right about the

[1] The Baambas are inhabitants of the forest region east of Ruwenzori Mountains. They eat every variety of meat, from that of the snake to the hyena. They were most probably cannibals not long ago, and are closely related to the Pygmy tribes.

tusks, it was a sow! After taking a photograph we continued our march.

Again I let a few wart-hogs go as they were too small. Soon we came upon some Jackson's hartebeest, and while the others decamped with grotesque antics, a large bull stopped to have a look at us. I should have liked to stalk him, but as this would have involved a very long detour I decided on risking a shot at a range of about 350 yards. I could only see his narrow chest, as he was turned in my direction to watch my movements.

I sat down and took good aim. He gave every sign of being hit and staggered away, to collapse after having done 50 yards. Another exposure and then nothing more tempted me to postpone our homeward march.

CHAPTER VII

The African Elephant

THE elephant is not only the largest, but surely the most interesting animal on the African Continent. Elephant shooting is so full of variety and incredible surprises, that it is no wonder that a hunter who has experienced its thrills will fail to be excited by the pursuit of other game. It is for this reason that I have made such a big skip in zoology, from the lion to the elephant! In my opinion the elephant, and not the lion, is the lord of the African wilderness; and elephant shooting is the most exciting and the most virile of all sports.

Unfortunately the elephant areas are diminishing rapidly. The reason is that ivory has always been of great value, and consequently elephants have been exterminated in certain localities where it used to be easier to get them. For instance, south of the Zambesi River, where formerly elephants used to roam in vast herds, they are now comparatively scarce. In the books by old hunters like Cornwallis Harris, Gordon Cumming, and later F. C. Selous, elephants are mentioned as existing everywhere in South Africa in great numbers.

In Cape Colony elephants have been under governmental protection since 1830, and it is on this account that they are still able to live undisturbed in the forests of Knysna and Zitzikamma and the Addo bush. Recently, however, they have caused so much harm and damage, that the herd in the Addo bush has been reduced in numbers.

Certainly no other animal will do so much damage in plantations or be a greater enemy to human cultivation. But this is only a secondary reason why elephants have been so reduced in numbers, for even in many uninhabited, waterless regions there are none found now and it seems almost incredible that in days gone by they were abundant even in the coastal districts of Erytrea, where nowadays we can hardly imagine their ever having existed.

The famous discoverer of the Rudolf and Stephania Lakes, Count Samuel Teleky, saw daily hundreds of elephants round these lakes. To-day only white bones, crumbling to pieces, tell of former herds. West of these lakes, in Karamodjo, which was indeed "No man's land" before it came under British control, elephants were simply slaughtered. I need only mention that W. D. M. Bell returned from his second safari in this district with 14,000 lbs. of first-rate ivory.

Naturally those times have passed away for ever and although the large white spots on the map of Africa indicating "No man's lands" have not quite disappeared, they are now few in number. Rigid laws have now been enacted to protect these primeval animals from annihilation and so their survival is probably assured. A costly licence only allows two elephants a year and forbids the shooting of a bull whose tusks are under 30 lbs. each. Further, any underweight tusks are confiscated by the Government, while the hunter may also be fined for his rashness, though confiscation of the tusks would, in itself, seem a sufficient punishment.

In certain game reserves elephants are decidedly increasing in numbers; but large tuskers are ever becoming more scarce.

There are still herds of elephant to be found in the wild mountains of Kenya and Tanganyika, in the "subugos" (rain forests in the Masai language), in the bushy jungles of the coast of Jubaland, and in the uninhabited, waterless woodlands of the savannas. But a hunter whose time is limited will need great luck in order to shoot an elephant in Kenya Colony. To be sure of success he must go to the unhealthy "kibiras" (rain forests) of Uganda; for in those papyrus marshes and vast swamps, covered with elephant grass, he will still come upon very large herds; while the endless and unapproachable marshlands and great forests of the Eastern Congo will for a long time to come give refuge to the elephant.

There are several different types of African elephants. In Congo there is the dwarf elephant, whose height is but 6 feet, whereas in East Africa an old bull will stand more than 11 feet, and the largest elephants have been found on the borders of the

Sudan and Abyssinia, while it is an established fact that the African elephant is far bigger than the Indian, which is rarely 10 feet in height.

The difference between these two species is great in every way, but the most striking lies in the ears, which in the case of the African are much larger, and in the trunk, which ends in two finger-like excrescences, one in front and one behind, while the Indian elephant has only one in front. Further, the trunk of the Indian elephant is smooth, like a rubber tube, whereas the African elephant's trunk seems to be composed of rings fitting into each other like a telescope. Of course there is also a great difference in their weights. While an African will weigh from 12,000 to 15,000 lbs., an Indian will not be more than 8,000 to 10,000 lbs. As, however, it has never been found possible, either to weigh an elephant on the spot where he was shot, or to move his great body, these figures can only be regarded as being approximate. Even measuring an elephant's height is a sufficiently hard task.

The Indian elephant also has much smaller tusks than the African, and bulls without tusks are by no means rare in India. The tusks of cow Indian elephants are scarcely visible, whereas in Africa cows will often carry tusks of a respectable size. Mr. Pearson, game ranger in Uganda, shot an old cow in Masindi, whose tusks were 56 lbs. in weight each. The heaviest elephant tusk is in the British Museum and weighs 226½ lbs. This ancient animal was shot with an old muzzle-loader in 1898, below Kilimanjaro, by a native hunter.

Some years ago tusks of over 100 lbs. were not rare, but the hunter of to-day should be well content and feel very lucky if he shoots a 100-pounder. These weights refer always to one tusk, not a pair.

When I set out on my first expedition in 1903 there were still many elephants on the Kilimanjaro, and some very fine tuskers were known there. But in those days quite a lot of professional ivory hunters exercised a kind of monopoly over these parts and were helped by the native professionals, or "fundis."

Unlimited licences as to the number of elephants were also given to hunters who were not professionals, the only limitation being the minimum weight, which was at first fixed at 7 and later at 12 lbs. per tusk. For each elephant killed the hunter had to pay 100 rupees, or else forfeit the tusks.

The most fascinating of all studies of African wild life is obtained by observing a herd of elephants. I spent a lot of time sitting with a telescope on a hill-top or in a tree, watching elephants feeding or resting—sometimes from a distance, sometimes from quite near—very often at the expense of my work, as I thus lost precious time for collecting for the museum. But these hours of watching were the happiest I spent in Africa.

The habits of the elephant vary according to the different parts in which they live. In East Africa, in the Kilimanjaro country, I never saw more than fifteen to twenty elephants in one herd, while in Uganda and in Unyoro more than a hundred will keep together in herds. On January 1st, 1914, in the Lugogo papyrus swamps in Uganda, I saw a herd of at least six hundred elephants. E. C. Akeley must have seen the same herd in the Budongo forest (which lies to the north of Lugogo in Unyoro) and he estimated their numbers as being even higher, saying that there were seven hundred of them.

The elephant will travel far and these journeys are mostly made in quest of food, for he is a great gourmand and will go a long way to get fresh dainties.

In the neighbourhood of Kilimanjaro elephants used to leave the forest when the rainy period began and move towards the savannas.

When hunting in the "subugos" of the Mutyek Hills in the Great Rift Valley, I was told by an old "fundi" that elephants are forced to leave the jungle in the rainy season because of the "siafu" ants, which crawl up into their trunks and cause them great pain. It is true that we came very often upon caravans of these driver ants in the rainy season, but the theory of the old Saleh Sadiki cannot be quite accepted, although he certainly had great knowledge of the habits of elephants and rhinos.

Elephant tracks made after a rainy season in the usually waterless and semi-desert plains can often be seen many years afterwards and so it is possible to come upon elephant tracks in districts where they are now extinct. On the shores of the big

Natron Lake I came upon the track of a big bull elephant in 1910. A friend of mine had known this track in the year 1903, and it was old even then. Surely this track must have outlived the animal itself, which had probably fallen a victim to the poisoned arrows of the Wandorobos, as did most of the elephants which strayed into these parts.

Sometimes I came upon regular elephant roads which must have been trodden some ten years before, the surface of which was still a yard below the normal level of the rocky soil, for in the forest regions of the west, in the impenetrable "kibiras," the elephants are the only road-builders.

The natives try to protect their crops from the devastations of elephants at night by means of big fires and loud noises, but these are ineffective means of saving their sugar-cane, pig-nut, corn and potato plantations and banana groves, and sometimes their entire produce will be destroyed.

I once saw the havoc wrought by elephants on an area of about 100 acres of mimosa forest. The trees were pulled out by the roots or broken in two; the soil was trampled; and the whole effect was as if a typhoon had swept over the land.

In that district there lived a little "mami" (this distinction is due to landowners, while the peasants cultivating the fields for a certain share are called "kopis") who was unable to procure the necessary kopis because of the devastations of elephants, and so lived by himself on his "mayro" (mayro means originally mile, a word which has been distorted, but here it is used for property, a square mile), and in spite of the struggle for existence which he had to face from year to year, he refused to leave, saying that he had got it from the "Kabaka" (king of Uganda) and so never would leave it. When I passed, the shamba of the faithful mami was a pitiful sight. Except the hut nothing remained untouched. The banana trees were broken and trampled down; the plantations entirely devastated and deprived of their fruits; even the granary huts were simply brushed away by the huge visitors. This poor fellow had been summoned to go to his chief, and his sickly wife had been alone in the hut throughout the night of terror.

This country will live for ever in my memory, for a few days afterwards, when photographing elephants, a bull tried to get me and I was forced to shoot him, although his tusks were under weight. So it was not a lucky spot in which to begin photography!

Probably this herd had often been disturbed, for it was known to be ill-tempered. In Uganda there are some herds renowned for their viciousness; for instance, near Bombo there is said to be one which will charge the instant they get wind.

When following elephant tracks I have often been amazed by the size of the trees they have broken. Unfortunately I never took any measurements of these trunks, but my photograph of one of them will give some idea of the elephant's power.

Sometimes if an extra large tree is in their way, they will help each other in the work of destruction. Two or three of them will work away until they have loosened the roots to such an extent that the tree can be knocked out of its place. They then stand around and eat the soft green leaves, young branches and even the inner bark, before proceeding to fell another tree.

On occasions, however, they seem to be possessed only by the spirit of destruction, as in no other way could I account for the extent of the damage they did.

I was often surprised to find branches broken off very high trees and at first used to think that this had been done by some unusually large-sized elephant, but later I learnt through my observations that they sometimes stand on their hind legs and thrust up their trunks to snatch at a high bough, when the weight of their bodies will be enough to break down branches of great size.

A herd of feeding elephants will carry branches for long distances, and sometimes I found a broken one in semi-desert plains, far from any trees. If we lost the spoor of the elephants we were following on rocky ground we could often pick it up by these torn, broken and chewed branches, which they spat out again after awhile.

I could never tire of watching elephants at rest or when feeding lazily, and in Uganda I had very good opportunities of observing them. It was then that I came to realize what a marvellous organ an elephant's trunk is. He may be just putting a branch into his mouth, when a fly or some other insect disturbs him, when, using trunk and branch as a fan, he will reach back and drive it away. Sometimes he will puff dust over himself to keep insects off, and in so doing he will often betray himself when resting motionless, for seeing a little cloud of dust from a distance has many a time told us where to find them.

A herd of cow elephants with calves is very noisy, but the old bulls are quiet. There can scarcely be a noisier collection of animals than a herd of undisturbed elephants, and they produce a wonderful chaos of sounds. They trumpet and growl and bellow and rattle and shriek and scream; and then follow the formidable crashes of trees falling down and the thunderous reports of cracking branches. If one is not too far away one can even hear the rumbling sounds of their stomachs at work and the loud flapping of their ears.

I loved to see two grazing elephants meet. They both throw up their trunks and let them down again, at the same time lifting one front leg with a bow. I often saw this and always had the feeling that elephants greet each other in this way.

But the peaceful scene will change the moment the wind turns to our disadvantage. All the trunks fly up and death-like silence prevails. The trunks begin to turn round and round in the air—even the smallest calves will follow the example of their elders—and then holding the ends of their trunks backwards, they begin to retreat. First they go noiselessly, but when they think they are out of the danger zone, they will suddenly give vent to their bad temper and break into wild trumpeting as they march away.

With the same trunk with which an elephant can take hold of a coin (we can see this done at the Zoo), he can also uproot a large tree, and in addition to this it is a most wonderful organ for scent. Sometimes they will catch our wind and become aware of our presence at incredible distances, and I think no other animal has the same power of scent.

The elephant makes use of his tusks in procuring food. The pair are never of the same size and shape, one being used more than the other. Natives call the elephant right- or left-handed, according to which of his tusks is worn away at the end, and this is very shrewd, as he always uses one to dig up roots and cut open the bark of trees.

In Africa elephants without tusks are rare, although single tuskers will often be seen. In India, on the other hand, the "mukna," or tuskless elephant, is quite common. I once observed a large bull for three days without shooting him because he had but one tusk, but I afterwards regretted having done so, because this one tusk was heavier than the two of the next I shot.

The tuskless elephant is said to be savage, for it will charge without provocation, and hunters will naturally keep out of its way, lest they should be forced to shoot it. During my third expedition I was told of an old tuskless bull elephant living in the papyrus marshes of the Mara River (the Ngare Dowash River is thus called before entering the Victoria Nyanza). I did not feel inclined to look for him, although an Indian merchant promised to pay the licence and share the diamond he was sure to find in the skull of the elephant. For the old Sanscrit legend has it, that in the skull of a bull elephant which has never had tusks a great "lulu" (diamond or pearl) will be found. My Indian friend was disappointed at my refusing to hunt this elephant, as I told him that I would risk going into the marshes for a 100-pounder, but not for this mythical diamond.

In Africa there are also certain savage individual elephants, like the Indian "rogues." On the Ukerewe Island in the Victoria Nyanza, during my third journey, a bull out of a small herd which lived there got very dangerous and kept the whole population in a state of panic. The utter desperation of the natives induced the Government, after awhile, to grant permission to shoot it, provided the tusks were delivered up. Naturally this did not tempt me to travel to this remote island, even when later I was told I could keep the legs.

I love to listen to the chatter of my boys in the evening, sitting round the camp-fire; but I liked best to hear the stories of the trackers and gunbearers when we were elephant hunting. These men were well versed in the ways and habits of elephants, for many of them had been the professional elephant hunters of native chiefs. They always knew of some mythical elephant beside which a normal elephant would seem small and whose tusks swept the ground so that he could hardly lift his head on account of their weight. My best guide, Ali Dazma, told me of one of these monsters which lived by the papyrus marshes of the Lugogo. This elephant was called "Kafumbe," which means "bad odour," for it was said that he disseminated a very unpleasant smell. His tusks were supposed to weigh 300 lbs. each and three and a half foot-lengths of a man would fit into his track. I had already killed the two elephants on my licence when Ali Dazma told me this tale, but he added that if I ever went after Kafumbe, I must never mention his name, for if I were to do so I was certain not to succeed and even might come to harm. This he explained by saying that this wonderful elephant would hear himself mentioned and either travel away or lie in wait and kill his persecutor.

During my last Uganda expedition I asked my gunbearer what "Kafumbe" was doing. He seemed greatly surprised at my question and said he had disappeared. He had not been killed, his spoor had not been followed, yet nobody had seen him for several years.

They all spoke in utter seriousness about "Kafumbe" and it really was not their fault that I never quite believed in his existence.

There is an African superstition that the person who sees an elephant lying down will suddenly die soon afterwards. In hilly, wooded countries it really is a rare sight to see an elephant lying down and a mountain elephant never lies down. He is a splendid climber and I have seen tracks on the upper slopes of Kilimanjaro where even heather seldom grows and every dawn brings frost.

In swampy places, however, they seem to lie down, or perhaps they only sink into the soft soil, for if they are disturbed by something, the elephants, hitherto invisible, will suddenly show up, their backs sticking out 4 to 5 feet above the reeds and rushes.

It is the hardest work I know to follow elephants through papyrus marshes, and tumbling into the deep tub-like tracks will make you lose some of your weight, as I myself found out during my last trip.

An elephant's leg seems to be made for wading. When its foot goes down into the soft soil, it flattens out and keeps the heavy body from going too deep and when he pulls it out, it shrinks up into its natural width and comes out easily without sucking up the mud as does a human foot.

For the elephant's foot is constructed somewhat like a very

perfect pneumatic tyre. The large hollows between its toes are filled with a tough, elastic, fat-like mass, which slides over the toes when the foot is lifted and makes it possible for the huge animal to move noiselessly over dried-up grass; and the old, experienced bulls, when scenting danger, are able to fade away like ghosts.

I was once following a solitary bull on Kilimanjaro and, being exhausted, we lay down for a little rest. We heard a slight sound and one of our guides said it was made by monkeys; the other one thought it was a guinea-fowl; but later we found out that the elephant we were following had been standing only 20 yards away from us. He must have noticed us and slid noiselessly away and we never saw him any more, because he had travelled over rocky soil.

Natives cut bracelets out of this mass of elastic fat in the elephant's foot, which look like amber when dried. I saw rows of these bracelets on the arm of an old "makua" (elephant hunter) and he was proud of declaring that they stood for all the elephants he had shot.

Many native tribes of East Africa will not eat elephant meat. Mohammedans make no use of it because they cannot apply the ritual throat-cutting. Some tribes say it is like cannibalism, because the elephant has one hand—the trunk—and is the nearest relative to man.

The Eastern tribes, and especially the tribes of the forests of Congo or of the marshlands of the Upper Nile, are overjoyed when an elephant is killed, and they usually celebrate the event with great festivities.

I have often eaten elephant meat myself, but prefer the toughest beef to a slice of elephant's trunk. It is only fair to add, I had a very bad cook at the time. Old hunters like Selous have stated that the elephant's heart is an exceedingly tasty dish, so any hunter of an inquiring nature should try for himself. He will also profit by learning where to find the heart and what the size of the heart is; knowledge which may prove very useful to him. But elephant's fat is excellent, as may be confirmed by everybody who—though probably driven by necessity—has used it for cooking.

CHAPTER VIII

Hunting the African Elephant

WHEN talking about big game shooting with sportsmen at home, I have often been surprised to hear that they would like to shoot lions and buffalo, while elephant shooting is rarely one of their aspirations. I have a fancy that the elephant living in their imaginations is the domesticated Indian elephant which will carry tree-trunks to the saw-mill and even rock the "mahout's" (elephant driver) child to sleep. On this account they seem to regard shooting elephants as being unsportsmanlike. This is a great mistake. The more opportunity one has of hunting the elephant, the more certain one becomes that it is the finest and most dangerous sport imaginable; while the fact alone that an elephant will lead you through the most varied country adds to the pleasure. I have hunted this largest of land animals through gorgeous "subugos"; under dark cedars from which long beards of lichen were dangling down, glittering with pearls of dew, and underneath the damp ferns illuminating the cool darkness of the densely luxuriant undergrowth, reminiscent of the primeval fern forests of old. Again I have followed elephants through endless stretches of bamboo thickets where the noise of an alarmed herd is something indescribable, and where we often sat at night by our camp-fire shivering with cold and fatigue and oppressed by the wilderness of bamboo around us. And then again I have traversed anæmic, barren, sorry, thorny, waterless bush country, in the "nyikas,"—through parched, desert-like natron steppes, into the high elephant grass and papyrus swamps and, during my last expedition, even into the "Kibira," an extension of the Congo forests.

The modern elephant hunter is severely handicapped, for all elephants have disappeared from regions where hunting on horse-

SPOT FOR DEADLY SHOT (×) ON AN ELEPHANT FACING THE HUNTER

DEADLY SHOTS (× TEMPLE, ×× HEART, ××× LUNGS)
FOR AN ELEPHANT BROADSIDE ON

MR. HORTHY WITH ELEPHANT BULL IN THE SWAMPS OF BAHR EL JEBEL.

back was possible, after the manner of Selous and his companions in South Africa.   Worst still, elephants can no longer be found in healthy and easily accessible country.   The man who wants to succeed in shooting elephants will now have to follow them into the fever zone, or to the areas infected with sleeping sickness. Besides, licences are expensive and hard to get, while "underweight shooting" is heavily fined.   Those areas which can be termed "No man's land," in which no authority holds sway and where elephants may be shot without limit, are getting very few and far between, and those who have the luck to find some piece of country that has been overlooked on the map, will surely have every right to hunting what elephants are there.

The sportsman who comes to East Africa with the intention of shooting elephants must have ample time to spare, for if this is limited, he will have to give up shooting other game and go to Uganda or the Congo with nothing else in view but elephants. But even in Uganda conditions have changed much for the worse since 1913, when I was there the first time.

After the Great War the natives began to grow larger plantations, where they worked more intensely and on a larger scale, so that they could no longer endure the frequent raids of elephants. The authorities had to lend a helping hand (Uganda is only a protectorate, which is why the natives have great influence in the Government) and gave licences for twenty-five elephants a year to anybody.   (Why was I not there?)   Later they inaugurated a band of governmental elephant-hunters, with a number of natives in their service, and these, hovering round the plantations, could shoot any elephant irrespective of tusks or sex.

Accordingly, it is hardly surprising that a good tusker is nowadays rare.   Those which escaped being killed retired to the seclusion of undisturbed areas, from which they only emerged during the night.   They are also surrounded and protected by the cows and calves of the herd, and under such circumstances it is nearly impossible to approach near enough for a shot.

Young calves and cows, like all protected animals, will often be aggressive and act on the offensive, even without being provoked.   Most sportsmen who hunted in Uganda were compelled to shoot "underweight" animals—chiefly cows—in self-defence.   The tusks of a cow elephant will rarely be up to the minimum weight.

Uganda is surely one of the most difficult of hunting countries, because of the elephant grass, which grows to over 13 and 14 feet in height, which makes it hard to sight, and far harder still to judge the tuskers.   The judging of tusks needs great experience, and native guides, trackers or gunbearers are never reliable.   One can only believe in what one sees oneself.

The quality of ivory varies in different parts of the country, but there are certain rules, which when followed, will help one to judge the weight.   First-rate ivory—so called soft ivory—is heavy and the tusks will be thicker and shorter; poor ivory is hard and lighter in weight, and the tusks are long and thin.   In most parts of Uganda, Unyoro and South Sudan good ivory prevails, so if one sees about 3 feet of tusk one need not hesitate to shoot, for the tusks will certainly weigh over 30 lbs. each.

In East Africa soft ivory is mostly found, although the tusks are not so thick as they are in Uganda, but longer.

It is not hard to distinguish a bull from the cows in a herd and in open places, for the body of the bull is much bigger, while the tusks are easily recognized.   A bull's tusk is not as luminously white as a cow's, and is always thicker.

Tracking is the general method of hunting elephants, and it is easy to find out from the spoor if there is a big tusker amongst the lot we are after.   A bull's spoor is not only larger, but of an oval shape, in contrast to the entirely round, basin-like spoor of a cow.

It can be regarded almost as a rule that big spoors lead to big tusks, although one may sometimes be surprised by getting larger tusks than the spoor had indicated.   On rocky soil it is hard to follow and judge tracks, so one must be guided rather by the dung, which will always be more voluminous when dropped by a bull than by a cow; so much so, in fact, that it will tell an experienced hunter if following up is worth his while.

I always made my trackers bring a twig with which they have taken the measurements of the tracks they had come upon, so that I could judge for myself.

A track measuring over 1½ feet would be worth following, because that would represent a 45 to 50-pounder for certain.

Mr. Rowland Ward, in the eighth edition of his book *Records of Big Game*, states that the measurement of the largest elephant foot set up is 23 inches long. The foot of an elephant I shot in West Nile Province—now standing beside me as a waste-paper basket —is 20¾ inches long.

A fresh spoor picked up at dawn should lead one up to the elephant during the day, as a travelling elephant stops to feed and spends the midday hours standing about under the shelter of a big tree. A herd then gives the impression of a huge granite block, and nothing but the slight waving of ears will tell that there is life in it. They close up together like sheep. Inside the forest they go on feeding during the heat of the day to the accompaniment of much noise, and the sounds of branches falling and twigs snapping will bring the hunter to the right spot.

It is hard to overtake a herd which has had its suspicions aroused, or worse still, been frightened by some imprudence on our side. They travel steadily and even if after a while their speed slackens, it is only to retire into some marshy place, where it is impossible to follow.

One thing is essential and that is never to get to windward of the elephant, or their marvellous powers of scent will instantly give them complete control of the situation and all our trouble, fatigue and excitement will have been in vain. Natives throw up dust or seeds of grass to show the direction of the wind. But dust is no good when the breeze is faint, or when it rains, and grass seeds will not always be at hand. I always took a little flour along in a muslin bag, while a smoker will always be able to know the direction of the wind.

The eyesight of the elephant is rather poor, but not as bad as has been stated in some books, and an elephant will always notice a man moving from a considerable distance.

His sense of hearing is not very acute either, and it is true that a herd is so noisy in itself that it seems quite unnecessary to approach quietly. Probably this is the reason why we think that they do not hear well.

When following elephant tracks, the hunter and his boys must be well provided with water, for sometimes he must bivouac on the spoor for the night, and the tracks may lead him through waterless country.

Tracks will generally be first found close to a water-hole where elephants have been drinking at night. They consume incredible quantities of water, which explains why they can go for two or three days without drinking. Elephant hunters, but usually only natives, will often profit by the water supply inside an elephant carcase, as the last means for avoiding death by thirst. It is certainly neither a very appetizing nor refreshing drink, but surely better than being parched to death.

One or two blankets, and in some districts a mosquito net, will be of good service to the hunter on a trip after elephant.

Any modern magazine rifle of great penetration will be good enough for elephant, but soft-nosed or expanding bullets should naturally never be used, as they will be quite ineffective.

The pointed bullets of the latest high-velocity rifles are not advisable either, because they are badly balanced and will often turn over in the body and so fail to reach the vital spots, especially in the case of a head-shot.

It is hard to give advice as to the calibre which should be used. A deadly head-shot can be given with a small bore, and for head-shots such a rifle is preferable; but for shoulder-shots, which mean the heart or lungs, a large-bore rifle is better. My own personal opinion is that a small-bore rifle is what I want, but a beginner should take a large-bore double. Old-fashioned 4 and 8-bore "cannon"—the 10-bore Paradox was really classed amongst small-bore rifles—have gone out of use, although quite recently. On my first expedition I shot with a double 8-bore I had been lent, and on one occasion this "mzinga" (cannon) treated me very unkindly. I was following the tracks of a solitary mighty bull elephant at the foot of Kilimanjaro through thorny undergrowth. He had uprooted a large euphorbia. The tree came down with a crash, telling me exactly where to find him and so I got very close, but seeing nothing but his head I had to shoot into his trunk, as there was no possibility of getting to one side. As I pulled the trigger, I was nearly knocked over by the fierce blow, and the explosion seemed rather excessive. In the first place I could not see the elephant because of the smoke, and when I had recovered from the shock I realized that I had fired both barrels off at once, for I had stupidly cocked both hammers. I knew that this could easily happen with these double-barrelled big bores, and both hammers ought never to be cocked at the same time.

Very much to my disgust the elephant was never found. We followed all day long on his tracks and saw that his gait was, at first, unsteady. He swayed about and vomited a few times, thus showing signs of brain concussion, but we could not overtake him. In the evening we lost the tracks as they led over rocky ground. My ears sang for several days, while for more than two months I always blinked nervously before pulling the trigger.

I am still convinced that this was the biggest elephant I am ever likely to meet, as the tracks were far the best I have ever seen.

To give an idea of the "cannon" which hunters of former days used, I must mention that the 4-bore elephant gun Sir Samuel Baker had, which was made by Gibbs of Bristol, weighed 21 lbs., while the cartridge was loaded with 16 drams of black powder and the bullet weighed 4 ounces. That rifle must have kicked a bit!

The smaller bore rifles are much handier, because first of all, a well-aimed, steady shot can be taken, and secondly, because the penetration is greater—two essentials for elephant shooting.

The vital shots on an elephant are few and small. The head-shot is the best and least cruel, but it wants much practice. The elephant's brain is very small in comparison with his large skull, so the beginner will do better to try for the heart-shot. True that a bullet in the head is far more effective, for the animal will collapse on the spot and die in a kneeling position, so that his companions will not even notice his fate, while a bullet in the heart will make him rush away with piercing screams and terrify the whole herd. Then come the difficulties of finding him, for an elephant will rush away for some distance even with a well-placed heart-shot, and although it may be hard to believe, to find a dead elephant, if only 50 to 100 yards away from where he got the bullet, is often a tedious and trying task. Another advantage of the head-shot is that if the bullet fails to strike the right place the elephant will very soon recover, whereas a badly placed body-shot will often result in a long and lingering death.

Further, it is a fact that a head-shot will never make an elephant so dangerous as will shots in other parts of the body, and my own experience is that in this respect the liver-shot is the most provocative.

If the bullet does not touch the brain but passes very near it, the elephant will collapse, but come to himself again soon and take to flight. Should an elephant collapse to a head-shot and lie quite motionless, without the dangling reflex movement of the leg, as a matter of prudence one should give him another bullet or else he may be up and away in no time.

I shall never forget when one of my "kirongosis" (guides) ran up to the elephant we thought dead and began cutting off his tail. The elephant suddenly wriggled and was trying to get up, but my second bullet spared him further trouble. My man simply flew away in terror, and I am sure nobody could have caught him.

An elephant standing broadside on is the easiest to shoot in the head. We must then draw an imaginary line between his eye and the hole of the ear, and it is there, in the pit of his temple, that the shot must be delivered, a little nearer to the ear than to the eye. If the hunter does not stand quite broadside on but a little to the rear, he should fire into the orifice of the ear.

It is much more difficult to shoot an elephant facing one. Aim should then be taken at the root, and in the very centre, of the trunk, for that is the only spot leading to the brain. A little to the right or to the left would only give him a filling in one of his tusks.

The older an elephant is the thicker his skull bones are and the harder it is to kill him with a head-shot. Cows and calves, or in other words, underweight elephants, can, however, be killed quite easily.

There is a larger field of possibilities in a shoulder-shot. In this case a big cordite Express will be the thing to use, although an experienced hunter will get the same effect with a small-bore magazine rifle.

For the heart one should aim at the anterior and lower part of the shoulder, while for the lungs a little further back and higher up. Of course a shot will be fatal, even if it fails to penetrate the heart, but only pierces one of the big blood-vessels surrounding it.

If the elephant stands facing you with head lifted, a shot low down in the chest will be sufficient, and when it turns, wounded, to bolt into the thicket jungle, a bullet up the rectum, though never a pretty shot, will very often be opportune, for it will probably hit the spine and thus paralyse the animal.   Under such circumstances alone is it pardonable.

One should never do what is often done, namely, aim at the "elephant" in general.   It only would have the bad result of frightening the herd away and very often infuriating the wounded beast, which may lead to deplorable results.

With a charging elephant there is nothing else to do but to shoot as quickly and as often as possible, and his initiative will be checked by a few shots round his eyes.   Beyond a doubt, elephants of to-day, who have often been molested and feel responsible for their cows and calves, are more dangerous than they were in times of more primitive firearms.   I came to this conclusion through my own experiences after comparing my first and last elephant hunts in Uganda.

Solitary bulls, or small bands of two or three roaming together, will be much safer to follow than herds and will also lead to better results.   It is true that such old bulls, who have often been under fire, keep to the seclusion of the thickest jungles during the day and can only be approached with difficulty; but, on the other hand, if there is no herd, one need not fear that a straggler will get wind and alarm the rest or, what happens more often nowadays, charges the hunter and obliges him to shoot an underweight animal.

Sometimes I have seen troops of ten to twenty-five bulls, and amongst these there will always be one or two good tuskers. There is nothing that appeals more to an elephant hunter than to meet such a troop on favourable ground and then to be able to pick the best tusker out of the lot.

Sometimes an alarmed herd of elephants will start off in a terrible stampede, and this is a bad moment for the hunter.   If he is in their way nothing will save him from being trampled upon and I fancy the thought that it was not done with bad intention, but merely through unaccountable panic, will not console him any the more.

It is quite inconceivable how hard it often is to sight an elephant when he is standing motionless amongst trees. It has happened to me, when looking for a shootable tusker, that I have simply bumped into a cow, and I could not tell which of us was the more scared.

Those who have hunted elephant for long will have seen that pathetic sight of a wounded elephant being helped to his feet and escorted along by his comrades. I have witnessed it, myself, a few times in the papyrus swamps of the river Mara.

1911 was a year of drought, and even the swamps of the Mara were dried up. I wanted to take advantage of this to shoot a large tusker and eventually to catch a baby elephant.

When we arrived at the edge of the great swamp, where recently the grass and the reeds had been burned and the dried bottom lay parched in the sun, we saw natives in small companies digging and hacking in it. I thought they were preparing the ground for sugar-cane plantations, but when I asked I was told that they were fishing. They were fishing for "mambas." Although "mamba" means crocodile, they were catching lung-fish (*Protopterus annectens owen*). When the tropical sun has sipped up the water, these amphibious fishes dig themselves into the clay soil, where they build a kind of cement coffin out of their phlegm. They sleep in it, waiting for the rain to fall and fill the beds of the swamps and rivers with water. These cells have a little hole at the top for ventilation, and natives are very clever at finding these phlegm coffins of *Protopterus*. This reminds me of another surprising and unforeseen answer I once got far up in the north, on the boundaries of the Danakil Desert, during one of my collecting expeditions. From a great distance I saw large black and white birds moving about on top of the acacias, and in my whole ornithological experience I had never seen the like. Asking what they might be, I received the stupefying reply that they were goats! And then, looking through my field-glasses, I made out that what they said was really true. The Bedouin women of Danakil carried the young goats out in the morning and as there was no other pasture for them to graze upon, they placed them in the tops of these trees!

I pitched my tent in a village called Iregi, which was built between masses of granite blocks. One of these served as a watch-tower during the time of the Masai attacks and from this block I examined through my field-glasses the swamps lying some hundred feet below. I could see the white herons (*Bubulcus ibis*) fluttering up and settling down again and guessed as to the where-abouts of elephants. Later I spotted dark bodies, the elephants themselves, moving about.

The "Sultani" (the chieftain) was a humorous old gentle-man, usually rather under the influence of drink, but at times he would be sober enough to give me information as to the movements of the elephants. He told me that a few years ago elephants had been very numerous in his domain, but after Shundi's[1] makuas had come and cannonaded about from morning to night in the swamps as well as in the acacia woods round them, few elephants were left. While I was there the elephants left the swamps only during the night and returned to them before it was light.

One evening, while I was watching the swarms of thousands of bats following their customary aerial route from the village to the swamps, Malioba, for this was the name of the old chief, told me a very interesting story. He said that every Mara elephant had a hole in the tip of his left ear, and this was "Ho, oho" (this was one of his favourite expressions); "Nizimu yao," he answered, when I wanted to know the cause of this.[2]

This nightly migration of the bats was something I had never seen anywhere else. Every evening some thousands of bats punctually flew at the same time, and took exactly the same route. Swarms of hawklike, rapacious birds (*Machaerhamphus*) escorted them, pouncing down every moment on their prey, but, as I observed, without much result. This daily migration of bats only occurs in the dry season, and it is probable that bats living

---

[1] Shundi, a known personality all over East Africa, was a slave from the tribe of the Kavirondos. At first he was a kind of agent in German service on Kilimanjaro and monopolized elephant hunting in the whole district. One of his fundis shot the world record tusker near Kilimanjaro. When he was forced to leave he and his Makua gang tried their luck in other parts until they came to harm in Karamodjo, where the inhabitants, who had enough of Shundi's havoc, killed him and all his men.

[2] This is their totem, or family sign. Many native families have certain animals which are their "nizimus"; the eland, the bushbuck and so on. The "nizimu" animal may not be touched by them, while of course they would never eat the meat of one.

in the crevasses of the granite blocks find few insects after the
"ntama" (millet) fields are cropped, and so have to seek food on
the swamps at night.

The day after Malioba had told me the story of the elephants'
ears, I at last had the luck to arrive in time before the elephants
retired. They were not quite in the open any longer, but had
not gone farther in than the boundaries of the swamp and were
still standing about in the high grass, and it was not so hard to
follow them. I climbed on to the shoulders of my tall gunbearer,
and from there I killed a middle-sized tusker, which, nevertheless,
seemed to be the leader, with two shoulder-shots. The herd
then lost its temper and turned on us. I scrambled off my boy's
back in no time, and we sped away in the direction of the burnt
grass. There I had to give up running, because the grass was
tangled and matted, and so I turned and shot the leading cow
with two quick shots in the head from my ·475 cordite Express.
She carried one tusk of extraordinary size. The others all rushed
up to her and tried to lift her, while some stood around with
trunks raised, searching for the enemy. In the meantime we
had reached the mimosa wood which bordered the swamps and
from a projecting rock could calmly observe the elephants. They
were still trying to lift their leader. I had a splendid view and
made sure that there was not a shootable bull amongst them.
One or two would have struck the limit, which was only 11 lbs.
at that time (in the English colonies it was already 30 lbs.), but
naturally I did not feel very keen. It would have been quite easy
to shoot one or two, or even the whole troop of twelve elephants,
for they were so intent on helping their companion, that even
the few alarm shots I fired to see what would happen, only caused
some of them to run in our direction; but not getting our wind,
they returned to their dead leader. I waited an hour thus and
was very impatient to investigate my quarry, but they showed
no intention whatever of leaving.

Meanwhile a native honey hunter ran up to me, led by the
reports of my rifle, and told me that while he had been following
a honey-guide an enormous rhino had chased him away. I left one
of my men on the rock to watch, and following his directions, got my
rhino in a few hours. It was the heaviest rhino horn I ever got.

I had shot the elephant at about half-past six in the morning, and when I returned at four in the afternoon the troop was still standing round the carcase, and only three of them had moved a little farther. The man I had left on watch said that they strode round the dead one in large circles, trumpeting furiously and seeking for the enemy, and then would again try to rouse her with their trunks.

In fact, they only left when the sun was low and, while I risked a few snaps with my camera, I was still afraid of being disturbed by a group of elephants standing about 150 yards away.

This was the only occasion on which I have known such determination on the part of elephants in standing round the dead. I have seen them try to help their mate when wounded several times, both before and after the incident just described.

Next day the men who had cut out the tusks brought in the two left ears, to Malioba's great pleasure—"Ho, oho," said he—and truly there was a round symmetrical hole in the tip of each. Further questioning was quite useless as he only repeated, "Nizimu yao!"

I cannot say whether all the elephants of the Mara Swamps have got this totem, for I did not shoot any more.

The tusk of the old cow was comparatively big, weighing 28 lbs., but the other one was broken, and only weighed 18 lbs.

The German game laws were still very primitive when I was in German East Africa. One was still allowed to hire "fundis" who, with their ancient muzzle-loaders, were a regular scourge to both elephants and rhinos.

These professional native elephant hunters called themselves "makuas," because the best hunters came from a Portugal East African tribe, called the Makuas. So all the fundis from any other tribe felt entitled to bear the name of Makuas.

These men were certainly interesting. With their long, smooth muzzle-loaders, powder-horns and caps, leather bags containing iron bullets, in which they also kept the "cheti" or the game licence, cautiously wrapped into a tanned skin. This cheti was often out of date; sometimes it was only some piece of paper written all over, and I am certain many of the Makuas thought that there was some sort of "dawa," or spell, in it.

The "dawa" plays an important rôle in the lives of all natives, but never of quite such paramount importance as in the case of a "fundi." One would see Makuas wearing a whole collection of "dawas," which they bore on a chain round their neck or a strap over their shoulder, or on a lace. But dawas dangled even on the bracelets cut from the elastic mass of an elephant's foot or spun from the hairs of its tail—which bracelets are already dawas to the man who killed the elephant—and dawas were fastened also to the butts of their rifles.

This question of Dawa-collecting was many-sided. Many of them were placed in little pouches made out of the skins of the Varanus lizard; others in the horns of antelopes, gazelles and goats, and even in empty cartridge cases. Each "dawa" had a spell of its own. For instance, one would keep off man-eating lions; while another would save you from snake-bite. Against each dangerous animal there was an unfailing "dawa." One of them was even said to prevent the hunter from being disturbed by honey-guides [1] while following elephants.

If a Makua killed many elephants he retired and left the dangerous work to his pupils and went in for the business of "dawa" making. It was a safe and lucrative occupation.

These Makuas had detailed and intimate knowledge of the lives and habits of elephants and rhinos, which explains why, even with very primitive weapons, they were able to kill these very powerful animals. It is true that they also wounded many and left them to perish of their wounds, and it was impossible to shoot an old bull in the Kilimanjaro district without finding one or two Makua bullets in him. The Makuas put two or three very badly wrought, and comparatively small iron bullets, to a ration of 6 to 10 fingers high of black powder. Firing this cartridge out of a rickety muzzle-loader was not devoid of danger, and only a shot delivered from very close quarters would do its work.

There was a belief amongst the Makuas that any man among them whose wife was untrue would be killed by an elephant or buffalo.

[1] The chattering of the honey-guide is very disagreeable in tracking an elephant or buffalo, as these beasts know that the honey-guide is calling to man and will soon decamp out of the dangerous zone. I usually shot these birds with a little ·22 Winchester as they began to warble.

Tribes of native hunters like the Wandorobos use poisoned arrows, and sometimes they throw poisoned spears and naturally hunt the elephants without selecting the big bulls.

The most famous of these tribes is the Wakambas, living round the Kenya Mountain, who, during the rainy season, will go after elephant as far as Kilimanjaro. They use such enormous bows that I hardly think a white man would be able to bend one, while their poison is said to be most deadly.

But the majority of the elephants have been killed in traps, as the natives have invented two effective ways of trapping elephants. One of them consists of a heavy log to which is attached a big spear. This log is suspended from the branch of a high tree with the spear hanging downwards. When the elephant, following his usual path, brushes past and loosens the rope of liane which holds up the log, the latter falls on the back of the elephant with tremendous force and the spear kills him. The other trap is a large pit dug in the elephant's path and hidden with branches; but this is not very effective, and usually only young ones are caught in such pits.

Probably the stories of elephants helping each other out of pits may be true. The upper bone of the near hind leg of my West Nile Province elephant had been broken and had healed up many years before, and my experienced gunbearer said this was without doubt the result of having fallen into a trap when it was young.

Formerly in the Eastern Congo and Unyoro, and even to-day in some parts of the Congo, the natives adopt a very cruel method of killing elephants. There are vast areas where elephant grass grows to a height of 12 to 15 feet and finger-thick. The natives let it grow for years without burning it down, during which time it becomes a favourite habitat of elephants, for the grass is so matted and tangled that nothing can disturb them. The natives then fire the grass in a large circle, when the blinded and scorched elephants which break through the fire can be killed with spears; but most of them perish in the fire. An ordinary grass fire does not trouble animals, for it only advances in a thin belt, and they usually go on grazing until the fire is quite close and then just jump over it. But from this formidable conflagration there is no escape, and the dry grass bursting into the flames sounds like the rattle of numbers of machine-guns. This cruel way of killing elephants is now forbidden, but there are still some spots in Africa where the arm of the law does not reach.

In Unyoro the natives do not use arrows, but they sometimes hunt by throwing spears at the elephants when they come to raid their shambas. I once heard an almost incredible story in this connection and after the most searching enquiries I discovered that it was true.

In June, 1914, I settled on the edge of the Bugoma forest where I wanted to observe the life of one of the most interesting apes, the "tchego" (black-faced chimpanzee), while at the same time I hoped to do some good collecting work.

Good guides were badly needed, for, in the forest, tracks made by elephants and buffaloes are so entangled, that it is quite impossible to find one's way unless one has spent one's whole life in it.

I got two guides out of the village Kikonda through the "mami" of the village. Both of them were trappers and snarers, and I had to promise not to repeat anything I heard of their doings, should I meet any gentlemen of the "serkal" (authorities).

One of the two guides was the hero of the story. His appearance was repulsive and this is perhaps why I could never feel much sympathy for him. When still a child he had been bitten by a puff-adder (*Bitis arietans*), and although he eventually recovered after a long illness, the venom left horrible traces on him. He only had two fingers on his right hand, while the whole right arm was degenerate, being only the arm of a five-year-old child on a huge, big man. He had been bitten on the hand, but even the right side of his face was abnormal, being pulled to one side and motionless, and the eye was of a peculiar shape and had the expression of a snake.

At first he objected to enter my service, but the mami who had been ordered by one of the ministers of the King of Unyoro to provide me with guides, persuaded him. According to the mami, my guide knew the forest thoroughly, as he constructed the pitfalls and snares and planned and headed the great drives of the dry season. But just before I arrived, he had made a fortune and this was the real reason of his unwillingness to take service.

One night my man awoke in the hut of one of his wives to hear a few elephants destroying the little shamba round it. He ran out with his spear and taking advantage of the favourable wind, got quite close to one of the elephants which was just lifting its trunk to grab the crown of a tree, and threw the spear right into the animal's throat. The elephant managed to go for 400 yards, but then expired. It was a middle-sized cow.

He was a made man, for famine was reigning over the country at the time and he could sell the meat to the Wanyoros, who do not despise it. The "serkal" also paid the fourth of the real value of the tusks, giving him some rupees, and this was enough to keep him from being obliged to serve.

When war broke out, this one-armed fellow was the first to leave me. He was dumbfounded when last year I suddenly turned up before his hut after an absence of twelve years. He recognized me instantly and leapt into the thick elephant grass and it took a lot of persuasion to get him out. At last he consented to join me again as guide and told me he had speared three elephants altogether. Two years ago he was very unlucky, for his elephant spear was carried off by a Giant Hog (*Hylochoerus meinertzhageni*). He came upon a sleeping giant hog and thrust the spear into the nape of the neck, but as he missed the vital spot, the beast darted up and ran away, disappearing for ever with the spear.

To give an idea of the practice which spear-throwing requires, I can say that I once tried to throw a spear into the carcase of an elephant. I swung the spear so that its end vibrated and then threw it into the shoulder of the dead giant. After having split the skin it bent in a ring and bounced back, so that I only just escaped being knocked over. Of course the easily roused hilarity of my boys was let loose and they swore that a spear can only be managed by blacks, while the white man should keep to his "bunduki" (rifle).

One of them then took the crooked spear, straightened it out on a stone with another one, and threw it into the elephant behind the shoulder, where it entered to a depth of two feet. He was the smallest and weakest little man of my safari, but he knew exactly how to do it.

CHAPTER IX

After Elephant in Uganda

I WAS dogged by bad luck all through the hunting season of 1913–14. In October, 1913, I was out taking pictures of elephants. Having climbed an ant-hill I was in the act of focussing my camera on two bulls which were moving in my direction. Elephants in these parts are often nervous on account of continued molestation, so catching the sound of the click of my shutter, they got furious and, screaming formidably, charged me. To save my life I shot one of them at the base of the trunk, and as he collapsed on the spot the other one retreated.

It was a great misfortune, for I saw at once that the tusks were well under 30 lbs., and an old African like myself knew that shooting an underweight bull was bad work.

I did not know how the authorities would regard this shooting of a charging bull or what penalty they would inflict, or whether they would only confiscate the tusks. They would be in the right if they took the line that it was my fault in the first place for disturbing and infuriating the elephants by my photography. But, thank goodness, authorities were very fair and generous, as the following note from the District Commissioner at Kampala testifies:

"With reference to your letter of October 24th, 1913, I have the honour to inform you that the Governor has ruled that the elephant shot by you in self-defence need not be reckoned on your licence."

District Commissioners have a marvellous secret service, and he smiled when I told him the details of my sad adventure and said that he had heard all about it long before I had come. But I had to give up the tusks which weighed 28½ lbs. and 29 lbs. Still

I could consider myself lucky to have come out of it all so well, especially as the tusks of the two elephants I shot afterwards helped towards further expenses, for it seems unnecessary to mention that a wandering Hungarian naturalist was not over-burdened with worldly riches.

December, 1913, again found me in the swamps of Lugogo after elephant. I was continually on their tracks; but as I was very careful this time, I did nothing but study the size of the elephants and never could decide on shooting. It was then that I observed the capital one-tusker which I mentioned in the last chapter.

The last night of the year came round, but there was no elephant tail in my tent as yet and the events of New Year's Day were probably warnings of sufferings I had to endure later on. But sad to say I did not understand them.

The first rosy dawn of 1914 broke upon me, and while I watched the golden-headed Sun-god bathing in the Victoria Nile, I sent my love and thoughts to those who were sleeping soundly at home. Very selfishly I also asked him to grant me a little luck for the coming year. His look seemed to me cold, but it was only a playful breeze that had torn a rag of fog from the cloud lying over the papyrus swamps. However, it made me stop my invocations to the heathen god.

We had been hurrying for an hour in the chilly morning air over the hard-trodden elephant path when we were suddenly arrested by that peculiar sound which is emitted by the bellows of an elephant when full of water. Soon we found fresh tracks and half an hour later had overtaken the slowly moving herd. I had never seen such an enormous herd and I think that there must have been at least 600 of them.

When I had approached near enough I left all of my men behind except my guides and my cowardly gunbearer (those I left were carrying the water and the cameras). We then followed the herd, which was moving on slowly, breaking trees, feeding, trumpeting and screaming. The calves and younger animals especially made an infernal noise. In districts where elephants have been molested bulls do not travel alone or in small companies, but usually keep right in the middle of a vast herd, and are thus protected by cows and young bulls, so it is very hard for the hunter to pick out a good one.

Very cautiously—always keeping up-wind—for the slightest breeze from the wrong direction would have betrayed us, we tried to approach them. How often has the wind been my worst enemy! When sailing in an old dhow on the Red Sea or the Victoria Nyanza it was sure to turn against me or to drop dead. When I was stalking big game in the bush, the wind would turn and get me in the back and spoil my hunt!

But this time the wind was steady, so we were able to approach close to the herd, to the terror of my gunbearer. The guides, however, were less frightened and pointed out some larger bulls to me. Of course they pointed with their fists, because to do so with a finger brings bad luck. I had had experience enough not to place much reliance on the judgment of the natives and examined each tusker they pointed out to me through my field-glasses but failed to find one worth shooting.

The undergrowth of the thin savanna forest had been scorched by a recent fire, so it was not hard to distinguish the elephants and to make a choice among them. I made up my mind to use this wonderful opportunity to shoot a real big one. At last I made out a huge elephant, one whose tusks certainly weighed 100 lbs. apiece. "This is the right one," thought I, but he then disappeared among the others. "No matter; I shall see him again soon and get up to close range." My thoughts ran on.

The sound of running footsteps made me turn. The men I had left behind had been coming up, and one of them, who carried my bag—an amiable young fellow—pointed out a bull elephant which had stopped behind and so had been cut off from the herd, and was now coming up. I soon detected the giant moving towards us with noiseless steps; for he was indeed a giant even amongst his own kind. But to my greatest regret his tusks were not in proportion to his enormous body, for they were hardly over the limit, being about 35 to 40 lbs. each, and their value would not have been sufficient for half of the things I wanted.

Therefore I tried slowly to move away, but as he was down wind he had got our scent and was scouting cautiously in our direction and I suspected him of some evil intentions. My men had already fled, and worst of all, the gunbearer with my Mann-licher-Schönauer had gone too. I could not run away, for my nailed boots, and the cartridges jolting about in my pockets, rendered a silent retreat impossible. When the bull got near he suddenly changed his mind, and trumpeting like mad he came for me. It was a terrible yet wonderful sight to see this charging giant in his fearful rage, the incarnation of fury of the gods of the African wilderness! One of my fleeing men—almost the oldest—tumbled over a root and fell yelling: "Mama vee!" (Oh, mother!) because he thought the elephant had got him.

With his large ears flapped forwards and his trunk stretched straight forward the bull came at me. The end of his trunk widened, funnel like, and looked like an arm stretched out to grip something. Usually the elephant curls up his trunk when charging, now he was too near and was only extending it to get hold of my neck.

I waited until the very last moment in the hopes that he would change his direction and not until then did I fire my ·475 cordite rifle, hitting him in the root of the trunk. He came down as if struck by lightning and fell dead into the shrubs not six to seven paces from me. The report of my rifle was answered by a terrible noise; possibly some hundreds of elephants began trumpeting, roaring and screaming. This would have been the right moment to put down on paper the profound impression the whole scene made on me. Even then it would have been a vain attempt, but I could have described it better than I can now.

There is no doubt that this scene added materially to my stock of nightmares, although many past painful experiences already offered a wide choice! Anyway I could say that the new year began badly for me!

I was quite downhearted at having been forced again to shoot a bad tusker, but as it was useless to cry over spilt milk, I hurried on to overtake the others. I had some exciting moments but failed to get another sight of the mighty bull I had viewed earlier in the day.

Later in the afternoon I had a presentiment that another attempt would lead to better results, so I took up the pursuit with fresh energy, but my men were soon quite exhausted, as they had finished their water supply and therefore begged me to return. What could I do but turn back utterly depressed?

But New Year's Day had still another adventure in store for me which had its sad sequel the next day.

The sun had already set and only the afterglow and a bright crescent moon gave us light. My gunbearer, slowly striding before me, suddenly stares to the left and whispers "ndjofu" (elephant). Looking through my field-glasses in the direction indicated I very soon detected the noble beast. But suddenly our elephant split into two parts and then the two dissolved into four. Hm! As far as I knew only the lowest living organisms multiplied in this way, but I never thought elephants did. My glasses soon solved the secret. It was not an elephant but a herd of buffaloes grazing there.

I beckoned to my gunbearer, who followed me very unwillingly, for he did not like the idea of hunting buffalo so late in the evening. The buffaloes noticed something and faced suspiciously in our direction—an impressive sight in the twilight. Judging one of them to be a big bull, I fired. An incredible tumult followed! It seemed as if the earth was vomiting forth buffalo. Crashing, dashing in every direction, the black masses rushed about one after another. Then came a formidable stampede and the vast herd, numbering at least four hundred beasts, flew past us in a phalanx.

The bull of the herd seemed very infuriated by this intrusion and he sought the enemy with nostrils held high in the air. Seizing the opportunity I shot him in the shoulder. It was hard to aim in the dusk and my rifle was loaded with bullets intended for elephants, and as they do not produce such an immediately fatal effect as do soft-nosed ones, the bull did not turn over but came furiously for us. The flash of my rifle had betrayed us. I waited until he was quite close and shot him in the chest. At the shot his head went down and he seemed to stand on it for a second. Then the heavy body crashed over and the bull was dead.

Next morning loud trumpeting and screaming awoke me. The elephants had returned and made an infernal noise round my tent.

It was still quite dark, but even elephants which have not been attacked are nervous at night and often brush away anything in their path. I had seen plenty of instances of this. So I waited, rifle in hand, for day to break, cursing myself for having shot the buffalo, as I should have to return to its carcase before following up the elephants. As I had intended to stay a few days longer at Lugogo, I had not cut out the tusks of the elephant I had shot the day before, but in order to save this hard work, left it to be effected by decay. Natives in that country would not eat elephant meat. The upper tusk can be pulled out easily on the third day, while the one resting on the ground needs one to two days longer.

At dawn we went to the buffalo bull. I took some photos and then gave orders to skin him. On the evening of New Year's Day I had hit another buffalo bull and he could not lie far away as probably his collapse had frightened the others and made them turn in our direction, so taking my usual men along I went to look for the spoor. I called to my gunbearer to bring me my rifle, but the wretch was quarrelling with one of his mates, who was skinning the bull and paid no attention to what I said. My heavy cordite rifle was being carried by quite a "wild" man, who did not speak the Swahili language and so he took no notice of what I wanted either. I had just started scolding them when suddenly about 150 paces away from the bull's carcase I saw a dark mass break out of the bush, dash at us, and then toss the tall guide just ahead of me, although he tried to defend himself with his spear, carry him on its horns, toss him up and strike him again. Then it dashed at me. I sprang behind a tiny tree and before it could reach me, I was up in it. I tore my knee open on a long thorn, but who would think of trifles at such a moment? The buffalo—it was only a cow which was standing behind the bull and had been wounded by the bullet which went through the bull —seemed not to take any further interest in me, for with one dash it could have felled the tree with me in it, but ran after the others who were dispersing in all directions. Soon I heard the yells of one of my boys not ten paces away, and saw my gunbearer running away with my rifle instead of trying to save his unhappy mate.

The poor fellow was still being savaged by the buffalo, and I thought he must be dead. But then I saw the "wild man"—for my snobbish gunbearer called him that—running up with the heavy cordite rifle, and as I jumped off the tree, he handed it to me. Now I was master of the situation! Taking a quick aim my rifle spoke and the buffalo went down bellowing, with rattling in its throat, beside its victim.

As I ran up I was relieved to hear the man's moaning. Of course his condition was very grave. The buffalo had first worked at the wallet he was carrying and pierced it through and through; then flattened my big aluminium waterbottle (the unhappy Izaja always carried these oddments). It was his good fortune that in my knapsack was my last tin of Californian fruit and two tins of sardines. These of course, as well as some periodicals, were horribly messed up, but all of them put together certainly saved Izaja's life by acting as a shield, and without them we should only have picked him up on the blood-soaked ground pierced through and through, and with a broken spine.

Even as it was he had a deep wound in his side and his kidney was also injured. We instantly made a litter and the boys carried Izaja to my tent, where I did my best to wash and dress his wounds. After that he was carried to Masindi, where he remained in the hospital for two months.

My tall guide was hardly hurt, for with the help of two men he got home on his own feet and even assisted at the skinning of the buffalo so as not to miss his share of buffalo fat. Of course I had to give up looking for my first bull, although I knew for certain that he was lying on the spot from which the buffalo herd had suddenly stampeded.

For a few days more I continued to look for elephants near Lugogo, but never found one worth shooting, although I came on many fresh tracks and even saw some animals. Sometimes the wind was bad, or the honey-guide's warble spoiled my hunt, or other unfavourable circumstances played their part in preventing me from shooting an elephant.

On the fourth day the tusks were so loose, that my men brought them home. But to my great disappointment they only weighed 40 and 39½ lbs.

At the end of January, 1914, I again returned to Lugogo from Masindi, where I had gone to sell the tusks, with the intention of shooting the second elephant on my licence.

Not two hours from Masindi I found fresh tracks, but as I saw that it was only a herd of cows and calves, I continued on my way, for I was in a great hurry to get back to the Lugogo swamps, where I hoped to find the big tusker I had to let go because of the other bull which charged us.

Next day we crossed the river Kafu and emerged on to the flat savannas where several varieties of antelope were abundant. I saw buffalo spoor also, but unfortunately I had already shot the four on my licence, so I could take no notice of any buffalo spoor, not even of those of a solitary bull.

After two days we reached a native village called Bumoni, where the "gombrola mami" (Waganda district chief) was said to be able to give full information as to the whereabouts of elephants. A native gentleman, one of the ministers (*sasa*, chief) of the King of Uganda and governor of a province, was staying there on some official errand.   Such native dignitaries travel with great ceremony, and lesser tyrants, who in their turn understand how to secure respect for themselves, received him with cringing humility.

After I had pitched camp I waited for the great man to pay his respects, but time passed and there was no sign of him.   At last a messenger came to say that the "Sasa" was coming, but his "boot-boy," whose duty was to put on the boots of his master, had not turned up in time.   After a while he came and I offered him coffee and tea, but he would only have whisky.   (It is strictly prohibited to give natives spirits.)   He promised me during his visit that he would give me a "mami" out of his escort to accompany me, who was also his own elephant hunter.   In Uganda and Unyoro only the king and the "sasas" had the right to keep modern rifles and get a game licence.   Of course the "sasa" seldom shoots his elephants himself, but sends his men out instead. These generally bring back a very good pair of tusks, but nobody knows how many elephants they have shot before they obtain that particular pair.   He also promised that he would order the mamis of the neighbourhood to be at my service, because during my first visit they did not show much desire to help me.   In return he asked me, the "great doctor," to give him the medicine, or if I had not got it to write to Europe for it, which would make it possible for his family to have many descendants.

At dawn we moved on and the sasa's man was already there to guide us. His name was Ali Dazma and his whole appearance and quiet bearing marked the brave soldier and suggested a good elephant hunter.

We did not find elephant tracks until the third day and these came from the opposite bank of the marshes. On our side they separated into three parties. First we came upon a herd of cows and calves, so we proceeded quickly in order not to give them a chance of detecting us and betraying our presence. I must admit that I was rather impressed by the bad luck I had had with elephants. It was not so much my own skin that I was concerned about, but that I did not want to shoot another young bull or cow and have trouble with the authorities. And what was more, I was very much in need of rupees, which only a good pair of tusks would bring me.

Day after day I had further proof that my new guide was an excellent man and at last he led me very skilfully into a herd which included some good bulls. We were squatting behind a bush and had a splendid view of the elephants, or rather of their tusks. I raised my rifle a few times but always lowered it down in the hopes that a larger bull would show up. In the meantime Ali Dazma crawled forwards and signalled to me to follow, pointing with his fist at an elephant. Coming up I tried to get full view of the mighty beast, but could not see his tusks, and because I never had confidence in the judgment of natives, I did not shoot. Had I only made an exception in Ali Dazma's case! The elephant turned round for an instant and then got behind some others. In that one single instant, however, I did see its tusks. They were *enormous*! But it was too late! The elephants began to get uneasy and moved off, while we, careful of the wind, followed them as close as possible.

Once I felt sure of getting the old tusker again, but a stupid accident upset all our plans. We wanted to get behind an ant-hill and shoot from there, but as my guide reached it three wart-hogs jumped up from behind it and ran into the herd of elephants with much noise. This created an alarm. A wretched young bull, with head uplifted, came up in a fury towards the ant-hill, and I was already prepared to shoot, but seeing my guide's calmness

I waited. I did well, for when but a few yards away from the ant-hill he stopped, and probably catching the scent of the wart-hogs, turned to pursue them. Ali Dazma's calmness was wonderful! To lie quietly behind an ant-hill but a few yards away from an infuriated elephant proved that he possessed, not only good nerves, but also a generous amount of fatalism. He beckoned to me smilingly and we ran after the elephants again. But it was in vain. We saw a good bull several times but we never got within range, and at last we got foul of the wind, whereupon the herd started trumpeting and fled, breaking down everything in its way.

Next day we continued our pursuit, but again without result, for the cows gave us a lot of trouble. During the hunt we had to make long and tiresome detours in order to avoid cows which stayed behind because their calves could not keep up with the rapidly moving herd, and we again returned late at night without having fired a shot.

The elephants did not like being worried two days running and seemed to have left the country altogether, for I did not see a fresh track for days.

But we found compensation in shooting "situtunga" (*Trage-laphus spekei*) in the papyrus swamps, and as this is a very rare antelope, I was very pleased, and in two days I shot the four heads allowed on my licence. One of which was the record.

At last on January 31st I shot a bull elephant.

Of course I never thought that this would be the last elephant of my fourth expedition.

That same day at dawn my cook came up to my tent saying that he had heard an elephant screaming from a great distance. Then the mami came with the news that his men had also heard "elephant talk." I left my gunbearer, who was of no use because of his cowardice, at home to finish the preparation of the situtunga hides and took the cook along instead, who was not altogether overjoyed by this honour being conferred on him.

We marched as quickly as we could in the direction in which the elephants had been heard, and we had hardly been gone a quarter of an hour when we met two greatly perturbed natives who were running to summon us, for the elephants had raided their fields. A neighbouring mami whose potato field had been devastated by elephants had sent them. A native had even speared one of the raiders which only stumbled, and then carried on. The spoor showed that it had been lamed and the bent spear was found 20 yards farther on.

The elephants had done their work thoroughly. Although there were not more than twenty-five in all, the field seemed ploughed up, and not one single potato was left; only masses of dung, which proved their good digestion.

Again we continued the pursuit. My guides decreed an incredible pace, which was only possible because it was cloudy and rainy weather. We were not compelled to follow the tracks at first but could go straight ahead to the spot where we knew we should come across them again.

I had already given up hope of catching them up because in rainy weather elephants will travel great distances, especially when alarmed, as was the case after one had been speared.

At last, at 1 p.m., climbing on an ant-hill, I saw them in a scattered mimosa jungle. The herd consisted of twenty to twenty-five bulls, some of which were quite young.

My cook gunbearer felt sick when we sighted the elephants and retired, so I crawled forwards with Ali Dazma, and, as the wind was favourable and the soil soft, we managed to get quite close without making a sound.

I again took my pick of the tuskers. Not one of them was as big as the animal we had seen a few days ago, and I was beginning to give up hope of shooting one when an elephant appeared whose tusks would, I thought, weigh 70 lbs. each. I did not want to spend any more time on hunting elephant, so decided to fire. I was already on aim when Ali Dazma checked me, pointing out another whose tusks seemed bigger still, probably about 75 to 80 lbs. each.

He was standing in a favourable position and as I saw his head clearly I could aim at the spot between eye and earhole. I pulled the trigger and he collapsed where he was. All the others lifted their trunks looking for the enemy, but were then suddenly overtaken by frantic terror, turned, and dashed away, razing down everything in their path, and only began trumpeting when they had stopped a mile away.

The dying elephant wriggled and kicked, but could not get up, so I gave him another bullet in the head. Hearing the report, the others, which were by this time far away, started screaming afresh as if to send a last farewell to their mate.

So at last we stood over the elephant I had longed for so intently. We looked to see if there was any "matcho" on the tusks, which is the first act of every elephant hunter. A "matcho" is a little channel going through the whole tusk which forms a little hole at the ends and takes away half the value of the tusks. But fortunately there was no such fault in mine.

We left some men to cut out the tusks, and carrying the tail along, hurried back to camp.

My men arrived the next evening with the tusks and then came a fresh disappointment as the tusks only weighed 53 and 53½ lbs. The internal hollow was larger than usual, which is why I overrated them.

In July my licence expired. I took out another at once, for I was in good elephant country and thought I could get two easily. After a fairly long time spent in the Bugoma forest I got a report that two enormous bulls had been seen. Trackers I sent out brought back confirmation of this and the tracks I picked up were quite abnormally large.

I sent my safari to the banana shamba which the two giants had devastated and was just going to start myself when I was summoned to go immediately to Hoima. I only found out there why I was summoned so urgently! The War had broken out and I became a prisoner. . . . Bad months, bad years followed, and after four years in India I was very glad to be allowed a rubber catapult with which to shoot some birds for my collection.

A rubber catapult after a Mannlicher-Schönauer and a Magnum-express . . . "Sic transit gloria mundi!"

CHAPTER X

Elephant Hunting in the West Nile Province

WE had been hunting near Lake George [1] but had not decided the future movements of our safari.

Licences were strictly limited and hard to obtain, but having got two of them the most interesting parts of Africa were open to us: to the West, or rather South-West, that wonderland of possibilities and eventualities, the Eastern Belgian Congo; and to the North-West one of Uganda's closed provinces, the West Nile Province. [2]

It was hard to make up our minds where to go. Two days' march from our camp into the blue hills of the mysterious Eastern Congo the endless dark forests offered, not only grand bull elephants, but other animals peculiar to the Eastern Congo, the rare and wonderful okapi and the bongo (*Boöcercus euryceros*), which inhabited the great volcanic mountains of Lake Kivu, while on the bushy, bamboo-covered slopes of Mikeno and Karisimbi [3] we hoped to see the mountain gorilla (*Gorilla beringeri*). But the West Nile appealed to us also; for there, beside numerous elephants, we should find the white rhino, and Mr. J. Horthy had obtained permission from the Governor of Uganda to shoot one of these rare animals.

Unfortunately time was short and the expedition into the Congo was put out of question by one of our party suddenly falling ill, and so we turned north towards Fort Portal.

The peaks of Ruwenzori are usually hidden by clouds and mist,

---

[1] Lake George has an area of about 120 square miles and lies to the south-east of the Ruwenzori Mountains.

[2] The West Nile Province lies to the north of Albert Nyanza and west of Bahr-el-Jebel (Rocky Nile). On the west it is bounded by Congo and on the north by the Sudan.

[3] Mikeno is 14,540 and Karisimbi 14,780 feet in height.

but now, as if to cheer us up, they emerged for a brief spell before sunrise and sundown, showing us their beauty. From a serrated edge of snow-clad ridges there towered the two big peaks, Margherita and Alexandra.[1] Although we had been camped right under them for nearly two months, we had never seen them, and perhaps it was for this very reason that they were called *Mons Luna*.

On arrival at Fort Portal we dismissed our porters as we could not take them with us into the West Nile Province. We could only take our gunbearers, personal boys and cooks; and even these had to pass a severe medical examination, as a precaution against the introduction of sleeping sickness.

On February 5th we started for Albert Nyanza via Kampala with one of our own and one hired motor-car. Our own second car had been smashed during our absence by the drunken native chauffeur in Fort Portal. This "dereva" (a word distorted from the English "driver") was the worst of a bad lot we had engaged. A true " communo-socialist" in the worst sense of the word, and not a very "noble product of modernized Africa and missionary education"!

The journey of 207 miles from Fort Portal to Kampala took a day. During the long drive I dismissed the alluring prospect my imagination had pictured of pursuing the okapi in the jungles of Ituri accompanied by the dwarf hunters of the forest (the Wambutie), and began to see myself on the track of huge tuskers in the scorched savannas and papyrus swamps of Bahre-El-Jebel, guided by spindle-legged Nilot "negroes." . . .

As soon as we had done our business, we were glad to leave Kampala.[2] A big town like this always had a bad effect on the riff-raff lot we had in our service.

On February 9th we arrived at Masindi [3] where we visited the office of the Provincial Commissioner who received us cordially and gave us a permit even to go into the danger area. Everybody going into the West Nile territory has to deposit £50, but an exception was made in our case.

---

[1] Margherita 16,794 feet and Alexandra 16,726 feet high.

[2] The largest town of Uganda with 200 to 300 European inhabitants. The number of motor-cars registered in Kampala in January, 1926, was about 3,000, not counting motor-cycles.

[3] Capital of Unyoro Province.

J. Horthy got his licence for the white rhino on payment of £25. The Uganda Government only grant two or three licences a year for white rhino, and even then only in exceptional cases.

The Provincial Commissioner spoke in warm terms of one of our Hungarian sportsmen, the late Mr. Oscar Vojnich. He told us that Vojnich met the late President Roosevelt and was very surprised to find that Roosevelt knew so much about Hungarian history and Hungarian conditions. I knew Masindi in pre-war days and it had not changed. Only the mouldering elephant skulls which bordered the roads leading to official buildings had been removed. The neighbourhood of Masindi was formerly perhaps the best elephant country in Uganda, and even now there are vast herds—sometimes consisting of some hundreds of elephants—but for this very reason it is hard to shoot a good tusker.

It is worth mentioning that Masindi was discovered by Sir Samuel Baker in 1864 when he was looking for the Albert Nyanza. His heroic wife, Flora Sass, of Hungarian origin, was also there with him. Sir S. Baker had great difficulties in Masindi and could not get away for a long time, but the Wanyoros were very afraid of the "Muleju" ("the bearded one") and finally asked their king, Kamrasi, to let the "Muleju" go.

Lady Baker's memory still lives among the Wanyoros, who called her the "Morning star." The English also honour her memory; they called her an Austrian lady, which was a great mistake, and I always pointed out to my English friends that she was Hungarian.

From Masindi we went on to Butiaba the same day. This is a port on Lake Albert Nyanza where we took up our quarters in the rest-camp to wait for our ship, the *Samuel Baker*, to start. The country around Butiaba is excellent hunting ground, and buffalo were plentiful, while we found some good elephant tracks too.

I was tempted to fish in the renowned Albert Nyanza, but my efforts met with no result. This lake is an El Dorado for anglers, as it holds the Nile Perch and the handsome tiger-fish. The largest Nile Perch caught at Butiaba with rod and line weighed 197 lbs. Both fish are said to be good fighters and to give grand sport, so I made up my mind to get some lessons in angling from an expert after my return home.

On February 10th we shipped our belongings on board the *Samuel Baker* and started north after midnight. The small boat was overcrowded with passengers, and there was not much accommodation on it for Europeans. Our travelling companions were very interesting people; among them was our old friend Captain S., who is known all over Uganda under the name of "Bwana Samaki" (Mister Fish). Captain S. is a well-known elephant hunter and now a game ranger. Once a wounded elephant caught him round the neck and flung him away, but somehow or other he escaped with only some scars on his neck.

Mr. B. was also on the steamer. He is one of the men who know the West Nile Province most thoroughly and he gave us some very useful information. He seemed rather doubtful of our success in shooting elephants. We had only fourteen days to spare and still had five elephants to shoot, Horthy having shot one near Lake George. Mr. B. warned us not to waste too much time in picking out big ones as anybody would be glad nowadays to get a 40- or 50-pounder. Thank goodness, we not only shot our elephants, but got fairly good ones.

Taking Mr. B.'s advice we asked the captain of the ship to put us out at Relli, a place in the danger area on the left bank of the Nile (lat. 3° 23' N.) at which ships only occasionally stop, and to pick us up again when coming back in a fortnight's time on his return journey. The captain consented willingly.

The steerage was crowded with natives. It is wonderful how they can squeeze up into such a small area, and they even seemed to enjoy the pleasures of travelling. Natives are very fond of society and take delight in it even when obtained in such a floating hell as an overcrowded Nile boat. The native contingent on the boat was composed of various tribes, yet they always understood each other in that East African esperanto, the Swahili tongue, which was here of course very mixed up with the Kiganda dialect and Arabic. It is sometimes very interesting to get behind them unnoticed and listen to the stories of a "safiri" (much-travelled man), or to watch them imitating a white man, sometimes the listener himself, with the most perfect mimicry, causing the bystanders to roar with laughter.

The voyage was rather monotonous. We did not see any

elephant, although they are said to be a common sight on the Bahr-el-Jebel in the dry season. But as there had been abnormally heavy rains the previous year, the elephants found water enough without being compelled to come down to drink at the Nile. We saw many herons, but otherwise few birds; also hippos and crocodiles, but the latter were much smaller than those I saw on the Semliki.

Our steamer stopped at a few places to get the necessary fuel from the wood dumps. Hundreds and hundreds of natives wait with great excitement and noise to watch the arrival of the steamer, for she comes only once in every two or three weeks.

Here we had already reached the land of the Nilotics. They have tall, slim figures and their skin is black as ebony. They wear no clothes except that on their upper arms they carry thick ivory bracelets, which show how rich their country is in elephants. The women also go about naked, unless the string of beads, or the thin cord of grass tied round their thighs, can be called a frock! They sell victuals—chickens and eggs—and soon the bargaining among the natives begins with all the customary noise and yelling. They try to get the better of the despised "msenzi," but this is no easy task.

The voyage on the boat was not very pleasant. It was exceedingly hot, and there was little room, but lots of mosquitoes, and we wondered what it would be like when we got on shore. I was glad I had provided my boys with mosquito-nets, for without them we should not have been able to exist a fortnight in the West Nile Province.

We arrived at Relli on February 13th at 4 a.m. We unloaded our luggage, consisting of sixty loads and our rifles, by the light of our hurricane lamp. I was nervous about this disembarkation, but it all turned out better than I anticipated, and nothing was lost. Close to the bridge, built on piles leading to the dam, we found the skull and other bones of an elephant, and the remains were now disseminating a fine smell. It had been shot by a highly-placed English official from out of a herd bathing hardly ten days ago. We took it for a good omen, as evidently there were elephants about. But it was also true that many officials come into this province to hunt, for it is easy for them to get a permit.

THE HUNGRY MADIS ARRIVED IN WONDERFULLY SHORT TIME

TUSKS OF MY FIRST WEST NILE ELEPHANT
Weight of the pair 162 lbs., Length, measured along curve of largest horn, 89 inches

CHARGED BY A RHINO IN THE THICKS

COUNT SEILERN'S SECOND ELEPHANT BULL.

I engaged some of the crowd of onlookers to carry our belongings to the rest-camp, which was about two miles away, so that when the sun rose we could pitch our tents. The rest-camp was well built and clean. There were two large airy sheds built to shelter our tents against the sun and wind, but I wanted them for a different purpose, intending to keep one for working on the white rhino's skin, while in the other I thought of drying the skin after it had been thinned, stretched and preserved with alum and salts. This shed was really a wonderfully useful addition to our camp, for a skin ought to be dried in a shady place and then any skilled taxidermist will be able to set it up afterwards in an artistic way.

Mr. Horthy had decided to give the white rhino's skin to the Hungarian National Museum, thus renouncing a most beautiful trophy, the well-set-up head of a white rhino. It was a magnificent gift.

While our men were pitching the tents I was making up to the "sultani," distributing cheap cigarettes amongst his councillors, and shaking hands with everybody. The Swahili language was of little help here, so I had to put in a few half-forgotten words of Arabic. In a word I adopted the tactics of politicians at home during election times when they want to secure the votes of influential peasants.

I sent two long-legged boys—who were in hopes of getting good baksheesh—to a place eight miles away to fetch a man named Langa-Langa, who was said to be a very good tracker. Then we tried to get information about elephants. I was told that there were plenty and the measures they indicated with their sticks were so large that we should have been well contented to see animals half the size. Of course these reports had to be taken "cum grano salis." The natives also knew of many white rhinos and said one "anassa" (white rhino) could often be seen quite near camp, especially in the dry season.

Hearing this, I at once sent trackers by twos and threes in all directions, promising them a handsome reward should they bring me reports of a white rhino. The youngsters ran away in the best of spirits, which showed that there were real possibilities, but I never dreamt that they would return so soon with good tidings.

Hardly two hours later one of them returned, quite out of

breath, saying that the "anassa was ready" and not even far away. In reply to my question whether the horn was big he said it was, but later admitted that he had not seen it, but "his body was enormous." I knew this and ran at once to Mr. Horthy's tent and in a few moments we were on our way after the white rhino which was said to be quite close.

Count Seilern did not come with us, but he asked to be informed at once if we succeeded in shooting the rhino. We took along our gunbearers and our half-witted skinner, whom I made carry my camera. The tracker had reported that the "anassa" was grazing in an open spot and so I thought that I might get close enough to take a good photo, while Mr. Horthy—in whose sureness of aim I had full confidence—would protect me in case of danger.

I told the guides to invite the men of the neighbouring huts to follow us at a distance and in case they heard a shot, to come up and help to skin the animal and carry home the great hide. I promised them the meat and sixpence each, while those who brought along a sharp knife would get a few cents more. I must admit that my promise had no great effect. At first only children tried to come and it was hard work to drive them home. Later I found out that only few of the Madis [1] eat anassa meat and nothing but heaps of meat would induce them to work.

Our guides advanced quickly. First they led us through cut durrha fields, then through burned savannas and a bushy mimosa forest. Tracks of game were everywhere. A herd of Uganda kob and one or two good bushbuck bolted out of the jungle, while old elephant spoor were all over the place. From these we were delighted to see that there were still some big bulls about. Rhino spoors only were conspicuous by their absence, although we had already been pursuing this supposedly "near" rhino for a long time. At last, after two hours, we found the old spoor of a rhino, and beside a small bush we saw the soil was dug up and there was quite dry dung lying close by, from which fact we concluded that the white rhino also digs in the earth while busy, just like his smaller relative, the black rhinoceros.

---

[1] The Madis who inhabit the neighbourhood of Relli are negroes of Nilotic appearance. Their language is quite different from the languages of their neighbours and there was no European yet who could speak the language of the "Madis."

I asked the man who had brought us the news to tell us where he had seen the rhino and he assured us we would soon reach the spot where he had left his companion. This "soon" proved more than a good half-hour, and when we did reach the place we did not find the man. Probably the rhino had got his wind and gone on. We looked at each other. Perhaps the rhino had been badly frightened, in which case we should be sure not to see it again on that day. But I knew it would really be best to shoot the white rhino as soon as possible so as to get on with the preparation of the hide and be free to go after elephants, for our time was strictly limited.

It was very hard to find spoor on the dry ground, but luckily, after whistling for the man for some time, we got an answer. But it was not the watcher who answered, it was Langa-Langa himself, who came after us with the two men I had sent for him. He at once showed us a few certificates of which he seemed very proud, but even without these it was obvious that he was a man who knew his business. The impression his brand-new khaki suit made was less favourable, for Langa-Langa seemed to have been badly spoilt by some sportsmen. Luckily, he did not stay with us, but entered the service of an American sportsman, who had travelled with us on the boat and in whose safari he had spotted a few boxes containing cash. Later on we got hold of some very good guides and trackers, who had smaller pretensions.

Langa-Langa at once took charge and very soon the watcher turned up also and said that the rhino had gone into a darker and thicker part of the mimosa jungle. We then noted the direction of the wind and sent even our gunbearers back. My hero was of course rather frightened, though the white rhino is not particularly dangerous. We then set out under the guidance of Langa-Langa and the watcher.

I had already perceived that my hopes of photographing the rhino could not be realized, so I left the camera with the men who stayed behind. I was just giving up hope of our ever overtaking the rhino, when our watcher stopped short, then getting behind me, said that the rhino was standing before us. I could not make it out and even Langa-Langa looked in vain in all directions, until at last he pointed and said he had now spotted the animal standing under a leafless mimosa tree. But by then I had seen it myself and if I had not known that it was a white rhino I should have mistaken it for an elephant, so much taller was he than an ordinary black rhino.

I beckoned to Mr. Horthy, who had also detected the beast and stood with the ·465 Holland & Holland rifle raised to his shoulder. We could not as yet see the horn, so I got a few paces nearer and saw that it was a bull and saw the rear horn, but could not get a glimpse of the front one. So I tried to get still closer in order to get a good view, but at that moment Mr. Horthy took aim and fired. With a snort the animal bolted away, but he at once got the contents of the left barrel. Both shots hit him in the shoulder, so he only advanced a few steps and then rolled over with all four legs in the air. It turned out that Mr. Horthy, who was standing a little to my left, had made out the horns of a mighty bull, and so he did not wait longer.

We ran up to the carcase and stood over it in deep emotion. The rhino had a very strong, thick horn, 28 inches in length, so I congratulated Mr. Horthy most heartily, all the more because I believe he was the first Hungarian ever to have shot a white rhino.

The men came up and the work of skinning began. First of all I had all the ground in front of the rhino cleared, because I wanted to take a few photos and because I was afraid that the big bushes and stones would be in our way during the work of skinning. While I was taking my photographs I asked the gunbearers, who had never seen a white rhino, what they thought of its size. They admitted that it was very large, but declared that they had seen equally large ones round the Kenya, Kilimanjaro, and other parts. Of course we laughed at their fibs, and when I showed them that the white rhino had a square mouth, whereas the upper lip of the black rhino curls up into a kind of a short trunk, they understood that this kind was not the same as they had seen in East Africa.

After I had taken some photos we took measurements and then we cut the skin open and began work. I longed for the men who had worked with me for years on the Ruvana Plains. How well they had learned the art of skinning! With them it would not have been a hard task, but with these "war-volunteers"

—as Mr. Horthy called them—crowding around, it proved very heavy work cutting the huge skin off the heavy body. But we got through it at last, although Langa-Langa was very fussy about the men going to drink. Happily I did not let him influence me, or I should never have seen them again, as those who were sent to fetch water never returned. At last I succeeded in bribing a few old men and little boys to bring some water and without it I doubt if the skinning ever would have been completed.

And then came the task of transporting the hide into camp. It weighed some hundredweights. Long poles had already been cut beforehand, on which the hide was laid; then some men went ahead and cut a way with bush-knives through the undergrowth. I must confess that I was very relieved when we arrived at last in camp, late at night, with the hide undamaged.

Just before we started our homeward journey one of the men who had gone into the jungle to fetch some bark for ropes came running back with the news that he had seen another rhino lying up not far away. The idea of taking some photographs appealed to me, but Johanna, who was now no longer frightened, stopped me by saying in an ironical way: "Wapi?" (Whither?) "If you leave, sir, the hide will never reach camp!" so I had to give up my plan, as he was undoubtedly right.

As we emerged on to the road I was tempted once again. In the Nile swamps below us I saw two elephants, and it was assuredly the devil who whispered, "Perhaps one is a record tusker!" But I continued my way.

Next day I engaged as many men as I could to scrape and thin the hide and I am thankful to be able to relate that I succeeded in bringing it home undamaged. The skull and leg bones also arrived safely in Budapest, but I must mention that the total costs of transport were about £100.

Seldom have I got into my bed under the mosquito nets with feelings of greater satisfaction than I did on the night of February 13th! For I had never dared to hope that we should get a white rhino on our first day in the West Nile Province, and succeed in bringing the hide into camp on the same day.

I had put quantities of salt all over the hide (alum should not be used at first), folded it up and had it laid in the airy shed. The "fundi"—our skinner was so called by our other men—had to sleep by the hide and the leg bones to protect them against hyenas. These brutes could do little damage to the skull.

I did not get to sleep for a long time. The humming of mosquitoes all around me, which developed into a regular roar, did not trouble me; on the contrary, I derived a certain fiendish joy from hearing their unavailing song, and felt as if I were sitting in a warm and cosy room while the wind howled outside, beating snowflakes against the windows.

Everybody was astir early next morning. All the gunbearers had to work on the skin and even the boys, after they had finished their work in camp, were set at it too, while the natives who swarmed around in curiosity got sixpence if they took their turn. So every one scraped away at the skin, for it had to be made quite thin and flexible in order to let the solution of salts, alum and arsenic work well into the pores. The fundi had the hardest task, as he had to work at the skin of the head, while the gunbearers had to take the bones out of the feet, which was also a difficult job. The others sat in a row and, under my guidance, scraped away at the skin which was about two fingers thick. The "sultani" also turned up and promised to have bars fixed along the rafters on the sides of the barn so as to enable us to use them to lay the hide on and keep the air circulating underneath.

In the forenoon we got news of elephant. Natives had seen six elephants, one or two being good tuskers, on the plains of Bahr-el-Jebel.

So Mr. Horthy left his gunbearer, who proved to be a much better skinner than gunbearer, behind, and set out with the natives who had brought the news. We waited anxiously for the report of the "mzinga" ("cannon," as the natives call heavy cordite rifles), and the men of the Madi tribe were especially keen, for it meant a heap of meat for them; and I am sure that, had we heard it, they would have left off work at once. Mr. Horthy returned in the afternoon soaking wet and muddy all over. The elephants had gone into the papyrus swamps and he could not get a glimpse of their tusks, so he had had his trouble for nothing.

When it was nearly sunset I stopped the work of scraping and rubbed the skin with the preserving solutions. Every part had to be well rubbed, more especially those where it was not quite clear of flesh and fat, such as the parts round the mouth and ears and the feet. After this was done, we folded it up again and laid it on the drying table. We could have scraped it down still more, but I was afraid it might begin to decompose.

As there was still half an hour left before dark I strolled down to the Nile for a walk.

Here and there Uganda kobs were grazing on the scorched soil; then oribi were startled by my approach and took to flight in ones and twos. I would gladly have shot one of these succulent little antelopes for the pot, but the proximity of elephants made this impossible. Even a lion with a fair mane would not have tempted me to fire.

To my delight we came upon the comparatively fresh tracks— about two days old—of an enormous bull, which was decidedly reassuring.

It was dark when I returned and in the high grass near camp some animal sprang away; I could not see anything, but it was probably a leopard.

During supper we made our plans, as usual, for the following day and decided that Mr. Horthy and myself would start off in a northerly direction before sunrise with the new kirongozi, who had been out with Mr. Horthy that day and had shown much jungle craft and knowledge and was not half so fastidious as Langa-Langa.

It was still dark next morning when the new man, Masuramke, presented himself with his followers at my tent. We started immediately, Mr. Horthy carried his ·465 cordite Holland & Holland, while I had my 9·5-mm. Mannlicher-Schönauer.

Only Mr. Horthy's gunbearer was with us as mine was left behind to help the fundi in the further preparation of the skin, so Masuramke had to carry my rifle too.

Our guide had long legs and we had to step out at our best to keep up with him. He explained that we should hurry because later on in the day the elephants would go into the papyrus swamps.

After almost running for an hour and a half we came to Masuramke's cotton-shamba and his huts. He had sent trackers out in the night and had ordered them to meet here with their reports.

We had only waited a few moments when one messenger came trotting along. He had seen three elephants on the banks of the Nyanza (the Nile is here called Nyanza), one of which was a large tusker. So we started off again at an even greater speed.

We saw lots of game on the burnt savannas and swampy flatland; mostly Uganda kob, of course, but also some waterbuck, whose horns were much smaller than those of the Semliki water-bucks. Harassed bushbuck flashed past us and a fine buck stood on the top of an ant-hill so as to get a good view of us, but of course we could not think of shooting, although I would have been extremely glad to get one, as this variety is confined to the West Nile Province. Next we saw a big wart-hog digging away 150 paces from us and when he spotted us he dashed off with tail uplifted.

We saw many fresh and old elephant tracks, and judging by these there seemed to be some good elephants waiting for us in the swamps of the Nile.

On reaching the papyrus swamps we saw the first giant feeding quietly and fanning himself with his mighty ears. His back was turned, so we could see nothing of his tusks and he was heading towards the part of the swamp where the reeds were even thicker.

The wind was right and steady, so we ran as fast as possible, but it was no use, for the bull had already entered the high papyrus and we only could guess his whereabouts by the white herons fluttering up and settling down again, and the swaying of the papyrus bulbs.

On reaching the edge of the swamp I ordered all the men back, even Mr. Horthy's gunbearer, and we only took the two guides along with us.

The ground was favourable for an advance, for the papyrus had been trampled down by elephants in great patches, and the six elephants were not very far ahead of us. Once we saw a head and then a back. At last Mr. Horthy saw a blazing white pair of tusks and asked me in a whisper if I judged them as being good. I thought them too thin, so we let their owner move on without shooting.

Two of the elephants had very large bodies. In former days it would have been an easy matter for a hunter to get the best, for he would have shot all the six and then examined their tusks. Now it is a strain on one's nerves to select the best tusker of a herd, and it needs much practice and a quick eye.

We hovered round those elephants for a long while, and they never were more than twenty paces away. They were moving on all the time, and as we followed them steadily, we had to cross a stream, which was most disagreeable, for the feet of elephants make deep holes, tumbling into which means water up to one's chin; and how hard it was to get out! Mr. Horthy, being taller, had the advantage here, while I was better off in thick jungle.

After we had crossed this stream our hunting ground improved. Patches of trodden-down grass were of larger extent, and sometimes we saw all the six elephants at once, while a pair of white tusks would flash up for an instant, only to disappear again, and we could not really tell which was the best bull. It was a trying time for our nerves!

We came to a spot overgrown with ambatch bushes, and an elephant bull which was taller than the rest, though he was not the biggest, stood on it, breaking branches off an ambatch tree, and I could see his tusks clearly for a second. Masuramke saw them also. I judged the tusks to be something like 75 lbs. each and whispered to Mr. Horthy, but he had been watching another tusker, and so he waited to form his own opinion, and then the chance was gone! The bull went in after the others, so shooting it was impossible.

Meanwhile the small herd had become dispersed, and we began to get anxious lest one should get our scent and had to exercise the greatest care, constantly testing the wind by throwing up ashes we had brought from the burnt plains. One bull had strayed away from the others and was now feeding alone in an ambatch thicket. I got quite close to him through a tunnel of bushes and papyrus broken by the elephants and judged his tusks to be 55 to 60 lbs. in weight. I beckoned to Mr. Horthy, but he was of a different mind, so we waited for the one we had seen before.

Then the elephants appeared to grow restless. They were

lifting their trunks, scouting, and moving in our direction. They stepped out of the jungle and crossed the trampled-down clearing. First came a small one, a 30 to 40-pounder; then the second one, a fine 60-pounder.

As he passed Mr. Horthy fired and the bull went down on his knees, but stood up again and turned towards us. The other elephants seemed terrified and ran up to the wounded bull and dragged him along. He then received the second bullet in the shoulder. Mr. Horthy's first shot had hit a trifle far back, for the elephant was in the act of striding forwards as he fired. This will show how very small is the vital area compared to the whole head of an elephant.

Masuramke and the other guide who had bounded away during these exciting moments had now returned and looked reproachfully at us, just like my dog when I miss a woodcock at which she has pointed. No wonder! A mountain of meat and baksheesh was in their grasp, and now it was gone for good!

Mr. Horthy thought his second bullet had hit in the right place, so we followed the spoor of the wounded bull. This was hard work in the matted papyrus jungle, and there was but very little blood to be seen. Elephants do not usually bleed much, as the thick skin and masses of fat soon close the wound. We could not keep on the spoor for long on ground that had been trampled down so much, and we began to lose confidence.

"Let us return to the stream," said I, "from there we can send back for our men and then send out trackers in pairs, who will soon pick up the blood spoor again."

When we arrived at the stream, the men had already come up, in the belief that the two shots they had heard had done better work. With Masuramke's help as interpreter I made them understand what I wanted; but hardly had they dispersed when we heard noises and they ran back in terror, saying that the elephants were charging us.

We ran to meet the animals crashing along, and then saw that it was not the herd, but only the wounded bull returning. He had obviously heard the hated voices of men and came to wreak his revenge. It was a wonderful sight! Those who have seen an infuriated elephant charging will think far less about the lion as king of animals, and even the ways of the buffalo will seem tame in comparison.

At first I thought it was not the wounded bull, as its tusks seemed smaller, but when it turned after the fleeing men I recognized it. Before it could vanish behind a papyrus clump Mr. Horthy fired twice, giving him two bullets in the shoulder. He slowly went down, tried to get up again, but two more shots finished him.

The natives, who a few moments before were in a state of panic, now yelled out with wild shouts of joy. I gave a quick glance at the tusks and congratulated Mr. Horthy, but could see a regret in his eyes, as this meant the end for him of this most exciting sport, for he had now shot his second elephant.

Then followed the photographing of the grand quarry, and of course we had to cut the papyrus all round so as to get a good general view.

At first we thought that we would not take the tusks out, as we were still staying at Relli for a few days. If the tail of an elephant is cut off it is a sign that the tusks are somebody's property and then nobody will touch them. But Masuramke said that the Eastern Madis, hearing the shots, would cross the Nile in canoes and steal the tusks. So we cut the feet off and just then a man turned up with an axe who was said to be a tusk-cutter. The cutting off of the feet is no easy task. The feet of the first elephant which Mr. Horthy had shot in Uganda, near Lake George, could not be preserved because we had waited until the next day and hyenas had damaged them seriously. But these three thieves had been killed by Count Seilern, who had found them on the carcase, with three well-placed shots which—as he remarked—were surely directed by the hand of Justice.

It was noon when we finished cutting off the feet and then Masuramke's younger brother arrived saying he had seen more elephants. When Mr. Horthy saw me preparing for a start he seemed doubtful as to the result, especially as the place indicated lay among the pale blue mountains very far away.

"When hunting elephants every chance must be taken!" said I, and it was only this maxim which made me start off again.

Mr. Horthy, seeing I was determined, was kind enough to

lend me his heavy cordite rifle, even though he was left without a weapon, and had some hours' march ahead of him before he reached camp.

I thanked him warmly for the loan of this fine Holland & Holland rifle, but as there were only two solid bullets left, I pocketed a couple of soft-nosed cartridges also.

My band was soon made up. Masuramke carried the cordite rifle and his brother, Abisai, the Mannlicher-Schönauer, while two young men, chosen by Masuramke, carried a gourd of water and my haversack. My camera, with one or two film packs, was put into the charge of a native called Langa-Langa—not the same man whom I have mentioned before. This was a tall man, although compared to others of his tribe he was small. Later I got very fond of this Langa-Langa, and he turned out to be one of the best of trackers, who could keep on a spoor in a marvellous manner. Sad to relate, he had the early symptoms of elephantiasis (a disease caused by the filaria), and his feet would swell up so that he could not always come out with us. After a longer expedition than usual he had to stay in camp for several days, where he helped to prepare the elephants' feet.

So we started. I asked Masuramke if he thought it likely that we should see elephant that same day, and he and his brother both assured me that we would if we did not waste any time, so we strode off at a tremendous pace.

We must have been a funny sight. The four long-legged fellows, with me in their midst, shouting and gesticulating, while Langa-Langa trotted behind with my camera and tried to keep up with us. Somebody who did not know what was happening, would have thought that these wild natives had caught an unfortunate white man, had taken his weapons away, and were now dragging him before the chief of their tribe.

Goodness knows how, but the Madis had found out about the elephant, and we saw them approaching from all sides. Evidently Masuramke was a man of importance, for each band of Madis we met greeted-him warmly, and listened to his instructions with humility. Probably he gave them orders about his share of meat, which would have to be respected.

Usually my boys had to be very silent, but I did not mind their chatter now, for noise enough was made all over the place by the Madis flocking to the scene, and the elephants we were after were still a very long way off. I was amused by their lively gesticulating and expressive sounds. Abisai was especially very noisy. There was such a lot of sporting spirit in this young man as in a good fox-terrier! Loud yells of "Taa-taa!" were meant to represent the report of the cordite rifle, then one or the other would stretch out his arms in imitation of the elephant's tusks, and tumble forwards, to show how an elephant falls.

The heat was terrific! I had made it a "quinine day" (usually when we had hard work to do we took one gramme of quinine every Monday and Tuesday), and I was beginning to feel the effect; ears singing and hands trembling. Luckily the good humour of my men helped me to get over this horrid feeling.

We had to follow the "bara-bara" (road) leading towards Dufile for a while and then left it again and headed straight towards the mountains in the west.

The character of the country had entirely changed. The barren, scorched slopes were covered with a leafless mimosa forest. It was a tedious sight, with nothing to give a little relief to the eye but one or two "ntugu" (borassus palms), which made small patches of green in the uniform grey, and some fruit-trees on the banks of a little stream. Elephants like the stringy fruit of the borassus palm, which is as large as a man's head and has a very agreeable odour, but its taste is rather bitter. And not only do the elephants eat it in the dry season, but the Madis also in times of want, for often a drought ruins the few crops they have left after the elephants and hippos have done their bit.

We saw dry spoors of buffalo and white rhino everywhere, and even more elephant tracks, both old and fresh. On the slopes of the hills, in stony soil, the tracks mould out a path nearly a yard, or even more, in depth. These elephant paths must certainly be several hundred years old. Broken and uprooted mimosa trees, and some hundred acres entirely trampled down, show that elephants still visit these regions annually even now. Amongst other game I saw the little dik-dik (*Madoqua*), the dwarf antelope of the waterless savannas, leaping and bouncing like a rubber ball and vanishing in a few moments.

I felt a few painful stings that reminded me that we were in tsetse-fly country. Soon they came in crowds, and it was hard to protect oneself against them. We had green branches in our hands and tried to drive them away with these. I did not even want to find out to which species of the *Glossina* family these flies belonged, as it was better to believe that they belonged to the species of *Glossina morsitans* or *Glossina pallidipes* rather than to *Glossina palpalis*, which spreads sleeping sickness. Those who get nervous about the bites and their consequences ought not to hunt in the West Nile Province.

The nearer we got to the mountains the more flies there were. The dry river-beds and shady trees simply poured them forth, and they stung even through my linen suit; but my poor men, who, with the exception of Masuramke, were quite naked, had to suffer even more. Langa-Langa had nothing on but a leather belt with a knife hanging on it and a brand-new red fez. Some elephant hunter had given Masuramke a winter coat and a helmet, and he never took them off in this Equatorial heat. I wondered how he could bear them, but now I began to understand the practical side of a winter coat in this hot climate. While we had to protect our whole body against the flies, he only had his legs and arms to look after, for he had cut out the sleeves of the coat in order to secure freedom of movement.

We found a beautiful spot in the bed of the river Endeni. The water accumulates there in the rainy season and forms a waterfall of about 45 feet in height. This waterfall had washed out a large basin in the rock, which contained water quite unusually clear for Africa.

This was the drinking and bathing place of elephants and all kinds of game from the country far around.

It would be a wonderful spot for a camera hunter. His films would be worth anything. In the high rocky wall it would be easy to find a niche for the operator, and from there wonderful pictures of game could be taken as they came up to drink. The photographer would have to sit under a mosquito net, which is certainly very hot, but it would be well worth while. Nobody could stand the bites of tsetse flies for hours, and what is more, sleeping sickness would be a certain result.

My men drank eagerly and filled their calabashes with water. They wanted to bathe, but Masuramke pointed out a protruding rock, fairly polished by a crocodile, which evidently sunned himself there every day, and so dropped the idea of getting into the water. Unfortunately every pool has got its crocodile! This old "undertaker" was reputed to have pulled down a few men already. Fortunately for him, he did not show up, for I would have been greatly tempted to despatch him, as it always gave me a special pleasure to shoot a crocodile. On subsequent trips I came upon a few similar water-pools in the beds of periodical rivers, and each seemed to have its own crocodile. In very dry years, when the water-beds are dried up, the crocodiles will creep into holes under the banks and pass their time in hibernation, and I came on similar cases on the Ruvana Plains.

We continued our march, still fighting against the tsetse-flies. My hopes were waning, although the kirongozi still swore that we should see elephant that very day.

On one of the hill-sides, some way off, we saw a big grey granite block under large shady trees and thought it was an elephant. This took us out of our way. I had observed it through my glasses, and as the leaves of a tree were moving in the light breeze, I mistook them for the movement of an elephant's ears. I examined my rifles, went through all the cartridges of the Mannlicher-Schönauer (this is very important with Austrian cartridges, in which the bullets are not held sufficiently firmly in the cases and often slip down, thus causing the greatest difficulty in reloading), and then set out towards the quarry that seemed so certain. I was so surprised by the unexpectedness of this solitary elephant that I never considered the possibility of his tusks not being good enough. All the greater was my disappointment when on our approach my glasses showed me quite clearly the mistake we had made.

After this episode Masuramke and myself climbed to the crest of the hill and continued our way along it, while we left Langa-Langa and a young boy to wait for us and look out for any elephants below.

On and on we went. The sun was sinking when we suddenly heard loud shouts. Abisai turned back, and running towards the sounds, started yelling in his turn. I tried to quiet him, but in vain, so I also ran in the same direction and found that it was the boy who was shouting, that elephants were standing about in the shade of the valley and that Langa-Langa was watching them.

We soon reached him and found him hiding behind a tree with his red fez pressed under his arm. Further, we soon saw the elephants and also got somewhat nearer to them in order to obtain a good view of their surroundings. They stood in four different troops. The three nearer troops consisted of cows, calves and two young bulls. The fourth troop was some way off under a large shady tree and two of the elephants in it seemed very big in the body. I thought they must all be bulls, although I could not see their tusks.

To my great distress a herd of Jackson's hartebeests was standing about between them and us. We could not avoid them, and on our approach they bolted, and for long while we could not tell whether we should be able to approach the elephants or not. But this danger passed, for the hartebeests did not bolt in the direction of the elephants, and so the latter remained undisturbed.

We got nearer and nearer to them. Behind the first lot of elephants I saw a waterbuck beginning to show signs of anxiety. We had to do something, so we crawled into the dry water-bed running between the elephants and ourselves. Of course the descent and ascent of the banks were noisy operations, and as we crawled out over the farther bank the startled waterbuck dashed away and caused the nearer elephants to take to flight also. But luckily when they reached the fourth group of bulls they stopped, and lifting their trunks, began looking for the reason of the stampede. The wind was right, so they did not find out from where the danger threatened.

What happened next I do not know. The elephants were probably warned by the waterbuck, or perhaps they caught a slight whiff of tainted breeze; they stood up in a fan-like formation,— there were about thirty,—and lifting their trunks advanced towards us.

We had to draw back, for if they had got our scent, it would have been dangerous, as the cows seemed very angry. Masuramke was very busy keeping the men in rear from running away, when

MARABOUS

VULTURES ASSEMBLING OVER AN ELEPHANT CARCASS

Rest camp, Paludjo

Madi huts and barns

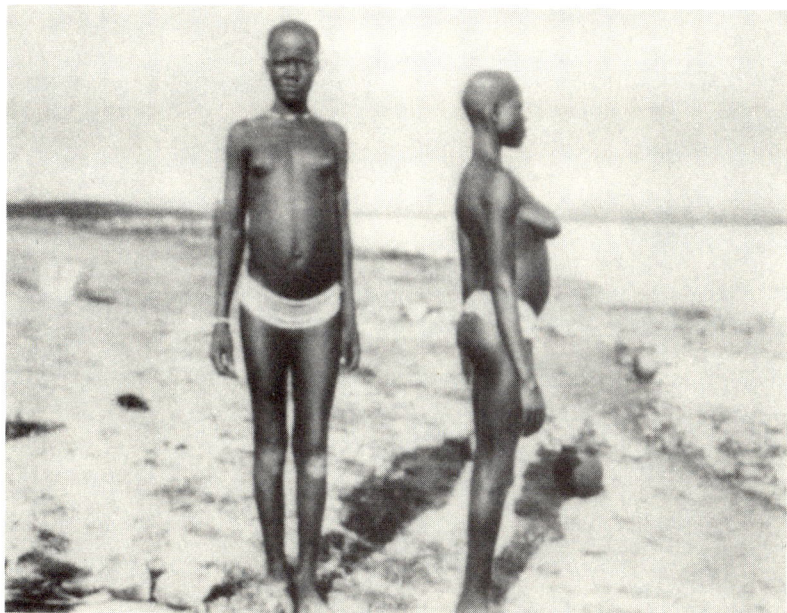

MADI GIRLS

MADI WOMEN CARRYING WATER ON THE BAHR EL JEBEL.

MR. HORTHY'S WEST NILE BUFFALO HEAD, SOMEWHAT RESEMBLING A RED BUFFALO

RESULT OF TWO WEEKS' HUNTING IN WEST NILE PROVINCE

the elephants would certainly have spotted us. With much difficulty we then climbed back across the river-bed.

I had the cordite rifle in my hands while I watched the suspicious herd. I thought I had seen two good bulls, but they were always hidden from sight by the cows. I raised my rifle a few times, but only to lower it again, as a cow or a young bull always seemed to be in the way. As I was watching them, my men began to whisper to me to shoot, for the great bull suddenly showed up. As though I had not seen him already! He followed in rear of the frightened herd, but stood in a bad position, so I waited for him to stand at the right angle. My men were so excited that I was afraid they would drag at my arm while I was aiming, but at last the moment came. As the bull crossed in front, I aimed at his shoulder and gave him both bullets in quick succession. I could not well see the effect of my shots, for the elephants closed round their patriarch, and what was more, I had to dash after the kirongozi, who ran away with my Mannlicher-Schönauer. I caught hold of him, shoved the empty cordite rifle into his hands, and ran back with the Mannlicher-Schönauer.

There was great commotion amongst the elephants. Fortunately the wounded bull was so much taller than the rest, that I did not lose sight of him, and the moment I got an opening I gave him another bullet from the Mannlicher-Schönauer. This shot made them all run round and round, and I got a fleeting glimpse between two old cows of the vital part of the head of my bull. So again I fired, this time right into the temple pit and he collapsed moaning. His companions tried to help and he struggled to get up, but another head-shot finished his efforts.

Then a good-sized elephant, I do not know whether it was a young bull or an old cow, stopped by his side trying to lift him to his feet, but finding its efforts useless, went to seek vengeance.

Critical moments! Fortunately the cordite was not loaded, or the kirongozi, who was trembling all over, would certainly have fired it off in his fright. The elephants seemed extremely scared and were working round behind us, which would mean getting our wind, so I waited till the dead one was left alone and then we ran down the river-bed, and making a large detour, got back to the dead elephant. The herd had at last crossed over to the other side.

We could congratulate ourselves at having shot such a mighty bull. There were no flaws in the tusks, which were, I was sure, not under 80 lbs. each. We cut off the tail, but did not attempt cutting off the feet, for it was late and we were few.

Unforeseen and sometimes disagreeable circumstances make up the luck of a hunter. I was disheartened when the waterbuck stampeded the elephants, yet in the end this turned out for the best, as the big bull was hiding behind the others and might not have shown himself, when I should perhaps only have shot one of medium size.

To please my men I shot a wart-hog on our way home. The bristles of the wart-hog would seem to be greatly valued by the Madis, as they were quite overjoyed, and hung up the meat on a thorny tree as a protection against hyenas.

The setting sun was shedding its last rays when my tired feet at last reached the bara-bara and the long-legged natives cheered me up with wonderful good humour and almost dragged me back to camp. Mr. Horthy noticed the elephant's tail in Abisai's hand at once and congratulated me heartily.

The dawn of next day saw us already on our way to the dead elephant. Again I had a proof of the rapid means of intercommunication used by natives. From all sides hungry Madis were closing in on the carcase. I was afraid they would begin to chop up the meat before we got there, when I would not be able to take any more photos, and feared that they might damage the feet. (These make very nice trophies, for they can be used as waste-paper baskets or liqueur-stands, etc.) But Masuramke assured me that he had left a sign on the carcase and no Madi would touch it before he came. And true enough crowds of Madis were sitting around it when we arrived, but had not touched it; nor had it been damaged by hyenas.

I took a few photos and then left my gunbearer there in charge of the work and I went on. Late in the night they brought home the tusks; the two together weighed 162 lbs.

The Madis are very fond of elephant meat and fully appreciate it, for at times they are not far off starvation. Drought and devastation of their crops by elephants and buffaloes will often bring them into sad straits. So the killing of an elephant means a great deal to a Madi village.

It is wonderful how quickly they get the tidings, and then they all set out with knives and spears sharpened up for the occasion, while the women and children carry curiously-shaped baskets in which to bring home the meat.

The women and children take no part in the cutting up of the carcase, but they hover around and must be ready to catch the pieces thrown to them by their husbands or brothers. One can see women, smeared all over with blood and the contents of the intestines, fighting over one piece of meat. If one of them has once secured a piece and puts it down in safety somewhere under a tree or on a stone, none of the others will touch it. It is now a question of honour, and it would be stealing to take it away from there.

My gunbearer, or rather my guide Masuramke, ordered them all to put their knives into one heap and wait until the tusks were cut out and the feet cut off; then the fundis took their part of the meat, and after this a signal was given, on which everybody else might seize their knives and start worrying the carcase. But they displayed a most sporting spirit in waiting until the sign was given.

Sometimes these fights had serious consequences, for instance, when my elephant was attacked by the crowd, one man had two of his fingers cut off and another man had a piece chopped out of his calf by the hungry crowd. But they do not seem to worry about such details, which never stop the wild work for a moment. The wounded man will put the bark of a tree or leaves on the wound and continue, or if he feels very ill, he will sit by the fire and devour fat fried over it.

The most comical incidents occur at the very beginning, when they open the body of the elephant. Usually the elephant has lain dead for several hours before the cutting out of the tusks has been completed; by that time the stomach of the large animal will be full of gases and when they open it with a knife all this quantity of gas is suddenly freed as if by an explosion. Some of the contents of the stomach are scattered around, and those nearest are covered with the evil-smelling filth, but they do not seem to mind. Nothing matters so long as they can secure a big portion of the stomach, which is what they like best. In a few hours the whole elephant will be chopped up, and then everybody is busy packing the meat for transport. Sure enough, not one pound of any of our elephant's meat in the West Nile Province was wasted.

Our stay in the West Nile Province was very limited, and we could not defer the day of departure, for the boat was coming to fetch us at Relli on the night of February 27th. We had still three elephants to shoot; Count Seilern had two in hand, while I could still get a second.

On February 18th we left Relli and went to Paludyo, where we pitched camp. The "sultani" of Relli gave us the necessary help and we got porters, who returned afterwards, to carry our loads back. The white rhino hide, which was not dry yet, the tusks and a lot of unnecessary baggage were left at Relli. The reports from Paludyo were favourable, and on our march there we saw that they were true. Only the plague of tsetse-flies was worse than ever.

On February 19th Count Seilern shot his first elephant. The tusks weighed 120 lbs. together; they were very short but thick. On this occasion the stampede of the herd drove me into a very unpleasant situation. Fortunately my previous observing place, a heap of granite blocks, saved me. This herd consisted of from thirty to thirty-five elephants, and I saw behind them a white rhino feeding calmly, so they evidently get on well together.

On February 20th six elephants were seen quite near to our camp, so I set out at once. They stood in some elephant grass which had been left untouched by the grass fire, but I could not make them out until I climbed a Kigelia tree. There were only four young bulls, so I did not harm them. The best was perhaps only a 40-pounder.

On the 21st we pushed far into the mountains and Abisai found quite fresh tracks. Although they were only spoors of cows, we followed them, hoping to find others later, but we could not overtake them. Following the greyish spoor of the elephants in the ashes of the blackened soil, we came upon the spoor of a solitary buffalo, which had recently crossed the elephants' path. I saw that it was very fresh and looked round for my gunbearer Johanna, who was not near me with the rifle. The kirongozi before me was so intent upon tracking, that he nearly bumped into the bull. I shouted to him and the bull turned on us. I jumped back for my rifle, but when I had it in my hand, the buffalo turned angrily away. I did not shoot, because I already had the four buffaloes allowed on my licence. This provided yet another object lesson how a hunter ought always to carry his own rifle.

Later I came upon a white rhino lying under a tree. I got quite close and took five photos. Unfortunately they did not come out, for there were no plates in my slides and film packs are no good in Africa; at least that was my experience wherever I went.

On February 22nd—although it was a quinine day—we set out before break of dawn. At first we found no tracks and got no news about elephants from the Madis we met on our way. So we entered the mountains by a path that had been trodden out by the natives when they carried away the meat of the elephant shot on the 19th. We found a fresh spoor here but could not keep to it, and as we were losing time looking for it, I proposed to Masuramke to go straight towards the borassus grove, for elephants like to feed on this fruit.

We met a quite "wild" Madi on our way. Masuramke said that some Madis cannot get used to "culture" coming to them in the form of taxes and have retired into the forests, where they live without paying either taxes or homage to "culture."

This "msenzi" brought delightful news. He had seen many elephants not far away, and in hopes of meat and baksheesh said he would guide us. We were delighted! Something bolted away with a great crashing, and the kirongozi said they were white rhinos. Buffalo spoor were everywhere, and the scenery was wonderful. There were a number of enormous wild-fruit trees, and on them clustered thousands of green pigeons and many kinds of bright-coloured birds. And what was more, there were no tsetse-flies!

Then we heard an elephant screaming. We followed up the sound, but Johanna hissed at us to stop. On our left there was a herd of elephants! The wind was favourable, so we got quite near the elephants, which were resting in a dry, rocky river-bed. Two shootable elephants towered up between the others. The nearer of the two stood in a convenient position, so that I could have given him a shot in the side of the head, but I thought that he was not big enough, and waited. Abisai was whispering to me all the time, "Kuba sana" (very big), so, when the elephants began to decamp, I shot him in the shoulder as he was climbing up the bank. He screamed out and began to run, so I sent two more bullets from my Mannlicher-Schönauer into him. Then we ran after the wounded bull and I do not remember ever having sweated as I did then. I gave him two more shots, but by then he had already slackened his pace and very soon stopped. In our eagerness to get up to him we ran into a herd of buffaloes, which did not seem to have noticed the firing.

I had five more shots at the elephant and at last he collapsed. He was a tremendous beast, but the tusks were not very big; only 46½ lbs. and 46 lbs.

As we were cutting the feet off we heard another elephant scream, for scarcely a mile away another herd were cooling themselves in the shade of trees. There was a good bull amongst them also. Shortly after we heard elephants from two more sides. I could have taken my time and picked out my bull at my leisure had I known that I would come upon so many elephants, and regretted having shot this one, for it should not have been hard to find something better.

The men who had been cutting the feet off made a little fire and roasted the fat glands from above the elephant's eyes and ate such quantities that I felt quite sick watching them. One can always see some oily liquid pouring out of an elephant's temple. This is particularly noticeable when the skin is dry and dusty. In Indian elephants these glands have been observed to grow larger during the mating season, so it seems probable that they have some connection with the animal's sexual life. Probably when rubbing against trees the smell of this secretion will attract the opposite sex and thus enable them to meet.

On February 23rd Count Seilern shot his last bull elephant and then we waited anxiously for the *Samuel Baker* to turn up. For the West Nile Province is a grand place as long as you are elephant hunting, but it turns into an inferno of tsetse-flies and mosquitoes the moment hunting is over.

CHAPTER XI
The Buffalo

W HEN I first set foot on African soil, nearly a quarter of a
century ago, the results of the great outbreak of rinderpest
in 1890 were still apparent, and buffalo were rare in German East
Africa, so I only read and heard of the fierce, cunning and relentless
character of this dangerous beast.

An attack of fever resulted in my going to the hospital of the
"boma" (here the word means a fortification) at Moshi under
Kilimanjaro, and in the passage leading to my room there lay,
ready packed for transport, the trophies of the late Captain Merker
(then only lieutenant), the well-known Masai scholar. Captain
Merker was not a keen hunter himself and most of his trophies
had been collected by his askaris, and amongst others the head of
a buffalo. This was the first buffalo shot in Kilimanjaro after
the great epidemic. An askari had shot it during a surveying
expedition on the Pangani River, and it was a good average-sized
bull. We saw the mark of the lead bullet of an 1871-model Mauser
in the forehead, right under the boss of the horns, and of course
someone at once declared that the askari delivered this masterly
shot after the bull was dead.

In Mombasa, and later in Moshi, I saw great quantities of
big elephant tusks, but none impressed me so much as that buffalo
head, and I never tired of standing before the black, uneven,
massive horns, while my fever-stricken imagination wound the
most fantastic stories around them. Throughout my stay I was
quite bewitched by this head, and when I was getting convalescent
I often took out my Mannlicher and aimed at it, studying the best
spots at which to shoot, in case a buffalo should ever charge me.
For in those days the thought of a non-charging buffalo never
entered my head. Formerly, and even now, by some hunters,

a buffalo was supposed to be the most dangerous of animals, and so it is not surprising that I was deeply impressed when I studied this head and later, too, when I followed buffalo spoor in the bush. That was long ago, and since they have increased in numbers and I have had opportunity enough to gain experience, I have come to the conclusion that buffalo are not so black as they are painted.

The way they have increased in number during the last twenty-five years is wonderful, with the result that in Uganda and in some parts of Kenya Colony they have been outlawed, as they really did a lot of damage to cultivation and even became a menace to human life.

Their habits have also altered in a very interesting manner. On my first expedition I never saw a buffalo in the open. We could never be out early enough, for they retired into dense jungle while it was still dark, and only came out late at night. Tracking was the only possible way of hunting them.

During my third expedition I sometimes saw them in large herds in the early morning or late in the afternoon. But I always tracked down those I shot; and I shot a great many buffalo, as otherwise I could never have obtained the cattle necessary to provide milk for my antelope calves and other young animals. The chiefs of the warrior tribe of the Wagayas would willingly give us cows in exchange for buffalo hides, from which they made their shields.

Later on in Uganda I saw great herds of buffalo, consisting sometimes of several hundreds, and they were much in our way when elephant hunting. And on my last expedition I saw many buffalo, notably in the Semliki Valley, although there had been another epidemic of rinderpest a few years previously, which had decimated them; but naturally this second epidemic was not as devastating as the first.

It can now be said that buffalo are to be found all over East Africa, either in the forests, swamps, elephant grass or bush; if there is water and shade, buffalo will be found.

The African buffalo can be classified into three main groups. One is the *Syncerus caffer caffer*, the largest in size and very black. His habitat extends from South Africa to the northern boundaries of Kenya and westwards up to the forests of the Congo. There are varieties even of this buffalo.

In the Cape of Good Hope buffalo now only exist in reserves like Knysna, Zizitkama and the Addo forests, and they are as strictly protected as the few surviving elephants.

The northern type, the Sudan buffalo (*Syncerus c. aequinoctialis*), is found in Abyssinia and the Sudan, and is much smaller, both in body and horns, than his southern brother. I saw a few on my last journey in the West Nile Province, although I think there must have existed there, as I believe there does in Semliki, a cross between the *Syncerus c. caffer* and the red Congo buffalo (*Syncerus c. nanus*). This is the smallest kind of buffalo, and its habitat comprises the Congo and West Africa. They are almost quite red, especially the younger ones.

On my early expeditions I only shot buffalo by tracking, apart from the few occasions when after I had tracked a bull down he entered some thicket and then had to be driven out. A buffalo is an easy animal to drive provided the thicket is not too extended. If the beaters were up wind, it would come out even before the drive began, and I generally noticed that drumming and yelling had less effect than giving scent.

On my last trip I shot all my buffalo without any tracking. (I should explain that I was only allowed four buffaloes on my licence in Uganda at first, but that afterwards this number was increased and ten heads may now be shot.) At dawn, in the morning and afternoon, in fact at nearly any time of the day, great herds will graze on the fresh grass of the burnt plains. Slowly the old conditions are returning, such as we read of in the descriptions given by hunters in former days, although twenty years ago I never thought it possible that I should live to see this change.

Hunting buffaloes to-day is far easier than it used to be, for, after one had tracked them down, they would often break away with a tremendous crash, without letting one so much as get a glimpse of them. And if one did sight them they were usually already in full flight; and it is hard to aim accurately at a black mass of bolting beasts in thick jungle.

It is not worth while following a herd in thick jungle because it is impossible to select a good bull, so I always tracked solitary bulls, or two or three old ones living together. I think the hearing of these old bulls is not as good as that of younger ones. The buffalo has wonderful powers of scent and good sight, while his hearing is also astonishing. All these qualities make him a dangerous antagonist when he is up against you.

In former German East Africa there was no limit to the numbers of buffalo one could shoot, and I shot as many as I needed, for, as I have already mentioned, I purchased my cows in exchange for buffalo hides. The sportsman must be very careful about the wind when after buffalo, and for this reason I invariably carried a little bag of flour, small grass seeds or some fine cotton, and when I approached the herd I always stopped to see if the wind was right, as it constantly changes in dense scrub.

If the tracks begin to turn round in a circle and the buffalo or buffaloes one is tracking stop once or twice and then turn again, it is always a sure sign that the herd is somewhere near. Flies will also give them away and sometimes one can get their scent, which just reminds one of coming to a farm at home and smelling the cattle in the stalls.

Often great flocks of Buphagas accompany the herd and the chirruping of these birds sometimes betrays them, but will even more often betray the hunter, for they fly up at one's approach, when the buffaloes bolt.

In swampy country white herons are in constant company with buffaloes, just as they are with elephants. They make much less noise and will not put the hunter's chances in jeopardy to the same extent, and what is more, their white plumage shows up from afar and indicates the spot where the quarry is to be found.

Buffaloes living near swamps are more or less aquatic animals and will lie neck-deep in water all day long and only come out to graze late in the afternoon.

They leave their daily resting-place in single file, usually with an old cow in front and the bull of the herd in the rear. The master bull of a herd never seems to have such big horns as a solitary bull, and consequently if there is any choice, it is seldom worth while following a herd.

Solitary bulls are said to be far more dangerous than herd bulls, but my experience has convinced me that the former shows no more readiness to go for a man than does a herd bull, and what is more, the hunter does not run the risk of being trampled down by a herd which has been stampeded from some inexplicable cause. A stampede is far less dangerous, as a matter of fact, than it seems, for in the end they usually get one's scent and sheer off. Of course it would be insane to rely on this, but in any case, if you kill the leading cow, you can count upon the herd changing direction. The noise a stampeding herd makes as it crashes through a dry reed-bed or the bamboo thickets of the highlands is indescribable, something like the reports of thousands of pistols, and a stampede of buffaloes will test the nerves far more severely on such ground than on the open plains.

Solitary bulls living near human habitations are often extremely vicious, and are called "Rogues." They have usually been wounded at least once, and have therefore declared war upon everybody. In Uganda such dangerous and infuriated bulls were by no means rare.

There was a time when buffalo were not protected in Uganda and anybody could shoot as many as they liked. The Waka-virondos, a tribe inhabiting the country to the north of Victoria Nyanza, paid £10 to £15 for a buffalo hide, and many Greeks and Armenians used to send black hunters all over the country to get buffalo hides for them. Hence the numbers of wounded beasts.

"Rogue" bulls very often took up their abode in deserted banana shambas and they then were very dangerous, especially to women and children coming for water. These deserted shambas are untidy, artificial wildernesses overgrown with dense brambles, giant nettles, different kinds of thistle and other prickly and tenacious weeds.

I shot a solitary bull in one of these shambas which was reputed to have killed a woman and wounded a girl. I saw the wounded girl, who got a good deal of her assailant's meat and I thought that she ate it with a very good appetite!

During my last expedition I had a very interesting experience with a "Rogue" bull. On my way back from the West Nile Province I prolonged my stay in Uganda for a month to collect tchego (black-faced chimpanzee) and other forest animals of the Bugoma forests for the Hungarian National Museum. I had selected a site for my camp quite near a village, when some young men ran to meet me in such a state of excitement that they could hardly explain what they wanted. They said that a huge buffalo was devastating their plantations of beans, grazing on the leaves of their potatoes and had frightened away the men who tried to drive it out of the field. If the signs they made with their outstretched arms had given the true measure of its size, this bull would have beaten all records. They begged me to come and deliver them from the marauder which was said to be lying up in a deserted shamba not far away.

I would have accepted their invitation with pleasure, had I not shot all the buffaloes allowed on my licence in Semliki, i.e. at Lake George, so buffaloes were now "tabu" to me in the West Nile Province. I was sorely tempted, especially when Johanna started to unpack the cordite Express, which Count Seilern had given me.

I argued with myself that the District Commissioner would surely agree to my shooting a dangerous buffalo, when he had come to learn the state of affairs, but then again I thought better of it and tried to explain my difficulty to the assembled villagers.

Of course I asked the mami to send a report to the District Commissioner and ask for permission to shoot this buffalo and assured him that if this permission came, I would do my best to rid them of their enemy, and would also give them the meat; but the villagers seemed disappointed and thought that my refusal was based on other reasons.

During the next few days I saw the large tracks of the old solitary bull and I received reports almost daily about his doings, but the permit did not come. So I never went near the spot indicated for fear of succumbing to temptation.

Eight days later a coffee-planter friend of mine came to see me as he wanted to shoot an elephant and he brought the news that the District Commissioner had asked me to kill this marauding buffalo. The joy of the villagers was great! I sent out messengers to bring me reliable news of the whereabouts of the solitary bull, promising them good baksheesh, and thought that next day the bull would be mine.

I cannot say what happened, but after that very day the bull was not seen again. Although I stayed there three weeks longer, no one saw his fresh spoor. This story was retold over and over again round the camp-fire at night, and I think Johanna will still go on making up weird tales about the "sheitani" bull, which had felt the impending danger and left the spot.

When buffalo shooting was unlimited in Uganda, and was a profitable business, many who were not hunters tried their luck and a large proportion of such gentry had to pay with their own skins for their audacity, while even more of the native hunters were wounded and killed.

Uganda is a typical elephant-grass country and is the least favourable for buffalo hunting, which was an additional reason why so many hide-hunters came to a bad end. In those days I heard a good deal about two hunters who had been attacked by a buffalo. First one of them was badly wounded; then the buffalo pursued the other one and tossed him. Meanwhile the wounded one had climbed up a tree, but without his rifle, and from there had to watch the infuriated beast smash the body of his comrade, throwing it up and goring it to pieces for two hours. I cannot say whether the second man had tried to shoot the buffalo while it was attacking its first victim, but I think he had. When the buffalo had satiated his vengeance and left the spot, the man came down from the tree, but could find nothing of his friend beyond the blood-drenched soil.

On my fourth African journey I made the acquaintance of a Swiss on board the steamer, who lived in Uganda and was bringing out his young wife to Africa. When the War broke out business became slack and so he started buffalo hunting, although he had told me on the steamer that he never had any desire to hunt big game and would not spend money on a game-licence. Anyhow, he did little harm to buffaloes, for the first cow he went after, which he wounded and then followed up, killed him.

Some months later I heard of another tragic end to a buffalo hunt, which I was told by a missionary who came to see a friend of his while I was interned at Hoima.

This missionary had come on foot from Mubendi to Hoima by an old and overgrown path and came upon a deserted tent, from which a very nasty odour emanated, and when he approached he found a dead European on the camp-bed. He had been wounded by a buffalo, and his boys had carried him to his camp and had there left him to his fate, for fear of being called to account for the disaster.

Wounds inflicted by buffalo will heal much more easily than those made by lions or leopards, and I have seen many cases myself where similar wounds inflicted by a lion or a leopard would never have healed so well as those caused by buffalo.

During my own hunting two of my men were seriously, and one slightly, injured by wounded buffaloes, and had we been more cautious these accidents could have been avoided.

When following up a wounded buffalo the strictest precautions should be taken. Old hunters and natives declare that a wounded buffalo will usually double on his tracks and attack his pursuers from the rear, and I believe that there is a great deal of truth in this. But in most cases, even when wounded, the buffalo will avoid man and take to flight, and will rarely act on the offensive. Of course one should never count on this, for a buffalo has all the advantages of the situation in high elephant grass, reedbanks or bush, and it is on this account that the greatest care should be taken.

The blood spoor must be examined closely for very dark blood and eventually for little pieces of liver, as these mean a liver shot and my experience is that any dangerous beast shot in the liver will be a desperate opponent, because they must be maddened by pain.

One of the most effective precautions is to take a most careful aim for the first shot and to know where the bullet strikes. This is not so difficult for a cool-headed sportsman in the open, but is more so in dense scrub or high grass. A buffalo which is really charging can only be stopped by death, and I know of cases where the hunter has taken refuge in a tree and has been watched all through the night by the avenger. The buffalo, like the elephant, has a revengeful nature and will not be satisfied for hours when spending his fury on the body of a victim.

W. D. M. Bell, to whose book I have referred already several times, states that buffalo are not dangerous, and hunting them is only good sport in the thickest bush. But Mr. Bell hunted in countries where few predecessors had disturbed the game and taught it how to defend itself. I think he would have formed a different opinion in Uganda.

The buffalo is very tough and will carry on with desperate

Wagaya warriors in full dress

OL DONYO NGAI—"GOD MOUNTAIN" OF THE MASAI

Young buffalo bull shot near Ndassekera

My best bull

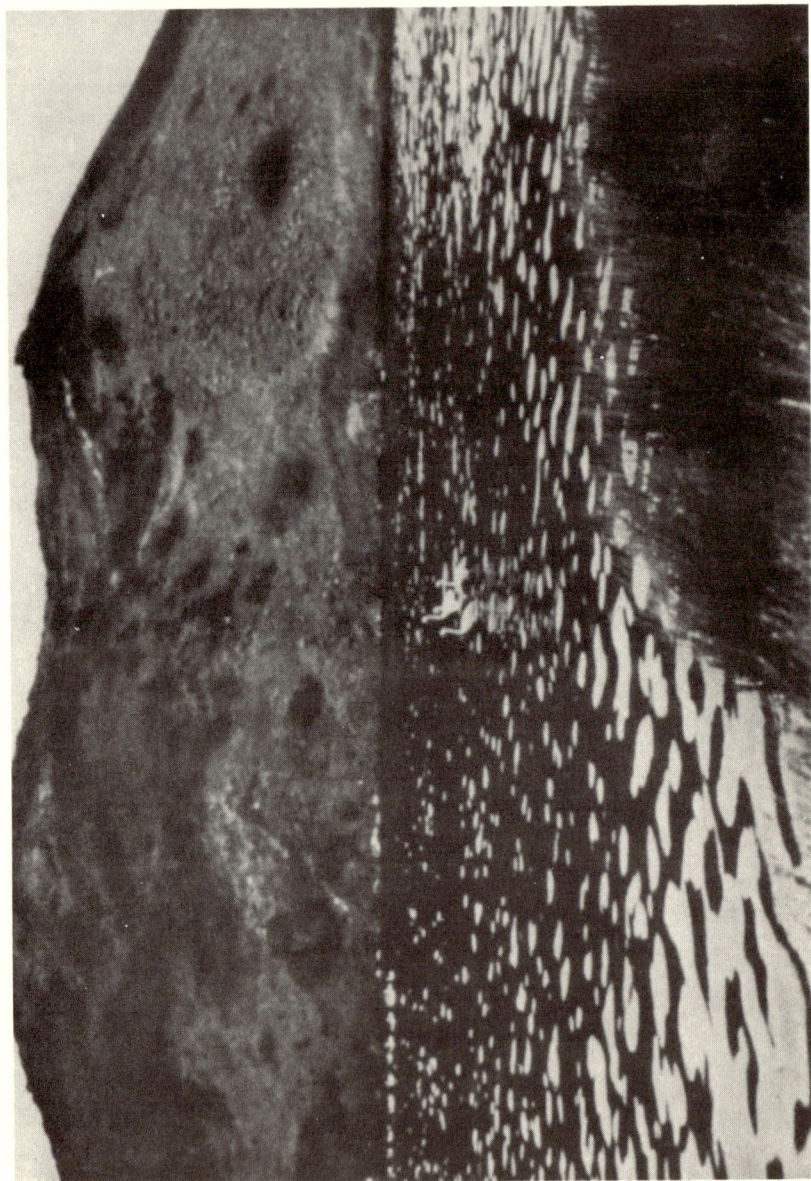

wounds. The shoulder-shot is always best. A head-shot is hard to place, for the forehead, especially in the case of bulls, is entirely covered by a horny boss, which acts as a protection, particularly when he lifts his head and nothing but the nose is visible. Head-shots are more effective at cows or the smaller red buffalo.

My experience is that a soft-nosed bullet from a big-bore rifle or a solid one from a small-bore are advisable. Which rifle to use is a question of individual preference. Personally I found that in thick grass or dense bush a double-barrelled big-bore was better than a small-bore magazine.

I have often eaten buffalo meat. An old bull's flesh is, of course, very tough, and I usually only kept the tongue and the marrow bones for my own use. The marrow I found excellent.

Sometimes we were compelled to use buffalo fat, but I must admit that I never liked it. A dish prepared with buffalo fat must be very hot and eaten quickly, or else the tallow remains on one's palate.

The natives sitting round the camp-fire will tell varied and fantastic tales about the buffalo. They believe that buffaloes persecute men adorned with horns even more than elephants will. Another story which natives believe is that when one takes refuge from a buffalo, one should climb a very high tree; for the buffalo will spray his urine up with the tassel of his tail and this has such an itching and burning effect that the victim will have to let go the branches and will fall down, only to be killed by the beast.

In certain parts of the country natives have no great awe of buffaloes. In Uganda, not far from Lugogo, I met a little "mami" who had speared ten buffaloes in the days when killing them was not limited and they were outlawed as vermin. He told me that in the early morning he would take two or three spears out and get as close to a herd as possible. Then he would throw his spear from ten or fifteen paces into the side of an unsuspecting animal. My black friend showed me his skill in spear-throwing, and the handle of one of his spears was actually shivered into bits by the violent vibrations. In any case, he would have won a prize as a javelin thrower! But to attack a herd of buffaloes single-handed and with only some spears in the hand must certainly require immense pluck.

CHAPTER XII

My Best Buffalo

IN 1910 I guided the expedition of Mr. B. Fernbach, a well-known Hungarian big game hunter, from the eastern shore of the Victoria Nyanza to the sea coast.

We had a large safari, for the country was trackless and uninhabited, and we were compelled to carry a huge supply of vegetable diet, for, as is generally recognized, natives cannot live entirely on meat but must have their "posho" made up out of corn, "ntama" flour or rice as well. That, of course, does not mean that they do not like meat, and to give an illustration of their appetite I need only state that the safari, consisting of 130 or 140 men, consumed three or four zebras, or an equivalent number of antelopes, or a buffalo, each day.

The most interesting part of our journey was the part which lay in the Great Rift Valley and its surroundings. The Rift Valley begins in Abyssinia, extends well to the south of the Equator, and is very wide. In it exist a whole chain of enormous lakes, notably the big Natron and the Eyasi lakes, which are surrounded by arid natron deserts, interspersed with dense forests, swamps and cane-brakes.

In these regions the old Earth still works busily away, and there were days when we passed as many as fifteen hot springs, while hot vapours issued from wide cracks in the ground. Small wonder that the Masai believed that their god "Ngai" lived on the volcano "Oeldoenyo Ngai" (God's mountain), which was continually belching out smoke.

The scenery is wonderful and the animal life abundant and varied. The Rift Valley constitutes a zoological boundary, but in it are to be found some species both of the Eastern as well as of the Western fauna. All the characteristic big game of Africa may be seen here: elephant; buffalo; rhino; hippo; the great cats, lion and leopard; the finest antelopes, the great kudu with gigantic horns and his smaller brother, the lesser kudu, and perhaps the situtunga which never leave the swamps.

This country seems to be the Creator's game reserve, and I trust that in time it will become a real reserve, when it will surpass America's Yellowstone Park.

While travelling in this fascinating country I determined not to shoot anything that did not make an exceptional trophy. So I went through the forests searching for tracks, admired the elephant paths which had been trodden into the rocky walls of the Great Rift in the course of centuries, and when I reached the lakes I revelled in the wonderful sight of thousands of pink flamingoes.

But on February 21st, 1910, after a silence of fifteen days, my rifle spoke again. I had noted in my diary that I had a pre-sentiment that something would happen on that day, and to prove that this presentiment was not false I will quote an extract:

Kiki Tinga-Tinga, February 21st, 1910. In the early morning I set out towards the low hills lying to the left of the camp along the elephant tracks we found the other day.

Soon we came on the spoor of two rhino, but lost it again on the stony soil. Then we found the track of an old, solitary buffalo bull, and followed it up into a large cane-brake in a river-bed. Never had I seen such tall reeds; they were at least 15 to 18 feet high. Of course it would have been quite useless to follow the buffalo into this thicket, so I lost some time in trying to drive him out, but at last I had to give it up and left the place in disgust.

Before ascending the hills we had to cross a plain covered with short grass where I saw impala, kongoni and zebra, and in the swamp below us a large herd of giraffe was watching us.

Once, just as we were scrambling through a river-bed—of course I was still at the bottom—we heard a great noise, which at first I thought was made by waterbucks, and I took my rifle from my gunbearer with little enthusiasm. And then I saw two great buffalo bulls, but I had no time to shoot.

We followed them easily in the sandy soil, and after about

two miles they slackened pace, so I gave them time to lie down and had my breakfast, and then started again.

The spoors of the two old solitary bulls led us into a dense thicket. I was anxious to meet them in a "good" place and was thankful to get through this bush without coming on them. Such hopes and fears are familiar to buffalo hunters.

Soon after that we emerged from another thick bush into a small clearing, when I perceived a grey mass on the other side, and an instant later one bull rolled over with a shot in his neck.

After this there was a great commotion, loud cracking of branches and clattering of hoofs, and suddenly to my utter astonishment two buffalo broke out of the thicket. They bolted past me and I rapidly discharged five shots. Both collapsed, but I saw one of them stagger up again and make off.

I then went to the place where I had shot the first bull in the neck, when I had another surprise, for he was not there and I could not even find any blood on the spot where he was shot.

Then I went to the spot where the other one had stumbled, but again no bull and no blood. Following on both spoors, we found some blood later on—light coloured, frothy blood from the lungs, and some bad, dark blood from an internal wound. I must here note that I was using an 8-mm. Mannlicher-Schönauer. It is better, anyway, than the 9-mm. Mannlicher-Schönauer, but is not half as good as the 6·7 mm.

I halted again to give them time to stop and give myself a chance of thinking over the next move; but the minutes dragged by and I was extremely vexed. At last I thought it was time to follow the bulls up. We had hardly gone 200 yards through the undergrowth surrounding the swampy forest when we noticed that the two tracks separated. I followed one and my Umbugwe guide and a man the other. I told them to be very careful to follow up the blood spoor and always to keep close to trees, but it was quite unnecessary to preach caution to these men.

We advanced silently on the spoors and hardly a thousand yards away from the place where he had first been hit the wounded bull started up quite close to me and ran on, but I could not see in the high grass. At the same time I heard a bellow from the other track and more loud crashing. I ran forwards only to see the hindquarters of the bull, but fired a snap-shot and thought I had hit him in the shoulder. I saw by the waving of the grass that his speed relaxed and then he stopped altogether, so I climbed up a tree in the hopes of getting a glimpse of him from above, but as I could see no better I came down, and as my foot touched ground I heard the groan of the dying bull.

My men wanted to run up to him, but I ordered a halt for a quarter of an hour, and when the time had passed, I crawled in the direction from which we had heard the moan, and soon I stood over my best buffalo. He was already quite stiff. I was deeply impressed by the sight of those enormous horns, and the only thing that detracted from my pleasure was the fear that I was not likely to find my second wounded bull. My men promised to get him—the larger one—but unfortunately my fears proved correct. We cleared the undergrowth round the body so as to be able to get some photos of my record buffalo. But the light even then was bad and the photos were failures.

I found four bullets in the body: one in the neck, one in the hip bone which had paralysed his hind leg, one in the horny part of the forehead and one behind the shoulder.

I sent some men back to camp to get help to carry the buffalo's head, hide and meat home and then followed the blood spoor of the other wounded bull.

We kept on it for a good while. He had advanced but slowly and stood for long in one place, circled round, and there was every indication that he was very sick. But night came and we had to give up the pursuit, leaving it for the next day.

On our way back we startled two more buffalo bulls out of the bush, but it would have been useless to try a shot.

February 22nd, 1910. We set out at dawn with Mr. Fernbach, for last night I advised him to try these low hills, which were full of buffalo. After we had crossed the stream we separated, and he headed towards the hills while I took up the tracks of the wounded bull.

After a short ten minutes I heard Mr. F.'s heavy Express twice in quick succession, and soon after this two buffaloes bolted before us, but I did not see them. On arrival at the spot where we had left off tracking last night I saw with regret that Mr.

Fernbach's shots had frightened my wounded bull away, as was shown clearly enough by some fresh drops of blood. Had I but gone a few yards farther last night I would have got the other bull also, and what a bull! However . . . "Amri ya Mungu!" (It was the will of Allah!).

We found the spoor and then lost it again. Then some more shots from the other side and a bullet whistled over our heads. We at once fell flat on the ground and signalled to the others to let them know where we were. Then the shooting began again, so we jumped up and ran in the direction of the shots. Then came one more shot, shouts and the moan of the dying bull. As we came up we were told that Mr. Fernbach's gunbearer, Osmani, had been knocked down by the buffalo. I examined him but found no broken bones and judged him to be not seriously injured.

What happened was this. Mr. Fernbach mistook a cow for a bull, because amongst ten others she stood the tallest and the first rays of light falling on her made her seem the dominant individual of the herd, so he gave her two bullets. He then followed her up and wounded her again; at last she drew into a very thick patch and lay down. Mr. Fernbach then handed his rifle to his second gunbearer and stepped on a tree-trunk, hoping to see better, but Osmani, thinking that the buffalo was dead and taking no heed of Mr. Fernbach's repeated warnings, entered the thicket. The buffalo got up and charged him. Osmani fired from a distance of two paces but missed, and the second barrel went off as the buffalo had him on her horns. This was the bullet we had heard whistling over us. The second gunbearer was a cowardly Usukuma who ran from the scene of danger, taking the rifle along with him, and so Mr. Fernbach had to run after him first to get the weapon and not until then could he give any assistance to the other man who was in such a tight corner. It was wonderful how many mortal wounds this miserable cow received without losing the will to attack.

Osmani felt his bruises for about a fortnight, but was then quite well again. He was an experienced old fellow, who had before been once picked up and flung away by an elephant, but fortunately the dense elephant grass softened his fall and he was unhurt. In 1912 Osmani accompanied me home to Budapest with a number of live animals.

After having made a litter for Osmani we again went after my wounded buffalo. However, my boys were rather upset by Osmani's accident and did not follow me with much enthusiasm. We kept on losing the spoor every minute as so many old and new tracks ran across it, so I had to give up tracking and went on ahead trusting to luck.

There were numerous buffalo tracks all over this ground, and finally we turned homewards as heavy clouds rolled up. I let my porter, who had just been promoted to gunbearer, carry my rifle, and I myself followed Magambo, who had a wonderful sense of direction. Coming to a place covered with elephant grass, he suddenly started back, whispering: "Kifaru!" We all stepped back while I tried to load my rifle with one solid bullet, thinking that there was but one rhino in front of us. I had forgotten, however, that the rifle had already been charged with six soft-nosed bullets, so in my hurry the cartridge stuck in the breech and the bolt would not move either forwards or backwards. (The same thing happened to me or two subsequent occasions, and I then gave up the bad habit of putting six cartridges into a Mannlicher-Schönauer.) A nice situation! We were standing on natron-covered soil, without the least possibility of hiding. I drew behind a dry thistle, but at that moment a rhino burst out, scarcely giving me time to step aside, and then the second rushed out, scattering my men in all directions, while my gunbearer sprawled on the ground beside the rhino, and I thought he was killed.

But later they all appeared again, grinning happily at their escape. Even my gunbearer had escaped without a scratch. He had been knocked over and the cartridge bag had been trampled on, but he came to no harm.

And then the gates of heaven were opened and torrents of rain poured down and we were drenched.

Thus does my diary describe the episode of my best buffalo.

CHAPTER XIII

Tracking Buffaloes

A SMALL safari was approaching the usually dry bed of the Ruvana. When it reached the river-bank, vultures which were perched on the old mimosa trees of the forest opposite, flew up with heavy flappings of their wings.

We knew what such an assembly of vultures meant! A tragedy had taken place during the hours of darkness and these hungry scavengers were at work clearing away the remains. Prompted by curiosity I took the rifle from my gunbearer's hand and sent him to investigate. I knew that the killer would no longer be found on the kill, for the vultures already seemed to have satisfied their appetites. My man came back with the news that the victim was a hartebeest, but that the other tracks were no longer distinguishable, as the birds had dug up the ground all around. We did not want to lose any time as we had a long march before us and the object of our expedition was something quite different. So my men put down their loads and went to get water in the river-bed of the Ruvana; and refreshed by the short rest and the thick, yellow water of the Ruvana—inhabitants of the African plains are not fastidious regarding water—continued the march over the rough ground near the banks.

But they seemed relieved when we were again on the flat, treeless plain free from all obstacles. The heat was terrific! All vegetation had been burnt to a dull yellow colour and large cracks in the ground yawned up at us.

The killing temperature also had its effects on the game, for it had retired into shadier places and only the Thomson's gazelles and topis grazed in the full glare of the Equatorial sun. Black and grey masses of animals could be seen under the large acacias— zebras and white-bearded wildebeests. They stood in a dense row facing the open, their pointed horns side by side, and looked like a phalanx, through which nothing could penetrate. At our approach an old bull would bounce out grotesquely, then slowing down to a sedate pace, approach us, then suddenly stop short and watch our safari with obvious curiosity as it passed quietly by.

We were marching in single file and my gunbearer behind me said: "You have swerved off the right path, sir. Keep in the direction of the three white birds standing on the banks of the water."

He knew as well as I did that there were in reality no birds and no water, and that the fleeting vision is but the magic play of the mirage which conjures up lakes in the parched desert and transforms the white bones of lions' victims into fluffy white egrets. The Fata Morgana is a wonderful conjurer! Even I, who know every movement of those delightful birds with their virgin-white plumage, began to wonder whether one was not really in front of me, for I thought I saw its graceful fluttering gait, and then again I seemed to see the sudden, quick peck it makes when catching a fish. Its movement is as fast as the slash of a venomous snake when it strikes its prey: the human eye cannot follow it. Farther away on the lake of Fata Morgana there swims a solitary fishing pelican created from the white skull of a long dead rhino; and there are the reddish ruins of an old castle formed from a small herd of hartebeest grazing not far away.

We marched on and on for hours on the arid, colourless, lifeless, parched desert, until at last a black line showed up and finished the pranks of the Fata Morgana. We had reached a forest skirting the bank of a periodical river. After that we crossed through badly cultivated dhurra fields and then arrived at a very miserable native village, where we hoped to get some guides. This was a hard task, for the men had gone somewhere "pombe," i.e. to drink, and nothing but women and children could be found. So I left my wily old munyampara and gunbearer to get all the information they could, to find a guide and get the necessary "dhurra" flour for my men, and told them to come to my tent before dawn broke.

My old munyampara again showed his cunning. Hyenas were still howling and jackals wailing when they stood before my tent, which we had pitched a couple of miles away from the village on the Ushangi River, which is usually dry. He called me aside and said that buffalo were near and the guide at hand, but as the natives of this country were not very friendly towards us, I should have to handle this man carefully. I then had a look at him. He had brought two young men along and was now squatting near the fire gnawing at a piece of meat. His name was Mgunane, which means "eight feet," and he did not inspire much confidence, for his face was sly and cunning.

We then started and during the first hour, when whispered conversation would not disturb the game we were after, my men promised our guide all sorts of rewards if he would lead us to success. But he seemed quite unmoved, while his spiteful demeanour only depicted feelings of malevolence. Close to a scattered acacia jungle he found a fresh and very big spoor coming from the direction of Ushangi and heading towards the jungle. His face brightened up at this and he declared it to be the spoor of a very big solitary bull, which had only passed a few minutes ago. After examining it thoroughly I recognized it as the spoor of an eland, that giant amongst antelopes.

Then I saw clearly that the guide intended to mislead us. Perhaps he had no confidence in me, or perhaps he was afraid of buffalo. So I then addressed him in an exaggerated friendly manner and said that I thought it was no buffalo track, asking him to give it another look. He fell into the trap on seeing my smiles and hearing my friendly tones and went on lying to me until I told him that he might get a good box on the ear if he told any more lies. My own men, who knew my ways, were, of course, giggling all the time.

"Are your senses returning to you?" I then asked him, whereupon he nodded quickly, turned at once in the opposite direction, and walked away.

The dew was already vanishing, but a lot of wonderful waterbuck were still grazing, and every moment we saw wart-hog, that ugliest of African animals, while once an old boar sped away with uplifted tail, and then a small sounder seemed very uneasy at our approach and came up trying to find out what we were. Their short-sighted little eyes are not much use, but the long and broad snout is all the better, for the slightest scent will warn them of danger. We stopped in a swampy opening of the forest, where there was the spoor of a vast herd, which might have been village cattle. One of my men instantly took off his sandal and put his toe into the dung; but it was cold and so this big herd must have passed hours ago. I had already suspected this from the look of the spoor, but this was not the reason why I gave up following them. The truth was that I never found it worth while to hunt a herd of buffalo, as it is so difficult to pick out the best bull in thick scrub when so many beasts are moving about. Then again herd bulls never give such fine trophies as do solitary bulls.

So we continued our way. My guide's face showed slight irony because he evidently thought that I was afraid to follow the buffalo herd, and I chuckled unto myself, thinking, "Wait, and you'll see!" And just then I stopped short, for on the hard stony soil I had spotted the spoor of two large solitary bulls. The boys would not believe at first that the scarcely visible little scratch was a buffalo spoor, but some paces farther on, where the soil was soft, the tracks could be clearly seen, and the dung we found also showed that both bulls were of exceptional size.

We took up the tracks and followed them. It was half funny, but half annoying to see what great respect my new guide, Mgunane, and Pandasaro, my second munyampara and gun-bearer, had for buffaloes; for if a bushbuck or waterbuck started up in the scrub they at once took cover. Pandasaro was never afraid of lions or rhinos and his awe of buffalo proved to be a fore-boding, for sure enough, some months later, he was badly injured by a buffalo bull.

We crawled, sometimes on all fours, through some very thick patches, often losing the track and finding it again. I sent my men forward with Mgunane to follow the track and in the meantime I put my boots in order. As my men did not return I continued tracking myself, and found the spoor after a search of ten minutes, but could hardly follow it in the dense jungle. It was very hot and I was exceedingly thirsty, so without thinking of possible bad consequences (dysentery, etc.) I went to the bed of the Ushangi River for water. I found a hyena's spoor in a dry hollow, and knowing that he must have been on the same errand as I was, I followed its tracks and soon came to the spot where it had begun digging for water. The sand at the bottom of the hole was damp, so I had only to continue digging, but before I began my men came along with the evil-smelling, warm, but boiled and filtered water which they carried.

My boys had found the tracks again, which led towards a very extensive thicket, where we could follow easily, for it was a "good" thicket with relatively little undergrowth, but full of the thorns which are so prevalent in East Africa. We put up so many waterbuck that I began to lose hope of getting the two solitary bulls.

At last we came to a very nasty patch, and I was just expressing a fervent hope that they were not in it, when Pandasaro leapt back. I saw a black moving mass and sent an 8-mm. Mannlicher-Schönauer bullet in the direction where I judged its shoulder was, but saw no result. I followed up at once but could not find a drop of blood, so began to think that I had missed. The buffalo made some wide circles which raised my hopes, and then I heard a slight noise! I crawled nearer and saw that the bull had been hit, for there were two large pools of blood. Again we followed and about 500 yards farther away the bull started up once more. We went on and on until at last I felt inclined to turn back because we were a long way from camp and it was now 3.30 in the afternoon; but I decided to keep on for another half-hour, after which, if I had not found him, I would leave the search until the next day.

In a clearing I came upon a small wallow. The wounded bull had naturally lain in it and had we not a few minutes before startled a herd of about twenty waterbuck, we should surely have found him there, and naturally we felt rather incensed against these waterbuck which had appeared at just the most inopportune moment. Two white-headed fish eagles sat on a large tree near the pool, speculating how to get a fat sheat-fish which was wriggling about in the shallow water. Our Ikoma guide killed the fish, which had already been wounded by the birds, with his spear. I did not want to spoil my men's enjoyment, yet it was a pity to waste time over that fish, so I went on with Pandasaro, leaving our guide to amuse himself to his heart's content.

Unfortunately we then diverged and it was Pandasaro who

started the buffalo up again, and had to run for me first, so that I had only time for a very quick shot at the disappearing bull. Then I ran as fast as I could after the noise made by the beast. When we saw it again it noticed me first and turned away, so I had another snap at it without being able to say whether I had hit it or not. I sent my men back to the spot where the track started again and I myself went to where I thought I heard the last snort, when I heard a weak rattling sound and then silence. It was a very thick bit of jungle and it was some time before I could crawl into it, to find the buffalo dead. I covered it with my rifle as I approached, but seeing that life was extinct I whistled to my men, who soon joined me. We gazed with much pleasure at our "first" of Ushangi, which was very large in body and carried quite good horns too, black, pearled, broad, but a little too short. I left three of my men, Mgunane amongst them, to guard the buffalo, while the rest of us returned to camp. We arrived late at night and the lions had already been roaring for a long time.

The Ushangi River later became one of my favourite buffalo grounds, and Mgunane was always pleased to accompany me. We had many an interesting adventure together and were in one or two tight corners.

The following experience also occurred on the Ushangi River: In 1910 I was already occupied in catching animals alive, and was very pleased that the good buffalo ground by the Ushangi River was hardly a day's march from my collecting camp on the Ruvana Plains. The rinderpest had been quite forgotten; buffalo had again multiplied to such an extent that the German game laws—which, however, were not irreproachable—did not limit the number of buffaloes which could be shot. So I was able to take my share in this fascinating sport, while every buffalo killed meant quite a little fortune. As I have already mentioned, I was catching animals alive, and was in need of milch cows to bring up the young animals, and these were hard to get, for the natives would not sell them willingly, and when they did, they only sold the worst cows they had. But when I arrived at Shirati, a place on the shore of the Victoria Nyanza in the former German East, with a few buffalo hides, I was very differently treated, for the elegant Wagaya swells would exchange two young cows for a hide. They made their wonderful big war shields out of these hides; that was why every sultani tried to get as many as possible for his warriors. I took advantage of the meeting between the three Wagaya chieftains who bid against each other, and in the same way was also enabled to get porters for my safaris.

So October, 1910, again found me hunting buffalo on the Ushangi River. The first day passed without seeing any, but on the second day one of my trackers spotted three solitary bulls in a little acacia jungle. I got the news too late that day for it to be worth my while to go out again, and as my men swore that the buffaloes had not noticed them and had not stirred, I felt sure of finding them the next day. My trackers could be relied upon to tell the truth, for I usually looked into their reports closely and if one proved false—the spoor would always tell exactly—they had a bad time of it, for I always enforced rigid discipline.

On October 12th I set off for the acacia jungle which the trackers had mentioned. Quite near my tent I saw a "pigeon tree" covered with ripe berries. There were, in fact, more berries than leaves, for the green pigeons had flocked to the tree in thousands and had already broken off all the twigs. When we approached there was a loud fluttering and many hundreds of birds flew up, while just as many remained. I was glad to find that they were so near and decided that, on my way home in the evening, I would shoot half a dozen with my Winchester-Automatic. As these birds live only on berries and fruit their flesh is very delicate, especially that of the young ones.

My tracker then showed me where the buffalo had been lying the day before, which made me very angry with myself for having been elsewhere, for I certainly never could have found them in a more favourable place, so I invoked the goddess Diana to let me see them in a similar spot. My prayer was granted, for I saw them in an even better place, but through my own stupidity I failed to appreciate the situation. But let my diary speak:

"First we followed yesterday's tracks, but getting tired of this, I left three men on them and we went to look for more recent ones. So we reached the 'bara-bara' and crossed the Ushangi.

On the farther bank there was also game in abundance, wildebeest, zebra, hartebeest and gazelles of all kind, and before daybreak lions had been roaring there. Then I returned to the old trail. Without noticing it we missed my men's spoor, and going a little more to the north, we found ourselves on the fresh tracks of a solitary bull, which had only just passed along the bara-bara and headed for the acacia jungle. We followed it up at once. After about 50 yards the two other bulls had joined him and they all three continued their way together.

"After a while my Ikoma guide bent forward, and following the direction of his intent gaze, I saw a dark mass on the ground, which my field-glasses told me was a buffalo. I left my men behind and crawled up quite close—about 15 to 18 yards—when I saw that all three bulls were resting together. So I tried to pick out the best one and advanced one or two steps nearer. For a long time I could not make out which was its shoulder and which its hindquarters. I was getting rather impatient when it turned towards me and lifted up its head, as buffalo do, and saw me. Prompted by a sudden impulse I aimed from a sitting position at its head—although it was partly hidden by a small tuft of grass—and fired. The bull jumped up like lightning and after staggering about a bit, disappeared. Its retreat was, however, too precipitate to give me a chance of a second shot.

"I followed up at once, but how angry I felt with myself for not having chosen one of the other bulls or taken a more careful aim. I should have been consoled had my bullet been deflected by a branch when at least I should not have wounded the beast. This thought, however, had hardly occurred to me when we found some treacherous, slimy blood on the soil. My bullet had apparently hit him very low in the head, or perhaps had failed to penetrate the horny mass of the forehead.

"Nevertheless we proceeded. About 250 to 300 yards farther on a waterbuck sprang up, and shortly afterwards there was more rustling in the underwood. I pulled Pandasaro back, for he thought it was another 'kuru,' but I had seen a large body which I took for that of a rhino and only realized it was the buffalo as it dashed past me, when I fired a hurried shot without any effect. Contrary to my usual custom, I was using solid bullets. I gave the wounded beast an hour's interval, and in the meantime we caught a waterbuck calf hardly a day old, which I sent back to my tent with a man. The waterbuck calf is the prettiest of all the antelope calves. An hour later we were again on the track of the buffaloes through both scattered and dense bush. We followed them in this way for two more hours, but zebra and waterbuck always kept coming between us and frightening the buffaloes more and more. Again I tried dashing after them, but through the broken and bent branches only succeeded in seeing in which direction they had gone on. At length I returned with Sindano to the spot where the three bulls had been lying up, in order to investigate the blood spoor more closely, when Sindano stepped back suddenly and whispered ' buffalo.'

"Almost immediately I recognized the animal as a rhino, which had got our scent and was charging with loud snorts. I at once fired, and hitting it behind the ear, dropped it on the spot. Then we realized that it was not alone, for its mate stood near at hand in the bush and on the report of my rifle dashed past us snorting and puffing. I sent a bullet after it, which it acknowledged with a squeal but without stopping. We pursued at once, and soon we came out of the bush and saw our rhino in the open. As it was wounded and the wind was wrong, I had to risk a long shot (about 200 yards) and felt that my bullet hit too far back, whereon he came at us squealing and snorting like a motor-car gone mad. We were lying flat in the scanty grass of the plain, and as I tried to reload my Mannlicher-Schönauer I found that the magazine had jammed.

"Then came some thrilling moments. The rhino was charging with a terrific noise and I was tugging away at my rifle in feverish anxiety. I hoped that Sindano would jump up and run away and turn the rhino's attention from me. It was not an altruistic wish, I admit, but he would have had more chance than I had. But Sindano had sense enough not to stir and lay flat twenty paces behind me. Suddenly the rhino swerved, slid forwards and collapsed, not to move any more. How relieved I felt! A few moments later I managed to free the bolt and my rifle was all right again.

"The horns of the two rhinos were good ones, especially those of the cow, and when they had been taken off we returned to our buffaloes. Half an hour later they again made off through the bush without my having seen them. We followed them till late in the evening, but in vain. To-morrow if we can still find the tracks, we will continue."

The second day of tracking also passed without bringing success, but a few months later we got the bull that had been wounded.

I was then hunting buffalo again on the Ushangi. In the early morning I saw three solitary bulls on an open plain, right among some herds of wildebeest and zebra.

I knew that I should not get the buffaloes while the herds of wily zebra and wildebeest were near them. Zebras are not very shy animals and they are easy to approach, but if one of them gets suspicious, they will start their barklike neighing and alarm the whole countryside. At length the herds of game began to move slowly, the zebras and wildebeests heading towards the open plain, while the three old bulls made for the mimosa forest.

We were hiding in a fold of the ground and waiting for the herds to retire and leave the buffaloes alone. While I was watching them through my field-glasses I saw two cheetahs lying in wait for a troop of Peters' gazelle. I could have shot one, but of course did not do so on account of the buffaloes. We waited a long time and at last the wide plain was cleared of all game and we tried to cut off the line of the buffaloes, making use of even the smallest shrubs as cover.

Unfortunately a rainstorm took us by surprise and interfered with my getting a good aim. I tried, therefore, to get still nearer to the buffaloes, but they spotted something and dashed off very noisily. For some hours we followed the spoor, and in the meantime the storm cleared and a light favourable breeze blew in our faces.

The buffalo eventually returned to the place where I had first met them. They were going slowly now, so I made sure that they would settle down in the acacia forest. The tracks showed that they stopped frequently in search of a convenient resting-place. But what was that? The footmarks were impressed deeper into the ground. They seemed to have been startled by something, and had suddenly dashed away at a great pace towards the Ushangi scrub jungle. Soon we found the reason for this, for we had not gone many steps farther when we met one of my men who had been left at home and had come out to look for honey! This evil-smelling wretch had frightened the buffaloes away! I will leave our conversation after this meeting to the reader's imagination!

After reaching the scrub, the buffaloes separated. We followed the largest of the spoors which led into a dense patch of jungle, something like wild holyhocks about ten feet high. I knew this spot well, and knew that it would be useless to follow. A drive was the only hope of success. I told my men to go round the patch so as to get up wind and scare the buffalo out of the thicket on my side, and waited in a small clearing where the buffalo had entered.

The drive began. My seven natives shouted and yelled and threw stones and branches down from the surrounding trees into the thicket, but for a long time nothing could be heard. Then one or two braver fellows—thinking that the buffalo had already gone out—penetrated into the thicket. Suddenly the great bull broke out not very far from where I stood and as he crossed the 25 yards of the clearing I sent five bullets into his shoulder. When he reached the edge of the forest he stopped for a moment, to get two more bullets, and then collapsed.

I was very glad to get one of the three at least. He was a very fine bull, and his horns were large also, by far the best of all I had shot on the Ushangi. The distance from tip to tip measured 3 feet 6 inches. When my men had cleaned the skull I saw that the bull was an old acquaintance, for behind the horny mass of the root of the horn, and in the forehead, I found my deformed 8-mm. Mannlicher-Schönauer bullet.

On October 10th, 1910, three days after I had shot two rhinos instead of a buffalo, I had another experience with rhinos while following buffalo tracks. The day before had been a quinine day and I awoke in the morning in a heavily drugged condition. The effects of quinine are the most unpleasant of all similar types of

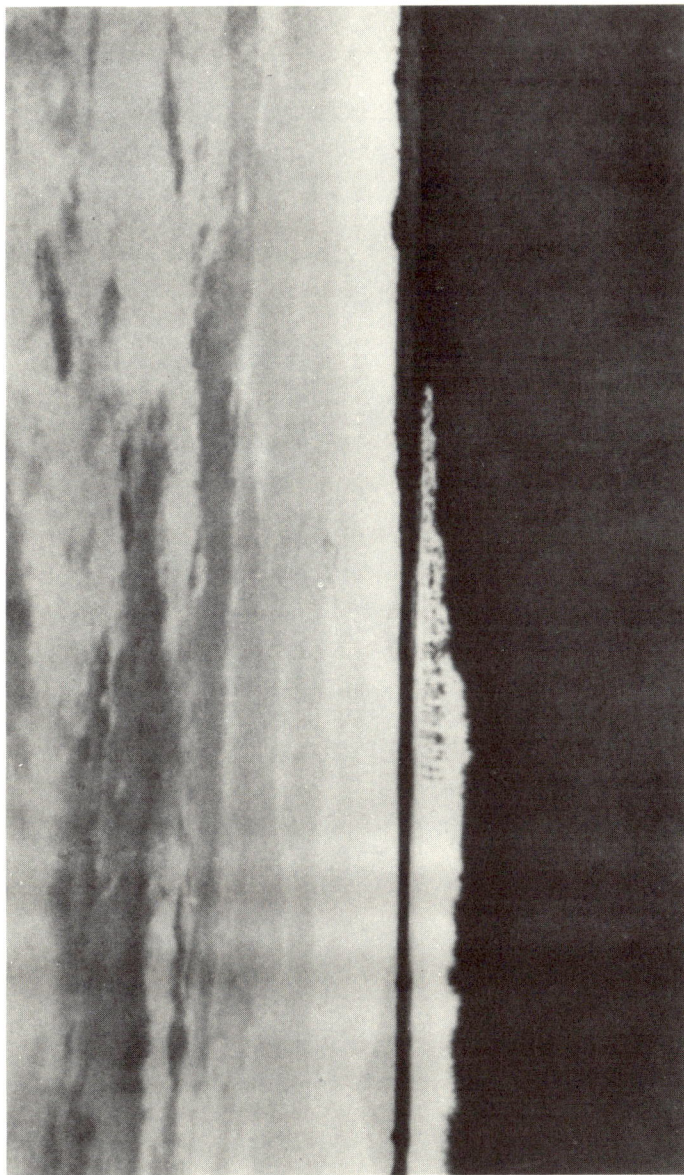

FLAMINGOES ON A LAKE OF THE GREAT RIFT VALLEY

THE "FIRST" OF USHANGI

BUFFALO BULL SHOT ON THE USHANGI
The hide was prepared for the Hungarian National Museum

CAGE FOR TRANSPORTING BABY RHINO CAUGHT ON THE USHANGI

BAAMBA MAN IN HIS CLUB CHAIR

BAAMBA WOMAN POTTER. ON THE LEFT THE CLUB CHAIR, UNOCCUPIED

dizziness, and when your ears are singing and hands trembling, a fair amount of fatalism is needed in order to make one follow a solitary bull into thick jungle.

Although I sent the usual trackers out in the morning, I had a sneaking hope that they would not find anything, and I myself set off for that part of the Ushangi forest where the evening before I had heard the "rrow-rrow-rrow" of some colobus monkeys, as I wanted to get some specimens of these monkeys, with the wonderful fur, for my collection. In these parts the natives hunt them with poisoned arrows, because their fur is used in their war dresses, and consequently the monkeys are very wily. I shot two big males and one female, and had the good luck to secure a baby monkey as well. Curiously enough, the young ones of these black and white monkeys are quite white, only the face being black.

I was just about to turn homewards when a man rushed up with the tidings that he had found fresh buffalo tracks. Of course I set out immediately, and after finding the spoor I examined my rifle and while doing so I had a curious presentiment that something was going to go wrong.

The spoor led through reeds to an area covered with elephant grass where we also came upon a fresh rhino track. I made a detour round this area covered with elephant grass, as I knew that if the bull got my wind, he would probably break out towards me. I was a good prophet, for that is what happened. I had hardly taken cover behind a small mimosa tree when the tall grass parted and a huge bull buffalo dashed out and then turned towards me. When hardly six paces off he got my bullet in the neck. He stopped short, staggered and turned slowly away, showing his shoulder as he went. I should have had ample time for at least ten shots, but again a cartridge jammed, and while I was working away at my rifle in nervous haste I saw his strength returning rapidly. At last I succeeded in getting my rifle into working order and, almost beside myself, I ran after the retreating bull. I saw him standing 400 yards away in the open, but I foolishly enough did not fire but ran up in the hopes of getting nearer. The bull began to move, at first slowly but then faster, until at length he disappeared in the bush. At first we found plenty of blood, but then none at all. My hopes of getting the buffalo began to fade, and he was a very fine bull. Never before nor after have I seen his like, and I cannot describe the anguish I suffered at losing him; it was physical pain.

I continued following the bull in the scrub in this state of mind. My rifle was loaded and the magazine charged with soft-nosed bullets. I actually thought of changing them, for I realized the possibility of meeting a rhino. Once a waterbuck started up noisily. I had an idea that it was the wounded bull and ran in its direction. On one side the jungle was nearly impenetrable, but ahead, where I heard the buck running, it was quite passable. Suddenly an inner voice seemed to whisper, "Look to your left!" And there, hardly four paces away, was a bull rhino, his head thrown down, snorting furiously. As is usual in moments of danger many ideas flashed through my brain. I realized that the soft-nosed bullet would not penetrate the skull, but also that there was no time to change; so I aimed and fired into his forehead. The beast collapsed as if struck by lightning, and as he tried to get up, I slipped a solid bullet into the chamber and shot him behind the ear. His horn was a very good one and weighed 14½ lbs., but it was a very poor substitute for the wounded buffalo.

I left a few men at the carcase to cut off the horn and legs and parts of the skin out of which sticks and whips are made, and we continued on the trail of the wounded buffalo. The bull went round and round in large circles, but always very slowly. After the shot he seemed to have redoubled his pace, but kept to the thickest jungle, so that sometimes we could hardly follow. When night fell I had to give up, but intended to continue the tracking the next morning.

At daybreak we did indeed follow the track of the wounded bull, but lost it at seven o'clock. Meanwhile we were attracted to a rhino's resting-place by the rhino birds fluttering up and down, but it was in the middle of such a repulsive thicket, that it would have been foolhardy to approach, as every advantage was on the rhino's side, and the birds would have given us away at once. I tried to drive the rhino out by sending my men up trees so as to give it their wind and telling them to throw down stones; but it was useless. It acknowledged every stone with a furious snort and ran to where it fell, but would not leave the thicket.

Sindano, who was sitting on a tree, made signs to me that he could see the animal from where he was, so at last I made up my mind and climbed up to him. I hated doing so, because the tree was covered with red ants and thorns. I saw very little of the rhino, and the swaying of the grass alone showed where it was. "Wait a bit," thought I, "I shall frighten you out!" So I fired a shot in its direction to frighten it which made it come towards us, but although I only saw it for an instant, I realized that my shot had wounded it slightly. It began to emit piercing shrieks and ran out of the thicket into the open, when I noticed that the shrieks came from somewhere else.

When I crept down to examine the spoors, I saw that it was an old cow with a young calf not more than six or eight months old trotting behind her. Now I understood why she was so reluctant to leave the thicket.

After taking their full ration of water for the use of those who were still to accompany me, I sent back some of the men to my tent to bring help, water and food after us and, with the few I had selected, we hurried after the rhino mother and baby.

A wounded rhino will travel far; and this one certainly did. We ran across the open bits where the spoor was easily read. Only two of my men followed me, the others went to seek water or else were too exhausted. I could not overtake the rhinos before sundown, and as the rhino birds betrayed me again, I had to take two shots at long range. The cow seemed severely wounded but still went on, while I followed as fast as possible. But we could not get up with her again that evening. We found water in the bed of the Ushangi and stopped there for the night. My little ·22 Winchester-Automatic again proved its use, as with it I shot a Thomson's gazelle for supper without disturbing the silence of the veldt. I may add that I missed salt and other cooking ingredients very much.

Early in the morning we were on the tracks again. Great herds of gazelles and wildebeest had crossed over the spoors, so we often lost them, but one of us always found them again. Finally all traces disappeared and we separated to search for them, when I saw a dark grey mass on the river-bank and recognized my rhino at once. I fired instantly. The rhino was mortally wounded, but turned on me. I stepped aside and gave her three shots in the shoulder, when she fell close to my men who had taken refuge in trees.

I laid down my rifle and field-glasses and so did my two men, and at a given sign we fell on the calf which was standing near the dead cow. It was already a strong animal, but we very soon overcame it, and we tied it to a tree with strong cords made out of sanseverin fibre. We cut off the old cow's horn, which was 2 feet 3 inches long, and then my other men came up, and finally Najsebwa appeared, leading those I had left at my tent. We built a cage out of creepers for the little rhino and carried it back to camp.

Next day we were heading towards the Ruvana Plains without the record bull's head, but with the baby rhino, which was an even better acquisition. But my pleasure was short, for hardly did we undo the cords and open the cage than the little animal began to tremble, breathe heavily, and in a few moments it was dead. This is often the fate of older animals, which can only be caught after a strenuous resistance.

At the end of October, 1910, I returned again to the Ushangi to hunt buffalo and, if possible, catch a young rhino. I had shot three buffaloes already during this trip. The two last I shot in one day; but it was a wild chase, and I had worked hard to get them. I could not return to my tent, but had to pass the night in the open. Of course, that night there was a heavy storm, which put out our fire, and we had to wait for dawn, wet to the skin and trembling with cold. The disagreeable results soon showed themselves. I had another bad go of fever and my old dysentery broke out again. On October 30th I woke in a bad state of health. I had passed an almost sleepless night, very sick, and when I did fall asleep bad dreams pursued me, and I was glad to wake again. A feeling of horrid fright—of growing terror—overwhelmed me, and I doubt if the greatest coward has ever felt such pangs of fear as are induced by fever-wrought dreams.

At dawn I did not even think of leaving my bed. But then one of my men ran to me saying that he had seen a big buffalo bull quite close to camp. So I staggered to my feet and started with my men after the buffalo. I certainly did not go with much enjoyment, but I hated the idea of appearing as a "goy-goy" (weakling in Swahili) to my men.

The bull meanwhile had gone into a thicket of "buffalo grass" which was growing over an area of about 50 or 60 acres not 600 yards from my tent. The wind was wrong, so I could not follow it into this thicket, and my men advised me to wait on the side opposite to where the bull had entered and to let them drive the grass. I did not like the idea, and was sure it would have a bad end, but I took my stand on an ant-hill, which was covered with bushes. The drive began. From where I stood I could see all my men as they approached. I heard a noise in the grass and lifted my rifle. But it was only a fine wart-hog which dashed past me, and not the bull for which I was waiting.

I was relieved when my men closed up, and I then called them together and told them to set fire to the grass at noon, for this seemed the only way to get the shrewd old fellow out. My boys did not think it a good plan, for they did not want to wait until noon, and said that the bull might leave the thicket before then. They begged to be allowed to follow the tracks into the thicket, for they thought it very probable that the bull was no longer there.

As we had not had any trouble with Ushangi buffaloes hitherto my men regarded the bull in a somewhat light-hearted manner. I did not want to spoil their humour, so I let them do as they pleased, stipulating only that they were to keep together, for a crowd is in less danger of being attacked than a solitary man. Once more I took my stand on the ant-hill, but soon had to retire again, not feeling at all well. I waited for the beginning of the drive, which would be signalled with a bugle, and the shouting and yelling that ought to follow, for in this case I had expressly told them to make as much noise as possible and keep together; but instead of this I heard cries of terror and pain.

Running back to the ant-hill I saw, not 300 yards away, my men scattering, and in their midst the bull with one of them on his horns and about to trample on him.

I fired and heard the bullet strike and saw the buffalo stagger. He left his victim and strode towards the river. Again I fired and again I heard the clap of the bullet. I could have given him still a few more shots if one of my men, the silly Tchandaro, had not been in the way, covering the bull with his body. I was still shaky from the terrible sight I had just witnessed, so I dared not fire. The first shot had been risky enough, for all the men scattered round the buffalo were in danger of being killed by my bullet and the victim was still on the buffalo's horns when I fired.

The bull disappeared in the river-side jungle and I ran to the unfortunate man who had been wounded. It was Pandasaro, my second headman. His head was injured but not very severely. A native's head will stand much and in a few days his wounds were healed. But what was worse, his right leg was broken above the knee and he had some bruises on his side, though they proved to be not as bad as I thought at first.

We carried Pandasaro on a litter to my tent, and while I wrote a letter to the Utegi settlement's physician for sleeping sickness (it was seven days' march from where we were) my clever old Najsebwa made splints, between which we then set and bandaged the broken leg. I had given poor Pandasaro a glassful of whisky before we started this operation, but even thus fortified he yelled until we had finished. Then eight of my men—four at a time— carried him to Utegi, where German professors of great knowledge were striving with German thoroughness to check the terrible scourge of sleeping sickness which was raging amongst the native population. Pandasaro was laid up for a long time and when after four months he came back to me again, though his wounded leg was shorter, he was still the best runner amongst my men.

I could not even wreak my revenge on the bull, for by the time we had finished dressing Pandasaro it was late in the afternoon. My men were downhearted, and so I only took Sindano along—but even he hung behind—so I went alone on the track, until it led into a clump of wild mallows, where it would have been foolish to follow, so I put it off until the next day.

On October 31st I wrote as follows in my diary:

Yesterday's bad bull is surely helped by Satan! I was on his track early this morning. It is hard to find the spoor because the cunning beast is striding along as cautiously as a cat, goes up and down and round and round again, so that it is nearly impossible to keep on the track. At last I succeeded in finding the right spoor which led out of a network of tracks, when a swarm of infuriated bees came upon us. Sindano started yelling and dancing, and we took more than thirty stings out of his head afterwards. Some also stung me on the head and hands, which was all the more painful on account of the great heat. I set fire to the dry, tall grass and this saved us. My face swelled up to such an extent that I could not see and could only grope my way home aided by Sindano. The swelling only went down the following evening, so I had to stay at home.

My men were extremely downcast, and I could frequently hear them say, "Khazi ya Seitani" (Devil's work), and they showed every inclination to turn home. I had to do something to buck them up, for their good temper was essential, as it was nearly impossible to get men for animal catching or for the hunting of dangerous game in these parts.

On November 2nd, although my eyes still had a very Mongolian look, I started again to hunt for the wounded bull, but without the slightest hope of finding him. My men only came reluctantly, as if under sentence of death, so I made my mind up that after we had found the track I would go ahead alone and leave them to follow behind at a considerable distance, for I knew that they would not be of any use, as they were so listless and frightened. Hyenas were holding a concert when we started, and we saw a lot of game during our march, especially impalas. But we could not find the track of the wounded buffalo, and it was not until much later that I came upon the first fresh buffalo spoor. Of course I stuck to my plan and left my men behind, to which they agreed joyfully.

Hardly had I gone one or two hundred yards into the bush, when I heard the snorts of buffaloes, followed by much noise, but the cover was too dense for me to see anything, although the buffaloes were only ten yards away. Some 400 yards farther on I again walked into three buffaloes, without seeing them, and again later I startled a small herd, but only saw a passing flash of black. For awhile I kept on the tracks, but then I returned to meet my men, and on my way back I came upon fresh tracks and followed them again.

A honey-guide joined me and his warble awoke the sleeping jungle. I tried to frighten him away, but the only result was that he got noisier still. A buffalo lying in his resting-place jumped up at the note of the honey-guide, holding his nose up high, but fortunately I noticed him in time. I never favour a head-shot when a buffalo stands facing one with raised head, but I could do nothing else but to take a careful aim under the brim of the horny part of his forehead and fire. The bull dropped without a sound, and then I saw that another and a smaller bull had been standing behind him, and was now facing me. I shot him sideways in the shoulder and as he bolted, I gave him another bullet. The bull thus received two good shots and fell down after having gone about 30 yards and gave his death-groan.

Aroused by this, two cows and two calves came for me from the right like a tornado. I shot the first in the forehead and she also came down. The head-shot is easier in the case of a cow, for she has less of the horny mass over her forehead than a bull. I shot the second cow at three paces from me, so when she slid down I had to jump away to avoid being knocked over. This was the last cartridge in my rifle. The two calves stood about twenty paces away from the two dead cows and only left when I shouted at them. Of course I did not want to shoot them.

After this was all over my nerves began to suffer from a reaction and in a few moments I felt cold shivers running down my back. I had to whistle and shout for an hour before my men appeared on the scene, for on their way towards me they had been frightened up trees by a cow with a calf. They were greatly pleased to see three buffaloes lying nearly in a heap, and a little farther away a fourth. Old Najsebwa said: "Sir, we are quits now with the buffaloes."

We prepared the largest buffalo's hide in the hope that the Hungarian National Museum would have it set up in its zoological department.

MR. HORTHY AND A BAAMBA GIRL

BAAMBA WOMEN FOLK

SOLITARY BULL SHOT NEAR FICUS CAMP

BUFFALO COW SHOT ON THE SEMLIKI

WAMBUTI ARCHER

WAMBUTI PIGMIES IN THE BAAMBA FOREST
My gun-bearer, Johanna, of average size, seems a giant standing between them

BANANA PLANTATION IN A CLEARING OF THE BAAMBA FOREST

CHAPTER XIV

Some Buffalo Hunts during my Last Expedition

THINGS usually turn out contrary to one's expectations in Africa, and we experienced the truth of this when diverse reasons compelled us to change the direction of our journey.

In Uganda, as elsewhere in Africa, conditions have greatly changed since the War. Formerly it was easy to secure porters there, but nowadays it is almost impossible, even when one offers very high wages. The reason is that since the War cotton-growing has proved to be a very lucrative business and most of the natives have taken to it.

Moreover, in the previous year there had been an exceptional rainfall in Uganda, so everything was fresh and green in December and the savanna fires had not begun. It is not exactly pleasant to hunt in elephant grass of from 13 to 16 feet in height, so we were forced to go to Fort Portal, at the foot of the Ruwenzori Mountains, in order to organize our safari. At Fort Portal we really got the men we needed, and were soon able to start for the Semliki River.

First of all, however, we obtained all the information we could about the hunting conditions and learned that the small West African red buffalo crossed the river Semliki in great herds in the month of March, migrating eastwards, and that the Semliki buffalo is probably a cross between the red buffalo and the large black buffalo.

It is a pity that this interesting local species provides an inconsiderable trophy compared with the East African buffalo, especially as the game laws of Uganda only allow four buffaloes on a licence, a regulation which is hard to understand, as buffaloes are the most widely distributed game in Uganda. We were told that this would soon be altered and that ten would be allowed, but during our stay in Uganda the law was not changed.

During our first few days at Semliki we did not actually see a buffalo. The herons betrayed their resting-places more than once in the tinga-tingas of the Semliki River, but it was hopeless to follow them in these primeval swamps.

On January 6th, after a very hard day, we at last came up with some. We had started early in the morning. We had seen white herons quite close the edge of the marshes above the tinga-tinga on the borders of the area covered with elephant grass. I was sorely tempted to go there, so we studied the direction of the wind once more and set out. It is unnecessary to explain how cautiously we advanced. There was a little clearing which could not be seen from outside, and over this clearing the birds kept fluttering, and my men closed up behind me saying, "Mbogo" (buffalo). It was curious how easily they were misled through the respect they had for buffalo, for as a matter of fact the alarm was caused by four innocent wart-hogs.

They were ashamed of having betrayed fright, for they dislike exposing themselves to the white man's contempt—so they pulled themselves together and approached the next flock of birds on the edge of the papyrus swamps with more determination. But this time a herd of waterbuck, and not buffalo, had attracted the birds. Aroused by the noise of their retreat an elephant screamed inside the papyrus swamps, or perhaps it was beyond the Congo boundary. The elephant poacher must have had an easy time before any agreement was made between the Congo and Uganda Governments.

For once the herons had pulled our legs and we came out of the tinga-tingas without our hopes being fulfilled. We then went to the place where the Wahimas reported they had seen both elephants and buffaloes in abundance. The sun was high when one of the Wahimas who had been sent out tracking came running back, saying he had seen five buffaloes and one elephant "quite near." His companion had remained on the spot to watch the elephant.

"Quite near" turned out to be very far, and the long-legged Wahima ran ahead of me so fast that I found it very hard to keep up with him in the great heat. After hurrying on for nearly an hour and a half I saw the sentinel on the top of an ant-heap. He pointed out a black mass lying in the tinga-tinga and said it was the elephant which he had been watching since his comrade had left him. Through the field-glass I could clearly discern the huge animal's back and flapping ears; and then another pair of ears and then still another. Evidently it was no solitary bull. Perhaps a few good tuskers had crossed over from the Congo side, and I had to find out what sort of tusks they carried. The wind was favourable, so we started. After the first hundred yards I saw the nature of the ground made our scheme hopeless, but as we had already set out I determined to stick to it. Sometimes I was nearly submerged in the water-holes which are formed by the footprints of elephants and my companions told me that the water-rills were full of crocodiles, a bit of information which did not increase my enthusiasm. But most horrible of all was the fact that on the tops of elephant grass are formed the nests of the vicious red ants and these plague one incessantly, although, curiously enough, natives do not seem to mind them.

Quite close to the elephants there was a small patch of dry soil, and finding a firm footing, we stopped on it. From here I saw that five elephants were feeding ahead of us. I could have shot the largest, but I had not seen his tusks, so I stole nearer and climbed on the shoulders of a tall Wahima, but even from this eminence I failed to make out the tusks. Getting impatient, I whistled, hoping that the elephants would lift their heads, when I could see their tusks, but they took no notice whatever at first, and then suddenly threw up their trunks and dashed away without showing their tusks. It was very difficult to get out of the tinga-tinga on their track, more difficult even than it had been to get in.

On the edge of the swamp, where the spoor could be made out quite well, I saw that all five were cows! Thus the three hours' march in the swamp—which I shall never forget—was quite in vain.

On our way home a reedbuck jumped up before us. It is a rare animal on the Semliki River, but as I wanted meat for my men, I fired at a range of about 200 yards. My bullet hit it too far back, so I had to give it another to bring it down. As I was getting my camera out, my guide whispered in excitement: "Sir! Buffalo!"

At the report of my second shot and not far from the place where my men had mistaken the wart-hogs for buffalo, a herd of buffaloes came out in single file. I judged that there were about sixty and was surprised to see so many red and dappled-red ones among them.

We instantly retreated behind an ant-heap and from there observed the herd, which seemed uncertain as to their next move. They started off, but then stopped again, and at last seemed re-assured and lay down on the dry bed of a river. One or two of them—probably old cows—remained on the bank and kept a sharp look out, although we were at least 800 yards away, and down wind.

I sent a Wahima lad back to camp for Mr. Horthy. It was four o'clock in the afternoon, and I knew that Mr. Horthy could not join us before sunset, that is, at about six in the evening. But I trusted that the lad, who had not been with us in the tinga-tinga, would be as quick as possible, and hoped that he would find Mr. Horthy in camp. Anyway, I decided to wait until a quarter to six, when there would still be a quarter of an hour before sunset.

I tried to doze behind the ant-heap, but curiosity kept me wide-awake, and every ten minutes I climbed up to have a look at the buffaloes, and then I would direct my field-glasses towards a cluster of the three borassus palms from which Mr. Horthy was likely to approach. It was not yet half-past five when I saw some men appearing from this direction who proved to be Mr. Horthy with a few porters and the Wahima guide.

I gave him a brief account of the situation; not many words were needed, because the buffalo were beginning to move and soon walked out of the river-bed in a long file. We still had to wait a little because Mr. Horthy had been met by my messenger on the way and had sent a man back to camp for his cordite rifle since he had only gone out to shoot antelopes with his 6·7-mm. Mannlicher-Schönauer.

The brief period of daylight we had left was slipping away rapidly, and, as the man with the rifle did not return, Mr. Horthy had to set out without it. We were down wind so we could advance without risk. Advancing cautiously from bush to bush we followed the buffalo herd which was slowly moving away. When at last we got up to them they became alarmed at something and dashed away in a stampede. I had already given up all hopes of a shot and we went through a patch of elephant grass and came to a big ant-heap which I was just about to climb when Mr. Horthy, who had already gone round it ahead of me, turned back, saying: "Here they are!"

And sure enough there they stood in a dense, motionless mass. Amongst them I noticed one whose colour was striking, for his hind part was quite red. Mr. Horthy aimed at him and a second later the bull sank down on his forelegs. The shot was followed by a scene of incredible confusion, yet the herd did not leave the place, but merely turned towards us with heads uplifted. A big black beast was in the front line—certainly the leading cow—and began to move in our direction, but I shot her in the shoulder.

Was I too hasty? Perhaps! But I already had experience of the danger of being suddenly trampled down by a stampeding herd.

After I fired the whole herd turned away, but still remained standing in the same spot. Again we saw the red bull and Mr. Horthy gave it another bullet, when the huge beast fell over on its side. And still the rest stood motionless. I believe we could have continued killing them without their thinking of saving themselves. It was nearly dark, and we were still waiting for the herd to move off, but they showed no inclination to do this, so at last we stole away unnoticed. During the march home we discussed the whole adventure and made up our minds never again to shoot anything but solitary bulls, and we stuck to this resolution during our stay in Africa.

The horns of the cow were similar to those of the Congo buffalo, although its colour was quite black. It was the leading cow, which explains why the others did not move after she had fallen.

A day or two after this first experience with buffalo we went eastwards and took up our quarters at Ficus Camp, which is already known to the reader. On January 9th Count Seilern and I started for a morning stalk. When scarcely half an hour away from camp we saw a herd of Jackson's hartebeest, among which was a fine bull. Accordingly Count Seilern and his Masai gunbearer began to stalk it while we sat on a little hillock in order to watch the proceedings.

In the meantime the hartebeests had moved on, but neither Count Seilern nor his man turned round, so I could not signal to them. Soon I heard a shot and at once sent the Wahima guide after them. An hour passed, then a second, but the Count did not return. At last the guide came back saying that he had not found the Count and had even lost his spoor. After hearing this I gave him five porters, hung my water-gourd round his neck and sent him in another direction to search for the lost Count, while I returned to camp.

Suddenly I saw the men, who were just passing through a patch of buffalo grass which had been left over by the grass fire, scatter in all directions. At first I thought a hooded snake had alarmed them and then the idea that it might be a lion flashed through my mind and I seized my rifle. I never thought that a solitary buffalo would lie up in such a tiny patch of grass. I was not ready with my rifle when a bull buffalo jumped up out of the high grass and made off towards the scorched plain, stopping from time to time. He was a long way from me and long shots at buffalo are against my rules. So we followed him in the hopes that he would soon lie down again, for the heat was great. Meanwhile he had disappeared behind a rise in the ground and the spoor led into another patch of buffalo grass. I now hurried after him as he was heading towards the Wasa stream which was the boundary of the game reserve.

Close to an ant-heap was a mimosa tree which had been broken by elephants, and one of my men had crawled up it and was now signalling to me that he could see the buffalo from his perch. As I could see nothing from the top of the ant-heap I, too, had to climb the tree. The branches and twigs were broken and entangled to such an extent that it was quite hard to get up, but with the help of my men I suceeded. At first I did not see much from there either, although the man above gave me detailed directions as to the whereabouts of the buffalo, but in spite of this I did not feel inclined to crawl up any higher.

At last the bull rose and gazed in the direction from which we ought to have appeared and I could then see him well. He was an old bull, but his horns were exceedingly short. I took in the whole situation and studied the ground in search of a place from which I could get a certain shot, but the grass was far too high for me to be able to approach unobserved.

So, as he stood with his shoulder turned towards me, I took a deliberate aim and fired. He acknowledged the shot plainly by stumbling over, but then recovered himself and dashed towards our stand. I saw the frothy blood coming out of his nostrils, and every moment expected him to collapse, but he continued his thunderous approach and the man above me began to yell: "He is coming!"

I had now to shoot hastily in order to avert a panic amongst the men who were squatting behind the ant-heap. I could only see the brute's nose and horns held up on high, flying through the high grass, so all I could do was to shoot him in the nose. This turned and stopped him, but unfortunately a bush stood between us, so I could not fire again, although he was not 30 yards off. He stood there for fully ten minutes and then went off again at a stiff gallop, and this time I only saw the grass swaying above him as he went.

We found plenty of blood at the spot where he had been hit first and more after the shot in the nose, and were following up the blood spoor when one of my men said that a white man was approaching. It was Count Seilern, who was calmly walking straight on to the wounded buffalo's horns, and we made frantic signs to him to "get out of this."

I went up to Count Seilern and told him what had happened, and although he was thoroughly exhausted he wanted to stay with me and follow the wounded buffalo, a course of action which is not without danger under ordinary circumstances. Of course I would not hear of this, but gave him some water and begged him to return to camp with a guide. At last he followed my advice, but left me his cordite rifle, which would be more serviceable in the high grass than my Mannlicher-Schönauer.

While we were following on the blood-tracks, my gunbearer touched my shoulder, whispering, "Hark!" and with a very life-like expression he imitated the dying bull's moan, pointing out the exact spot from which he had heard it. I had not heard anything, and it was quite out of the question to go into that dense jungle.

So, with my rifle at the ready, I waited with every nerve on edge and once or twice thought I heard a groan, but the wounded bull never appeared. My gunbearer, who always treated buffalo with great respect, began to lose his nerve and slowly stole off, while the way he climbed up a thorny tree would have done credit even to an old baboon. He then signalled to me from the top of the tree to go to the right, where there was an ant-heap. I got there with great difficulty and the bull must have got my scent, for he began to snort, but did not appear. So at last I went back to the tree in which my gunbearer was perched and made him give me a detailed description of the ground behind the thicket. As I came up he signalled to me that he could see the horns of the buffalo, which had now come out and was slowly approaching the spot where I had been standing before. He invited me to come up to him, for I could have a good view from there. I did not even try, as I could never have succeeded in surmounting those thorns and creepers, so I told him to stay where he was and point out the direction to me.

Hardly had I advanced a few steps when he beckoned to me to come back as the buffalo had re-entered his hiding-place. By this time my men had come up and advised me to burn the buffalo grass round the bush. I agreed and went towards the ant-heap, but Johanna begged me to climb a tree instead, saying I should be sure to see much more from there. So I clambered up a mimosa tree which was covered with ants, Johanna having enthroned himself above me in order "to see better." Soon the fire was ablaze, but the buffalo did not move. I had foreseen this, being certain that he would not be so foolish as to leave his damp and marshy retreat, where fire could not harm him; but I hoped that it would be easier to get him after the grass all round had disappeared.

But the veering wind, and possibly the awkwardness of my men, turned the fire towards our tree with dangerous rapidity and soon we had to jump down and seek safety. So nothing was left but to return to camp and come back for the wounded animal in the evening. On our way I remembered that we had once found the steel jacket of an expanding bullet under the skin of a buffalo cow just where it had entered the body; so evidently this expanding bullet (Hirtenberg) was not the right one for buffalo. I had noted this fact at the time, but unfortunately forgot about it afterwards.

A CULTIVATED CLEARING IN THE BAAMBA FOREST

A Baamba family

Ferns on the Karanghora pass

MR. HORTHY'S FIRST UGANDA ELEPHANT BULL, NEAR LAKE GEORGE
Note the three spotted hyenas lying on the carcass, shot when damaging the hide

SOLITARY BUFFALO BULL, SHOT NEAR LAKE GEORGE

BAAMBA HALF-DWARF EX-CANNIBALS
They file their teeth to make them sharp

BAAMBA WOMEN TRANSPORTING SALT

At five o'clock I was again at the scene of action, and reached my ant-heap without hearing anything. Johanna and the rest of the men perched on the trees signalled that they could see and hear the buffalo. I strained my eyes, but in vain. I heard a slight rustle in the bush, but it was only made by birds. The dark spot Johanna had mistaken for the buffalo turned out to be a tree-trunk and the reeds in front of it, shaken by the breeze, gave it apparent movement. At last, however, when I had climbed a higher ant-heap I spotted the wounded bull. He was in the open, 300 yards away from his former resting-place, and lying in the shade of an umbrella acacia. At last!

I waved to Johanna who, not doubting the change in the situation, followed me; but the moment he saw the buffalo, he retreated behind an euphorbia bush. He was more afraid of the buffalo in the open than he had been in thick jungle. I approached within 120 yards, but it required five well-placed shots before we were sure of him. This was the last occasion on which I shot a buffalo with an expanding bullet, and in future I always used solid bullets with good results.

This solitary Semliki bull was a very old beast, and his colour as well as the shape of his horns were those of the black buffalo, but the horns were a very poor trophy in comparison to those of an East African buffalo.

On leaving Ficus Camp, we went north-west into the Baamba forests. In those parts of the wonderful Ituri forests, which extend into Uganda, okapi (*Okapia Johnstoni*) still exist. This part of our expedition was very interesting, but entirely without result from a hunter's point of view. Much time is needed for hunting in the forests, and unfortunately we had very little at our disposal, so we left the country of the formerly cannibal and pygmy Baambas (the Baambas living in the Congo are still cannibals) and headed east towards Lake George.

Our porters had a hard crossing over the Karanghora Pass in the Ruwenzori Mountains, for it poured with rain while we were ascending the western slope. On our way through the bamboo forest we saw no tracks whatever and only once did we hear a troop of monkeys escaping through the bamboo. Natives living west of Ruwenzori eat any kind of meat, so they hunt monkeys as well as other game, and this was why the poor monkeys were so easily frightened. In the eastern parts of the district monkeys will take no notice of man's approach, because the natives never harm them, for they would not eat monkeys even in times of famine.

The Karanghora Pass was quite a lively spot. We met a few native safaris coming from Katwe, on the northern bank of Lake Edward, carrying salt. In the western part of Ruwenzori, and still more in the Belgian Congo, salt is of very great value and almost the only form of exchange. We also met a few Wambuti women, who, laden with their heavy loads of salt, tripped along behind their tiny Bakondjo husbands, who seemed dwarfs beside them. As it was raining I could not take any photographs of them. The Wambuti dwarfs, who live in the Ituri forests, are famous hunters with the bow and arrow. In the Baamba forests only one or two Wambuti families are left, the others having died out from sleeping sickness. The Wambuti women were stolen by the Bakondjos, but they seemed quite content with their fate.

Pitching camp was quite a difficult matter, for we did not find a clearing large enough for three tents and all my men had to work with bush-knives and sticks to clear away the thick underwood. A brook with icy cold water rippled not far from our tents and on its bank grew wonderful ferns, some of them 12 to 15 feet high. The scenery reminded me much of pictures of landscapes during the carboniferous period of the earth. At night we sat round the camp-fire shivering with cold, for we were 9,000 feet above the sea. Next day we passed through more bamboo jungle and reached the eastern slopes where a wonderful panorama unfolded itself. The eastern slopes are steeper than the western and our nailed boots proved very useful.

When we reached the bara-bara (road) we experienced but were not surprised by a sign of the changed times, a strike! Our porters declared their intention to return to Fort Portal for a few days to see their women and have a rest after a month's safari. Of course we could not agree to this and so we wasted a whole day in discussion, and it was not until we had driven out the ringleaders that we could make the men continue the journey.

After the strike we made a stiff march of three days, when we came to the hills on the south-western banks of Lake George, where we pitched camp at a village called Muhodja. This ought to have been a good hunting-ground, but the frontier of the Lake George game reserve lay to the north and the sleeping sickness enclosure on the south. Tracks and local information told us of one or two huge bull elephants which were in the habit of raiding the banana shambas from the forests on the hills. One or two elephants from the reserve also visited this village, and there seemed to be many and good buffalo in the neighbourhood.

On January 27th I made my way at dawn towards the southern part of the lake because I had had reports of elephants. I found that elephants had certainly passed in great numbers, but the spoor told me that there was nothing shootable in the herd. On my way home I went along the lake, where I saw numerous elephant skulls bleached by the sun. My men passed them quite indifferently, not like those of a former safari round Kilimanjaro, who always threw a green twig or a bundle of grass on the white skulls, saying they were "Dawa." The word "Dawa" has a very wide meaning amongst natives, for it means any kind of medicine, or spell, and sometimes some ancient rite of a very primitive religion.

We passed through some wonderful euphorbia groves along well-beaten elephant and buffalo paths. Once an African cobra (Naja haja) darted out and slid away. The East African tribes of hunters, and especially the Wandorobos, believe this to be a bad omen. Later on we saw one or two "sunus" and a few waterbuck, but nothing worth shooting. The heat was terrible, and just as severe as it had been in the Semliki valley.

In the afternoon, just as I was approaching a herd of waterbuck with my camera, I was attracted by a curiously-shaped ant-heap in the reeds which seemed partly covered with papyrus. At first I had thought it was an elephant feeding, but it seemed too small, although it might have been knee-deep in the swamp. When I came nearer I saw with my field-glasses that I was mistaken, but at that moment my men began to shout "Mbogo!" A solitary buffalo bull was moving through the reeds. I ran after him at once, but he suddenly disappeared in a quite unaccountable way. We looked for him right and left, but saw him nowhere! I sent one of my men up a thin acacia tree to search the ground from there. Johanna crawled up too and when up the tree heard the buffalo wallowing. I was almost on him before I could see him and fired at very close range. The solid bullet caught him in the shoulder and killed him on the spot. He was a very old, solitary bull, but unfortunately his horns were small. In the south much better heads could be found, but the thought that I would soon get a licence for more buffaloes consoled me; as when we came to Uganda everyone had assured us that the law would be altered.

We asked Johanna why he had climbed the tree too, and he answered reproachfully: "Because I was anxious to see his horns and was just going to stop you from shooting, when you fired." And he nearly boxed the kirongozi's ears because the latter seemed just as sceptical about this as I was! I never could have imagined how hard it would be to get the bull out of the mud wallow, but after a lot of "guvu, sava-sava, hooo" yelling and shouting we succeeded at last. I returned to camp late to hear the good news that Mr. Horthy had shot a bull elephant. So the Naja haja did not bring bad luck for once.

On January 29th I went tracking elephant towards the edge of the game reserve in the north. We had gone a long way and I had found fresh tracks, but not big enough to rouse my enthusiasm, and so after awhile I gave them up.

We had tramped for nearly ten hours without stopping when from the top of an ant-heap I noticed another ant-heap of curious shape and watched it through my field-glass for long. The high grass was waving in a light breeze and this gave it a semblance of movement. Then I made out a tail switching and very soon the ant-heap turned into a grazing buffalo.

I was far from camp and it was already four o'clock. I thought of sending a quick runner for Count Seilern, who had not yet shot a buffalo.

But two hours for the long journey there and back seemed too little and so I determined to have a look at the horns first. As I stole along three wart-hogs jumped up and rendered a closer approach impossible. There was, I admit, a little malice behind this manœuvre of mine, but I wanted to see what excuse Johanna would make for staying behind. When the "giri" started up the buffalo lifted his head and advanced a few steps in our direction, and Johanna at once flattened himself down behind a clump of grass. The whole situation, as well as the 40 yards between us and the buffalo, allowed me to risk a little fun, and so I spoke to the bull: "Mbogo! Are you looking for Johanna?" I will never forget the reproachful look shot at me from behind that grass patch. At the same instant I shot the bull in the chest, but at the next I, too, threw myself down, for as the bull came down, another one which I had not noticed, stood up. It would have been very awkward if I had been compelled to shoot this one too, for I had now completed the number allowed on my licence and had shot my fourth buffalo. But the second bull seemed only to want to find out the cause of the noise and then, to my great relief, turned away. Meanwhile the first bull, which had a bullet in one side of its chest, had also disappeared, so I began to regret the joke I had made, but after a short yet quick bit of tracking one of my men saw the wounded buffalo and I was able to finish it with a neck-shot.

He was an old bull, and his horns were short and blunt, but better than those of the last one.

As he gave his last groan, something crashed through the thicket at our backs and startled my men, and they began to shout that the other bull had returned. And then a pair of horns appeared, followed by a red body, and a long-horned Ankolean ox stood before us. A few days before some natives had been trying to drive this ox through a river, when it escaped and was lost in the jungle. An inexperienced hunter might easily have been tempted to fire, and great would have been his astonishment when standing over his prize!

Soon after this we were on our way to West Nile Province, hoping all the time that the game laws would be changed soon, but unfortunately for us this only came about after we had left and so I could not shoot any more buffalo during my last visit to Africa.

CHAPTER XV

The African Rhinoceros

MR. THEODORE ROOSEVELT, in his book *African Game Trails*, wrote some words below the photograph of a rhinoceros standing in the open plain which well characterized the individuality of this curious animal: "Lost in prehistoric thoughts." Anyone who sees a rhino for the first time must surely derive the impression that it has been left behind from an earlier age.

The black rhino is not at all rare either in Tanganyika or in Kenya Colony. The northern parts of Tanganyika used to be very prolific in rhinos, but in the south of former German East Africa they were not so common. In Kenya—except in the coastal areas—it is ubiquitous, especially so in the northern regions near Lake Rudolf.

In Uganda there are no rhino at all, and the Victoria Nile is the western limit of their habitat. There are various types of the so-called black rhino in different parts of the country. In the mountain forests its horn is thin, long and flattened on both sides like a sword, while those found on the plains have short and thick horns. In the north round Lake Rudolf and in Somaliland they are smaller in body. Formerly all mountain rhinos carried horns of nearly the same shape, and for this reason scientists called them *"Rhinoceros bicornis holmwoodi."* Nowadays, however, the forest rhino often seems to cross with the rhino of the plains, as the spread of civilization drives the latter into the forests on the mountains.

The black rhino is no more black than the white rhino is white. Its upper lip protrudes and it only feeds on twigs and leaves, which fact explains why it dwells in thick bush. In very dry weather great numbers collect in the subugos of the mountains. The white rhino is much larger than his so-called black relation and is the largest land animal with the exception of the Indian elephant. In colour it is grey, slightly lighter in shade than the black rhino. Besides this difference the white rhino has a straight cut upper lip without any protrusion and so it ought to be called the wide-mouthed rhino, and as a matter of fact many hunters do so call it. It does not feed on twigs, but entirely on grass. In South Africa the white rhino has been extinct for all practical purposes since the middle of last century, but in North-Eastern Mashonaland there are one or two protected specimens and perhaps a dozen more in the swamps round the junction of the Black and White Umvolosi Rivers.

Sir Samuel Baker was the first to realize the possibility of the white rhino's existence in the north, and he drew his conclusions from a few rhino horns he saw in the Lado, for the white rhino of the Lado hardly differs from the extinct species of South Africa.

I only made the acquaintance of the white rhino during our last trip to Africa and I have already given my experiences with it in Chapter X. In Uganda, the Sudan and the Belgian Congo laws have been made to protect the white rhino and this will probably save them from extermination for many years yet. During my first, and more frequently during my third expedition, I saw innumerable black rhino and shot a good many. But I would not do so to-day, even if the shooting of rhino was unlimited, as it used to be in those days. To shoot them now would give me no pleasure, and I would only do so in special cases when one was needed for museum purposes or if I were trying to catch a baby rhino.

When I established my camp under Kilimanjaro in 1903, one or two Europeans living there who were not hunters, described the rhino as being one of the most dangerous kinds of big game and warned me to be very careful when I met a "kifaru." They spoke of the elephant as quite a harmless animal in comparison.

The reason of their great respect for the kifaru was that a European had been killed by a rhino not long ago, and that the noise of the safaris crossing from the coast to the Kilimanjaro district would often disturb a sleeping rhino which would at once scatter them in sheer fright and blind rage.

To be truthful, I must admit that I believed the rhino was a dangerous animal for a long time, chiefly because I happened to see and shoot my first few rhinos from a distance of but a few yards in the thickest thorn scrub. I had either followed them or run against them in the thorny bush. Later on I learned that by no means every rhino which I thought dangerous was so in reality, but when a large-bodied animal charges down on one, snorting and puffing, at close range, one hardly has the time to appreciate its real intentions or to judge the danger of the situation.

The rhino has a peevish, sullen temper and avoids the society of other animals. I have never seen any feeding with other animals but have often noticed one about a 100 yards away from herds of antelopes and zebras, and when the latter became aware of my presence and fled, the rhino would notice it too and dash away. Rhino are usually found alone or in pairs, and once I saw three together, but I have been told that where they are very numerous, troops of five have been recorded. A troop of three will generally be composed of a bull, cow and a calf; but sometimes of a cow with a nearly full-grown calf and a new baby of a few months.

In unfrequented districts rhino will be on the move until eight or nine o'clock in the morning; then they rest in thickets or under the shade of trees on the plains, and do not move again until late in the afternoon. Whether it is asleep or on the move the faithful rhino-birds (*Buphaga*) will never leave it, and the cry of these birds warn it of the approach of an enemy. The rhino-bird will also accompany other animals to pick the ticks and other parasites off them, but such coalitions are never so common as in the case of the rhino. When these faithful and vigilant attendants are not present it is very easy to approach either a resting or grazing rhino and to get up within a few yards of the animal, provided the wind is favourable, for the kifaru has very poor eyesight. His powers of scent, on the other hand, are excellent and the faintest breath of air blowing it towards him is enough to rouse him from his deepest sleep. Then he tries with snorts and puffs to find out the whereabouts of the enemy and finally dashes away with tail uplifted. In most cases he dashes straight for the human scent, though possibly intending no harm whatever and perhaps only driven by curiosity. And very often this stupid habit is his undoing.

He will behave similarly when the rhino-birds fly up with scared cries, but lies down again the very moment the birds seem reassured and settle on him once more. I have noticed that the birds only give alarm at the approach of man; they take no notice of antelopes or other animals.

Rhinos do not do much harm to the shambas of natives in general, and only once or twice did I hear complaints of a few kifarus which had taken to the ntama plantations and done a lot of damage.

We often found the spoor of rhino far away from water-holes in the waterless savannas, and we often came upon water when following their tracks. Rhinos visit water-holes soon after sundown, so they often have to start in that direction in the early afternoon, grazing on their way; but if they are a very long way off they will march along without stopping for a moment.

In the daytime the rhino is of a quiet and silent disposition, but round the water-hole at night he becomes a very noisy customer. Our night's repose was often disturbed by rhinos drinking from the water-hole near our camp, and it is not advisable to pitch camp on old rhino tracks, for the rhino may return at night and give the safari a few anxious moments. This happened to me once, but as we heard him approach in time a few alarm shots had their effect and made our unbidden guest change his direction.

He will keep to his well-trodden paths and return to the spots where he leaves his droppings. These latter are usually under a bush or tree and, as the kifaru throws earth over his excrements with his hind-legs, in time he digs a deep hole. My Masai friends told me an interesting fable explaining why the kifaru (or in Masai language, the "amuny") digs up earth after this act of his which is, I think, worth recording.

In olden times the rhinos were of bad character, even worse than nowadays, and they attacked men and scattered their herds until at last the men got tired of it and went out to revenge themselves. But in those days men were very stupid—as my historian asserted, "even the Masai"—and always mistook the elephant spoors for those of the rhino, and in following them up they would often rouse the poor elephant out of his afternoon sleep. These continual molestations made the elephant beg the rhino to behave himself better and leave man alone; and if he could not bring himself to do this, then at any rate he should leave some kind of sign which would enable man to recognize his spoor. Of course the wicked rhino did not heed these words and merely made a number of impertinent remarks; so the poor elephant had to suffer further molestation.

At last the elephant lost his temper and meeting the kifaru uprooted a young tree and gave him a sound beating with it, and since then the rhino has always covered his dung and scratched the earth away all around it; and also since then he has kept out of the way of the elephant. . . .

The natives believe that the rhino avoids the elephant and is also on bad terms with the hippotamus. I cannot say whether this is true or not, but the bodies of many rhinos I shot were covered with scars, and my boys declared that these scars were the results of fights with hippos; but personally I think that they were caused by fights between themselves.

Once I shot an old bull rhino whose ears and tail were missing, and feel sure that these injuries were inflicted by a lion, in which case he had probably got them in early youth, because it seems hardly possible that lions would attack a full-grown rhino.

The rhino is unpopular because in his blind fury he will often charge safaris. If the porters save themselves in time by climbing up trees or hiding behind bushes they come to no harm, but a lot of damage is always done to the loads they carry, for everything is thrown away at such a moment. The consequences of a rhino charging a safari are worse when the loads are carried by animals, as the terror-stricken beasts will stampede in all directions and it is hard to catch them again; much time will be lost and even more damage will be done to the loads. During my absence my safari was dispersed twice in this manner. The first time only a few bottles of alcohol containing some specimens were broken, but on the second occasion the breaking of my last two bottles of whisky affected me more deeply. And besides, I was so far from civilization that I could not replace them for a long time—I was then on the Ngare Dowash near the British frontier. I happened to see the last act of this tragi-comical play—the porters flinging away their loads and the dust kicked up by the two vanishing rhinos. On that morning I had gone on ahead, starting well before camp was broken up, taking a guide and gunbearer with me in the hopes of meeting some worthy game, but especially rhino, for in the country through which we were travelling numerous mouldering skulls showed that the Wandorobos had killed many.

My round in the early morning gave no result; we saw nothing worth mentioning, not even a rhino spoor. At seven o'clock, while waiting for the safari to join us, I sat down under a shady tree on top of a hill and soon fell asleep. My guide awoke me after an hour to tell me that the safari was coming up. I was very glad to hear this because I had not had breakfast yet, when suddenly a terrible noise broke out from the direction of the safari, and I then saw the scene which I described above. Curiously enough, we had passed by the very bush behind which the rhinos had been sleeping, but they did not notice us and we did not catch sight of them. Of course I felt very inclined to take my revenge and, making my safari pitch camp, I followed the spoor; but it led over rocky soil and I soon lost it.

Meeting kifarus often brought about comical situations. On the Ruvana Plains I once shot for the pot a male dik-dik, which is a tiny little animal hardly bigger than a hare, and one of my men asked for one of the little horns, because he wanted to put into it a recently acquired "dawa," which would keep him safe from the rhinos. I granted him his request, gave him the skull and let him pull off one of the horns, hardly two inches long, and he hid his new treasure in it.

Next day while we were looking for buffalo spoor in the jungles on the banks of a river-bed a rhino got our wind and charged us in the most unexpected manner. The man with the "dawa" was the only one who was in danger and he only escaped because the snap shot which I made at the last moment hit the rhino in the neck and killed him on the spot.

At night my men sat round the fire, living again through the adventures of the day, and pulling the thorns and thistles out of the soles of their feet after they had been softened by the heat of the blazing fire. I went up to them and, amidst peals of laughter from the others, I told the man with the magic charm to claim back what he had given for the "dawa" and to give the "nganga" (magician, physician) a good flogging for having sold him such a useless "dawa." But he seemed quite offended and said with conviction: "No, sir. Who can tell what might have happened to me without this 'dawa'?"

A similar comic episode occurred on the Ushangi River. One day just before an early start the man who usually carried my camera, came to my tent wrapped in a blanket, and leaning on a stick and said that his leg hurt him. It is interesting to note that if a native ever reports sick, he always has a blanket to cover himself and a stick to hold himself upright, whatever his ailment may be. A blanket and stick are the insignia of the sick just as a hurricane lamp in the hand denotes the boy (private servant) and the tea kettle indicates the pishi (cook).

I examined my man and found that he was malingering, so I hung my camera round his neck and he had to come along with us, which he did sadly enough, never forgetting his limp.

We had been tramping along for nearly an hour when we came to that part of the watercourse where our guide had seen buffalo spoor the day before. The more open places were covered with high buffalo grass and on the banks of the river stood a dense forest interlaced through and through with great creepers.

Tensely we examined every footprint and noted every sign, and so we did not keep an eye on our limping companion, who tried to slip away unnoticed, for he did not like the idea of having to play up to his part all day long.

Suddenly we heard shrieks of terror and calls for help and the enraged snorts and grunts of a rhino. As we looked in the direction of the noise, my gunbearer handed me my ·465 double cordite Express and then we saw our poor lame friend dashing towards us as if on wings, and not far behind him came the thundering giant in full pursuit. Happily he had taken our direction and my bullet brought the beast to a stop just as he had nearly caught the man up. The grass was high and this interfered with my aim, so my first bullet was rather too far back, but anyhow it made the rhino swerve. I seized the chance he then gave me and shot him in the shoulder and killed him. The terrified man did not stop, but sped on until he found a mimosa tree and fled up it with great agility, and it needed much persuasion before he would come down again.

After he had recovered from his fright he regained his voice, and using it to good effect, told us that having loitered behind he tried to catch up by taking a short cut when suddenly a rhino stepped out from behind a bush and charged him. The rhino's horn was good; my camera in its strong case came to no harm; and my man's bad leg was healed; so this little incident had a lucky ending in every respect.

When in the open, and especially if his truthful companions, the rhino-birds, are not with him, it is not hard to stalk and shoot a rhino—in fact, this affords little sport. Following him in the bush, on the contrary, will always be dangerous and exciting. There was a time when my nerves were very badly shaken by rhinos, but it must be remembered that I shot about 80 per cent. of my rhinos in the thickest bush or in the dense undergrowth of the riverine forests; and also that in that part of the country there were many rhinos which had been wounded and infuriated by the poisoned arrows of the natives. Such harassed beasts have, of course, a worse temper than those which have been left alone. I often found points of arrows in the bodies of my rhinos or else very nasty wounds full of pus. I have stated that the rhino is one of the most irritable of animals, but experience proves that nothing can be more easily checked than a rhino's even most serious attack. It is nothing compared to a lion's or buffalo's vicious charge, and either of these animals will follow his enemy like a bloodhound. An alarm shot or even a loud shout will often be enough to turn the rhino off his course.

It is also my experience that a rhino is very easily killed, though this fact seems quite inexplicable. A shoulder-shot, even if not very well placed, will finish him. If the bullet does not touch his heart he will give a shrill squeal, just like a pig when it is stuck with a knife; he will then run on for about 100 paces and collapse. No other animal leaves such an abundant blood spoor as the rhino in the event of a shot in the lungs.

I have also tried head and neck shots with good result. The head-shot can be difficult at times, because the spot nearest the brain is partially covered by the horn. I had a very thrilling adventure with a rhino once which taught me how hard the horny parts are to penetrate. Under the Ngurumini Mountains the natives had seen a rhino cow and calf in some thorn scrub, so the next day found me on their tracks, although I could not make out from the spoor, which was on dry, stony soil, whether the rhino calf was worth catching or not. I had already covered quite a nice distance through the "wait-a-bit" thorns, when suddenly the rhinos started up quite near us and dashed away with the usual grunts. Just at the moment of their escape I was on all fours getting through a tunnel in the thick bush, and as I heard that they had stopped not far away, I did my best to reach a clearing where I hoped to see something. When at last I could stand up the kifarus started off again, but now moved parallel to us. I ran a few steps forward to get a better view and a chance of a shot, when a silly accident occurred, for a branch tipped my wide-brimmed felt hat over my eyes, so for a moment I could not see anything. The rhinos passed close by me, but I could not shoot, much to my men's surprise.

After various explanations we then found out that the kirongozi who had brought news of the rhinos had not seen a cow and a calf but two full-grown animals. But we continued to follow the tracks, as one of my boys said that one of the rhinos had a very long horn.

The tracks of the alarmed rhinos led through quite an open space into a big area of bush. In this bush we found a clearing where we rested and had lunch, during which I read a Hungarian daily paper a few months old which had been used to wrap up the food. It contained an instalment of a novel by Stacpoole about Africa called *Pools of Silence*. The translation was indifferent and "buck" was always translated as "roebuck," although the scene was laid in the Congo. On the subject of rhino the writer explained to the tyro, that a rhino must be shot in the neck. "Not bad advice," thought I, but at that moment I had to jump to my feet, for a snorting rhino thundered down on us at full speed. After we had sat down to rest the wind had begun to veer about in every direction. As a matter of fact this was one of the reasons why we thought it would be a good time for lunch, but when the wind grew stronger it brought the rhinos with it.

Fortunately my rifle, an 8-mm. Mannlicher-Schönauer, was at hand, and I shot the rhino galloping for me in the head. I felt that my shot had gone home and so I was rather surprised when the beast did not collapse, but only swerved slightly and then turned round quickly and went off with its mate. I just had time to send a snap shot after it into its shoulder, which it acknowledged with a loud squeal. It left a profuse blood trail which we followed for about 100 yards and then found it lying dead.

We easily found the shot in the shoulder, for frothy blood was oozing from it, but we did not find the head-shot until much later, although it ought to have been on the forehead. But at last, right in the middle of the front horn, we saw a trace of the first bullet. The horn had stopped the bullet, which was intended for the brain, and it is interesting to know that the solid bullet failed to penetrate the horn, although at this spot the horn was not more than four inches thick. On the opposite side of the horn a slight bulge and a few splinters were all that showed the effect of the bullet.

A few months later I had an interesting experience almost in the same place with a three-parts-grown rhino. I had killed the cow, but this calf did not want to leave the body and with uplifted nose tried to catch our wind, anxious to wreak vengeance. We shouted at him, but the only effect of this was to make him come for us, whereupon my men fled up some trees on either side, and as I did not want to use my rifle I, too, climbed up a small tree. The young rhino vented his rage on the fresh spoor of my men and dug them up; then taking one of the smaller ant-heaps for his antagonist he attacked that. It was very interesting to watch the kifaru's charge. His head was bent down low and on reaching the heap, he butted his horn into it, while his tail, which was held straight up, went down and then up again. This movement was somewhat like the left hand of a fencer who makes a point, but the usual exclamation "La" being replaced by a furious snort. As I sat in the top of a miserable acacia tree not 7 feet high, I could see all this very plainly.

My men, who were all perched on surrounding trees, saw a good opportunity for a bit of fun, a thing which the native will never miss—he would rather lose a dish of pombe, which means a lot. One of them, the quickest and cleverest of the lot, began the game. When the rhino turned away, he crawled down from his tree, picked up a lot of stones and then quickly climbed up again.

All the others followed his example and very soon the young rhino became a target for a regular fusillade. Every stone that fell made him turn against it and he kept dashing from one to another, puffing and snorting wildly. This gave the playful boys a new idea. They began to throw stones at each other, which made the kifaru dash at the occupied tree and the man on it had to climb a few branches higher up for safety. This amused me at first, but I soon began to dislike the game because the kifaru came very close to my tree sometimes and little was wanted to shake me off it! So I seized a favourable opportunity to jump down and shot him through the ear. This, coupled with an alarm shot sent after him, made him go at last and we could approach our quarry.

I only once had a man of my safari seriously wounded by a rhino. This accident occurred on the Ruvana Plains. I had taken out my newly recruited Wagayan porters for their first essay in hunting and we were marching along unconcernedly and not heeding the wind, because we had never seen rhino tracks near the little acacia forest through which we were travelling. I had left my gunbearer at home to superintend the preparation of a cheetah skin and untrained men were carrying my rifles. When the rhino charged us I threw back my ·22 Winchester and reached out for the double cordite Express, but in vain, for the "msenzi" who had been carrying it had bolted. So I ran towards the thorny thicket to get one of my rifles and avoid giving the rhino my scent. The inexperienced Wagayas sped across the open plain right into the wind, while the brass rings they wore on their arms and necks jingled and rattled. I had warned them to leave these at home because they might prove troublesome in the "pori" (wilderness), but they thought it bad "dawa" to take the rings off, and as I did not want to appear too strict at first, especially as it was very hard to get men at that time, I let them come out with all their dangling finery.

The man carrying my Mannlicher-Schönauer got caught in the thorns and I overtook him, but at that same moment I saw that one of the others had been overtaken and trampled on by the rhino. The Mannlicher-Schönauer was loaded with soft-nosed bullets, but of course there was not time to change them, only to send five

EUPHORBIA COPPICE NEAR LAKE GEORGE

ELEPHANT SKULLS BLEACHING IN THE SUN

HEAD OF BLACK RHINOCEROS
Notice the trunk-like protruding upper lip

HEAD OF WHITE RHINO
Notice the broad upper lip and straight mouth

MR. HOBLEY'S WHITE RHINO

bullets as quick as possible into the rhino's side. The rhino squealed at the two last shots and disappeared into the thicket.

Reloading my rifle I ran up to the man feeling quite certain that he would be lying mangled and quite dead. Great therefore was my joy at seeing him stagger to his feet. His head was covered with blood, but experience had taught me that at first sight such injuries very often seem worse than they actually are. And this was the case again. The rhino had split the calf of his leg open, but as he only butted at him while passing him on one side, the wound was not very deep. It was this blow that knocked the man down.

It was the man's extraordinary good luck that the back parts of a rhino's legs are like pneumatic tyres and that the soil was damp and soft from the previous night's rain, so the rhino's legs slipped off the man's head. No other part of his body had been touched. There was a big gaping wound on his scalp, but the Wagayan "club-proof" skull will stand much. The man soon recovered and only a large scar remained to remind him of his adventures for the rest of his life. Next day when we found the old bull rhino he got the best parts of the meat, and I can vouch that he seemed to like it very much.

One should use solid bullets for shooting rhino, and the bore of the rifle is a question of individual taste. Personally I do not think big bore necessary, for, as I have already stated, the rhino is not tough, and I have always found that a shoulder-shot with a small-bore rifle is sufficient.

The native hunters, the Wandorobos and the Wakambas, regard the rhino as an easy quarry, for if the rhino-birds are not about, they can steal up to the drowsy beast and shoot their poisoned arrows into him from very close quarters. The Wandorobos use also poisoned spears for rhino hunting.

The Wakamba hunters sometimes cut down euphorbias, because kifarus are very fond of the soft, fresh sprouts of these trees, and when they are feeding on them at night they shoot them from ambush with their arrows.

The Wandorobos have been killing many rhinos lately, for the horn is now a popular article of trade. Formerly they hunted rhino on account of the meat and did not care much for the horns, only snuff-boxes and clubs being made out of them. During my first trip I saw many such articles made out of rhino horns by the Wandorobos and Masai.

But even then rhinoceros horns were of very fair value, and if one was over 32 inches long it was even more valuable than ivory. At the last ivory and rhinoceros horn auction in London the latter were sold at a higher price than the ivory.

Rowland Ward states that the record black rhino horn is 53½ inches; the southern white rhino record is 62¼ inches, while the northern white rhino is only 41 inches. These measurements are of course those of the front horns, for as a rule the rear horn is much shorter, although it does happen in some parts of the country that both horns are of the same length and occasionally the rear one is the longer. Nowadays a horn over 30 inches is rare. Generally a cow's horn is longer, but thinner, than a bull's. Better sticks and whips are made from rhino hide than from hippo hide. The belly of the rhino and the back of the hippo are the choicest portions of hide used for making these articles.

CHAPTER XVI

The Leopard

IN order to complete the list of African big and dangerous game we must include the leopard, which is the smallest in size but has the most handsome skin, and is to be found all over Africa. The leopard is more common than the lion and it undoubtedly has the most extended habitat of any of the cat tribe. In Africa —except the coastal parts of Northern Africa—one can still find leopards everywhere, even where the last roar of the lion was heard a hundred years ago.

The leopard's distribution through East Africa is very general, and there is no part of the country where its tracks would not be found: in the great dark forests, in the riverine jungles and the arid plains, high up in the mountains—even up to the snow-line—and on rocky hills or in swampy plains. Human habitations will not disturb him and he will even break into East African towns, for one can often read in the local papers that a leopard snatched a dog away from the centre of some town.

Differences have been established between leopards of different countries. Those found in the mountain or riverine forests are larger in body, their skin is darker and the spots are bigger; while the leopards of the plains are of a lighter colour and smaller in body. Melanism in Africa is rare and in East Africa only one or two black leopards have ever been shot. In Abyssinia it is a more common occurrence.

There is but little difference between the African and Asiatic leopards. In Asia—with the exception of Tibet—leopards are known all over the continent from Asia Minor to Manchuria. The larger ones are called "panther" and the smaller ones "leopard" by Indian sportsmen, but zoologists do not distinguish two varieties and classify both leopard and panther as one species. Their colouring and size differ according to the country in which they live, but even in the same country they vary greatly. The difference in size is very striking. While the male—so my experience goes—will sometimes weigh as much as 200 lbs. and even more, the female will seldom exceed 75 to 85 lbs. In Rowland Ward's *Records*, the record African leopard is 8 feet 11 inches, and the record Indian leopard 8 feet 6 inches, measured from the tip of the nose to the end of the tail.

Although leopards are more numerous than lions, the European hunter will meet them less frequently. One might imagine that the spotted skin would show up very easily, but in actual fact it melts into its surroundings in an astounding way and so one may often pass by a leopard without noticing it. In the daytime they will often be perched on a tree with thick foliage, when the hunter will usually only become aware of its presence when it leaps off the tree like a yellow shadow to vanish into the thicket below. Seeing a leopard is mostly a matter of luck. And when the meeting does take place it usually comes so suddenly and is such a surprise, that one has not time to shoot before it has gone. And very often one comes upon it when pursuing more interesting game and so has to keep silent. This is why many European hunters, who have spent years in the wilderness, have never met a leopard, although they often have heard its angry purring growl quite close and have been irritated by its daring robberies.

The quickness and audacity of a marauding leopard are incredible. Daily complaints can be heard of a leopard snatching up a goat or a ram in full daylight while the herdsman was driving his flock into the village, and vanishing with its victim like a flash. They seem to prefer dogs to anything and their boldness in seizing dogs surpasses all else. When bent on getting a dog, a leopard will even enter human dwelling-houses and I have heard of one snatching a dog away from his master's side while the latter was marching along with a caravan.

When hunting elephant in 1903 I once pitched my camp by a village called Kindi at the foot of Kilimanjaro and on the "bara-bara" (road) leading to Arusha. This bara-bara was the best place for finding tracks, because the elephants usually crossed it when coming down from or going up to the mountains. It was known that this district would soon be proclaimed an elephant reserve, and the corporal of the garrison of Moshi wanted to make the best of his last chance of getting an elephant. Corporal L. was an old African, who began his service under Von Wissmann. He pitched his tent a few hundred paces away from mine on the bara-bara, so in the evening I went to see him and we agreed that one of us would track along the road to the right and the other to the left of our camps. I stayed up late with the old African that evening, as I greatly enjoyed listening to his tales.

About one o'clock in the night I was awakened by rifle shots, and next morning I discovered the reason. L. had an old bulldog —I even recall his name, "Simba"—which slept in his tent under his camp-bed. Although the flap of the tent was let down, it was not fastened and the leopard stole in and pulled the dog out, although fires were blazing all round the tent. Of course many shots were fired in the direction of the noise, with the result that the leopard let go his prey, but the poor dog was already dead.

At night leopards are very audacious and will enter human dwellings and will often kill human beings. Leopards turn into man-eaters more frequently than do lions and such man-eaters are harder to kill. Soon after the occurrence I have just related, I had an experience myself which greatly impressed me with the silence with which a leopard conducts his thefts. We had built a collecting camp on the Daryama River at the foot of the Letema Mountains. On the first day of my arrival I shot a striped hyena (*Hyæna Schillingsi*), which had been discovered by Professor Schillings. I wanted to set it up later, so I had to prepare the skin. I shot the hyena after dark and my men laid it down between them where they slept round the fire. In the morning the hyena was gone. My men at once began to talk of some devil's work, for the thief had made no sound and had left no spoor. Not far away, however, we found the trail of something that had been dragged along and 100 yards farther on we found the hyena fixed between the branches of a smooth-barked mimosa tree at a height of about 12 feet.

It is a well-known characteristic of leopards that they will carry their booty up a tree for the purpose of securing it from hyenas, jackals and vultures. Natives say that they do it so as to be undisturbed while feasting, as their prey is often stolen from them by hyenas. When wandering in the wilderness one often comes upon such remains, deposited between branches, and I have always wondered how the leopard was able to drag the body of a bushbuck or an impala (which are as big as a fallow deer) up a branchless tree to a height of 10 or 12 feet.

The tracks of a wounded buffalo once led us from the open plain into a forest skirting the dry river-bed of the Ushangi. We were intent upon the tracking and watched the thickets on the bank with the greatest attention, because these river-side thickets are often the most dangerous places, as wounded beasts will frequently lie up in them. As we were crouching down and piercing into a dark tunnel formed by the undergrowth, a leopard suddenly sprang off a tree not two paces from me, and disappeared with an angry growl. It happened so quickly that there was no time to be afraid. We had disturbed it while feeding on an impala which it had killed a short time before. Had I been alone I doubt whether it would have given up its kill so easily, but the approach of six men was too much even for the "tchui." (Tchui means leopard in the Swahili language.) I set a trap under the tree, but of course the leopard never returned. It would seem that they often give up their kills in this way, because I have frequently found the bodies of antelopes which were as dry as mummies.

Another day while I was on the Ushangi I decided to drive a thicket to get out a solitary buffalo bull: and while waiting for the drive to begin I sat on a tree-trunk at the spot where I thought the buffalo would have to come out. Suddenly I heard a slight noise behind my back and had a feeling that many eyes were watching me. And in truth quite a lot of baboons were coming towards me, studying me with great curiosity, for probably they had never seen a white man before. I was greatly amused by these baboons. They sprang up a tree which had been struck by lightning and kept on crouching down and jumping up again while gazing at me. One old man baboon caught hold of a youngster's tail who was occupying the best seat and pulled him down, only to take his place himself, but at the next moment they all turned terrified looks in another direction and then fled with barks and shrieks. Instead of the buffalo I was waiting for, a beautiful male leopard stepped out and passed by me not more than 25 to 30 yards away.

I was sorely tempted to send a bullet into his shoulder, all the more so as the buffalo spoor was not very fresh and we could not tell for certain, the soil being dry, whether the buffalo had not already left the thicket. But unluckily I gave up this certain trophy for a very uncertain one, and the fine leopard went on unharmed. Later on, when the beaters came out, we learned that the buffalo had not been in the thicket and all our exertions had been in vain. I have always regretted having missed that chance of shooting a leopard, for since then I have never had another.

Leopards are very fond of hunting monkeys, and it seems that they hunt them with success, for the monkeys betray great anxiety when a leopard is near. When a troop of monkeys begins to yell in rage and terror, it is always a sure sign that they have spotted a leopard and this is the moment for the hunter to snatch up his rifle and run to the scene of the commotion. Many leopards have been bagged in this manner. All monkeys, especially the long-tailed monkey (*cercophitecus*), are sure guides, and they seem to utter a special sound when signalling a leopard.

It was interesting to note that while I was drying skins of lions or other beasts before my house in the Letema Mountains, the long-tailed monkeys kept me company, looking down at me from the branches of the mimosa trees, but the instant I laid out a leopard's skin the "tumbilis" came up closer and closer and made a terrific noise, abusing the skin of their enemy with furious gestures.

I owe my first leopard to monkeys. In those days (1903) I lived the life of a Robinson Crusoe in my camp at Letema, for I was compelled to exercise the strictest economy. I had built a hut out of banana leaves and after it was finished I dismissed all my Manyamwezi porters (the Manyamwezis were the best porters), keeping only a few cheap Mtchaga boys. The Watchagas who live on the slopes of Kilimanjaro are an ingenious and diligent people. In those days they had small pretensions, but were not adaptable to safari life, for the moment they left the hills and came into the plains, they caught the "kunguru" (malaria). In other respects they also feared safari life, for they were frightened of animals and also of their great enemies, the Masai.

On one safari when one or two of them fell ill, they thought they had had enough of camp life and I woke one morning to find that my Watchagas, together with three Arushai natives who had enjoyed shelter for the night, had eloped. Hard times followed, for I was alone in the vast wilderness. But a month and a half of seclusion passed very agreeably and I shall never again get the same chances of shooting lions and leopards as I had then. But as I wanted to save myself the trouble of preparing their skins single-handed, I did not go after them.

The night before the episode I will now describe I had stayed up late busy with the preparation of some birds I had had the luck to get for my collection, and although I was dead-tired I was glad to be up, for the concert the lions gave was exceptionally fine. When my work was done I at last retired to rest, but had only slept for a short time when a hippo shuffled into the yard. He snorted and I shouted at him, when he turned round quickly and trotted back to the river. I had hardly fallen asleep again when my hens started making a hideous noise. A serval, which frequently visited my poultry yard, had again got amongst them, and as a shot fired to frighten him had forced him to leave without his quarry, he returned twice that same night.

I awoke late next morning, for on top of a hard day I had had a bad night, and I did not leave my hut until the sun was high above the mimosa trees. I began my daily round by making some coffee, and the water was just beginning to boil when I heard the alarm cries of some grey meercats, which indicated the presence of a leopard. Snatching up my 7-mm. Mauser I ran out in front of the boma to find out the cause of the monkeys' shrieks, although I guessed that they were directed at a leopard returning from his nightly prowl. I was right, for very soon I saw the leopard stealing along the path like a cat, and careful of brushing his flanks up against the dewy grass on either side. He took no notice of the troop of monkeys, although some older males were hanging over him from low branches and abusing him roundly. For awhile I stood admiring the scene, but as he was already about 80 yards away, I fired. I hit him in the shoulder and he fell dead, and then I returned to my coffee.

The beautiful skin made me happy, only the thought of pre-

Skinning the white rhino

We reached the road with the skin

RHINO COW SHOT IN THE BURNT ACACIA FOREST

On its left is a dropped Ostrich egg

Rhino bull killed in a "good" thicket

The thickets were usually of this type

FINE LEOPARD SHOT NEAR NGARE DOWASH

paring it all by myself marred my happiness. But I was spared this work, for while I was at lunch an "olmuru" of Arusha-chini, with whom I was acquainted (an "olmuru" is a married Masai, who has left the ranks of the "elmorans" or warriors), came to see me, bringing some honey to exchange for iodoform, which the Masai value very highly. I gave him what he wanted and some other gifts as well, so he stayed and helped me with my tedious job.

Hard though it is to bag a leopard by fair hunting, it is quite easy to catch them in traps. I admit that the setting of traps is unsporting and I should never have done such a thing for a lion, but I cannot place leopards in the same category of game, and besides, at first, I was often so hard up that I could not have done without the money I got for the leopard skins.

I usually set the traps on paths made by antelopes and used a dead guinea-fowl or the intestines of game I had shot as bait. I have also often caught leopards with the carcases of hyenas as bait. I used not to fasten the chain down, in order to prevent the animal from trying with all his strength to pull his leg out of the trap, but let him go off with the trap on his leg. A leopard caught in a trap is the personification of rage. It will tear and bite the trees around him and if he sees the trapper approaching, he will receive him with furious growls. Of course the trap and the heavy clamp attached to it will slow down his speed, but he still may be dangerous and the greatest caution is advisable. It is not always easy to shoot a leopard caught in a trap, for it will generally crawl into a thicket and one only becomes aware of its presence as it actually springs at one. Besides, it is impossible to be certain whether the trap holds the beast firmly or not, and the shot will probably be a difficult one in the dense scrub, even if the charging beast is unable to free itself from the trap.

The first leopard I caught in a trap came at me with the heavy trap hanging on his leg with incredible rapidity and I missed him with my first shot. If the chain dangling behind had not caught in a tree I should never have had time for a second. My only excuse was that my men had reported that a hyena was caught, and as the ground was hard and dry I could not see the spoor, and only followed the trail left by the chain. I was then taken by surprise by the fierce growls of a charging leopard. We had caught three hyenas on the same spot and the bait was absolutely rotten, so the old theory that leopards will eat only fresh meat is certainly incorrect.

When camped on the Ruvana Plains my old munyampara, Najsebwa, used to do all the trapping for me, and he would kill a leopard in a trap armed only with two sticks. When the animal leapt at him, he held one stick before it while he smote it dead with the other, hitting it on the head or the spine. He said he never wanted more than two blows for a leopard, whereas three men's arms would get tired out thrice over if they tried to kill a hyena in this way. One day we saw an unusual sight on the Ngare Dowash when searching for one of the traps. As we approached the trap cautiously, we heard the forest guinea-fowls (*Guttera c. granti*) denouncing the leopard, and then we saw a whole troop of guinea-fowls huddled together with their necks stretched out, cursing their helpless enemy. Hatred had blinded them in the same way that it does magpies when they see an owl, and they did not even notice our approach.

The natives invariably trap leopards and their traps are something like our box traps. The "box" is dug out of the ground and covered with tree-trunks, and one large trunk makes the trap-door. When the quarry dashes at the bait, the trap-door comes down and the "tchui" is caught. Then, of course, the whole village becomes exuberant. Women and children stand around the prisoner abusing him and mocking at him, until at last, when they have had enough of this amusement, they finish him off with spears. It is a curious fact, but natives of Uganda, and even more those of Unyoro, have far less respect for the leopard than for the lion, although the leopard is known to attack human beings far more often. If they hear lions roaring they will not leave their huts; and it is certainly true that lions are frequently man-eaters. But they will always face a leopard bravely and often with no other weapon than a club.

During my last trip I was told by my old friend Mr. D. M. Stafford, a coffee-planter near Hoima, that a leopard had taken to attacking a herd of goats and had already carried off two of them. The owner of the goats, an old "Nyoro," vowed vengeance and sat in wait with a heavy stick. The leopard fell into the snare and was struck down dead, then the Nyoro swung him over his shoulder and took him to my friend for sale.

Another story is still more extraordinary and my friend recommended the hero of it for reward to the Provincial Commissioner. A leopard broke into a hut in which a sick woman was lying, while the men of the village were out hunting pig. The leopard injured the woman badly, but on hearing the villagers returning, took to flight. The men followed in pursuit but could not catch it, and while they were chasing it, it returned quietly to its helpless prey. A man passing by the hut accidentally heard the woman's feeble moan and opened the door to find himself facing the leopard. First of all he struck it, and then catching hold of its tail, he beat it to death.

I have only shot nine leopards, which is my smallest total of all the "big and dangerous game," although I trapped more than fifty. Leopards cannot be hunted systematically except by sitting up, and even those who would never adopt such means for shooting a lion, will sit up for a leopard. Personally I have never shot a leopard in this way, but I have tried driving them a few times, always without result. Beating for a leopard is far more dangerous for the beaters than driving a lion, for a leopard will always try to break back and will very often attack the beaters. I never experienced this myself, but I have heard of accidents during leopard drives. It is probable that a leopard will more readily act on the offensive than a lion.

If one comes on a leopard resting on the branch of a tree it is easy to shoot it. Unfortunately I never got the chance of shooting one under such circumstances, although I have often seen them so resting, but I never had my rifle handy on these occasions. The first leopard I ever saw was up a tree, but as I was collecting birds at the time and had no cartridges for my shotgun other than short cartridges loaded with dust-shot, I had to beat a retreat. This leopard was crouching on a branch of a mimosa tree near my camp on the Letema Mountains. It kept glaring at me with shining eyes and I felt very uncomfortable during my retreat. When I ran back with my rifle in hand it leapt off the branch and disappeared in the undergrowth before I had time to fire. It almost seemed as if these short cartridges filled with dust-shot had a particular attraction for the big cats because the same thing happened several times when I was after birds. My second meeting with a lion occurred under very similar circumstances and it also happened at my Letema camp, when I was collecting Nectarinias in a Tamarind coppice. Nectarinias are wonderfully coloured little singing birds and correspond to the humming-birds of the new world. I fired and all of a sudden a beautifully maned lion leaped out of the thicket, took a good look at me and then, to my great relief, disappeared.

It is more dangerous to follow up a wounded leopard than a wounded lion. A shotgun loaded with large shot is the best weapon for dealing with a wounded leopard, and although I have not tried it, I am sure that a charge of S.S.G. would have a tremendous effect on a leopard at a distance of 15 to 30 yards. British sportsmen often use S.S.G. when sitting up. I never had a serious encounter with a leopard, nor had any of my men. Most of them had had some adventure with, or had been mauled by, one of the big and dangerous game, but all the same I would never underrate the "tchui" as enemy.

I have met many natives who had been crippled for life by leopards, and once I was called to attend one who had been badly mauled, but I came too late. Neither I, nor even the greatest surgeon alive, could have helped him any more. I will describe this man's adventure, as it gives a good idea of the mentality of Bantus.

One and a half hour's march from my camp on the Ruvana Plains three men were working in the shamba of my friend, Matirigo, whom I have already mentioned. Of course, as was their custom, they had their bows and poisoned arrows with them so as to be ready for any emergency. It may be that a leopard came after the dog they had with them, or perhaps the dog spotted the leopard, but when it appeared all the three of them shot their poisoned arrows at it. Two of the arrows struck it and it crept into a thicket to die. It could not go far, for the poison had begun to work. The man who had missed it wanted to try another shot, so as to be one of those who were honoured when the feast in honour of the brave leopard-killers was held at the court of their sultani, Katutu. His comrades warned him of the uselessness of such a dangerous act as the leopard would soon be dead, but he thought that they were only trying to do him out of his share of the glory, and became more determined than ever.

The leopard sprang on him as he approached and would probably have killed him on the spot, had not his gallant dog come to his rescue, seizing one of the leopard's legs. On this the leopard retired again to the thicket and was soon dead. His two companions never went to help him because all three of them had had relations with the same married woman. There is a popular superstition to the effect that, under such circumstances, if one man were to help another in case of danger, he would only bring bad luck upon both of them. For this reason the two men did not go near the wounded one but returned to Matirigo's tembe[1] and sent out help to their companion, who in the meantime had crawled home.

After the fashion of natives they took the whole matter quite calmly and never thought of sending word to me. Matirigo told me that the wounded man did not want a white man's help, but tried to heal the wounds in the native fashion. They put butter, melted mutton-tail fat and the bark of trees on the wounds, after which came the real medical help. For they killed a fat goat and the wounded man feasted on it until he could hardly move! If a sick native possibly can—no matter whether he be suffering from malaria or a broken leg—he will always try to cure himself by devouring a goat. There is a certain sense in this, I admit, for a native in good health will hardly bring himself to kill a well-conditioned goat and so will seldom get a chance of enjoying its excellent flavour. And, besides, a Bantu is always able to eat and sleep.

Matirigo did not send for me before the fourth day, then I found the sick man in a hopeless condition. Even moving him to the nearest missionary station was out of the question, and very soon afterwards he died of his wounds.

In books dealing with African sport the authors usually give their opinions as to which is the most dangerous game animal. It is, however, hardly possible to give a definite answer to such a question, as the conditions of hunting are so varied that

[1] A low, flat-roofed hut, in which are many rooms, with a closed yard in the middle used as a shed for the cattle.

sometimes one and sometimes another kind of animal will seem the most dangerous. This is why the opinions of the best known and most reliable African hunters are so different, even if they have hunted in the same parts of the continent.

F. C. Selous, who is probably the most famous of all African hunters and is known to have been an excellent observer, places the lion first as the most dangerous animal and after it he puts the buffalo and elephant equal, while the rhino only comes in the last place.

Judging by his writings C. H. Stigand must also have been a very good observer, and he places them in the following order: first the elephant, the hunting of which cannot be compared to any other; then the lion, the rhino and last the buffalo.

Sir Samuel Baker also gives the elephant the first place, and next the rhino, while he puts the lion last.

Sir F. Jackson, a former Governor of Uganda and a wonderful observer of nature also, regards the buffalo as the most dangerous; elephant second; lion third, and rhino last on the list. It should be noted, however, that Sir F. Jackson shot considerably less than the others I have mentioned, and he had only killed ninety in all of the four species.

Personally I have shot about 200 head of the five dangerous animals, so I think I am entitled to give my opinion for what it is worth. In districts where elephants are often disturbed and the hunter has to pick out the largest tusker of the herd, on account of the limits imposed, elephant hunting is undoubtedly the most dangerous sport. In districts where elephants have been undisturbed—and they are now few—the danger is much less. I give the lion the second place; then the buffalo, and last the rhino and leopard. I must admit that I have only decided on this order quite recently, as there was a time when the list began with the rhino. This was in the days when I always tracked rhinos in the densest jungle, as I have already recounted in the chapter on that animal, and was so often in tight corners. At that time I thought the elephant far less dangerous than any other animal. I am convinced that a long experience will convince a hunter that the buffalo is less dangerous than one would imagine, and to-day I am of the decided opinion that hunting buffalo is not on a par with hunting elephant or lion.

CHAPTER XVII

Lucky Experiences with Leopards

DURING the first part of my third trip I had pitched camp on the Ngare Dowash River (Mara) on the frontier of British East Africa. At that time hardly any white men other than the officers of the Boundary Commission had travelled through these regions and they gave me very interesting reports of the fauna of this part of the country.

From the hunter's point of view the upper reaches of the Ngare Dowash were also reputed to be rich and interesting, and we heard of many herds of elephants between the Ngare Dowash and the Kisi forests. So it sounded an ideal hunting-ground.

The animal world, especially the world of birds, was extremely well represented. As a collector I was very successful, but less so as a hunter. I never even saw the spoor of elephants, although there was ample evidence that they must have been numerous some years before. And I had counted on elephants! When the sad truth became clear I called my camp on the Ngare Dowash "Camp Disappointment."

I had suffered many hardships while getting there. The last villages were in the Ngurumini Hills and here I had to provide food (dhurra flour) for my men, and engage headmen. The inhabitants of these hills were rather unfriendly, and so it was a long time before I could get what I wanted.

At last we started at the end of May, 1909. The almost uninhabited Wandorobo Plains begin under the Ngurumini Mountains and extend nearly to the Great Rift Valley and thence towards Mount Meru. Nomadic Wandorobo tribes of hunters wander about in this vast wilderness, and when white men approach, they instantly move into the wildest parts which are only known by them. They had driven the elephants away with their poisoned arrows and had almost exterminated the rhino in this part of the country.

On reaching the spot where I intended to settle down I sent most of my men back to bring the flour we had left behind in Ngurumini, and with the few remaining men we began to build our permanent camp. If we stayed in one place for any length of time I always built a grass house for myself as it was so much more comfortable than a tent.

When building one of these grass palaces I shot the finest male leopard I ever bagged. On June 19th, 1909, I roused my boy and the other men from their morning sleep to hurry them up with the work of building while I, myself, went to a rocky spot behind our camp to see if the meat I had put out for marabous was still there. When I reached the tree on which I had hung the meat I saw the head of a big beast of prey glaring at me through the high grass. At first I took it for a spotted hyena's head, but when it did not make off, but growled fiercely at me, I knew that it was either a very large leopard or a lioness.

I had no rifle with me, so I had to turn and run as fast as I could to my tent, which was not 60 yards away. I was in my pyjamas and one slipper flew off, but who would think of stopping for a slipper at such a moment? My boy Masakwanda, who was thatching the roof of a hut with grass, saw me, and guessing the reason for my haste, slipped off the roof and came to meet me with my loaded Mannlicher-Schönauer. We ran back but the beast was gone. I expressed my opinion of the situation in a few well-chosen Swahili and Masai words, when the animal suddenly reappeared and tried to steal away in the high grass. But I had got my sights on it by that time and a second later it rolled over with angry growls. But soon it was up again and with tail on end it dashed away. I sent two shots after it but missed, and no wonder, as I could only see the tip of its tail! Then I saw it climbing up a low ant-heap, on which a small bush was growing.

Having had some experience of the big cats when wounded, I did not follow at once but returned to my camp. My men,

NGARE DOWASH

NAISEBWA WITH LEOPARD SHOT ON THE RUVANA PLAINS

Native hut E. of Victoria Nyanza, built among granite rocks for safety against Masai attacks

DRAGGING A HIPPO CARCASS OUT OF VICTORIA NYANZA

I FEEL A DWARF BESIDE MY GIANT GAYA GUIDE

who were sitting on the top of the hut built for the boys, had seen everything and declared that the wounded animal was a fine lioness. A bit later I went to the spot where my first shot had hit the animal and found plenty of light, frothy blood. Nevertheless I did not think it was blood from the lungs. I examined the ant-heap through my field-glasses but saw nothing, and as I felt sure of getting him later on I returned to the river, where I bathed and fished.

My men declared that there were no crocodiles in the upper parts of the Ngare Dowash, and as I had not seen any myself, I used to bathe every day and enjoyed a swim in the cool water of the river. A bathe is a rare pleasure in Central East Africa, where the smallest pool in the bed of a periodical river is full of these vile reptiles. A few days before I left my camp for good I saw an old crocodile basking in the sun, which rolled lazily into the water at my approach. This was not 120 yards from my bathing-place!

After I had bathed and caught about 60 lbs. of carp and silure (sometimes called cat-fish)—not much of a bag in Central Africa—I headed back for camp. My men were far more industrious in discussing the adventure of the morning than in building the roof, and I found my boy Masakwanda fast asleep!

Three hours had passed since my shot, so I thought the time had come to follow up the wounded animal. We went through the high grass to the ant-heap, taking every precaution, and on going round it I found that our quarry had not left its hiding-place as yet. I examined the ant-heap from all sides but could not find any sign of the wounded beast. Cautiously, with rifle at the ready, I got nearer and nearer the "white ants' " fortress, but saw nothing. One more try! I fired my shotgun, but got no response. "Pangani," one of my porters and a reckless fellow, armed with his spear, was now quite close to the ant-heap, as he thought that the beast we were after must be dead. It was lucky for him that I called him back, for as I went round the ant-heap again, at last I saw a huge leopard crouching and about to leap at Pangani. I fired and killed it on the spot.

It was a very fine male leopard, its length being 63 inches from the nose to the root of the tail, while the tail measured 30 inches.   I am sorry to say I could not weigh it, but it seemed very heavy to us, although it was not full fed.

During my third trip in Africa I shot another fine male leopard which I saw by mere chance.   I was heading towards the Ruvana Plains in 1910, to settle down there and build a collecting camp. I had been on these plains twice before, so I knew their richness in game.

Our caravan was trapping over the hills dotted with the shambas of the Washashi tribe and as we descended the Washashi Mountain slopes above the Ruvana Plains we could see great herds of game and I was certain that we should hear a lions' concert that same evening after dark.

I had hoped to reach the Tirina River, but the fates had other plans in store of me.   We approached the place where we had camped in December and I went in front, as we hurried towards the Tirina, so as to be able to pitch our tents before dark.   After that work was over I wanted to take my Mannlicher-Schönauer and shoot one or two zebras or hartebeests for food for my safari.

As we neared the site of our former camp, the second headman, who was tramping along behind me, suddenly squeezed my arm and whispered, "Tchui!"   I snatched my Mannlicher-Schönauer from him, but on second thoughts remembered that I had not inspected my rifle since the previous night.   The packing and the loading up of our luggage and the engaging of new men had prevented my usual inspection and now that I thought of it, I remembered having seen a wasp buzzing round the barrel.   These wasps are dangerous and they will chose the most inappropriate spots for building their store-houses.   They have often filled the narrow muzzles of my modern small-bore repeating rifles with little balls of clay, in which they preserve spiders and caterpillars which have been poisoned by their stings.   They store them away in order to feed their young on them later.

What could I do?   Keeping one eye on the leopard, I pulled out the bolt, examined the barrel and then slipped a soft-nosed bullet into the chamber.   By that time the leopard had left his abode in the remains of my old kitchen and tried to retreat, but my bullet caught him up and he threw up his tail three times and gave a weak moan, after which followed absolute silence. We could not see him, for the grass was very high after the rainy season. My men wanted to run up to him, yelling "Here he is!" but I kept them back and stood motionless for at least five minutes, just waiting, but nothing came. Then I gave the order to turn away and pitch the tent. This was a difficult job as every moment they wanted to run up to where the shot had stopped the leopard. But I prevented them from doing so and the tent was up at last. "Come along, sir!" No! I sat down to table, asked for whisky and soda and only after I was refreshed, would I go to the spot. I began by throwing lumps of earth into the grass; then I advanced cautiously, rifle ready, and we found the old cat—he was already quite stiff. The shoulder-shot had killed him instantly.

It was an old male, but not as large as the one of the Ngare Dowash, nor so fine in colouring. When we opened his stomach we found that it was empty except for a pair of gazelle's hoofs. It was luck to have shot him dead on the spot, as otherwise he would probably have tried to charge.

CHAPTER XVIII

Hippopotamus

I NEVER could understand why the hippopotamus has deserved this name, as nothing could have less resemblance to that noble animal the horse. The old Egyptians called him "river hog," which is far more to the point than the Greek name. However, the Egyptians had time and opportunity enough to observe the ways of the hippopotamus closely, as in those times some even existed in the Delta of the Nile, whereas now none are to be found anywhere in Egypt.

In the rivers, lakes and papyrus swamps of East Africa the hippo is still very common, although in some regions, for example in Uganda, on the Victoria Nyanza, Albert Nyanza, Lake George and even on the Nile, there is still no limit to the number of hippos that may be shot. In the rivers and swamps of uninhabited districts where the hippo lives undisturbed, he moves about during the daytime rather than at night. In such places one can see them basking in the sun on the sandbanks in large schools quite close to crocodiles and water-fowl. Often one can see a baby hippo seated on its mother's back while she lies in the shallow water, or sometimes a red or a giant heron standing in solemn guard on the head of an old bull hippo. They swim with their nostrils and eyes just out of the water and come up full of curiosity to meet the approaching man. But in those districts where they have been frequently molested, their mode of living is quite different, and then they only leave the deep waters or safe swamps during the night in order to graze.

They do much damage to the sugar-cane and rice shambas of the natives, and it is for this reason that they are classified as vermin. A shamba ravager will always return to deep water, or into the unapproachable swamps, before dawn. During the night they will often travel a long way from the rivers and cover great distances. I have frequently found their spoor on steep mountain slopes, proving that they are good climbers, and I have often been struck by the quickness and agility which that big, shapeless mass of soft flesh shows on land. When alarmed, a hippo will make his escape through dense jungle, and take to water in a few seconds in order to hide in its favourite element.

Where the hippo has made the acquaintance of fire-arms he will be very cautious and never show up in the daytime. Deep tunnelled paths in the dense jungles of the river-side will tell us of his existence, and the fresh droppings splashed over the bushes, as his tail quickly wagged to the right and to the left, will give us an idea of his nightly wanderings. Even his deep bellow, the most impressive sound after the lion's roar, is seldom heard in those countries where he is often sought, while in places where he is undisturbed he will be very noisy and boisterous during the night, while even in the daytime his loud grunts and splashings will tell us of his whereabouts.

Hippo shooting, especially from the banks of a river, is no sport whatever and is merely target practice. A good head-shot will sink him without anything more than a toss of the head. A shot which is mortal but not so well placed will make him throw his heavy body from side to side and he will kick a few times with his hind-legs before he goes down. The sudden disappearance of a dead hippo, without giving any sign of having been hit, will very often lead to unnecessary bloodshed, for the beginner, thinking that he has missed, will go on shooting at all the heads that reappear to take breath. A few hours later, or the next day, a man will see with horror the extent of the slaughter he has done. In the dry period of the year the water of the rivers is confined to small pools and hippo will flock together into them when any number can be shot in this unsporting manner.

The carcase of a hippo will come to the surface in two to four hours after its death, according to the temperature of the water, and the condition of the animal's intestines. A hippo shot in the shoulder, especially if the lungs have been injured, will usually swim to land and die there. Many men who have never hunted in their lives are tempted to use their rifles to bag this easy and bulky quarry. The poor "kibokos" [1] which lived near towns were badly off, for it was enough for one of them to lift their nostrils above the surface in order to have a bullet whistle in its direction. It is true that the kibokos of such places are very knowing animals and that they have learned to pop up as seldom as possible—for they can stay under water for several minutes—and then even to hide behind a water-lily or nymphæa. In the old days in German East Africa I used to call the hippo the big and dangerous game of the holiday hunters!

Some people class the hippo amongst dangerous game because they will sometimes upset a boat or native canoe if roused. But such accidents are usually the result of the natives hunting them with harpoons thrown from their fragile dug-out canoes. These harpooners steal as close as possible to the animal while it is asleep, and throw their harpoons into it. The wounded hippo will sink and swim off under the water, but a buoy, made out of a piece of ambatch wood, is attached to the harpoon by a cord and shows which direction it has taken. When quite exhausted the harpooned animal will at last come to land and then the hunters spear it on the bank. It is a very exciting but cruel sport and can even be dangerous, for it may happen that the infuriated beast will bite one of his pursuers in two. Many canoes will also be bitten through by enraged kibokos, so natives use their oldest canoes for this form of hunting.

On the Victoria Nyanza and Bahr-el-Jebel natives do a lot of harpooning. When we left the West Nile Province we came down the Bahr-el-Jebel on the S.S. *Samuel Baker* and my attention was once suddenly attracted by a mass of something swimming, and it was some time before I realized that it was a harpooned hippo dragging along the floating ambatch. I felt very sorry for the poor beast thus sentenced to death. I once saw another rather disgusting sight on the West Nile. The Madis, who had shot a hippo cow the day before, were dragging the carcase out of the water in the early morning, and the little children, who had crowded up round the animal lying on its back, were

---

[1] Whips and thongs are made from hippo hide and so these as well as the strokes given and received with them are called "kibokos."

punching the dead mammæ and drinking with relish the milk which poured out.

A wounded hippo may sometimes be dangerous and will assume the offensive against a passing canoe even without the slightest provocation, and I once had an experience of this kind with a hippo on the Victoria Nyanza which might have had serious results, for it happened quite unexpectedly. It was at the beginning of my third expedition to Africa, and I had gone out with two canoes to collect birds and take photographs. I occupied the larger and better canoe, with two men paddling, while my gunbearer sat in the other canoe with two other men. Their duty was to collect the shot birds, which was no easy matter as I usually fired in the direction of the papyrus swamps on the beach, and I had no thought of shooting at a hippo.

We were attracted by two otters playing in the dark, quiet waters of a small bay covered with lotus flowers and my men did their best to get up as close as possible so as to give me a chance of shooting a specimen of such an uncommon animal. We sped on and every time the paddles struck the water the canoe seemed to leap forward, so that it was quite hard to keep one's balance. We were almost near enough for a shot when the men of the other canoe called out, "Angalia bwana!" (Take heed, sir!).

At that instant I saw a pink mass shooting towards us under the water; then came a shock and our canoe was lifted off the surface. I shall never understand why we did not turn over. The canoe sprang a leak, but my men did not lose their heads and handled it so cleverly that we reached a swampy part of the lake. We got out of the sinking canoe and with much difficulty extricated ourselves from the quaking soil of the papyrus marshes, wet and dirty. If we had been in the other canoe it would certainly have gone to pieces and the numerous crocodiles would have seen that this book would never be written. Fortunately my camera was in the other canoe and so my losses were confined to the shotgun cartridges, which I had placed in the bow of the canoe, and they flew in a big curve out into the deep water.

This surprise attack prompted me to seek my revenge, and that same evening I made a sort of bridge out of ambatch branches and papyrus stems, so as to enable us to approach the small bay dry shod and the next morning I shot our assailant in the head. The Wagayas who lived on the shore told us later that this savage kiboko had already killed a fisherman, who was putting out his fish traps. What happened to the man after his canoe was broken and he had been flung in the water nobody knew. Maybe he was bitten to death by the kiboko; otherwise he was eaten by crocs.

Near Shirati the shambas of the Wagayas were often damaged by hippos, so I was asked by the authorities to shoot one or two of the raiders in the hopes of frightening the others away. Of course I never derived any pleasure from shooting them, but the scenes enacted when dragging the huge body to shore and cutting it up were sometimes extremely diverting. Yelling, quarrelling and fighting were the order of the day, and yet that gigantic mass of meat would vanish in a very short time. I witnessed similar scenes years later round the carcases of elephants in the West Nile Province.

It is a rare occurrence, but sometimes a kiboko will attack man on land, though I am certain he will only do so if he is wounded. Emil Tallián, a Hungarian hunter, had some experience of this on the Athi River, and he was only able to kill the infuriated pachyderm at the last moment. All the time he thought he was facing a rhino, for he did not imagine that a hippo would come at him in the daytime so far from water. I should point out that this occurred in very thick jungle. Such attacks are more common at night and are usually directed against women returning from the shambas or going for water. Hippos never wound a man, for if they overtake him they will actually bite their victim in two. Those who have seen the hippo's mouth with all its large, irregular teeth will have no doubts as to how terrible the bite can be.

The crooked tusks of the under jaw may attain a considerable size. Rowland Ward gives a record of 64½ inches, but this is surely abnormal. A normally formed tusk is about 40 inches in length. Formerly these tusks were very valuable, for they were used for making false teeth, but to-day they are almost worthless in comparison.

Natives are very fond of hippo meat, as are some Mohammedan

MADIS DRAGGING A HIPPO OUT OF THE BAHR EL. JEBEL

COUNT SEILERN ON A HIPPO HUNT

SKINNING A HUGE GIRAFFE BULL.

tribes. Strictly speaking they are forbidden by their religion to eat the meat of an animal whose neck has not been cut open, and the body of a hippo only comes up hours after death. But the ingenuity of the natives surpasses that of the mediaeval monks, who could eat black-legged wild duck on fast days, for, seeing that the hippo spends most of its time in the water, they class it as a "fish"!

Disagreeable religious laws made by the Prophet are easily transformed by natives. As already stated, they are allowed to eat the meat only of those animals whose throat is cut when still alive. As nobody has the pluck to go up to a wounded buffalo to "hallal" it, they will wait until it breathes its last and when it takes no more notice of the kirongozi's spear tickling its side, and the bwana gives the "ruksa" (permission) to "hallal," Abdullah, Juma, or some other Mohammedan of the safari kicks the hind part of the carcase. This touch makes the hind-leg jerk as if the animal were still alive and the next moment they cut its throat with the fervent exclamation of "Allahu akhbar!" They do very much the same with the prohibition of alcohol, for although it is forbidden by the Koran, Mohammedan natives will get drunk just as often as the "Kafiris" (bushmen). One of my men was very often subject to alcohol poisoning—otherwise he was a very useful man—and so I tried to appeal to his religious feelings and drew horrible pictures of how he would pay for it in after life. But my words made little impression on him, and the old rogue whispered to me that he had learned a prayer from a "malimu" (teacher) for a consideration, which washes away all traces of sin from the soul.

The hippo has got no animal enemies. Even the lion can attack only very young ones with success. The crocodiles live on the best of terms with them, but the natives have told me that when a hippo cow drops a calf she drives away all the crocs which may be near her young one. The carcase of a hippo is soon devoured by crocs. They swarm up to it, guided by the blood flowing from the wound.

CHAPTER XIX

Giraffe and Zebra

THE most characteristic animals of the East African savannas and plains are the giraffe and the zebra. Although the two are very different from a scientific point of view, I have bracketed them together, both in this chapter and afterwards, because neither offers any real sport to the hunter.

Giraffes feed on the leaves of trees—mostly on those of acacia, mimosa and various bushes. I have never seen them feed on grass on the open plains. They are the tallest of all animals on the earth, attaining a height of about 18 feet, and are mostly found in the scanty savanna forests, rarely being seen on the treeless plains. The "tigerhorse," as the zebra is called, is perhaps the most common of all East African game, and is equally numerous on the savannas and on the open plains.

Throughout Tanganyika and Kenya varieties of giraffes exist everywhere, with the natural exception of the densely populated parts and heavy forests. In Uganda proper there are no giraffes. They mostly occur on arid plains, frequently far from any water, and I have seen them on rocky mountains about 6,000 feet above sea-level.

I saw herds consisting of sixty between the Ruvana Plains and the Great Rift Valley, but usually not more than from two to twenty will congregate together. The giraffe likes the society of different kinds of game and herds of oryx, impala, roan antelopes and zebras will peacefully graze with them.

In districts where hunting by natives is controlled, giraffes seem to increase in number, but wherever they can natives hunt them extensively and kill numbers of them by shooting them from ambush with poisoned arrows. They sometimes have to follow a wounded animal for hours, and it would seem that poison has a slow effect on giraffes. A giraffe is of great value to the natives, for besides supplying them with a quantity of meat, they use the hide for sandals and make neck and arm bands from the hair of its tail.

In South Africa this fine animal has been exterminated solely on account of its wonderful skin, because the Boers found that the best whips were made of giraffe hide, and in those days a giraffe represented a profit of £6 to the hunter. They hunted them on horseback and a good horseman could easily ride down a giraffe. In Kenya and Tanganyika giraffes are seldom hunted now, for no sportsman has any desire to kill this peculiar and harmless animal. Besides, they are protected by the new game laws and no one may shoot more than one a year, while the licence is costly (£15). Their existence in East Africa is thus assured, especially as they do no harm whatever in the plantations nor to the natives' shambas. They sometimes used to damage the telegraph wires, but this has been remedied by putting the wires up higher.

Travellers on the Uganda railway between Nairobi and the sea-coast, will be sure to see some troops of giraffes calmly feeding not 100 yards from the line. It is hard to believe, but even experienced hunters will sometimes fail to detect this large animal when it is standing motionless amongst the mimosa bushes; but the fact is that spotted and striped animals like the leopard and zebra melt completely into their surroundings in certain lights. The gait and motion of the giraffe are unique. When an old giraffe bull strides from one mimosa tree to another he is the personification of dignity, and the onlooker will not notice the slightest ungainliness in his movements or in his stature. But when a giraffe is alarmed and takes to flight it gives one a very different impression. He breaks into a gallop not unlike that of a camel, and his body then rolls from side to side, while his long neck goes backwards and forwards, reminding one of the mast of a ship in a rough sea.

When grazing, their long tails are in constant motion, for swarms of flies never cease tormenting them. The well-known Professor C. G. Schillings, who was the first to photograph African wild animal life, called these movements "tail language," as he believed that the giraffe probably signals with its tail to its companions, as it is literally a completely dumb animal. But it is hard to accept this theory, which was bitterly attacked at the time, especially by his compatriots, amongst them Captain H. Fonck in his book *Deutsch Ostafrika*.

The giraffe is certainly quite dumb, utters no sound whatever, and will even suffer the greatest pain without a murmur. I have observed them often, but have never heard them make any sound. Nevertheless my old munyampara, Najsebwa, declared he had heard our young giraffe calf call out before feeding-time, probably through hunger. When I asked him what the cry was like, he said "namna kondoo" (like that of a sheep). After this I watched our little "twigga" (Swahili for giraffe) even more attentively, but never heard him.

Giraffes living in captivity feed on lucerne and hay and are very much thinner and weaker than wild ones, which always seem to be in good condition. One never sees that thin neck on a wild giraffe, which is so typical on specimens living in captivity. A wild bull giraffe's neck is so thick that it does not even give the impression of being very long. In the third volume of Brehm's *Lierwelt* a giraffe is said to weigh 1,300 lbs. I cannot understand how this figure was arrived at, as even a thin one in some zoological gardens will weigh more than that, and I should put down the weight of a healthy, normal, wild bull giraffe as being over 2,500 lbs. The fresh skin alone of a giraffe will weigh some hundred pounds.

On the Ruvana Plains I shot a huge old bull and skinned him for the museum. The skinning was very difficult, although all my men were well trained to the work. In fact there is no more difficult job in field taxidermy than to skin a giraffe well enough for setting up later on by a professional taxidermist. The skinning of an elephant is about as difficult, but the skinning of a rhino is easier, for the giraffe's neck is very fat and under the skin one will come upon a thick layer of fat. Even Professor Schillings, who travelled with an enormous safari and every possible requisite, could not prepare a giraffe skin, although he tried over and over again. Schillings then enlisted a European taxidermist and he managed to send some entire skins of young bulls and cows to

German museums which had been wonderfully prepared and preserved.

At my camp on the Ruvana Plains I accumulated great quantities of salt and alum, and so I succeeded in preserving the large bull's hide and sent it home in perfect condition. I was very proud at this, although it turned out to have been wasted work, as unhappy circumstances prevented the big bull from ever being set up.

Lions will sometimes attack giraffes and I have found several carcases killed by lions. But I do not believe that a single lion can kill a giraffe unaided, for a well-aimed kick would stop him for good. The natives, especially the Wandorobos, declare that giraffes are often brought down by leopards, which lie in wait on a tree and then will leap on its neck and bite its throat open. This is not impossible, yet I can hardly believe that a fully grown giraffe could be killed by a leopard.

Except in quite uninhabited regions giraffes are very wary and wideawake, and I have had ample opportunities to judge. Their powers of scent are poor, but their eyesight is wonderful, and on account of their height they can see a very long way and detect the slightest movement. They are extremely tough and will go far even when seriously wounded. On account of their size, which is misleading, it is very easy to misjudge the distance when shooting giraffes.

When I first went to Africa there were almost no limits to the number of game one might kill, and even the shooting of elephants was not restricted. The zebra alone was protected by law in German East Africa, the idea being that zebras might be tamed and eventually replace horses and mules in the tsetse-fly areas. A lot of time and money was wasted in capturing and trying to tame zebras, but the only result was the discovery that the zebra is a vicious, ill-tempered animal, which can rarely be domesticated. It has no aptitude whatever for work and succumbs readily from heart-failure when given a heavy load.

On my third trip I took out a "big licence" (costing 750 rupees), which meant unlimited zebra shooting as well. In those times in German East Africa the shooting of game was quite unlimited, and the numbers of different head of game were only restricted in 1912, in imitation of the English Game Laws.

In English territory the zebra was also protected at first to a certain extent, and not more than two, then ten and afterwards twenty, were allowed to be shot on one licence.

Now, in "modern Africa," where alongside the railways and the roads tractors are turning the hunting-grounds into fields of wheat and maize, the zebra has been classed amongst the destructive animals and there is no longer any limit to the numbers one may shoot. Lovers of wild animals did their utmost to save this beautiful animal from extermination, but the authorities had to take notice of the complaints of farmers. Settlers in Kenya declare that the zebra does an enormous amount of damage, which is why it is detested all over the country. They often destroy completely whole fields of Indian corn and ntama, and it is believed that the zebras spread dangerous ticks, which are the disseminators of contagious diseases amongst domestic animals. But this is not all, for they do great damage to the wire fences enclosing the farms.

It has even been suggested that every hunter who shoots a lion should pay for it with fifty zebra hides; for, as lions kill many zebras, the good they do should be performed by those who prevent them doing any more. Travellers and all disinterested people will be "pro-zebra," but only so long as they have not settled down in Africa. The sportsman will derive no pleasure whatever from hunting zebra, as an animal which so closely resembles a horse cannot be regarded as fair game for the rifle, and he will only shoot them to satisfy the appetite of the pagazis, who eat the sweetish meat with relish, or when a bait for lions is needed.

A herd of zebras grazing on the plains or passing by at a thundering gallop is a most wonderful sight, but can very often be a trial when one is stalking other game. They are not easily alarmed and consequently are not hard to shoot. The leading stallion will keep a watchful eye on the hunter from a great distance and observe all his movements, and sometimes give a barking neigh, which alarms the whole countryside, especially the game which the hunter is after. Zebras are very sociable and are usually seen amongst herds of other animals, and many different kinds of game—ostriches, wildebeests, various antelopes, impalas and gazelles—will flock round them.

Some explorers have told of grey, zebra-like animals, which they thought were wild asses, but this could only have been due to an optical illusion; for in a certain light and from a certain distance zebras do give the impression of being grey, as the bright stripes melt into the colour of the ground. The habitat of wild asses begins much farther north, in Somaliland. In Danakil Land I saw the spoors of wild asses, but never saw the animal itself, and only once heard the noise they made dashing away.

The countries in which I have travelled are the habitat of Grant's zebra (*Equus granti*). This is far the commonest species and is the variety which is difficult to tame and, according to reports, will never be a useful servant of man. The same species is found in Uganda in small numbers. Here it is still protected; only one zebra may be shot on an annual licence. In the northern parts of Kenya, north of the Uaso Nyiro River, a larger kind of zebra, covered with narrower stripes, called Grevy's zebra, is found. This species seems to show a greater disposition for domestication, and under the present game laws six may be shot yearly.

In Swahili the zebra is called "punda-milia."

CHAPTER XX

Antelopes and Gazelles

EVEN if I were only to give a detailed description of the varieties of antelopes and gazelles which I have actually shot, I should require too much space, so it is clearly impossible to write of all the different types and species which are to be found throughout East Africa. For this reason I will only give a short description of the most striking and common kinds.

On the plains and savannas of East Africa antelopes and gazelles may be seen in incredible numbers. The plains and thin mimosa-wooded savannas are the real home of the antelopes; but there are some species which are only to be found in the dark forests; others only on rocky ground; others again which will seldom place foot on dry ground, but live only in swamps and papyrus marshes.

The diversity of species is reflected in the differences of size, shape and horns. For instance, the dwarf antelope is hardly as big as our hare, but a bull eland will weigh perhaps over 1,600 lbs. Sixty inches is no record for the horns of a greater kudu; two inches would be a record length for some dwarf antelopes. Their habits are also equally dissimilar.

THE GREATER KUDU

The finest of all the antelopes is the greater kudu (*Strepsiceros strepsiceros bea*). His head is royally adorned with great, spiral-shaped horns; his red-brown skin striped with white; and altogether he is perhaps the most magnificent specimen of all the African fauna.

Although the great kudu is known from Abyssinia to Cape Colony, it may be regarded as one of the rarest antelopes of East Africa, and its fine horns will be a trophy especially valued by

GIRAFFE SHOT IN THE GREAT RIFT VALLEY

CARRYING GIRAFFE MEAT: A HAUNCH AND SHOULDER

Zebra Stallion

A SAVANNA FOREST SCENE : THREE ZEBRAS WATCHING US

ELAND BULL SHOT ON THE RUVANA PLAINS

any hunter. It is not surprising that many a sportsman would sooner get a kudu head than the finest lion's mane, or even a buffalo. Throughout all my journeys I saw very few kudu and shot only one when I first went to Africa, south of Mount Meru, in the Marti Mountains. In Oeldoenyo Kisale I came upon some greater kudu, but they were only cows and calves. I was then guiding Mr. Fernbach's expedition, and we stopped there for two days, but could not sight a single bull kudu. The bulls are rarely seen, partly because they are more cautious and partly because they have been to a large extent shot off in recent years.

The best grounds for greater kudu are the stunted scrubs and slopes covered with euphorbia in the Kilimanjaro district. In the southern parts of Tanganyika they are more numerous, and there are signs of an increase in their numbers in the north of Kenya. To the south, in Rhodesia and Portuguese East Africa, they are still more common, as they also are in Abyssinia and Somaliland. In my experience the Great Rift Valley forms the western boundary of the kudu's habitat in the northern parts of former German East Africa, but farther south, the boundary lies considerably more to the west. Rinderpest has decimated the stock of greater kudus in general and exterminated them entirely in some parts. Even before the great rinderpest they were not very numerous, as the natives hunted them hard because they made their "buguruma" (war trumpets) out of the spiral horns, and this is why even to-day they are still eagerly sought for. The female sometimes, but very rarely, grows them.

Once when travelling in the Uganda train I had the unusual luck of seeing a wonderful greater kudu standing in the bush, in the last rays of the setting sun. This is a rare sight, even for those who often travel on this line. The Masai call the greater kudu "olmalo" and the Wanyamwezis "tandalla," and the men of the safaris usually call it by this name too.

THE LESSER KUDU

On the savannas of Kilimanjaro, overgrown with dense sanseviera bushes—the country of the Masai and Wandorobos—I often came across the greater kudu's near relation, the lesser kudu, which is his image in miniature. The essential differences between the greater and the lesser kudu are that the latter is smaller and has more white stripes, the mane being white also; and the line across the throat is missing. The difference in weight is enormous, for the greater kudu will weigh about 850 to 1,000 lbs., while the lesser kudu hardly more than 380 lbs.

The western limit of its habitat would seem to be the Great Rift Valley, for I cannot remember having ever seen one on the other side of the Rift. In the Great Rift itself they are common. Lesser kudus go about in troops of from two to five, but old bulls are solitary. They usually move in the early morning and late in the afternoon; and during the daytime they lie up in dense thickets. At first I could not get near one, until an old Wandorobo, whose wounded leg I had treated successfully, took me to a spot where they were to be found.

Near the Letema Mountains they are numerous, and I often walked into a troop when out collecting, or roused a sleeping buck. Usually I merely heard them break away or saw their horns flashing through the trees. It is very hard to detect a lesser kudu when it is standing motionless, for, like all other striped animals, its bright colouring melts into the patches of light and shade in the background.

The female lesser kudu has no horns, and the difference in size between the sexes is great.

The lesser kudu (*Strepsiceros imberbis*) is called "osiram" in the Masai language.

THE ELAND

The largest antelope is the eland (*Taurotragus oryx*). It received its name from the Boer colonists, who, when they settled in Africa long ago, named every animal they met with in Africa according to their knowledge of natural history. They called the giraffe "cameel," the leopard "tijger" and the largest antelope was called "eland" after the largest stag, the elk.

Of these old Boer names the "tijger" caused at first a terrible error in natural history, which even found its way into old school-books, and in the daily Press one can still find reports of tigers being shot by a hunter in Africa.

The distribution of the eland is very wide. It exists everywhere where the country suits its mode of living, from the Southern Sudan to Cape Colony.   The eland does not inhabit open plains, but is rather to be found in the bushy or thinly-wooded savannas. It feeds mostly on bushes and the leaves of trees.   It likes mountains and its spoor can sometimes be found at great altitudes.

The rinderpest of 1890 seems to have affected their numbers, though far less so than those of the buffalo, and to-day the "mpofu" (the name the men of the safari give it) is even common in certain districts.   During my third expedition there were times when I saw elands in herds of from fifteen to twenty.   It was rare to see larger herds, but once I saw some hundreds on the Ruvana Plains.   They had probably herded together, because they were all making for better pastures.

Old bulls go about alone or else join other antelopes.   The old eland bulls with their blackish necks and dewlaps bear a strong resemblance to our Hungarian bulls, and the sight of a herd of eland grazing will make one think of tame cattle rather than antelopes.   But this peaceful picture will soon be changed the moment they are alarmed, for they then dart off in a series of bounds like the bouncings of a rubber ball.   I have always marvelled at the wonderful muscular strength which enables these heavy animals to make such mighty skips.

All the senses of the eland are particularly acute, so one must be very careful about the wind, and as his eyesight is very good they will detect the slightest movement from a great distance. In open places one must usually risk a long shot and under such circumstances small-bore rifles are best.

My own experience is that this big animal is not at all tough, and an eland would be incapable of escaping with the same shot with which a white-bearded gnu could go for some miles.   It is also curious that so powerful an antelope, with horns so suitable for defence, will never show the slightest inclination to assume the offensive.   But between themselves the bulls must have some desperate fights, for broken horns are more frequently seen on elands than on any other antelope.   Eland cows have also got horns which are much thinner, and sometimes longer, than those of the bulls.   Abnormalities of horn are very common in the case of eland cows.

The meat of the eland is very delicate and all African hunters prize it highly. South African hunters, such as F. C. Selous, have described what an eland meant to them in the lonely veldt. They got fat for cooking, made candles out of the tallow and various things out of the hide. Unhappily the usefulness of its skin was one of the causes of its extinction in South Africa, as avaricious hide-hunters sought it chiefly for its skin.

The laws the English Government passed to protect the eland saved them from extinction and have even brought about a certain increase in their numbers lately. This is greatly to be desired, for the eland is easily tamed and would be a useful domestic animal in East Africa, especially in the tsetse-fly areas. Some farmers have already obtained good results with tame elands.

The eland bull is as big, and sometimes even bigger, than the Hungarian white ox.

THE BONGO

In the dense forests of the higher mountains in the east and in the "kibiras" of the west there lives a wonderfully striped and large antelope, the bongo (*Boöcercus euryceros isaaci*). Unfortunately I have never had a chance of seeing, let alone shooting, this coveted animal.

During my two journeys in Uganda I did my best to find their spoor in the kibiras, the dark forests of Uganda, but I could never come across a bongo track and so I had to believe the natives who said that bongo did not exist in those parts of Uganda through which I travelled. Mr. Cuthbert Christy, in his book *Big Game and Pygmies*, writes of the occurrence of bongos only in the Mabira forests, east of Kampala. I found the spoor in the forests of Ndassekera on my third trip, but as I had no good Wandorobo guides, I could never get a shot. True, my time was also very short, and it was often hardly possible to follow the spoor because of the giant nettles.

Before this fine antelope of the forest was discovered I had often heard of it from the natives. It was in 1904 that I pitched my collecting camp high on the slopes of Kilimanjaro (about 9,000 feet above sea-level), and from there I went out collecting into the heather zone which rose to about 12,000 feet. Here an intelligent Mtchaga guide told me about a giant antelope with a striped body and short legs, which had spiral-shaped horns like a kudu. He also said that the sultani of Kibosho would pay several cows for a hide of this animal, which when laid under a woman in childbirth helps her to bear her child with less suffering. I could not go after this mysterious animal because I had just recovered from some serious wounds and the malaria I had contracted on the plains plagued me badly. Besides, I was very sceptical. It is possible that my guide heard of the bongo from the Wandorobos and that the story about the magic hide came from the same source, for to my knowledge no bongo was ever shot in the forests of Kilimanjaro.

THE SITUTUNGA

Sportsmen making a trip to Africa will seldom shoot the antelope of the papyrus swamps and marshes, the situtunga (*Tragelaphus,* or in accordance with the new nomenclature, *Limno-tragus spekei*), as its habitat is sometimes entirely unapproachable.

The situtunga is a relation of the bushbuck; their horns, shape of body and even their colouring being very much alike. The situtunga, however, is much larger. Its black, white-tipped horns are as big as those of the lesser kudu. The difference in size between the male and the female is unusual, and the latter is hornless like the doe of the bushbuck. The most remarkable characteristic of the situtunga is its long hoof, which prevents it moving quickly over dry ground. Natives take advantage of this, and in dry seasons they set fire to the papyrus reeds when the situtunga drive begins. The beaters are armed with spears and are men who know every foot of the marshes—which patch of reeds will bear and which will not. They have their dogs with them and the pursuit begins. Patches of papyrus which survive the flames offer safe retreats to the situtunga, which lie neck-deep in the swamp, old bulls by themselves and younger ones in small troops with the cows.

When the situtunga are forced to take to dry land they soon meet their fate, as they stagger about helplessly with their long hoofs and are quickly overtaken by their pursuers and killed with spears. Like all the other forest antelopes, they are courageous animals, which will put up a stout defence if driven to bay. The difficult character of the ground and the situtunga's dangerously shaped horns can place the hunter in an awkward predicament, and I have heard of many natives being stabbed to death; but those who are swallowed up owing to an incautious step in the swamp are far more numerous.

I only saw situtunga during my fourth trip and shot the first bull I sighted. In 1914 I was hunting elephants in the swamps of the Lugogo. The spoor led over to the other side and we had to cross the river. My excellent guides told me where to step, but even so it was a very thrilling experience to walk over that weak platform of grass and weeds, under which lay the bottomless swamp and certain death. On reaching the other side I walked up the bank and from there made a thorough examination of the marshland through my field-glasses, while my men looked for the lost elephant spoor. Great stretches of the papyrus had been scorched by fire. I had no thought of situtunga but was searching for the king of the birds of the marshes, the Shoe-bill—abu markub (*Balaeniceps rex*),—and climbing on to an ant-heap I just saw a dark brown animal disappearing into a clump of papyrus.

I knew at once that it could only be a situtunga, for no other animal would go so far into the swamps, and asked my men if this antelope was known in these parts, when they told me that it was. But how was I to get him? After having taken good stock of the situation we all agreed that nothing could be done but to try to drive the swamp. In the meantime a lot of men had come up, who, anticipating baksheesh and good meat, seemed quite willing to undertake the drive. It was hard to reach the spot where we could get on to the tracks and I was already dead-tired when at last I found a firm footing and some cover on a little island of reeds. The beaters, who were down wind, began to come up. Of course the bare-footed natives carrying nothing but their spears and a long pole to keep them from sinking in case the mat of grass should break through under them, went along with much greater ease than I did.

I had not begun to hear the beaters when the patch of reeds I was standing on began to sink. I was already knee-deep in the marsh and had turned to break off a few papyrus reeds with the intention of making a kind of raft on which I could keep myself up, when I suddenly heard confused shouts, and the words "Angalia bwana" ("Look out, sir") came to me out of the distance. After this I heard something breaking through the reeds, which suddenly parted to let out a dark body. All I saw of the bolting animal was that it dashed into the half-burned papyrus bank, and when I saw for an instant that it was horned, I fired at it. I heard the bullet strike, but the wounded buck never stopped and on reaching the reedbank it was lost to view. My men came out of the reedbank on hearing the report of my rifle and we were all soon assembled by the drops of blood splashed over the grass. The buck was obviously hit somewhat too far back, but I felt sure of finding it. And I was right, for nearly 60 yards farther on we came upon it wounded. On seeing us approach it took up a menacing attitude, and as the spot on which we stood was by no means safe, I finished it off quickly.

I ran to my rare prize, but on my way I made a false step and was only saved by my guide's ready help. I saw at once that the buck was a very fine one with massive horns. We had the greatest difficulty in bringing it to shore, but my men managed it at last.

The following days I spent situtunga hunting and we had a few drives. They proved successful and I shot the four allowed on my licence. I prepared the skins of a buck and a doe for the Hungarian National Museum, and they luckily arrived at Budapest just before the War.

In times of great drought the sportsman is sure of getting a situtunga if he can spare some time for hunting in the Uganda papyrus swamps. But even then it is a difficult game, and one will always have the feeling of having well deserved a beautiful trophy.

On the northern islands of Victoria Nyanza there lives a sub-species of situtunga. This antelope does not live in the swamps, but rather on the rocky islands in the ambatch bushes. This one is easier to get and visitors to Uganda usually shoot their situtungas here. Of course this animal has shorter hoofs than his relative of the marshlands. The natives of the Victoria Nyanza call the situtunga "nzove." Its weight is about 300 lbs.

THE BUSHBUCK

The white-striped and spotted bushbuck is found all over Africa, from south of the Sahara to the Cape, and naturally over this vast area there are many sub-species of bushbuck (*Tragelaphus scriptus*) which differ greatly both in size and colouring.

Civilization has driven other antelopes into the reserves, but the bushbuck always keeps to its original habits and lives in bush and scrub, or even in the forests near human habitations. It does not mind the close proximity of cultivated land and is rather attracted than otherwise by plantations. It is a greedy animal and likes to visit vegetable gardens, and the natives' fields of bean and tchoroko (native peas) suffer much from their depredations. I, too, have felt sore sometimes with the "pongo" (Swahili for bushbuck), for it often came into my little vegetable garden, which had given me so much trouble, devouring my green peas, lettuces and radishes, and I had to go without these most welcome accessories.

The bushbuck, like all cloven-hoofed game, seek the open in the evenings and early mornings, and in undisturbed parts of the country it can sometimes be seen during the day.

They are the favourite prey of leopards and when they utter the short bark, which is so similar to the bark of a roebuck, a leopard is probably close at hand.

Very many local variations are known in colour and size. For example, the East African and Uganda buck weighs about 200 lbs., while the smallest kind, the harnessed bushbuck, weighs scarcely more than 100 to 120 lbs.

The meat of the bushbuck seemed excellent to me, although many natives would not touch it for anything in the world, because they believe that they would get leprosy from it. It is interesting how some tribes have certain superstitions which prevent them from eating the meat of antelopes with spiral horns. The bushbuck is called "ngabi" in Uganda, and the does are hornless.

THE WILDEBEEST

Visitors travelling for the first time on the Uganda train will notice two kinds of antelopes, the kongoni (*Alcelaphus cokei*)

Roan antelope

Najsebwa with an eland cow

Mounted head of my "record" Situtunga

White bearded wildebeest bull

UGANDA BUSHBUCK

BUSHBUCK SHOT ON THE NGARE DOWASH

JACKSON'S HARTEBEEST

KONGONI BULL

and the white-bearded wildebeest (*Connochaetes taurinus albojubatus*).

I have often travelled on this line with new-comers to Africa, and they have invariably mistaken the solitary old wildebeest bulls, or wildebeest herds, for buffalo. I admit that for those who have never seen buffalo this mistake is natural, for wildebeest do resemble the buffalo when facing one. But as soon as a wildebeest herd begins to move, this illusion is dispelled. The leading bull will step out at first with graceful strides, but on seeing a man it turns in flight with a series of the most grotesque leaps into the air. The rest of the herd join in the antics and all dash away, making sudden spurts and turns, only to stop again very soon and begin the performance anew. The wildebeest's funny action is known to every visitor of the zoo, for the smallest kind of wildebeest, the white-tailed South African species (*Connochaetes gnu*), moves in just the same way in his small paddock as his other relations do on the open African plains.

On the natron plains of the Masai highlands, wildebeest live in big herds, usually in the society of zebras, kongonis and gazelles. Such plains are filled with the humming noise of wildebeest, sometimes to such an extent that it is hard to sleep. They are playful yet quarrelsome animals and can often be seen engaged in serious fights with each other.

I learned to recognize the wildebeest as a very shy animal, which it is difficult to approach on the open flat plain to within a close shooting range of, say, 150 yards. I obtained better results when I came up gesticulating and talking. Their curiosity was then aroused, and if they started running at first, they would soon stop to wait for me and I then sometimes got within shooting distance. The wildebeest is extremely tough, and I know of no other African antelope which will travel so far with a mortal wound.

The natives to the east of Victoria Nyanza kill a lot of them with poisoned arrows round water-holes in the dry season and also by driving them. These drives assume the proportions of a small campaign, for many hundreds, and sometimes even many thousands, take part in them. As the tail of the wildebeest is the chief war ornament of some tribes they are greatly appreciated, and these giant drives are mostly arranged in order to obtain the tails.

The white-bearded wildebeest weighs about 600 to 700 lbs. Its Swahili name is "nyumbu ya porini" or simply "nyumbu." (*Nyumbu* means Mule, *nyumbu ya porini* means Mule of the wilderness.)

THE KONGONI AND HARTEBEEST

The most common of all the antelopes which inhabit the plains near the Equator is the kongoni. Although it is not exactly an inhabitant of treeless deserts as is the wildebeest, it is often to be found in them. These curiously built animals with long and narrow faces are to be found in the society of zebras, antelopes and ostriches, and their gait is just as grotesque as their figure. Kongonis are badly plagued by the larvæ of the osterus, and perhaps it is this that often makes them leap about in such an extraordinary manner. In countries where it is often molested, the kongoni is extremely shy and hard to approach. It is nearly as tough as the wildebeest, although it is so much smaller, and I fancy that its weight must be somewhere round about 350 to 380 lbs.

In Uganda I hunted the largest kind of hartebeest, the Jackson's hartebeest (*Alcelaphus jacksoni*). He resembles his smaller relation of the east in everything, but is much larger, and I would judge its weight to be about 500 lbs., while naturally it does not look quite as gaunt as the kongoni. The natives of Uganda call it "nangazi."

West of the Great Rift Valley towards the Victoria Nyanza we find the beautifully coloured jimela or topi with lyre-shaped horns (*Damaliscus corrigum jimela*). The jimela is much better proportioned than the other hartebeests, but its action and movements are just as characteristic as the kongoni's, and all its habits are entirely similar. They are shy animals and a sentry, usually an old hind, will stand up on an ant-hill and give loud warning should anything unusual come into view.

Hartebeest cows carry horns, and sometimes it is difficult to recognize the bulls.

WATERBUCK

Of all the varieties of African antelopes I think the waterbuck is most frequently mentioned in books describing African game. The name waterbuck (*Kobus ellipsiprymnus*) is not a happy one, as it certainly conveys the impression that this antelope leads an amphibious life. The waterbuck lives near the water and usually lies up in river-side forests during the daytime, emerging in the evening to graze and frolic about during the night. In the early morning hours it returns to the forest.

It is one of the medium-sized antelopes, its weight being about 450 to 500 lbs. and its bearing and general appearance are very much like a red deer, only the bucks have horns. Its habitat is very extended as it is found everywhere, from the Sudan to the Cape of Good Hope—i.e., had been found. In East Africa he is the most common of all the antelopes, for although it does not roam in such great herds as do the hartebeest and wildebeest, it is to be met with all over the country wherever there is water.

The waterbuck, like all antelopes, likes the society of other animals, and I have seen them in company with impala, zebra, wart-hogs and even buffalo. It is not very difficult to approach, but it must be remembered that the nature of the ground will always favour the hunter, because wherever the waterbuck is found there is sure to be plenty of cover. It is a very tough animal and will carry away a severe wound.

All over Africa there are many kinds of waterbuck, but the best heads come from the Semliki River. Sportsmen do not appreciate their meat because the buck has a penetrating smell similar to that of our Hungarian stag in the rutting season. This odour is sometimes so strong that I could often tell where a buck was lying up from a long way off. They go about in small herds of eight to twenty, and are usually led by an old hind. In certain seasons the sexes separate, and then larger herds of bulls, mostly young ones, are to be seen.

I usually built my collecting camps near rivers or periodical water-holes, so that I could always see herds of waterbuck grazing near my camp on moonlit nights or in the early hours of morning. They seemed to feel safe near my camp, and they were right, for

I only shot one occasionally for food. Another reason for their liking the vicinity of my camp was because I often had to burn down the drying grass round the camp in order to protect my grass huts from grass fires, and the new grass on these burnt patches made their favourite grazing.

THE ROAN ANTELOPE

The roan (*Hippotragus equinus*) is one of the largest antelopes, for it is not much smaller than the greater kudu, and its weight is over 750 lbs. It prefers bush and thin mimosa forests and the highlands rather than the plains. In fact, it is to be found almost everywhere where the eland is known, although it is not so widely distributed as the eland. For example, in the northern parts of former German East Africa and to the west of the Great Rift Valley it was fairly common in some places, but was hardly ever seen east of that valley.

A wounded roan will at times put up a desperate fight, so caution is advisable, for its strength is great and its horns are dangerous weapons. Natives declare that a charging roan will sometimes even bite viciously.

The sable is smaller in body than the roan, but carries much larger horns. The horns of the sable (*Hippotragus niger*) are the finest trophy after the greater kudu that an African hunter can get. Unfortunately I have never even seen a sable, let alone shot one. It is mostly found on the coast of old German East Africa and in some parts it is said to be quite numerous. I never hunted on the coast, for after disembarking, I was always in a great hurry to start for my collecting stations, and so I could never hope to add a sable to my collection.

THE ORYX

Amongst the old Boer names given to African animals, one of the most surprising is the denomination of the oryx, which they simply called "gemsbuck" or chamois. This huge animal, weighing from 500 to 580 lbs. and having—especially the South African sub-species (*Oryx gazella*)—horns more than 3 feet in length, has no resemblance whatever to the chamois of the high mountains of Europe and Asia Minor, and the difference is all the more marked since the oryx lives only on the plains. In the country round Kilimanjaro the Tuft-eared oryx (*Oryx beisa callotis*) occurs, which differs from its other relations in having much shorter horns and long bunches of hair on the tips of his ears.

In the Masai country I found oryx on waterless plains, sometimes a day's march from any water, in herds of from five to thirty-five, and very often in the society of Grant's gazelle and zebra. West of the Great Rift Valley I never saw oryx, for there its place is taken by the roan. The oryx is entremely wary and tough. In districts where it has been shot at a few times it is hardly possible to get within shooting range. The horns make a wonderful trophy and a good pair are the dream of every African sportsman.

The cows have horns too, but they are much thinner, although sometimes longer, than the bull's, and a beginner may very easily make a mistake in the sexes. The horns of an oryx make a dangerous and frightful weapon and often prove fatal even to lions. Natives have told me that they had sometimes found carcases of the victims of such a duel.

There was nearly an accident when I shot my third or fourth oryx. Led by an old Wandorobo kirongozi I stalked a herd of oryx and shot two fine bulls. One of them was still living when my Mohammedan boys, who had followed us at a distance, ran up and I had to allow them to hallal the oryx as they were so keen to get the meat. I was curious to see how they would do it.

My old Wandorobo caught hold of one horn and at the same moment my Manyema gunbearer got hold of the other. The rest of the men, six or seven in number, swarmed round and held the animal down.

When the Manyema cut the thick skin of the neck, the poor beast made a final effort, shook the men off and rushed after them with head down.

My rifle stood leaning against a tree, for I had gone up to the Manyema to lend him my knife as I could not stand watching them try to saw the neck open with a blunt knife.

I had to rush back for my rifle and I think my bullet was only just in time, as the oryx was on the point of piercing one of the men.

I have often watched the play and sham fights of oryx and marvelled to see how clever they were at defending themselves and avoiding each other's thrusts.

The Swahili name for oryx is "tchiroa," while the Masai call it "olgomoszorok."

THE IMPALA

In the scattered scrub jungle of East Africa, but always in the vicinity of water, the most common game is the impala, or as the men of the safari call it, the "svala" (*Aepycerus melampus suara*).

This most graceful representative of the African antelopes may be encountered both in small and big herds, and usually in the middle of a big herd made up of hornless does, there is to be seen the powerful buck, ornamented with lyre-shaped horns, striding along with majestic gait. In certain seasons young bucks go about together without any does but usually led by one or two old bucks. Sometimes several hundred can be counted in one herd.

A startled impala herd is a most wonderful sight. They leap and bound up to such heights that one might almost think they were flying over the ground. After the report of a rifle they will dart about in all directions, sometimes jumping over one another. This spectacle often reminded me of the playful porpoises on the mirror of the calm sea.

The weight of an impala buck is about 160 to 200 lbs.

REEDBUCK

Often in well-watered parts of the plains which are covered with reeds and high grass one will rouse a bright yellow antelope, bigger than a roebuck, which often jumps up at the last moment and utters a piercing, whistling sound. This is the reedbuck of East Africa (*Redunca redunca wardi*).

As its name suggests, the reedbuck lives amongst reeds, high grass and rushes. It is usually solitary, but will also go about in twos and threes. It comes out into the open in the early morning and late in the afternoon and lies up in the safety of the thickest patches during daytime. This mode of living assures its survival even in spite of increasing civilization.

Its horns turn forwards, taking the opposite direction to the horns of the chamois.

Various species of reedbuck are known and on the highlands I made the acquaintance of the mountain reedbuck (*Redunca fulvorufula chanleri*). This variety has a much smaller body and horns, while its colour is exactly the same as that of our roe in winter. In its movements it reminded me so much of our roe that I felt a special sympathy for it.

I usually found the mountain reedbuck in bands of four.

Its Swahili name is "tohe," and in Uganda it is called "ndiaza."

KLIPSPRINGER

We miss the crowned king of woods, the stag, the real wild-boar and that inhabitant of the high European mountains, the chamois, in the fauna of Africa.[1]

In East Africa there is a tiny antelope, which in many respects takes the chamois' place, and which was named "klipspringer" by the Boers (*Oreotragus schillingsi*). It is the same size as our roe, but differs from all other antelopes in the shape of the hoofs and the structure of its hide. The hoof is comparatively large, but it uses only the tip, so that the hoofs stand almost vertically above the ground when it walks. Its longish grey hair is of a strawlike texture and is attached to the skin in very much the same loose manner as is the winter fur of our roe. This tiny antelope is distributed all over Africa, from Abyssinia to Cape Colony, and many local variations are known. I was always charmed by the sight of the beautiful African chamois standing on some projecting block of granite, and when alarmed bouncing from rock to rock like a rubber ball.

The flesh is excellent, but most natives will not eat it and the South African Boers only shot them when they wanted their hair for stuffing their saddles.

Many klipspringers are killed by leopards, as rocks which

---

[1] In North Africa stags, and even boars, are known; but this region belongs to the Mediterranean zone and not to the African fauna.

are overgrown with dense tropical vegetation are favourite haunts of both these animals.

THE UGANDA KOB

The wilds of Uganda consist mostly of elephant grass, and as very few kinds of antelope will stay in this high grass, there are few antelopes in Uganda. On the riverine plains, where there is no elephant grass, or wherever new grass springs up after fires, one can always find Uganda's most common antelope, the Uganda Kob (*Adenota kobus thomasi*), which the natives call "sunu," while its Wanyoro name is "palaki." It is a good-looking, well-built animal, and the bucks alone have horns, which resemble those of the impala in shape, but are shorter and thicker, and not black, but horn-coloured. The kob is a medium-sized antelope which weighs about 250 to 300 lbs.

I have seen very large herds of Uganda kob, and sometimes the sexes were separated. On our last expedition we often became tired of "soonoo" meat and were glad to meet a herd of Jackson's hartebeest or some other antelope so as to get a change. The kob is easy to stalk, but hard to kill, as it will go a long way with a mortal wound. Many variations of kob are known, the most beautiful being Mrs. Gray's kob (*Onotragus maria*) which is found in the swamps of Bahr-el-Ghazal in the Southern Sudan.

GRANT'S GAZELLE AND THOMSON'S GAZELLE

Two beautiful kinds of gazelle live on the open plains ("mbuga") of East Africa, and in some parts they are very numerous. One of these is the fine Grant's gazelle (*Gazella granti*), and the other his little brother, the Thomson's gazelle (*Gazella thomsoni*).

The small Thomson's gazelle is distributed all over Masai land and can very often be seen quite close to their grazing cattle. This is but natural as the Masai are herdsmen and never hunt nor eat the flesh of game. "Tommies" (as they are commonly called in Africa) give, when grazing, the impression of domestic animals, especially as they do not seek shelter, but move about in the open and can easily be approached to within 120 to 150

IMPALA BUCK

PANDASARO WITH MY "RECORD" IMPALA BUCK

COKE'S HARTEBEEST CAPTURED IN LOOP-NET

SEMLIKI WATER BUCK

WATERBUCK SHOT ON THE MARA RIVER

MOUNTED KLIPSPRINGER FROM THE AUTHOR'S COLLECTION
The property of the Hungarian National Museum

UGANDA KOB SHOT NEAR ALBERT NYANZA

yards. When frightened they stiffen up and make a few awkward bounds before they gallop away with their heads bent down. On the Balangeti Plains I once saw incredible masses of Tommies. One troop passed before us after another, and there must have been thousands and thousands of them. At the time they were very much in my way, because I was tracking a rhino and the hoofprints of these gazelles ploughed up the ground and made further tracking practically impossible. The bucks of Thomson's gazelle carry comparatively large horns, and the does have horns too, but these are very often malformed. A buck weighs about 50 or 60 lbs.

The stately Grant's gazelle seems a giant beside its little brother and weighs about 200 lbs. The head of a good buck makes a fine trophy, as the horns are black and ringed, and of a graceful shape. The does also have horns but these are thinner and shorter. A local variety of Grant's gazelle is found east of Victoria Nyanza, the *Gazella granti robertsi*, and this fine gazelle was extremely common on the Ruvana Plains. The difference between this sub-species and the original Grant's gazelle is in the horns which half-way up take a sudden bend outwards. Thus the tips are wider apart, although the horns are much smaller.

Grant's gazelle is far more wary than Thomson's gazelle and is often hard to get in districts where they have been much hunted. They usually go about in large or small troops in company with other game, but I have never seen them herd together in such numbers as Thomson's gazelle. I have often seen a solitary old buck walking haughtily amongst Thomson's gazelles whom my men would call "Munyampara yao" ("Their munyampara"). One will often meet troops composed entirely of bucks. A solitary doe of either kind is a sign that her long-legged, large-eyed little fawn lies somewhere near. Does with young invariably live apart until the latter are strong enough to follow the herd. The Masai name for the Grant's gazelle is "engoli," and for the Thomson's gazelle "goilin."

THE GIRAFFE GAZELLE

The bushy patches of sansevieras east of the Great Rift Valley are the home of a very curious gazelle, the giraffe gazelle

(*Lithocranius walleri*), called by all sportsmen by its Somali name "gerenuk." When I first saw a gerenuk in the Letema Mountains, I thought it was a dwarf giraffe, as its very long neck and the shape of its head make it look very like a giraffe, especially when standing still or feeding on the foliage of trees. The gerenuk is also found in waterless deserts. It feeds mostly on leaves and foliage and when doing so will often stand up on both hind legs in order to catch hold of a tempting twig.

Old bucks are often solitary, but usually from three to six will band together. They are extremely wary and cautious, and a novice will usually only see a long shadow flash into the bushes, as a gerenuk stretches its neck forward and keeps its head low when galloping. In the country round Kilimanjaro they were very common, and there were days when I could have shot six or eight good bucks. Only the bucks have horns, which are markedly annulated and lyre-shaped with the points turning forwards. A buck will weigh over 130 lbs. The gerenuk is called "nyoga-nyoga" in Swahili and "nanyad" in Masai.

THE DIK-DIK

In East Africa live various kinds of dwarf antelope of which even a brief enumeration would be too long. So I will omit the varieties of the duikers (*Cephalophus*) and oribis (*Ourebia*) and only give a short description of the dik-dik (*Madoqua kirki*), which is called "paa" in Swahili, and so often mentioned in hunting literature. The dik-dik is very frequently met with in the dry bush-covered ranges of East Africa, even near the coastal towns. It is smaller than our hare and will not weigh more than 7 or 8 lbs. Its nose is shaped in a trunk, like that of a tapir, and on this account it is also called by German sportsmen the tapir-antelope. Between the two straight and nicely ringed horns it has a bunch of hair and because of this it is sometimes hard to make out the difference between the little bucks and does.

I always loved to study the habits of these little animals which would jump up at the very last moment on my approach and leap away with enormous bounds, only to stop dead behind a bush to peep out at me.

Many different kinds of dik-dik are recognized in those districts in which it is to be found. In Danakil Land there is the Somali dik-dik (*Madoqua swaynei*). This is practically the only game which is to be found in the scattered scrub of the Danakil Desert, so we fed on nothing else but dik-dik meat during our stay in those parts. It would really be better to shoot this dwarf inhabitant of the bush with a shotgun, but usually one has not got one at hand.

In the vast wildernesses of Africa, in the dark rain forests, in the bamboo thickets of the mountains and above the tree-line, as well as in the swamps, many unknown species of antelope may still be living and probably most of these belong to the families of the dwarf antelopes. Of the larger antelopes I hardly think a new species is likely to be discovered, although it is possible that the forests in the lowlands of the Congo and the swamps of the country round the sources of the Nile still hold some surprises in store for us. But it does seem almost impossible that a larger kind of antelope could have escaped detection. It is, however, different in the case of the dwarf antelopes. These tiny and inconspicuous creatures can live unknown and unobserved in the dark forests.

For instance, I lived for months in the Bugoma forest without seeing or shooting a silver-buck (*Cephalophus aequatorialis*). The natives on the Congo frontier call this animal "mboroko" and in Uganda "ntalaganya." This antelope, which is even smaller than the dik-dik, is comparatively numerous in the Bugoma forest and I very often heard the slight sound it made as it went off—not much more than the noise of a bolting squirrel—but the spoor told me that it was an antelope. In the dry season natives put up loopnets in the thickest parts of the forest and drive the little creatures into them in large numbers, for the "ntalaganya's" skin is of great value, and fine rugs are made out of them.

The duiker which lives in the forests is somewhat bigger and is also hard to get. These little antelopes yield tiny trophies, but their pursuit involves many hardships and requires much knowledge, while the possibility of discovering some new species adds zest to the hunt.

CHAPTER XXI

Cheetah, Caracal and Serval

THE cheetah, which differs from the true cats and the lynx in many respects, and although belonging to the family of cats, bears some resemblance to dogs, is to be found all over the East African plains where there is plenty of game. One great difference between the cheetah (*Cynailurus jubatus* or *guttatus*: *cynailurus* = dog-cat) and other cat-like animals is that the cheetah cannot entirely draw back its claws. Its shape is also different from that of a leopard as it is much taller and more slim; its head is smaller; its legs are longer and thinner, reminding one more of the legs of a dog than of a cat; and its skin is covered with simple round spots, not rosettes like the leopard. The cheetah is a typical dweller of the plains and one of the fastest of all animals over a short distance. It mostly runs its prey down and does not lie up in wait like other cats, but it is also fond of ambushing and stalking its victims.

It has long been believed that the cheetah cannot climb trees, and even Brehm makes this assertion. But this is wrong, for although it but rarely exercises such cat-like powers, it is quite capable of climbing a suitable tree if circumstances compel it to do so. I have seen some wonderful photographs in an English weekly showing a cheetah at the top of an umbrella acacia, whither it had been forced to retreat. These photographs were taken by Paul Rainey, an American, who hunted on horseback with a pack of splendid dogs on the Masai plateau between Naivasha and Nakuru, where tsetse-flies are not known, and after a run of a few miles the cheetah was forced to climb a tree. I fancy the cheetah utilizes this means of escape very often when run down by a pack of wild dogs.

Once when I was out on the Ruvana Plains trying to catch

animals and hunting, my trackers came back with the tidings that they had seen an old lioness perched on a dry tree-trunk on the bank of a periodical river. I would not have moved out of my tent for a lioness, but I was curious to find out what the animal, which they had mistaken for a lioness, might be. I asked them if it was not a big old leopard, for it is well known that lions do not climb trees. But they swore that it was a big lioness lying on a somewhat slanting tree-trunk. Unfortunately, as we stole up to it, the animal noticed us and slipped off the tree, but I could make out through my field-glasses that it was a cheetah. My men would not believe that they were wrong until we went up to the tree and I showed them the spoor. Probably almost every African hunter has at some time or another mistaken a cheetah for a lioness. I once shot two cheetahs in the firm belief that I was killing lionesses, and only saw the round black spots when I approached the dead bodies.

The cheetah is not regarded as one of the dangerous game, but when wounded it will sometimes charge man and I have had reliable information that some men have been seriously mauled. It is true that such cases are exceptional and personally I have never had any such experiences, although I have followed up many wounded cheetahs in dense jungles and high grass. They never showed the slightest wish to assume the offensive even when they could no longer escape and we had come right up to them.

The pursuit of cheetahs is, like that of the leopard, a matter of luck, even though they are generally about during the daytime. Cheetahs cannot be hunted systematically. For instance, of all the African beasts of prey, the cheetah alone never visited a bait and was never caught in any of the traps I set for museum purposes. But in spite of this I would not go so far as to say that the cheetah never touches carrion.

I saw a cheetah during my very first trip to Africa. This meeting was very interesting and I always regretted that this first one I saw went off with its fine coat. I was collecting birds at the foot of the Letema Mountains and was running after a beautiful starling (*Cosmopsarus regius*) when with a furious snarl a big beast of prey sprang up in front of me. At first I mistook it for a leopard, but then saw that it was a cheetah. Later I found out that the cheetah had been frightened off its fresh kill, a giraffe gazelle, and had stopped about 70 yards away. I had a gun in my hand loaded with small shot and so I made desperate signals to a man 50 yards away, who was carrying my 7-mm. Mauser. But the coward would not move. When at last I got my Mauser the cheetah had gone. For nearly three hours I waited by the carcase, but the cheetah never returned. I had no more time and had to turn homewards with a sad heart.

A few months later I shot my first cheetah, also in the Letema Mountains, and sent it to the Hungarian National Museum in 1905. During my third trip I had unusual luck in meeting this beast and shot eight.

I shot my first Ruvana Plains cheetah under interesting circumstances. I was on the spoor of a wounded wildebeest bull which led through the bush, when from underneath a thorny shrub a dik-dik sprang up. Out of mere habit I kept the sights of my rifle on it, not even thinking of firing. As the little antelope was passing a sanseviera bush, two fine cats suddenly broke out of it and in the next second it was torn asunder by them. I thought they were lionesses and, as there was no time for investigation, I at once let fly and the first cheetah collapsed at my shot. The bullet I sent after the other missed because of my great hurry—although no hurry whatever was necessary, but I had not had a chance of a "double" at lions before then—and so it made good its escape. I approached the dead "lioness" cautiously and only when I had got up within 50 yards of it, did I notice the spots on the skin and realized that I had shot a cheetah.

On one occasion we went out to catch roan calves on the hill slopes north of my camp. Sitting on a bad Masai donkey I saw something which resembled a cat sitting up. I thought it was only a tree-trunk and that the slight movement I had seen was only the grass behind swaying in the breeze. Nevertheless I got off my noble mount to find out what the peculiarly-shaped object was and aimed at it. The distance was great and the wind also made it difficult to take a steady aim, so it was not surprising that I did not hear the bullet strike and the object did not move. I gave it another bullet as I was vexed at not having hit a tree-trunk and I was not altogether sure whether it was a tree-trunk.

The reader will think: "Why did not you stalk nearer?" True; but the circumstances were unusual. I had had a "quinine day" and had just completed a series of long and fatiguing marches so I did not feel in the least inclined for a stalk. Therefore I fired for the second time, with the same result as before. "I must hit that damned tree-trunk," thought I, and took aim for the third time. This was not a good shot either, but it certainly went nearer the mark, for the tree-trunk leapt up and with a graceful bound disappeared into the bush. It was a big cheetah.

Cursing myself I went up to the spot with my men, and there we found the cheetah's fresh kill, a klipspringer buck. The cheetah had just began eating its hindquarters. A hundred yards farther on I saw it again and missed it once more! I then followed my men homewards in a bad temper and we were in rather a hurry because a grass fire which had caught the high, dry grass of the hill slopes, was threatening my tent. I only found time shortly before sundown to return to the cheetah's kill. To be honest, I had very little hope, because I was certain that my four shots had scared the animal away for good. Great was my surprise when cautiously approaching the spot, we did not find the klipspringer's carcase there. The track along which the cheetah had dragged away its kill was clearly distinct and following it up, I had the luck to meet the cheetah for the third time, when my bullet killed it on the spot.

I have seen cheetahs in troops of three to five several times. Once I saw four together quite close to my camp on the Ruvana Plains. I got two of them in spite of the fact that I had still to load my rifle as I was just starting out from camp.

My luckiest "double" was also on cheetah. While my men were pitching camp I went for a solitary stroll in the bush near the Ngare Dowash River. As I stepped out of the bush into a wide clearing covered with low grass, two cheetahs dashed out of the shadow of a mimosa tree. They were rather far away so I did not want to shoot, but suddenly the female stopped broadside on to me. The distance was more than 400 yards, so I knelt down and took a full sight. The cheetah went down. The report made the male stop too, but he was then 450 yards away, so taking a still fuller sight I fired again. Although I heard the bullet strike it had sufficient strength to run into the scrub close by, but after having gone about 100 yards, it died.

Very often I had to refrain from firing when I encountered cheetahs, as at the time I was on the track of more noble game, such as, for example, a buffalo. On other occasions I have let them go when we were on the march, and had no time to preserve their skins, for I never had the heart to kill such a wonderful beast merely to put it down in my game book.

It is well known that when cheetahs are captured young they can be easily tamed, and are used by Rajahs in India to hunt antelope. For cheetahs are also found in India, and, according to Brehm, the Indian variety is larger than the African; but this is not correct. Rowland Ward's record for the African cheetah is 7 feet 9 inches, while that for the Indian is only 7 feet. Unfortunately I did not take the measurements of my biggest cheetah, but I think it must have been near the record in length.

Twice I shot cheetahs when I was quite alone and had to skin them and carry the skins to camp all by myself. I must admit, it was hard work, especially on account of the ticks and the tick-flies which swarmed on them and plagued me badly while I was skinning and taking the skins to camp. The lively tick-flies, which are very difficult to catch, were especially annoying, as their bites swell up badly and leave behind them itching and little burning boils. The lion and leopard are also covered with these pests, but nothing like to the same extent as the cheetah. It is interesting to note that I never found any fleas on the big cats even if I ran up immediately after I had killed one in order to look for them on the body while it was still warm, for fleas will leave a lifeless and cold body at once. I may explain that I collected parasites and fleas for museum purposes also.

Recent English game laws protect the cheetah, and now a licence only allows the hunter to kill one cheetah a year.

The cheetah makes a very peculiar chirruping sound, at least those kept in captivity did, something more like the warble of birds than the imposing roar of other cats. When angry it puffs and growls-like real cats. The men of the safari call both the cheetah and the leopard "tchooi," but they will sometimes refer

Roberts' Gazelle shot on the Ruvana plains

Thomson's Gazelle

GRANITE ROCKS NEAR VICTORIA NYANZA

Uganda Leopard

Cheetah

Compare the spots with those of the leopard above

Hunting dogs

Making baskets for transporting animals

to it as "kingugwe." Professor Schillings was mistaken when he stated that this was the Swahili name for the striped hyena (*Hyaena schillingsi*) which he discovered. The Masai name for cheetah is "olginyalaho."

In East Africa there are yet two more big cats. The serval (*Felis serval*), or "tchooi barara" in Swahili, is rather common, but the other, the caracal or red lynx of the desert (*Felis caracal*), is very rare in the parts of East Africa through which I travelled. I have only once seen a caracal when I was out hunting for the pot in the Letema Mountains. It sprang up in front of me and darted away. I sent a bullet after it from my long 71 model Mauser which, because of its general utility, is called the "meat provider," but missed. I never got another chance of shooting a caracal.

The serval is a long-legged and fairly large cat. The male will weigh 25 to 30 lbs., so it is not only taller, but also heavier, than our Hungarian wild cat. Its fur is of a yellowish hue and is marked with black dots, or rather patches, but these dots are small on the western species, the servaline cat (*Felis servalina*); the fur of the typical eastern serval is finer.

The serval hunts by night, and this is why it is rare for a sportsman to get one, but as it is very common, any number could be caught in traps. Servals are a menace to poultry yards and the natives put up box-shaped traps made out of thick logs. Natives living near Kilimanjaro and the Meru Hills brought in hundreds of serval furs for sale. The price of these furs was then 1 r. 4 a., or for the finest ones two rupees. Of course this was long ago, perhaps in 1903–4, and nowadays they would probably fetch far more. At the foot of the Meru Hills servals were so numerous that I drove out a few every day. Once I shot three in one morning. In the higher regions of these mountains black servals were not uncommon and I trapped two. When holding up these melanistic skins against the light one could make out the spots, but otherwise they were of a uniform black. Near the coast they are said to attack herds of goats and sheep, and ostrich farmers declare that the serval is the most dangerous enemy of the ostrich chickens.

CHAPTER XXII

Hunting Dogs, Hyenas, Zibeth Hyenas and Jackals

HUNTING DOGS

WHEN travelling through the East African "pori" (wilderness), I had many an unexpected encounter with hyena dogs, or as they are generally called, hunting dogs, and have had many opportunities of watching them, as they ran down an antelope out of a herd, cutting it off, and pursuing it silently with long strides. The leaders of the pack usually keep to the right and left, close behind the hunted animal, while the pack follows well spread out and keep at a fixed distance. The leaders usually follow by sight—at least I have always noticed this—while the pack follows by scent, keeping their noses well to the ground.

Any animal hunted by hyena dogs is a picture of abject terror, and whenever I saw any they had already been torn by the fangs of their horrible pursuers. Sometimes they have passed me but a few yards off and on such occasions I lost no time in shooting— usually without any effect—but they never changed their course and continued the relentless rhythm of their hunt. If I shot one or two out of the pack, it made no difference to the rest. The one that went down received a few bites from the passing pack, and then on they went. The hyena dog would be the most ideal hound! The hunted animal will sometimes make its way through a herd of other game which is peacefully grazing, and even then, as the herd scatters in confused haste, the pack will not let their prey out of their sight. Nothing can divert them from their purpose, and sooner or later they will bring it down.

Often when watching such a hunt I thought that if I were an artist I would paint the scene as an allegorical picture of "Fate."

The distribution of the hunting dog (*Lycaon pictus*)—its Swahili name is "umba ya witu"—is very extended, and it occurs on the plains and savannas, in all countries from the southern borders of the Sahara to the Cape of Good Hope, wherever game is plentiful. In former German East, and especially on the Ruvana Plains and the surrounding savannas, I saw them very often. I have even seen them out of the window when travelling on the Uganda Railway. In Uganda I met them more rarely, and naturally only where antelopes were abundant and not in those districts which are covered with elephant grass.

The hunting dog is perhaps the most coloured of all beasts of prey, for it is dappled with white, black, bluish black and brown. In the case of very old males this colouring seems to vanish and they become almost quite black. These old animals have hardly any hair left and their skin is almost naked. From a distance a pack of hunting dogs looks like a pack of hounds with black bodies and white tails. In the Budapest zoo I saw a fine old male hunting dog. Its coat was thicker and longer than I have ever seen on its brethren of the wilds, even though cubs have thicker and longer hair than the old ones. I have seen them hunt in packs of from five to fifty, and I have also often seen a single animal chasing a reedbuck or impala. I never saw more than fifty in a pack, but reliable hunters declare that packs of a hundred are not rare.

Old books of natural history state that, according to the natives, hunting dogs even kill lions. I never heard of such a case; nor do I believe it possible. On the contrary, I have seen—as I have already recounted in Chapter IV—hunting dogs fly before lions, and the wonderful black-maned lion I got was shown me by the behaviour of the wild dogs. It is possible in districts where game is not plentiful, that the lion will leave the field to the hunting dogs, once they have made their appearance, for game desert such places. On the other hand, leopards and cheetahs are attacked by hunting dogs, and if they cannot take to a tree in time, they will be torn to pieces, though a leopard would probably leave also some wild dog carcases on the scene.

The damage these dogs do to game is really enormous, for they often kill more than they can eat. Besides, the appearance of a pack will cause the greatest uneasiness amongst the game.

While the sight in the daytime of a lion or lions approaching a thicket to rest causes antelopes and zebras merely to stare in curiosity, or sometimes even to follow a little way, the appearance on the scene of a pack of wild dogs will make them panic-stricken. Once or twice I have seen white-bearded wildebeests standing up in an impenetrable phalanx, horn to horn and shoulder to shoulder, defending the calves and weaker animals which were herded together in the centre of the circle. But usually these animals can be seen flying at full speed with their tails floating behind them.

I remember once seeing a most horrible sight, and ever since then I have done my best to kill as many hunting dogs as possible. One early morning I came upon some hunting dogs feeding on the hindquarters of a jimela buck which they had just brought down. The poor creature was still living and tried to defend itself by plunging its horns right and left. But it was too weak and missed, and each time one of the dogs tore a piece of flesh out of it. In fact, they literally ate it alive. They were so occupied with their voracious cruelty that they let me come up quite close. Shaking with indignation I let my Mannlicher-Schönauer speak for me and four of the murderous brutes met their death.

The greatest number I ever shot out of one pack was seven, and then I wounded three more. I came upon this large pack of thirty-five to forty dogs on the Ngare Dowash one late afternoon during one of my bird-collecting trips. I could hardly get my young gunbearer to come up to me, so scared was he by the noisy, restless pack, which was not 70 or 80 yards away. Of course the "tchootchies," as they are called by Washashis around the Ruvana Plains, only tried to frighten me and did not dare to come nearer than 50 yards. They threw themselves upon their wounded companions and began to tear them as they howled with pain, even though I kept on shooting at the assailants and brought down some of them also. My ammunition was running out—I only had fifteen cartridges for my Mannlicher-Schönauer with me—so I gave up firing, and some time later the pack also left. I have often had hunting dogs bark at me and after my first shot approach still closer, but never before nor since did they let me bombard them for so long as on this occasion.

Another time I saw four old bitches on the Ngare Dowash with more than twenty scarcely half-grown pups. The pups had thick, woolly, brightly-coloured fur, and were very different to the nearly black old ones. It is not at all rare to find the pups of two or three bitches in the same den, and the four families I saw together probably came from some such source. Hunting dogs are extremely fertile and a bitch has from six to eight pups.

Natives can always tell many stories about hunting dogs when they squat round the camp-fire at night, but only the inhabitants of the coast pretend that the "umba ya witu" can be dangerous to man. They also maintain that the leader of the pack leaps up at their quarry, tearing a piece of flesh out of his side. This he flings back to the dog behind him and this one devours it. Then another will spring forwards and do the same thing until the hunted animal comes down. The Washashis and Wanyamwezis do not consider them dangerous to man, but rather as friends, and so they chase them off their fresh kill without the slightest fear. But they always leave a leg behind for the dogs, for otherwise—so they believe—the "tchootchies" will tear the mean man to pieces.

My experience has certainly confirmed the belief that hunting dogs are not dangerous to man, although it might easily have happened that a few natives have been killed by them, especially if they lost control of themselves and ran away. In gameless countries these wild dogs will do a great deal of harm to the herds of goats and sheep. I never heard them give tongue when actually hunting, and it would seem that Brehm's description of them hunting their prey with loud howls and yells is incorrect. I only heard the "hoohooo" of hunting dogs when the pack had lost its leaders and seemed to be calling for them.

On two occasions I brought dogs which I had shot back to camp in order to take accurate measurements and to prepare the skins for museum purposes. Once I shot two out of a pack of four and the two others kept howling round camp the whole night and two days later we still saw these forlorn "tchootchies" slinking about in the neighbourhood of the camp. Another time I shot the leader of a larger pack late on a moonlit night and again the pack kept howling around for two days.

I have very rarely known hunting dogs feed on carrion, and I only caught one in a trap which was set close to a fresh bait of wildebeest. It would almost seem as if hunting dogs are sporting, in a way, to the marrow; for although they are terribly cruel, they always procure their own food; and this fact must be regarded as an extenuating circumstance when the damage they do is being considered.

HYENAS

In Kipling's *Jungle Book* the clever old brown bear, Bhaloo, the teacher of the jungle folk, spoke thus to the wolf cubs: "Feet that make no noise; eyes that can see in the dark, ears that can hear the winds in their lairs, and sharp white teeth, all these things are the marks of our brothers except Tabaqui the Jackal and the Hyena whom we hate." Yes, it is true that hyenas are the greatest outcasts of the animal world; and it somehow seems as if body-snatchers are despised, not only amongst human beings, but also amongst animals.

Whenever we set foot in any part of East Africa, we were certain to hear on the first night the ghastly voice of the big, spotted hyena (*Hyaena crocuta*), which afterwards so often disturbed our nights during our travels. It seems to say "ooi-ooii-ooiiii" and comes quite close to the tents at night. The Wanyamwezis squatting round the camp-fire used to comment on this with a laugh, and say that the "feesi" is howling for "tchoonwi" ("tchoonwi" means salt and at the same time the word sounds like the howl of hyenas). When quite close it is an extremely disagreeable noise, especially to the traveller or hunter who, tossing on his couch under the mosquito net, has been struck down by fever. One does not nearly so often hear the so-called laugh of hyenas which is invariably mentioned in books of natural history. It is anything but a "laugh," and is the most repugnant and most disagreeable sound of the African night.

I heard it for the first time towards the end of my first trip, but during my third stay in Africa I was given ample opportunities of listening to this ghastly sound. Personally I believe that hyenas only "laugh" when under the stress of great excitement. They do so in the rutting season—I have watched them when sitting up at night—and they will also make this noise in moments of annoyance when they dare not approach a large carcase, of which lions have already taken possession. And I once heard this laugh when my men trapped a "feesi" and had beaten it to death. This idea was initiated by my old munyampara, Najsebwa, in the Ruvana camp, partly because he was furious with the "feesies" for demolishing so many traps, and partly because in his youth he had been a great stick fencer and wanted to practise this sport on hyenas, and also teach the younger men how to use the stick. I have already said that they would finish a leopard easily, but to kill a hyena gave them hard work and their "arms tired three times" before they had finished.

The spotted hyena is a powerful beast which would, if it were not so cowardly, be in the front rank of the big and dangerous game. Their jaws and fangs are incredibly strong and even the bones of antelopes, or the steel-like leg bones of a buffalo, are smashed to pieces by them in order to get at the marrow.

At night the hyena is a brazen thief and there can be few travellers who could not complain of their nightly robberies. Sportsmen will soon learn by experience that trophies must be protected, or it might easily happen that a fine buffalo head, or a greater kudu's wonderful horns, will disappear during the night. Even if a track is found, the bones of the skull would be unrecognizable, thanks to the hyena's fangs. The space under the outer fly of the tent is no safe place either, for once an audacious hyena robbed me of my saddle which I had placed there. Luckily the marauder jerked one of the guy-ropes of my tent and I awoke in time to send a few alarm shots after it—of course without hurting it—but at any rate I got my saddle back, which it dropped in its fright. But the hyena's powerful jaws left their mark on my expensive saddle. The best way to protect horns against hyenas is to hang them very high up in trees during the night, and one must also be very careful of skins. Many lion, leopard and other valuable skins have been lost by sportsmen's carelessness, and even skins which have been already worked at with arsenic are not safe from hyenas.

The spotted hyena is common all over East Africa near big towns as well as in the wilds. They will roam the streets of towns at night just as much as jackals and from the hotels in both

Mombasa and Nairobi I heard their howls every night. They are also inhabitants of the dark rain forets, but are most common where lions are numerous, for they prefer the remains of lion kills. I saw more spotted hyenas near the Balangeti River, south of Ruvana, than anywhere else, and there I generally saw fifteen to twenty "feesies" in the early morning. But this country was particularly prolific in all sorts of game, especially wildebeest, and consequently lions were also very numerous.

The following story will give some idea of what enormous masses of meat hyenas can clear away. It happened on the Balangeti River, and the natives who had been helping to catch animals, begged for an eland to complete the feast I was preparing for them after their labours. The sun was just setting when I succeeded in bringing down a big eland bull. We were rather far from camp, and so I could not send for men to carry back the giant antelope. Accordingly we made a strong boma round it and left quite confident that our quarry would be safe until morning. Early next morning I went back at the head of a sufficient number of boys to carry back the huge carcase.

As we approached I saw several hyenas slinking away from the direction of the place where I had left the eland, and I noticed that they all seemed very well fed. I began to doubt whether the boma had kept the hyenas off my eland after all, and even thought that some natives must have seen us and opened the boma to steal some meat. On arrival at the spot we found the boma demolished. Thorny acacia branches, as thick as a man's arm, had been bitten and torn by hyenas, and lay scattered amongst pools of blood, the contents of the entrails, and a few bones. What numbers of hyenas must have collected for this free feast, and what a chorus of howls and yells the night must have heard! Farther on we found the skull gnawed and bitten all over.

These beasts of prey have enormous muscular strength, and they can, for instance, drag away a dead zebra quite easily. Nothing can give a better idea of this strength and staying power than the scene in *Travel and Adventure in South-East Africa* by F. C. Selous, when a hyena dragged away the skin of a big eland (shot the day before and weighing, therefore, at least 50 lbs.) which had been laid out in front of the horses inside an enclosure. The men poured boiled

Our Spotted Hyena as Watch dog

Men carrying Big-eared Foxes

A WART HOG.

Meat supply for my Zoo

Mounted Wart hogs in the Hungarian National Museum, collected by the Author

PORCUPINE

NAJSEBWA WITH AN AARDWOLF

maize on the hide, but the hyena was away with it like a flash, through the hole it had made in the fence. All this happened in the presence of a number of men while the fire shed its light on the hyena. Of course they all dashed after it at once, Selous with his rifle and the men with torches, and even the dogs were set free to join in the chase. It was easy to follow the spoor of the hyena as it dragged the skin over the recently burnt plain, but the dogs could not overtake it until it had to cross the bed of a river. Here they stood guarding the skin they had recaptured until Selous came up. The hyena had a start of but a few yards, yet it had gone 300 yards before the dogs could overtake it. Selous then kept watch over the skin and he was right, for an hour later the hyena returned for it and Selous shot it.

A hyena's gallop is very peculiar. The animal moves fast, but seems to progress in a series of jerks, for it keeps on looking back, and its head which swings from right to left and then back again creates this impression.

In spite of its great muscular power and turn of speed it will rarely attack a healthy beast or man. In some countries they are said to have dragged men out of their tents at night and done great damage to the herds of cattle. The hyenas of Ugogo and Ufiomi had a very bad reputation in this respect, but this can be explained partly by the fact that these tribes do not bury their dead as do the Masai and Wakambas, but put out the bodies into the bush as prey for hyenas. Bedridden sick natives will often fall victims to hyenas, and wounded, old or sick animals are also an easy prey.

The Somalis told me that hyenas only attacked their camels and mules when these had hobbles or shackles on. When they were let loose there was no reason for the owners to be anxious about them.

The "feesi" kills many new-born antelopes and devastates ostrich nests, on which account ostrich farmers hate them and hunt them as much as they can. If hyenas are not sufficiently careful when approaching a lion's kill, they often come to grief, and I found more than one hyena's carcase lying near the remains of a lion's kill. But hyenas very often chase leopards away from their kills, as I have often seen from the spoor as well as being told so by natives, and it is for this reason that leopards hang their kills on branches. However great the "feesis'" fear of lions, if they come upon a wounded lion they will attack and devour it.

Naturally the natives have many legends about this robber of the night. They say, for example, that it is a "ganga" (magician) who changes into a spotted hyena at night and robs children and men, and this is naturally one of the favourite topics of conversation with the men sitting round the camp-fire at night. It is an African edition of the German "Werwolf" saga.

I have also heard from my old munyampara, whose equal I never had and never shall have again, that the hyena can imitate a lion's roar. Of course I listened to this story with the greatest interest, as I did to all stories about the lives of African animals; but . . . I did not believe it! Yet A. Blayney Percival, about whose reliability there can be no question, has known it in Somaliland.

Round the safari fires there is always much talk about the "feesis'" voracity. The natives of Africa regard the appetite of hyenas in the same light as the Eskimos do the voracious capacities of wolverine (*Gulo borealis*). Once, for instance, I shot at a spotted hyena which was just running away with the leg bone of a zebra bait. The bullet caught it far too low and so only smashed his front leg. In his pain, as will almost all wounded beasts of prey, it snapped at its leg. But my men maintained that it mistook it for a bloody bone and wanted to eat it. It is a fact, however, that when a hyena is caught in a trap, the instant it is taken out of it and chained up, it will greedily devour any food thrown to it, while every other beast of prey when taken prisoner will rather die of hunger than touch food given to it. Its greed makes it very easy to trap, and I have often been very annoyed when I set traps for smaller animals I wanted for museum purposes, and a "feesi" got caught, and often even demolished the trap with its powerful jaws.

Once on the Letema Mountains I had a curious experience with a hyena. Two traps were set for leopards—leopard skins then represented an important source of my income—but the traps always remained empty, although the baits were carried away. This went on for nearly a month, and innumerable guinea-fowl and other leopard delicacies disappeared in the same mysterious manner; but no tracks of the thief were found.

I suspected an old "feesi" from the first, but my little Masai boy spoke about some Masai spirit. I then put a trap in a more open place and in the thick boma I tethered a live sheep. Next morning the sheep was gone, but there I found the old "feesi's" spoor. Of course it did not pass through the opening and over the trap, but demolished one wall of the boma. "Wait a bit!" thought I. I brought the other trap along and placed it in the opening of the boma which the old hyena had made and tethered a goat inside.

An hour after dark we heard the furious growl of the prisoner. The Masai youngster mistook it for a lion's growl and so did I at first. I ran up with a hurricane lamp—which often went out— with the intention of shooting the unknown beast. In those days I was very inclined to do such imprudent things! On arrival at the spot I heard chains rattling and was received with a furious snarl. My boy lifted the lamp, but it went out again. We crawled back, lighted the lamp anew, and then came forward again. By the light of the lamp I saw for a moment a reddish yellow something collapse at my shot, and was certain that I had shot a lion. When we were sure the creature was dead—in the meantime the lamp went out once more—we saw that what we thought was a lion was a large fat, spotted hyena. This beast had grown very fat on my baits! I then understood why it never stepped on the plate of the trap, for one foreleg was missing. Probably it had left it in a trap years ago. The goat tore itself free when the hyena was caught and ran home. Luckily it did not step on the plate of the other trap, and it came away with only one slight bite on one of its legs.

Besides the spotted hyena I shot two kinds of striped hyena in East Africa. Schillings' hyena (*Hyaena striata schillingsi*) was not rare in the Kilimanjaro district. It prefers waterless countries and its distribution is the same as that of some of the Somali fauna, such as the lesser kudu and the giraffe gazelle. I never saw this striped hyena west of the Great Rift Valley. This striped hyena is much smaller than its spotted relative and is a less daring thief. Professor Schillings writes in his book, that he had heard from his men that the striped hyena is even more aggressive than its bigger brother; but this, of course, was only the natives' tale, which they invented as they saw that their master was very interested in this beast.

Once I shot a Schillings' hyena at nine in the morning as it was slinking away. When we opened it we found its stomach full of wild fruit, so it seems that they will adopt a vegetable diet when in want. Besides, I have also noticed this with the common striped hyenas (*Hyaena striata*), for they were regular visitors to the palm coppices on the Danakil banks when the fruits got ripe, and I found that the natives had hung up empty tins and other noise-making contraptions on the leaves of the lower palm trees to frighten the hyenas away. On the Danakil coast the hyena lived mostly on what the waves washed up on the beach, and all kinds of scraps round the fishing huts.

At different times, and usually unexpectedly, I saw an animal emerging from its burrow which resembled the striped hyena, but was much smaller. This was the zibeth hyena (*Proteles cristatus*), or the "aardwolf" of the Boers. This long-maned, ferocious-looking animal is quite harmless, for its teeth are quite rudimentary and it feeds almost exclusively on white ants.

I met them most often on the Ruvana Plains, and on two occasions we dug them out and brought them to camp; but as they would not touch their food, they died, to my great regret.

JACKALS

An absolutely typical, as well as the most common, of all noises of the East African night is the cry of the jackal. The jackal (*Canis schmidti*) gives a disagreeable "beeh-beéhhh" sort of cry which will often keep the tired hunter awake. Its Swahili name is onomatopœic, namely "behaa." On the plains teeming with game we find them in astonishing numbers, and like the hyena, especially where lions are numerous, because something for the common folk will always fall from the royal table. The jackal, together with the hare, plays in native tales the same rôle as the fox does in our animal stories, and they are known as the followers and spies of the lion.

Although jackals roam about at night they may be seen in daylight, especially in the early forenoon and late afternoon hours, when they slink along, their tails between their legs, in the direction where the vultures are circling. Usually they hunt in couples and they must indeed be quick to get hold of a bone or a piece of flesh if vultures and marabous have already surrounded the carcase.

Even a delicate little creature like the Thomson's gazelle doe shows not the slightest fear at the sight of two or three jackals, and all I have ever seen them do was to stamp defiantly with a foreleg if a fawn was lying near by. But if an animal is wounded a jackal will sometimes show an unexpected boldness. Once at the foot of the Ngurumini Mountains I shot a reedbuck, which carried on with my bullet for about 200 yards, and then lay down. A jackal rushed on him instantly and bit its hind leg. The reedbuck tried to defend itself, but could not, and I ran up across an open place. But this did not frighten the greedy jackal in the least, and it went on tearing at the dying animal. As I was about 130 paces away I fired at him with my small ·22 Winchester-Automatic. At my shot it snapped round at its flank, and then—though staggering—continued to tear the buck. My second shot—which was quite unnecessary—dropped it on the reedbuck, which it did not intend to leave even when wounded to death.

At night they were most impudent and used to come right up to our tents round which the meat supply of the safari was drying and which, together with the trophies, gave out a strong smell. There were times when we caught a dozen of them in a single night with three or four disk-shaped traps. On hearing the cry of a trapped jackal my trappers ran up, and hitting the beast with a stick on the head, finished it, and set up the trap anew. Often they had hardly time to return to camp, which was not 50 to 60 yards away, before another jackal was caught.

My native skinners hated jackals because skinning them and preparing the skins gave them a lot of work. Jackals are usually very fat, and the slightest trace of grease left on the hide will produce sebacic acid which destroys the skin. Nice rugs can be made from picked jackal skins.

Various kinds of jackal live in East Africa and we also trapped some silver jackals (*Canis holubi*), which mostly live in the higher parts of the country.

When tramping across the plains we often nearly stepped on four or five tiny fox-like animals with upright great ears, which would run a few yards off and then stop and snarl at us. This always amused my men intensely, for they did not know of the big-eared foxes (*Otocyon megalotis*) and thought at first that the animals were young jackals. They invariably broke into loud cries of "Allah," and then followed peals of laughter. On the Ruvana Plains we met with many of these little animals, and there the natives called them "bruke." They are very neat-looking little animals, with quite rudimentary teeth, and they mostly feed on white ants.

That most characteristic beast of prey of the deserts, the desert fox (*Fennecus familiaris*), I twice saw in Danakil Land. Probably they had come for the ripening of the dates, because when cutting them open, we found their stomachs filled with dates. Before then I had never seen any in that country. The three I shot are mounted in the Hungarian National Museum.

CHAPTER XXIII

Pig, Aardvark and Porcupine

THE African fauna is quite devoid of real pig. It is true that in the forests of North Africa our wild boar is to be found, but those territories belong zoologically to the Mediterranean zone and not to the Ethiopian.

THE WART-HOG

The plains and savannas from the south of Abyssinia to Cape Colony are inhabited by the wart-hog (*Phacochœrus aethiopicus*), an interesting variety of pig. This animal is the incarnation of ugliness. Its head is far too large and is provided with powerful tusks and adorned by two ugly excrescences. Its ugliness is still further accentuated by the small eyes placed on the sides of the head. Its skin is nearly naked, but on its neck and back are a few long, stiff bristles, giving it a still wilder appearance. It is not so tall as our wild boar and its weight is also less, for I think an old hog would weigh about 280 lbs. The tusks, however, are much bigger than those of the European boar and also differ by the fact that the upper tusks are the longer. The record wart-hog tusk is 24 inches long.

It is comparatively a very common animal and may be met with any day, when the little sounders, numbering from three to six, can be seen in the open during the daytime strolling about or digging for roots. They keep away from cultivated land and therefore do little harm in the shambas. I have often seen them feed on carrion, a thing which our wild boar will also do.

They prefer to keep near other animals, like zebras and antelopes, probably because they cannot rely upon their own bad eyesight and so are in need of some friendly warning. When the barklike neigh of the zebras or the alarm snort of hartebeest gives

271

the signal of danger, then the sounder of peacefully digging "giris" is aroused as if touched by an electric current. Up go their ugly heads and tails, and after a few turns in different directions they thunder away, usually in single file.

Although it looks very ferocious, the wart-hog can under no circumstances be regarded as dangerous, as one very rarely charges even if wounded. I have only once known a wounded "giri" take the offensive. This rather comical adventure occurred near Ndassekera.

I shot a roan for meat for my large safari, but the beast carried on and I followed it for a long distance before I could finish it with two more shots. Contrary to my habit, I did not recharge the magazine of my rifle, but started homewards, leaving some men to bring in the meat.

Hardly had we gone 500 yards when I saw two reddish pig-like animals step out of a bush. I thought they were bushpig, and so I fired and one of them collapsed to the shot. The other one, perhaps confused by the report, took to flight in my direction and then I saw that the animals were no bushpig, but two young male wart-hogs, which had rolled about in the red clay after their wallow. As we needed more meat I shot the second wart-hog in the head, but at the instant I pulled the trigger, it lifted its head and so my bullet did not penetrate the brain. Then it came right on to me. Seeing that the situation was getting serious I reloaded, quite forgetting that this was my fifth and last cartridge, and that the magazine was empty. I tried to take a cartridge out of the cartridge holder sewn on my shirt, but it stuck and I could not get it out in a hurry. (I never found the cartridge holder sewn on the shirt of any practical value, for if the cartridges went in easily you always lost them, while if they stuck, you could not get them out in a hurry.) In the meantime the furious "giri" had chased me three times round a small tree, to the greatest joy of my men, who were standing near another tree. When at last I got out the cartridge and succeeded in reloading, the animal suddenly fell over dead. This determined attack was the last expression of his energy in life; it impressed me much and I shall never forget this young "giri," a sportsman to the last.

ZEBUS AND WHITE HERONS ON THE BEACH OF ALBERT NYANZA

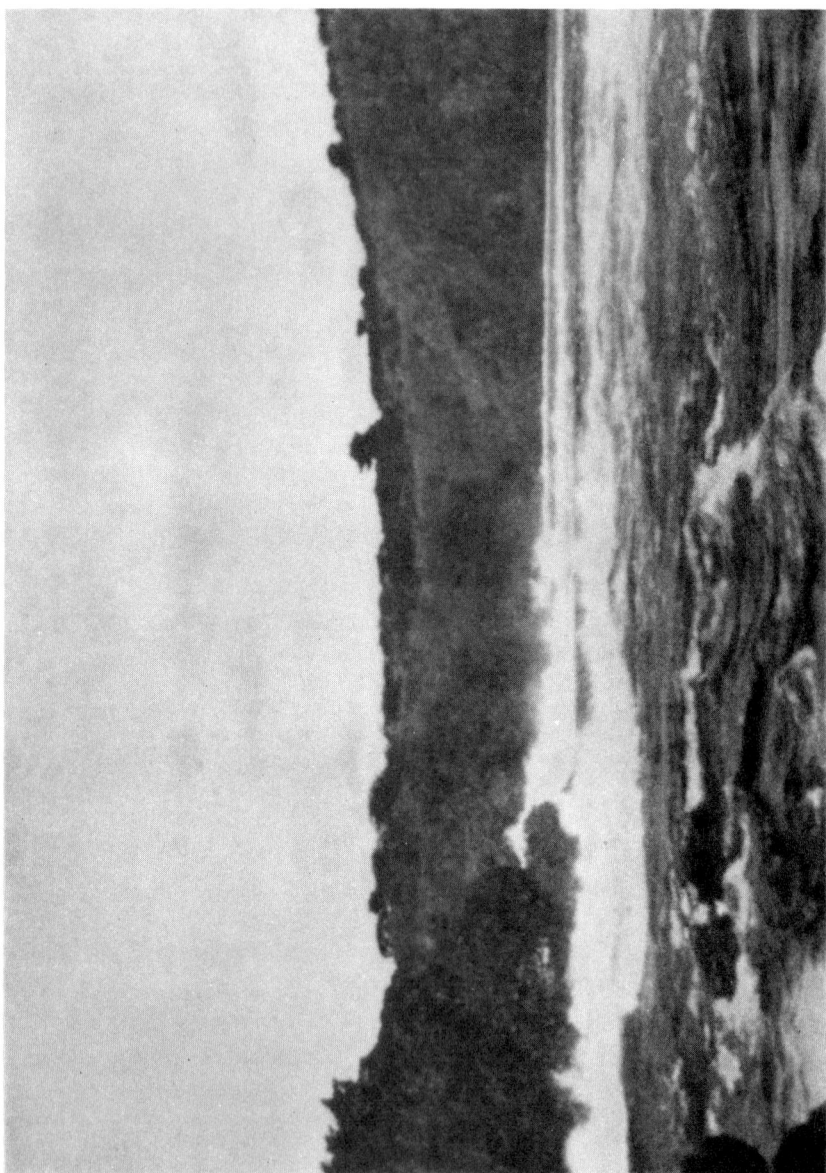

RIPON FALLS—ANOTHER VIEW

In the parts of Kenya devoid of tsetse-fly, where during the last ten years so many new farms have shot up, settlers started that most popular Indian sport of pig-sticking, and a "giri" run to bay will charge the horseman armed with a spear and thus gives very good sport.

A wounded wart-hog very often takes refuge in an aardvark's burrow, and it is very interesting to notice how it will invariably turn round before the entrance of the burrow and go in backwards. Then of course the pursuing enemy—let us say a dog—will get a very hot reception.

In any case an aardvark's burrow is a favourite resort for wart-hogs and they will very often farrow in one. The ugly little pigs are very frisky animals, and unlike true pigs, they are not spotted or striped, but quite uniform in colour.

Strolling over the plains—especially when thinking of other things—the hunter will often be startled by the sudden and vehement upburst of a solitary "giri," or a whole "giri" family, which will dash away enveloped in a cloud of dust.

My experience is that wart-hog are not very tough and do not carry on with as serious wounds as the wild-boar will. The meat is white, but of nasty flavour; I at least did not like it. The men of the safari do not care for this meat either and most of the tribes do not eat it at all. I am naturally not speaking of Mohammedans, who sometimes objected even to touch a killed "giri" if they had to skin it or cut its head off.

There is surely no African hunter who has not been roused by his boys with the exciting news that a great big-maned lion had been seen a moment ago, and on arriving at the spot has seen an old "giri," or only found its tracks. From a certain distance in a bad light and in the high grass it is not difficult to make this mistake, and more than once in a thick fog I have taken a wart-hog crossing before me for a rhino, and was not the only one to think so, for my men did the same.

Rinderpest causes great mortality among wart-hogs, but as, like all pigs, they are very prolific (six to eight young pigs being born in a litter), they always make good their losses very soon.

THE BUSHPIG

The hunter will meet the bushpig (*Chœropotamus chœropotamus*) more rarely, as its habits are very like those of the European wild boar. It leaves the bush or thick forest after dark and returns to them before daybreak. The damage these pigs do in the plantations are so serious in some parts—especially near the coast—that the natives have to relinquish their shambas because of the devastations of the sounders of "ngruve."

The bushpig resembles the wild-boar in his external aspect much more than the wart-hog does, but it is considerably smaller, and an old male will weigh only about 200 lbs. Further, it differs from the true pigs in that it has only forty-two teeth instead of forty-four, and on its ears there are big bunches of hair.

I have seen but few bushpig by chance, usually when I was stalking elephant early in the morning and so could not risk a shot. In districts where natives complained about the damages done by bushpigs I had some drives with good results. It is easy to shoot them by sitting up, but there is no sport in such a method and in Africa it is not worth one's while to feed the mosquitoes for the sake of a pig.

Natives put up nets in the dry season after the grass is burned down, and drive the bushpig into the nets, killing them with spears. These small beasts are brave and of an aggressive nature and the beaters are often injured seriously. I knew a one-legged man in Uganda who had been wounded so badly by a bushpig that his leg had to be amputated.

It is fortunate that they have many enemies in the animal world—especially the big cats—otherwise all the plantations in the coastal areas would be devastated. It is on this account that the cocoa-planters are so displeased when somebody shoots a lion in their neighbourhood.

THE GIANT HOG

About 1903 in the same district where the East African bongo was discovered, a large black pig was discovered in the dark "subugos" (rain forests) which was the so-called giant hog (*Hylochœrus meinertzhageni*). It should be realized that though the giant hog is larger than a wart-hog, it is by no means a giant, being hardly as large as a wild boar.   When one gets a glimpse of the animal in the depths of the forest, and sees for the first time its massive, black body and the long bristles which make it look still larger, one is inclined to believe it a real giant.

It is astonishing that the giant hog was not discovered until 1904, for the native hunting tribes have always known of it. Further, its distribution is wide, as its habitat extends from the forests of Southern Abyssinia, throughout the subugos of Equatorial Africa to East Kameroon.

In former German East Africa I believe I was the first to notice its existence, but unfortunately I could not shoot a specimen to prove what I had discovered.

Once in 1911 I was returning to my camp on the Ruvana Plains from a shooting and animal-catching expedition.   My way led me along the Ngare Dowash.   Of course there was no question of any definite road, not even of a path beaten by natives, for this wilderness was only crossed by some Wandorobo hunters.

At one spot where the forests of the Ngare Dowash banks widened out I went to the head of the safari and we tried to get through the thickets, taking advantage of buffalo and hippo paths, as the jungle was woven through and through by creepers, "wait-a-bit" and other thorny plants, which made it nearly impenetrable.

Suddenly I was stopped by a black mass standing about 25 yards away from me.   I bent down to make out what it was and as it seemed to be a buffalo calf I did not shoot.   But at the next moment the black mass grunted, jumped up, and was gone.   On reaching the spot I saw by the spoor that the animal was a giant hog, a specimen of which I was seeking so intently.   Of course after I had lost this chance there was no hope of coming up with it again.   During the next two days I tried to come across one but without success.   Nor did I see any while hunting and collecting in Uganda in 1913.   My Wanyoro porters declared that in their country the giant hog, or as they called it, "tsenke," is not rare and I fancy this is true.

I pitched my collecting camp in 1914 in the Bugoma jungle and heard with pleasure that the giant hog was by no means rare in these regions.   It is true that hunting it was very tedious in the dark forests, but neither this nor the fact that some of those regions were infested with sleeping sickness kept me from trying my luck.

Incidentally the natives were very keen on hunting the "tsenke" and mostly used traps constructed of heavy tree-trunks. I found many of these traps in the forests and some were so wonderfully hidden that without a good guide it would have been risky to stroll about in the forest.

On June 14th, 1914, I was awakened by the shrieks of "tchegos" (chimpanzee). I dressed hurriedly and went in the direction of the sounds, hoping to be able to observe their ways. Unfortunately when we reached the spot they had already entered a thicket of date palms standing in a little swamp formed by a forest brook, and so I had to give up following them.

On returning to my camp I was visited by a native chief, with whom I had to discuss the food supply of my men. So it was late in the afternoon when I went for a little stroll in the forest.

In these rain forests, the "kibira," game is relatively very scarce. One or two kinds of dwarf antelopes, bushbuck, pigs, buffalo and elephants are the sole inhabitants of the Bugoma forest, so my men got meat very rarely, especially as I had shot all the buffaloes allowed on my licence. Accordingly I had no great hopes when I started on this stroll. I merely set out in my customary direction to a place where I had recently noticed the tracks of a giant hog.

As we were tramping along on the well-beaten elephant track, we were suddenly startled by the sound of breaking twigs, snorts and smacking of lips. We stood motionless and the sounds came nearer. At last I saw a black lump which I recognized as the head of a "tsenke." I covered it with my rifle instantly, and after the report the giant hog was kicking its last. Its mate was feeding near, but I did not shoot it, and let it dash past me. I then ran up to examine my first giant hog.

My men were very noisy in their hungry excitement about meat, nevertheless the second hog again appeared suddenly. I could not tell whether it bore any unfriendly intentions towards us or not, but yielding to my men's persuasion I fired. The bullet was acknowledged with a great squeal, as the thick undergrowth had prevented a clear aim, and so I gave it another shot.

I at once sent two men back to camp to fetch others to carry home the meat of the sow and cover up the hog's body with branches, as I wanted to prepare his hide for our museum. My men came home very late saying they had lost their way, and to my bitter disappointment brought home the meat of the hog, after having chopped up the hide irreparably.

The hog was a huge specimen. Nine men were needed to bring in the body even after it had been cut into pieces. The head was very much like a wart-hog's, but the warts on it were not as long, only broader. The tusks are also of the same shape as the wart-hog's, only they are shorter and thicker. The thickness of its nose was quite remarkable.

The giant hog, as I observed later, likes to live in caves formed by the protruding banks of forest brooks. I also found more traps set for "tsenke" in such places. Usually they would be easy to shoot early in the morning and late in the afternoon on the little forest openings covered with elephant grass. Fresh shoots of elephant grass and the roots of a kind of giant artichoke—I called it elephant artichoke—growing on these clearings seem to be their favourite food. According to the natives they do not do much harm in plantations.

My experience is that the "tsenke" is not aggressive at all. I once had to follow a wounded giant hog through the thickest undergrowth, where we had to creep along on all fours and often the wounded animal only jumped up at the last moment with a snort, but never turned against us. Even when at last we came upon it in the bed of a brook, from which it could not climb out, it showed no inclination to charge, and I finished it there with a bullet.

The natives—contrary to all my experiences—described it to me as an aggressive and dangerous animal. Natives usually hunt them with dogs and probably a "tsenke" brought to bay will turn against the pack and defend itself. Cuthbert Christy also mentions in his book, *Big Game and Pygmies*, that he was attacked twice by wounded giant hogs.

During my last trip I had not the luck to meet a "tsenke,"

although I had taken it for granted that I should be able to secure one or two specimens for the Hungarian National Museum in the Bugoma forest. But not only had the rinderpest decimated them in those parts even more than in the country to the west of Ruwenzori, but the lions had acquired the habit of hunting them. I also found lion spoors in the Bugoma forest in 1914, where I had never seen any before.

I once heard a hog bolting away in a swampy part of the forest, and we ourselves were compelled to fly as swiftly as possible from the spot because of the tiny red forest ants which covered us. These tiny ants are even more disagreeable than the frightful hunting ants, because it is easier to escape the caravans of the latter than the bites of these forest ants, which cover every twig, leaf and blade of grass. Their bite is not so painful as some kind of poisonous excrement they produce, which causes the sores to itch and burn intensely. The forests are full of all kinds of pests of this sort. Masses of tiny ticks will invade you and cover your body day after day, and these tiny parasites will get into most unexpected places, and on several occasions I woke in the night to find one established inside my nostril. In the Bugoma forest I came across another very nasty plague, a hairy green caterpillar. During my last excursion I did not see any more of these, so probably their season is in June and July. These creatures are generally on the underside of the leaves, and when touched they cause the same burning pain as nettles, and great restraint is needed to keep one from scratching. And if one does scratch, the pain grows worse and the swelling spreads.

It seems that the rinderpest has appreciably diminished the stock of giant hogs. According to Cuthbert Christy this is also the case in the Nandi forests, where buffalo and giant hog were nearly extinct after the great outbreak.

Natives prize the meat of the "tsenke" very highly, and I found that it was much more tasty than that of the wart-hog.

THE AARDVARK

If we ask European sportsmen how often they have seen a badger—the hermit of our European woods—there will be few who have observed the life of this very common nocturnal animal.

This merely shows how hard it is, even in our country, to sight any animal which lives the life of a recluse and goes about at night. How much harder must it be then to get an idea of what animals of similar habits look like and how they live in exotic territories. To secure a specimen of one is the greatest luck.

The aardvark (*Orycteropus wertheri*) is the real hermit of East Africa. Professor Matschie gave a very good description of this curious animal when he stated that the nose is like a pig's, its head that of an antbear, the feet those of an annelid, the body that of a kangaroo. It lives nearly exclusively on termits (white ants), and only leaves the labyrinth of holes it has dug for itself after dark and returns before daybreak. Never did I nor my men meet with a late aardvark hurrying home after dawn, though we sometimes had the luck to meet a porcupine.

The distribution of the aardvark is very wide. From Abyssinia to Cape Colony it may be found everywhere. In German East Africa Captain W. Werther discovered a variation in the family of aardvarks, and the type has been named after him. I have killed a few of these and also brought some live ones home to Budapest.

I tried to get one during my first trip, but never succeeded, although they were not rare at the foot of Kilimanjaro, as I could see from their tracks. There they were called by the men of the safari "mühanga."

On the shores of the Victoria Nyanza during my third expedition I often found the spoors of the aardvark. It walks on its claws and so the footprints it leaves are very much like those of a bustard. I have often shown the spoor of aardvark to Europeans, even to very experienced sportsmen, but none recognized them. Even native trackers and gunbearers knew very little about them.

Professor Schillings states in his book that the aardvark only goes out for nourishment in the dark of night and in the rainy season. Probably the aardvark is about more in this season, because it is then that the winged ants swarm and so an ant-hill gives it ample food. But it wanders about also in the dry season, as can be seen from its tracks. Besides, the first aardvark I got was shot on a moonlight night during the dry season.

This nocturnal stalk will live for ever in my memory. I was

taking my collection back to Shirati, where I celebrated my meeting with the District Commissioner and a settler, and of course we did not drink water. My two friends went to rest with fuddled heads, while I took my rifle and started for a stroll. I had told my friends that I would go out to shoot an aardvark, but they laughed at the idea.

Hardly had I got beyond the booths of the Indian merchants, when just as I was passing the wretched shambas of the askaris, I heard a peculiar grating noise. I knew instantly that a porcupine was coming towards me. But I did not hurt this second hermit of African nights, and through my field-glasses I could see quite clearly how he was digging out the sweet potatoes in the plantation.

When the porcupine had shuffled away panting and rattling, I stalked on and then sighted my long-wished-for aardvark near an ant-hill. But it had also seen me and hastened towards its underground fortress. I fired, but missed and then fired again. The second bullet hit the aardvark in the shoulder and finished it on the spot.

Hardly had I run up to my quarry to fasten my handkerchief on it as a protection against hyenas when I heard the alarm bell from the little fortress and the bugle sound the alarm.

I was now in a nice mess, as I had forgotten to let the guard know that I was going out hunting, although I knew quite well that two reports in the night was the alarm signal.

My crime weighed heavily on me as I returned to camp feeling almost indifferent about my precious bag. When I reached the boma the guard was already dispersing. The District Commissioner received me with indescribably polite words, for they had just managed to arouse him up from his heavy sleep. Of course I could not escape punishment, and I had to pay for the drinks they took after breakfast, which amounted to something like the price for a fine-maned lion's skin!

During breakfast I heard of the humorous scenes the alarm had provoked. Lamenting Indian merchants fled loaded with their goods into the boma, thinking that the Masai or Wagayas had fallen on them.

I got several aardvarks by digging them out of their burrows. It is hard work, because the underground tunnels and passages

Baboons shot on the Ngare Dowash

My tame Baboon, "Sheikh"

The pasha of the Bugoma baboon troop

OUTSKIRTS OF THE FOREST SCORCHED BY GRASS FIRES

A LITTLE CLEARING IN THE BUGOMA FOREST

BLACK MANGABE MONKEY FROM THE BUGOMA FOREST

COLOBUS MONKEY FROM THE BUGOMA FOREST

of their buildings are so complicated, very long and branching off in many directions; and when pursued the aardvark goes digging on and on.

It may be interesting to mention that I never saw the remains of an aardvark which had been killed by a beast of prey. I tried to feed my captured lions and hyenas with the meat of aardvarks, but they always refused it and would not even touch it, although my hyenas and jackals devoured anything in the way of meat and bones. I tried over and over again, but always with the same result. Probably the strong smell of musk makes them refuse it, though South African farmers like the greasy meat of this animals which weighs about 180 lbs.

Once—I could not say in which year it was—an order was issued in German East putting the aardvark on the list of vermin, and a reward of three rupees was even offered for every aardvark killed. I really do not believe that anybody got that money, for few men have killed any. But this case is a typical bureaucratic blunder which even the thorough Germans committed. For judging by the aardvark's huge claws, which he needs to dig with in the ant-hills, the creators of this order had erroneously supposed he could do a lot of damage in plantations.

THE PORCUPINE

The porcupine (*Hystrix africae-australis*) is more common in the countries through which I have travelled than the aardvark. The most certain signs of its presence are the long bristles it loses, which can be found on paths winding along on hill slopes, or on tracks beaten by game through the bush.

Natives know it well under the name of "noongoo," because it is a frequent visitor to their mohogo and potato shambas, where it does much damage. As a matter of fact it would be easy to prevent this damage, because the lowest thorn fencing would make it impossible for these short-legged animals to enter. The "noon-goo" lives exclusively on plants, especially on knobs and roots.

Natives catch them very often, for a porcupine surprised in the moonlight on an open place and far from his hole cannot escape. But as a rule they are caught in traps.

The sportsman will rarely meet a porcupine, unless he is an early riser or by chance comes across a late "noongoo." But if somebody will devote one or two moonlit nights to sitting up in a place where they are numerous, he will surely have the opportunity to observe their nightly rovings. The appearance of one is soon announced by the jingling and clanking of the bristles as they scrape up against each other; further, on its tail it has a feathery spike, forming a rattle, which it brings into action if scared or roused into emotion. Then its bristles, standing up on end, make it seem twice as large as it really is.

Most native tribes appreciate its rich, white meat. I myself think it is rather like roast goose. My men did not even skin the "noongoo," but only plucked him and scorched off the remainder of the bristles and hairs.

Beasts of prey, especially the great cats, are also fond of the "noongoo," though its bristles often wound them disagreeably. In the paws of my leopards and even lions I always found one or two broken "noongoo" thorns. Natives believe that it can shoot its bristles out at an enemy, wounding him gravely. But this, of course, is only a myth. One thing, nevertheless, is true, namely, that the porcupine can get very angry and—I observed this on my captives—in his wrath he shakes himself and then some bristles may fall out. This is probably the origin of the native belief.

We often found an aardvark and porcupine in one and the same burrow, for the porcupine will often take possession of the ardvark's hole, though he is a good digger himself, like all the burrow dwellers of the "pori," such as wart-hogs, and often also hyenas.

The last twenty years have brought many alterations in Africa. The vast continent has changed greatly since the War. Hundreds and thousands of tractors have transformed great wildernesses into fertile country. Many thousands of motor-cars speed over endless roads traversing some hundred miles daily where loaded safaris used to crawl along, not long ago, at a rate of 10 to 20 miles a day. The cars and the travellers in them know nothing about the "telekaza" marches and the killing thirst, when the safari rested during the day and crossed the waterless deserts in the night and early morning.

In this "changed Africa" the rain forests and the great papyrus swamps are still full of mystery. There still may exist bigger nocturnal animals, awaiting detection. Thus, for instance, in the subugos of Kenya, namely in the Nandi forest, natives speak about a curious animal that goes about at night and I was told that some settlers have also seen it, and there are many explorers who seriously believe in its existence. This mysterious animal is the "chimiset" or "Nandi bear," which according to natives lives on trees and resembles in many respects the apes.

Time will perhaps show us what the "chimiset" really is like, and it is possible that the description of it given by natives is not far from the truth. Then, probably, more will be found out about the animal life of the rain forests and the marshlands of the west. Then we shall know whether the water elephant of the great forest rivers, and the "water tiger," the descendant of giant lizards, as well as the "chimiset," are real animals; or whether they live only in the overheated imagination of natives, which is sometimes influenced by alcohol or the love of rousing sensation.

In the seclusion of a solitary hunting camp, or when sitting up over some bait, and more often still during my sleepless nights, I have thought about some sounds I have heard during the African nights. Sounds I could not place amongst any of those I knew, and even the greatest efforts and most minute investigation did not bring me any nearer to positive knowledge. The opinions of natives were also very divergent.

Once in the vicinity of Disappointment Camp on the Ngare Dowash I saw something just for an instant, which often returns to my memory, and I would give anything if I could get some certainty about what I saw there!—And then?

CHAPTER XXIV

Monkeys

GERMAN settlers in former German East Africa, when writing home, used to say that the "Spell of the Black Continent" held them fast. But when they were home-sick and tired of Africa, they turned against it, and called it "Monkeyland." This shows that Africa is well stocked with monkeys.

I will begin by telling of the most common kind of monkey (*Cercopithecus*).

The first mammal I set eyes on when landing in Mombasa was the common grey monkey (*Cercopithecus rufoviridis*), appearing and disappearing in the dark green luxuriant foliage of huge mango trees.

The "tumbiris" (the Swahili name for this monkey) are only found in the riverine and mimosa forests and on the outskirts of the rain forests.

They do a lot of harm to the shambas of natives. I have often watched them when, after a given signal, they would plunge off the tops of mimosa trees, and make a dash for the maize field underneath, leaving, of course, some of their number on guard. With thievish little hairy hands they would tear off the ripening ears of the plants and stuff as much of the milky grain as possible into their mouths. Whenever the sentinels left on the trees noticed something unusual and gave warning, the whole lot would leap back with shrieks of terror into the safety of the mimosa trees.

Women and children guarding the shambas did not alarm them and they continued stealing before their eyes, but if a man appeared on the scene, especially when he was accompanied by some jackal-like dogs, then panic came over the band and they were very quick in escaping.

Leopards are best signalled by the "tumbiris," and for many of my leopards I have to thank them.

Near my Letema camp the giant trees of the forest hang across the Daryama River on both sides, so that the monkeys had a splendid bridge spanning it. When a troop of monkeys frolicked on these overhanging branches, there would soon appear one or two triangular heads of crocodiles on the surface of the water, hoping that some of the quarrelling monkeys would fall into the river. But in a moment the monkeys would notice them and then began the wildest imprecations and shaking of branches over the heads of the crocodiles.

These antics never failed to amuse me, and they were still funnier when, instead of the "tumbiris," a troop of baboons crossed overhead.

In the district of Kilimanjaro and westwards to the Victoria Nyanza the blue monkey (*Cercopithecus albogularis*) lives in great numbers in the darker forests. These monkeys have beautiful fur and are somewhat larger than the "tumbiris," but less lively and do comparatively little harm to the shambas of natives. At one time fashion wanted its fur and recently game laws have restricted the numbers which may be shot.

Round the Victoria Nyanza one can find the red-tailed monkey (*Cercopithecus schmidti*), which is very like the blue monkey, but differs from its eastern relatives in having a heart-shaped white spot on his nose. The more we go to the west the more often we find this fine animal in the rain forests, where many varieties of monkey exist.

In the forests of Kilimanjaro and the Meru Mountains colobus monkeys (*Colobus caudatus*) were plentiful in the days of my first African trip, though they have been eagerly hunted for their beautiful fur. With their velvety black backs and long white manes hanging down on both sides and covering their bodies as with a cloak, and their long, white, flag-like tails, they are the most beautiful of all monkeys. The most remarkable peculiarity about them is that on their hands they have got only four fingers, the thumb being quite rudimentary and lacking.

A favourite subject for discussion round the camp-fire of a

hunting safari is the natural history of animals their master—or former master—has killed or observed during the trip. A "safiri" (man who travelled far) will also ask questions if his master is a beginner, such as: "Where are the mammæ of the 'noongoo' or the elephant?" Should the answer be that they are in the usual place, all will burst into laughter; for the "noongoo" has them on her sides and the elephant between her two front legs.

"Which is the monkey without a thumb?" was also one of these ticklish questions.

The colobus, or "mbega," as the men of the safari call them, live in the tops of the largest trees of the forest. They come down very rarely and avoid all cultivated land, which is why they never do any mischief in human cultivations.

They feed mostly on young twigs, leaves, and wild fruit. In the daytime they are rather silent animals, so that it is hard to detect a troop in the tree-tops. An alarmed troop of "mbegas" seem to fly along with their white tails floating behind them like ever so many white flags. After a short rush they will suddenly hide behind a thick branch or a knot of creepers and then it really wants an experienced eye to find them, especially in districts where they have been much hunted. Where they have not yet made the acquaintance of man they will peep curiously down out of their hiding-places, but their curiosity is not of the insolent kind that baboons show.

The presence of these otherwise silent monkeys is betrayed by their morning and evening chorus, which is one of the most characteristic sounds of the African jungle, beginning with a suppressed "ro-roo-rooo," and getting louder and louder, until it stops suddenly, only to begin anew. They repeat this concert till the sun is up above the trees, and in the evening they go on singing in this peculiar way till sunset.

The beautiful fur of these monkeys became fashionable and many have been killed. Natives also wanted them, as these furs were used for their war fineries. The "monge" (a decoration round the ankles) of the Masai and other tribes imitating the Masai were made from colobus skins.

English game laws protect them very stringently, but unfortunately only against the white man's weapons, for it is impossible to protect them against the uncontrollable hunting tribes, such as the Wandorobos.

West of Kilimanjaro another variety of the colobus, the *Colobus palliatus*, is known. This monkey has shorter white hair on its sides and on the end of its tail it has only a white bunch of hair.

I found this colobus monkey, which has many sub-species in the western and north-western forests, very often even in quite insignificant riverine forests. They were numerous in the Balangeti forest, though natives hunted them eagerly with poisoned arrows and exchanged the skins for goods with Masai and Wagaya.

In these regions natives hunt them with very light arrows made out of reed, in the end of which is stuck a short piece of wood, pointed at both ends and dipped in poison. This was a very primitive weapon in comparison to the other arrows they used on other animals or in war. When I asked why it was so, they answered that too many got lost in the dense foliage.

It is interesting to note that I often heard the "ro-roo-rooo" of the colobus monkeys from the vast papyrus marshes of the Mara River and according to natives they were numerous on the few sickly mimosa trees that grew in the more dry parts of the swamps. In papyrus swamps I have even seen them swinging themselves about on papyrus stalks.

The young colobus monkeys are quite white at first, their faces alone being black and the black hair on their backs comes out gradually later.

Monkeys are no fit object for hunting. Their shooting is no sport, and their death is so human that for a good time you will not want to shoot one again.

Sometimes shooting baboons (*Papio*) may be classed in a different category, though the death of an old baboon, especially after the wicked expression of its face is softened by death, is even more human than that of smaller monkeys. Of course if one sees the damage they do to the shambas of natives, and even to the plantations of white man, these feelings may become changed.

A wandering explorer must try to be on the best terms possible with the natives, who can be of great help to him in his scientific researches, and so I often used my rifle to save them from these disastrous monkey raids. The monkeys which I shot, and which were not needed for museums, were used as leopard baits.

In certain parts of Uganda—for instance, round the Albert Nyanza—the coffee-planters are fierce enemies of baboons and usually engage native hunters to prevent them from devastating the plantations.

The life of baboons differs from that of other monkeys in that they spend the greater part of the day wandering about on the ground, whereas other monkeys spend it in the tops of the trees. Baboons spend the night in trees, and if some enemy approaches they also take to trees during the day.

In a troop of baboons, which will sometimes count some hundred head, there are about half a dozen old males, compared with which the others seem quite small. These big males rule over the whole tribe with great severity and cruelty and the fangs of such old "pashas" are stronger and longer than those of their worst enemy, the leopard.

A baboon troop is very noisy as they emit very varied sounds. The old males give deep growls like those of the leopard (which even sometimes misled my well-trained ears), and these growls always dominate the barking of the others and the screams of the little ones.

When the troop of baboons invades a plain, catching grasshoppers and other insects, they always leave vigilant sentinels situated on different trees or rocks. On the whole they are very quick and they leave nothing unnoticed. They like grasshoppers, but eat anything they come across. Every bird's nest, either full of eggs or young birds, will be emptied by them. They get hold of smaller mammals and it is not impossible that they kill and devour dwarf antelopes also, as described in some books written by African hunters. Naturally their chief nourishment consists of fruits, roots, and fresh shoots.

They are incredibly insolent thieves and know quite well from what distance natives can harm them. They take little notice of the womenfolk's shouts and cries and will even turn menacingly against women and children on guard. Theodore Roosevelt mentions in his book that R. J. Cunninghame, the

AN ANT-HILL

PAGODA-SHAPED ANT-HILL IN THE BUGOMA FOREST

Tchego shot in the Bugoma forest for the Hungarian National Museum

JOHANNA AND JUMA WITH THE TCHEGO

THE TREE OF THE GREY PARROTS IN THE BUGOMA FOREST

My collecting camp on the Ruvana plains

well-known African hunter and scientist, had seen two women killed by baboons in Uganda. In that country baboons had become too audacious and kept the whole village in terror. The villagers had come to Cunninghame asking him to save them from this plague, as not only had the two women been killed, but some children also had been mauled by baboons. Cunninghame spent a week in that village and killed enough of them to frighten the rest away.

I have never experienced anything of the sort myself, but I learned how impudent baboons can be in 1914, in a village near the Bugoma forest, where I wanted to put up a collecting camp. Famine, caused by the great drought, and by raiding elephants, had come over that part of the country, and the poor natives, who had lived for weeks on nothing but roots, could hardly wait for the crops to ripen. They had learned by sad experience that they must cultivate larger areas, and so big green fields of potato and native beans stood at the disposal of the troops of baboons. Baboons especially relish green beans. The Wanyoros living there are no bowmen, and the baboons knew exactly how near they could venture to keep clear of the spears thrown at them.

When I arrived the natives received me and implored me to help them, and of course I promised to do my best, as I was chiefly dependent on their friendship.

I warned my guide to be very cautious and we hastened towards the shamba, which was filled with the chorus of monkey voices; but my guide said that there was no reason whatever for caution, as the baboons would not be frightened by our approach. I could not believe him, and all the less because a crowd of villagers had come with me to seek revenge.

But my guide was right. The troop was not more than 60 to 70 yards away from us and went on calmly ravaging a bean plantation on the border of the forest. My appearance only caused a little uneasiness, or rather curiosity, and they kept on looking at me, while they seemed to give me all kinds of selected baboon epithets. Probably they had not seen a white man before.

They only began to realize danger when the third veteran had dropped off the tree-trunk he was seated on, never to rise again. The next time I came they showed greater respect and hurriedly left the place.

It is not pleasant to follow on the track of an alarmed troop of baboons through the thick undergrowth, for the foliage is smeared over with their nasty-smelling excrement.

These apes soon recognize fire-arms in countries where they have been hunted by white men. I even noticed this on my first trip, for when I was out catching butterflies I could shoulder the handle of the net without even giving them a start—on the contrary, they grew more impudent still. But when it was really the barrel of a rifle, they would not gnash their teeth at me with hair standing up on end any more, but scamper away pell-mell.

Baboons running over ground hasten on in a one-sided gallop, turning their heads back from side to side all the time just as hyenas do.

We once had a very peculiar experience with baboons caused by an optical illusion. First Bálint Fernbach, then I, and finally the whole safari was deceived by it. . . .

In the early morning we had rather a ticklish adventure with buffaloes. Mr. Bálint Fernbach had killed an infuriated old cow not three paces off, as she came thundering down on us. I had followed a wounded buffalo through the luxuriant undergrowth of the "subugo" and woke an old bull rhino, which came at me in great rage. I fired at him when he was but eight yards away, and as I had no clear opening through which to take a good aim, my bullet struck the skull, but not the brain. The rhino passed me bleeding profusely and masses of blood were splashed all over the bushes, as is often the case with a head-shot. I knew that it would be useless to follow, but my men urged me to do so and so I went on for half a day over swamps and wooded, undulating country. I only returned late in the afternoon to camp—tired to death. While I was taking a late meal, Mr. Fernbach told me that after his return to camp the men reported that a herd of buffalo was grazing on the opposite slope. He thought it was funny that the herd consisted mostly of calves with only one or two incredibly large bulls amongst them. This occurred in the hills of Ndassekera on the western side of the Great Rift Valley, where it was generally foggy, and there was a slight veil of mist hanging over the landscape at the time.

We were taking our afternoon tea, when our men shouted "kifaru," and we saw an old rhino bull trotting over a little clearing near camp, so we set out to follow him. Coming to the spot where he had entered the forest, my men pointed in another direction, saying "ollarok" (buffalo).

I sent word to Mr. Fernbach, but he was too tired and did not come. I had to hurry on, for light was failing rapidly, and running down the hill-side I saw that we should have to cross a swamp, so I took my Zeiss "Silvamar" glasses up again, to have another good look at the buffaloes and stalking conditions. But what did I see? One of the buffaloes climbed a rock and there began scratching itself like a baboon. It was this troop of baboons that Mr. Fernbach and the safari had held to be buffaloes, and this explained why he thought he had seen mostly young calves and only some very big bulls, as the old baboon veterans are very much larger than the rest.

When I told my men what a mistake they had made they would not believe me, but later, when all the apes had installed themselves on protruding rocks, they had to give in. Coming home I told Mr. Fernbach and we discussed the question and came to the conclusion that the mist had brought about this optical illusion; but as the natives had been deceived too, there was no reason to feel ashamed. Our men, however, did not get over the episode as we did, for after having talked about it over many camp-fires, they agreed that it had been "devil's doing" (*khazi ya sheitani*), which usually solved every problem.

Tribes imitating the Masai, and later on even the Masai themselves, wore enormous shakos made out of monkey skins, and this is why old baboons were very valuable. Formerly these head decorations were made out of lion manes and only the lion killer had the right to wear it. But time has altered good morals even in Africa, and even the proudest Masai "elmorans" wear "lion's mane" made out of the fur of baboons. Imitation furs —*tout comme chez nous*—can be found even in the heart of Africa!

Many native stories are told about baboons, and natives believe that they have once been human, but as they refused to work and would not give up stealing, they took up quarters in the wilderness and turned into "nyanyis" baboons.

If one of our men was very awkward or forgetful and we called him names like buffalo or rhino, he seemed greatly pleased and honoured. But if he was called "nyanyi" or "tumbiri," he would be deeply hurt.

Natives often brought young monkeys as a present or for sale, and I usually had one or two in camp. The baboon baby with its little wrinkled old face is a very comical creature. They are easily tamed and become attached very soon, but they can never be taught cleanliness in the rooms and will always steal things.

I had one grown-up baboon with my safari. This ape had once belonged to a small garrison, and the askaris had taught it various little tricks. I still remember the first impression we made on Wazanak territory. The Wazanaks, who lived on the eastern shore of the Victoria Nyanza, were a mountain tribe with a bad reputation. I intended to create a great effect when first appearing before their invariably drunken sultani, so I promoted three of the best-dressed porters to the rank of gunbearers. They strode along behind me proudly, shouldering my fire-arms—but with slight feelings of awe—while by my side, carrying my Winchester-Automatic, came my fourth gunbearer, the tame baboon. At this sight, soberness came upon the sultani and his court, and I do not think that a dozen askaris could have caused greater respect than my baboon gunbearer.

In the rocky mountains of Danakil Land the collared baboon (*Papio hamadryas*) is common. I observed that these apes helped their wounded along, a thing I have never witnessed with any other variety of the monkey tribe. I was told that common baboons will also do this, but I never saw an instance of it myself. I was also told that the old males will even frighten away a leopard and thus rescue a comrade from its jaws. When baboons are tramping about on the ground they carry their babies on their backs and are regularly ridden by them, whereas all other monkey babies will hold on to the hairy breasts of their mothers.

In the western parts of East Africa I collected a few different kinds of mangabey (*Cercocebus*). They have very long legs and

WASHASHIS FEASTING ON ROAST ZEBRA

A YOUNG RHINO, TWO MONTHS AFTER CAPTURE

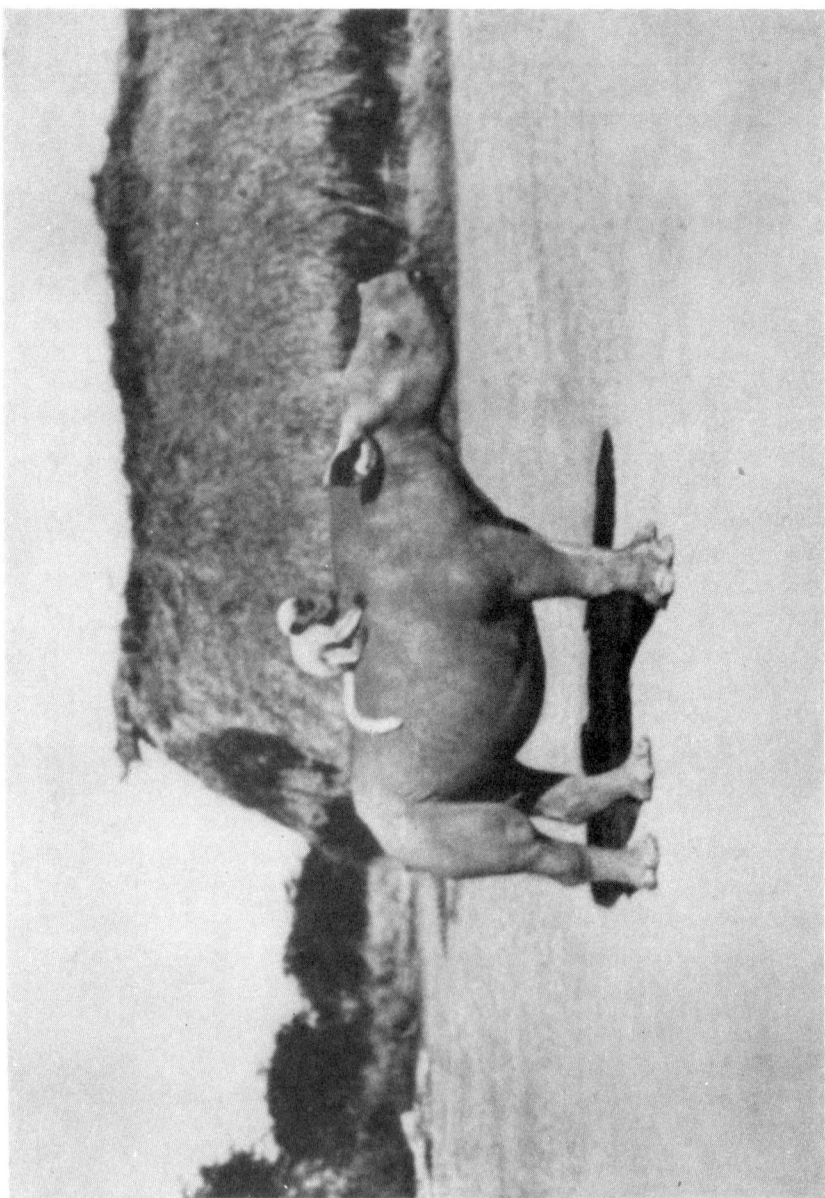

THE SAME RHINO THREE MONTHS AFTER CAPTURE

very long tails and have the same habits as meercats. On old males long, mane-like hair over the shoulders is very characteristic.

In 1914 I collected a very interesting and perfectly black specimen of mangabey (*Cercocebus albigena ituricus*) which I only saw in the Bugoma forest. But my fine collection became a victim of the War.

During my last Uganda trip, however, I again got three of these for the Hungarian National Museum.

The most interesting of all monkeys are the anthropoids, the true apes. It was only on my two last trips that I had an opportunity of meeting one kind, the "tchego" or black-faced chimpanzee (*Anthropopithecus troglodytes*).

Apes live in East Africa's western districts in the prolongation of the Congo forest ranges. For a long time it was thought that the largest ape, the gorilla, lived only in the forests of the western coast, till in 1903 Captain v. Béringe killed the first East African gorilla on the slopes of the Sabinjo volcano, near the Kivu Lake. This mountain gorilla was called *Gorilla beringeri* after him, and was much larger than its western relations, differing from them also in many other respects.

The mountain gorilla cannot be found everywhere in Africa. Until recently it has been seen only in the bushy forests of Lake Kivu's volcanic surroundings and in the forests on the western shores of Lake Tanganyika. Cuthbert Christy states in his work *Big Game and Pygmies* that the Ituri forest is also the home of the mountain gorilla, because he saw two gorillas there, which probably belonged to the *Gorilla beringeri* species.

Unfortunately I have never hunted in regions where they are to be found and consequently never met with mountain gorillas, this most interesting of all apes. The chief object of my fourth trip was to observe apes, and this is why I went to Uganda, i.e. to Unyoro. When at last I was in a position to observe the lives and doings of tchegos day after day, the outbreak of the War put a stop to all my activities. So I could not realize my hopes of observing the tchego and gorilla and could not secure any for museum purposes.

During our last trip we came very near the gorilla ranges,

which have since been allotted to the Belgian Congo, but again, owing to unexpected circumstances, we had to change our plans.

Former explorers have described the gorilla as a wild and very ferocious animal which would have to be given the first place amongst big and dangerous game. Now that we know so much more about apes, especially about the gorilla, we know that the thrilling stories written about it are merely tales, and that the powerful, evil-faced ape (an old male gorilla will weigh about 400 to 500 lbs.) is of a peaceful disposition. Hunting literature never mentions any European hunter who has been killed by gorillas. That one or two natives have fallen victims to them is probable, but surely the gorilla is not the terrible animal described by the first European gorilla killer, Paul du Chaillu. The clue, however, to these descriptions, as C. Akeley mentions, is that du Chaillu's publisher is said to have returned his manuscript twice, not finding it sufficiently exciting.

The black-faced chimpanzee has a wider distribution in East Africa, and on the outskirts of the Congo forests it can be found in many parts, though it is not common. In the "kibiras" of Uganda, strictly speaking, I never came across tchegos, and the natives indicated the Bugoma and Budongo forest as the real home of "kiteras." ("Kitera" is the Bunyoro name for tchego; the men of the safaris call him "soko" or "sokomoto.")

I found the first signs of the kiteras in a narrow riverine forest on the bank of an insignificant rivulet, but at the time I did not know that the spoor I found was that of a chimpanzee. On the trees quite close to each other I saw nests of birds of prey, and was astonished, because birds of prey never live in flocks as far as I know, and my men did not enlighten me as to what they were. Probably they did not know themselves that the nests we saw were flat couches made out of branches by kiteras. This place was near a coffee plantation and a long way from the Budongo forest, a fact which helped to confuse me. I was the guest of my friend the planter, and one morning when his old Nyoro night guardian reported that he had heard the cries of kiteras I would not believe it. Then I had to leave and it was not until later, one or two months after this had happened, that I found out that what I had mistaken for nests of birds of prey were the sleeping-places of a little troop of chimpanzees. There must have been only females and young ones in this troop because the males require larger nests and never build them up as high as these were. So the old watchman had been right.

I had already been camped for a long time near the Bugoma forest, when one day, at dawn, I heard the distant cries of kiteras. It is hard to describe them as they sound more like human cries than a chorus of animals. Hearing them made a deep impression upon me. Later I had opportunity enough to hear these cries, mostly towards sunset and again at daybreak, nearly at the same time as the chorus of colobus monkeys. Sometimes the "goma" (dance-music or song) of the tchegos is accompanied by drumming, because they beat mouldy tree-trunks with the palms of their hands. This drumming always means an outbreak of emotions, I suppose.

Their spoor has taught me that they spend the greater part of the day on the ground and not on trees. When running away they will also rush along the ground and rarely take to trees, especially the old ones. At they run along they use their hands to part the foliage and bushes, and it is very rare for them to proceed on all fours. This I could see very well in the marshy riverine forests which were overgrown with wild date palms. It was there also that I made out clearly that the chimpanzee does not step on its open palms, but on the outside finger-knuckles of the half-closed hand.

They feed mostly on wild fruit and young shoots. I believe that the fresh shoots of the wild date palms attract them at certain seasons. They keep away from cultivated land and consequently do no harm in shambas.

Male veterans grow sometimes to an enormous size, and even an experienced hunter will find it difficult to distinguish the male tchego from a gorilla in the depth of the forest. The foot-prints of these old veterans can also sometimes be quite discon-certing. Once, for instance, I was following a troop of tchegos through a swampy wild date thicket in a narrow forest adjacent to the Bugoma forest. In this noisy troop of apes there were some old males and had I not read Captain v. Wiese's book on tchegos and known their huge measurements from the book by the Prince of Mecklenburg, I should surely have mistaken them for gorilla tracks.

The kiteras lead a roving life in the Bugoma forest. They will be missing from one part of the forest for months, then they will suddenly appear there and camp there for days, as long as the ripe fruit or the fresh shoots of certain trees have not disappeared.

They usually live in smaller or larger troops, and veterans are sometimes alone or in pairs. The largest troop I have ever seen comprised in all about sixty to eighty animals.

Their nests, or rather couches, are green twigs and branches carelessly put together, probably only for one night's use. I have also noticed that they made similar resting-places for the day. These beds were in the forest, and generally on young trees, and the old males did not put them up higher than 9 to 12 feet above the ground.

In the year 1914, when I had finished the building of my elephant grass castle on the outskirts of the Bugoma forest, two kiteras always made their nests on trees round my camp. Probably they felt interested in our doings or were attracted by the great illumination, for sometimes even hurricane lamps would shoot out rays of light from my house.

Curiosity is a very characteristic trait of all monkeys, and kiteras are no exception. The first one I ever saw was peeping at me from between two branches. The almost human face showed such curiosity, that it seemed to ask me: "What sort of creature are you?" For more than fifteen minutes we stood staring at each other, and then, wanting to see how it moved away, I walked up and shouted at it. It let itself slip slowly down at first, then swung from branch to branch, and when it gained the ground it scampered away and disappeared in the dense undergrowth.

To-day apes are protected in the English colonies and a licence to shoot one for scientific purposes can only be obtained with difficulty. When I was in Africa the last time a game licence entitled its owner to shoot one tchego, but now this has been prohibited. This is quite right as the tchegos are harmless animals, and there is no reason whatever for killing them, especially as such killing seems so akin to murder.

OUR BIG RHINO FASTENED WITH STOUT ROPES

MY BIGGEST RHINO BULL

ESCORTING THE BIG RHINO BACK TO CAMP

SAFARI CARRYING THE LOOP-NETS

SETTING UP LOOP-NETS

I only killed two chimpanzees. One before the War and the other during my last trip in 1926. The skin of this one I brought home, and it is waiting to be mounted for the National Museum by our able taxidermist, S. Ory. This experience of mine with the tchego deserves a short account.

On my return from West Nile Province I stayed for a month to visit the Bugoma forest, where the War had surprised me in 1914. The sole purpose of this extra trip was to collect a few interesting animals for the Hungarian National Museum, as my collections of 1914 were lost.

Soon I saw that the results of the trip would not come up to our expectations. My time was short, and ample time is essential for collecting in the forests. Circumstances seemed altogether against me on this occasion. It was just the season of the cotton crops. Big and small were transporting cotton to the Kiziranfumbi cotton market. (In 1914 there had been no idea as yet of cotton-growing in these parts.) Natives were not in need of money for the moment, and so I could only get guides and porters with the greatest difficulty.

It was especially hard to get guides. My guide of 1914, whom I mentioned in the chapter on elephants, and who had been bitten by a poisonous snake and had a mutilated hand, was still alive, and I succeeded in finding him on March 10th, after I had induced another native to show me the path leading to his new hut. But it was hard to come to any arrangement with this curious fellow. He ran away as we came up to the hut, because at the outbreak of the War he had been the first to desert my camp and had also taken some things along with him. Now, he thought, I had turned up only to avenge his unfaithfulness. At last he calmed down and accepted two shillings from me. But his conscience seemed very painful, for I could see his heart beating under the black skin in suppressed excitement. Then he simulated lameness, and limping along before us, took me to the site of my former camp, which I should never have been able to find by myself. Twelve years is a very long time! The elephant grass fires and twelve years' rainy seasons affect a place so much that it becomes quite unrecognizable.

He took me to a place I remembered vaguely, where there was

a narrow peninsula-like space covered with elephant grass in the forest. There he lifted the matted grass and exposed a reddish strip of burnt clay. These were the only remains of my once so stately home, the best collecting palace I have ever built for myself. I was taken prisoner out of this magic spot, where I could shoot giant hogs at every stroll, where I heard the concert of tchegos every night and knew that two record bull elephants were near, which I could have got, had the order for my arrest come twenty-four hours later.

Five and a half years' captivity had started on this spot. I was overwhelmed by disagreeable memories and retraced my steps hurriedly. As we passed by the kirongozi's hut, he left me without a word. I did not stop to look at him, but said that if he had looked me up in Europe I would have killed an ox in his honour, while he did not even present his old friend "rafiki" with one or two eggs. These reproaches made seemingly little impression on the man, but to my greatest surprise he suddenly turned and ran back to me, forgetting his limp, and presented me with a stick carved in Arab fashion. So peace seemed restored between us and he sometimes guided me in the forest—though not very willingly—where, so he said, he seldom went, as the setting of traps had been severely prohibited. Of course trapping was no longer of much use, as the giant hogs had been decimated by the rinderpest.

On March 19th I started for a collecting excursion under the guidance of my one-armed kirongozi. It was late in the morning, for at dawn it had been pouring, as the rainy season had begun. I found curiously-shaped ant-hills on the border of the forest and inside it also. They were shaped like Chinese pagodas and I took some photos of them and then we went westwards over unknown tracks. The usually silent forest seemed full of sounds. I heard a small animal scuttle away, and the kirongozi said he had seen a "kadjodjo," which means little elephant. I scolded him for not having called my attention to it before. This little animal interested me greatly, but I never could catch or kill one.

I made my men tell anything they knew about the little "kadjodjo," and as far as I could make out it was the hero shrew or elephant shrew. Meanwhile rain started again in large heavy drops. When it stopped a curious chaos of voices was heard. All my men said it came from kiteras, but I had never heard anything like it from a chimpanzee.

Of course we hurried in the direction of the sounds at such speed that I cannot remember having ever felt so hot and so short of breath as I did then, except perhaps when hunting situtunga in the Lugogo swamps or when I shot my last elephant. We lost the direction sometimes, and then when the sounds struck our ears again, we continued following them. My gun-bearer Johanna was so excited that he forgot to leave the signs we used to make when tracking and ran on in front. I think the zeal he showed was chiefly because he wanted to make up for having been drunk during the past few weeks. Again rain fell, but we seemed to get nearer to those sounds, which some-times seemed to come from man. My one-armed guide did not like the pace at which we were going, for he, being an expert, always went slowly through unknown forest, breaking branches and marking trees on the old elephant path we usually followed. But at this pace it was quite impossible to take these necessary precautions.

The kiteras had stopped on trees on which grows a mandarin-shaped and coloured, but hard-skinned wild fruit. Under these trees lay empty cores of the devoured fruits. After a chase of three hours we came up quite close to where the kiteras had settled. Every tree was crowded with them. The shrieking, yelling, growling and drumming was terrific. Another shower came down and the noise made by the apes became louder.

At last I could see some of the troop. They were mostly females and young animals. Their movements were quite different to the movements of monkeys. I did not see the daring swings and bounces which the colobus and others take when flying from one tree to the other. The tchegos walk along on thicker branches on their hind legs, keeping their balance with their arms or sometimes holding on to leaves.

At last I saw one of them which seemed much larger than the rest as he looked down at me curiously. I recognized him for a male and shot him in the chest. A frightful discord of voices followed! I was howled at from all sides in terror-stricken and furious tones and the angry drumming was redoubled. The storm was raging and rain gushed down. I saw the wounded tchego drop off the tree, clutching at the branches in his fall, and then I also saw a very old male sitting on the crown of a young tree quite close to me and realized that I had been over-hasty in shooting. When this huge animal, which was nearly as big as a gorilla, saw me, he came off the tree with a swing, tearing off nearly half of the tree's crown and scampered away over the ground. I could not shoot because I had already exhausted my licence with one tchego.

I followed them for a good while yet, for I wanted to note their doings while running away. I came to the conclusion that the old animals ran along the ground, while the young ones took to trees in their escape. We discovered one or two quite young members of the troop, babies in fact, on the very tops of the trees, hanging on to a branch, quite motionless. My kirongozi said that the kiteras leave the babies behind when they escape and come back to fetch them after the danger is over. Had I asked for a special licence, I could have caught these young ones by shooting the branches off the trees, but as it was I could do nothing more.

The one I killed was a young but quite full-grown male. Its great lips fell and I felt so sorry for it when I came to look into its human face and held its human hand.

To my greatest regret it was pouring all the time, so it was impossible to take a picture of the dead tchego, for in such dark forests I had to take time-exposures even in bright weather. So we shouldered our quarry and doubled back on our tracks. After going for an hour the kirongozi announced that he had no idea where we were or which was the right direction! My compass had been stolen from me on my West Nile trip, so we had to face one or even more nights in the forest. And still another bad surprise was in store for us. My boy had forgotten to put the matches into my wallet. I always used to look through it before starting, but this time I had been forgetful myself.

My kirongozi bemoaned our fate and I hoped that the sky would brighten to give us a chance of seeing where the sun stood and perhaps take a few pictures. But the rain went on without stopping and we tramped on at random. We crossed a brook and a swampy spot. Here we came across a broken twig and then my kirongozi was reassured and knew where we were.

Before dark we arrived back in camp. The clouds had lifted a little so that the last rays of the setting sun enabled me to take some photos. I then took the measurements of the tchego by the light of a lamp and my men skinned it.

The tchego is covered with a thick fur overcloak, and no wonder, for the forest nights, especially in the higher mountain regions, are very cool and sometimes the thermometer will sink below freezing-point. I thought of the hothouse air in the menageries in which our apes at home must live, and was not surprised that they die of lung complaints, because these artificially heated glass palaces must hold the germs of every disease.

I thought it curious during my last trip that we saw no tchegos in the great Baamba forest which is connected with the Ituri forest, whereas the Ituri forest itself, as well as the forest on the Ruwenzori Mountains to the west, is full of them. I could not interrogate the Baambas well enough as to the reason for this; whether their forests had always been devoid of apes, or if they had only disappeared lately. It may be that sleeping sickness has done away with them as it has decimated the tribe of Wambutis, the dwarf hunters of the Baamba forest. This is a daring supposition, I know; but why impossible?

That the inhabitants of the forest have made up legends about the apes is not surprising. It is a general belief that the veteran male chimpanzee will steal young girls if he gets the chance. I asked Johanna how and when this had happened for the last time? He answered that in his country (Uganda) it only occurred in times long passed, but in the Belgies (Belgian Congo) it still happens every day. He seemed offended when I risked a joke that probably the tchegos ceased to steal their girls because the Uganda Government had prohibited it. His reproachful eye seemed to say: "You, sir, are always joking!"

Another belief is that gorillas and chimpanzees will come round camp-fires and warm themselves on chilly nights. The raconteurs could never agree whether the apes kindled the fire and put logs of dry wood on it, or not. Some said yes and some said no; the latter using the argument that the fact that they did not do it was the proof that they were not quite like man.

All agreed that kiteras are folk of honour, never stealing anything, and not like baboons and other monkeys. If tchegos do visit a plantation they will at the most take but one tomato each, and their leaders see that none of them takes more.

As my men were skinning the tchego I noticed that Johanna was scraping the ribs off very carefully, and I found out that when carried next one's body, the ribs are an effective medicine, and that the Wanyoros prize this "dawa" highly, and would pay for it well. So my Johanna assured for himself a little profit.

CHAPTER XXV

Capturing Wild Animals

I CALLED my collecting camp on the Ngare Dowash "Camp Disappointment," because so many hopes failed to materialize there. It is true that I could have made no more perfect collection of birds in any other part of East Africa, for a greater variety of species could not be found anywhere else; yet I was most disappointed, for I expected more, especially in the way of sport.

Even so, I left the spot with a heavy heart after having spent a few months there, for I knew that with better men I could have done good work. I gazed at my deserted camp with feelings of sadness, for I realized that in one or two days all our buildings would be burned down by the Wandorobos. I could never gain the friendship of this tribe in this region. If I made out some Wandorobos through my field-glasses, I shouted all kinds of enticing promises in their native language, but without result; for they fled and hid like hunted game of the jungle.

I definitely left the camp on November 20th, 1909, and headed towards Shirati. Owing to the sudden death of Bálint Fernbach more than a hundred porters were available, so I engaged them at once and began to organize our safari for a fresh trip.

That same day I was met by the man whom we had sent for our mail and amongst other letters from home I had one from an old friend, Dr. Aladár Kovách, who told me that the Zoological Gardens at Budapest were going to be reorganized by Dr. Adolph Lendl and would be opened in May, 1912. As a member of the new management he asked me to bring them some specimens of East African animals. I was overjoyed to get this commission, for I love nursing young animals, and always had a few tame ones about the camp.

Of course I could only think of commencing operations after

the hunting expedition we had planned was over, but I immediately forwarded my application for the licence necessary for capturing game.

Although my outfit was entirely lacking in the most essential items, containing nothing else but two cases of tins of condensed milk for baby animals, beginner's luck smiled upon me, and the first animal I caught was the most valuable I could have hoped for in the neighbourhood of the Ruvana Plains.

At the beginning of August I received information that a few rhinos had been observed in the thick bush-covered slopes of the Tyamriho Mountains, three hours' march from our camp, and I heard later that these rhinos had actually knocked over a couple of men who were marking out trees for the building of an Adventist mission.

So I set out with the idea of shooting rhinos which could then be prepared for museums, not even dreaming of catching one alive.

After pitching our tents I had a quick lunch, as I wanted to do some scouting, but was still drinking coffee when Pandasaro came rushing up. Snatching up my rifle I ran to meet him, for I was certain that a rhino had been seen. While we ran along together, he whispered that while he was putting up a leopard trap he had heard the sound of a rhino feeding.

Very cautiously we stole up to the spot he indicated, when I, too, heard the loud chewing and masticating of a rhino feeding. A dry branch cracked under the weight of my foot and I heard its angry growling snort. Pandasaro, as quick and clever as a monkey, fled backwards to hide behind the trunk of a tree, holding the lowest branch within reach with one hand, so as to be able to swing himself up at the first sign of danger.

I pointed my rifle in the direction of the snort but without being able to see anything. So I waited in suspense, but as the rhino did not get our wind, it was reassured and went on breaking off branches and eating them.

I crept up unobserved and was not more than 2 or 3 yards from him when he saw me, and would have gone for me; but as I had seen his head a solid bullet did its duty.

The report of the rifle and the crash with which the enormous

OLD WILDEBEEST BULL CAUGHT IN A LOOP-NET
The native on the right is holding a captured jackal

CARRYING TO CAMP A JIMELA CALF, CAUGHT IN A LOOP-NET

ARRIVAL AT THE PADDOCK

MY FIRST CAPTURED WILDEBEEST CALF, WITH ZEBU CALVES

THE SAME, 1½ YEARS LATER

This animal lived for some time in the Zoo at Budapest

IN THE PADDOCK.   WILDEBEEST AND AN ELAND CALF

body came down was followed by the frightened shrieks of monkeys and the red-feathered turacos, which uproar was followed again by the great quiet of the jungle. Only the rhino's head twitched from one side to the other with convulsive movements: this was all that could be heard.

The men I had called up at once began to skin it with great skill, and went on working late into the night. The heavy hide could only be brought to camp next morning, where they continued scraping it. After a week's hard work it was prepared so well that it could be made life-like again for any museum at any time.

In the afternoon I strolled towards the other part of the forest, although without the slightest hope of seeing anything. But I had hardly advanced more than a few hundred yards when a furious snort from the burnt buffalo grass made us jump.

The wind was wrong, so I made a big detour and tried to crawl up to the spot from which the snort had come. It was not easy because we could find no tracks. The rhino had come in from the plain, and this being down wind, we could not take advantage of the spoor. While my men were dispersed and looking for the tracks, I heard some scuffling in their direction, and running up to them, found Pandasaro perched on a thorny mimosa tree, while the cool-headed Sindano was scraping the thorns off another mimosa tree with his knife, so as to have a more comfortable retreat in case of danger.

The man on the tree signalled that the rhino was quite close. When I made it out I advanced a few steps towards it, but it moved on also and then stopped again. In vain did I search in every direction, but could not see it, although by this time I knew I must have been quite near it. First Sindano and then Pandasaro followed me in the belief that the rhino had gone. Then suddenly Pandasaro spotted it and pointed in the direction of a large grey mass, which I had taken for an ant-hill.

I raised my rifle, while my men took refuge behind all kinds of bushes in every direction. At the shot the rhino swung round in a flash and disappeared in a thick cloud of dust. As we heard nothing further, I concluded that it had rolled over and was lying dead.

But as we cautiously followed up, a furious snorting made us stop. My two men vanished from my side and I was ready to fire when—Good gracious!—instead of the mighty rhino I was expecting, a wee rhino baby dashed out of the reedbank! The next moment I had put my rifle to "safe" and thrown it down, and as the youngster passed by me I pounced on it, closing my arms round its neck, and our struggle began. The little rhino fought a desperate fight. I could never have imagined that this creature, hardly two months old and weighing but about 150 lbs., could exert itself to such a degree. Very soon I was on the ground, and as I hung desperately to it, it dragged me about over the sharp buffalo grass. I was covered with bruises and scratches and my clothes were torn, but I knew I was holding a treasure and I did not want to lose it. The little rhino was squealing, while I shouted to my men for help. At last they appeared and fell on the little beast with such determination that they rolled it over and then held it down. We had no rope with which to bind it (later, when I was a real animal catcher, I made every man carry a few yards of rope on his body), but I held on with one hand and took my putties off with the other. We then succeeded in binding the little pachyderm, but when we tried to lift it on our shoulders and carry it to the tents, we could not, because the moment it began to kick we were scattered all around. So we had to undo the knots fastening its legs and twisted the putties round its neck like a collar. Two men clung to it right and left, while I took hold of its tail, and in this manner we managed to take it to our camp.

On reaching the camp, we bound it to a tree and put rugs over it, for the poor little animal was quite exhausted by excitement and fright, and was panting and trembling all over.

But what did we look like? Our clothes—I mean mine, because the others had none—were torn; we were smeared all over with blood, dust, and the sticky, slimy perspiration of the rhino. We were in a disgusting state. The carcase of the old rhino cow was already cold and stiff, but we could pay no attention to it, and I consider I was very lucky to find the horn next day.

The baby cried for a few hours, but by nightfall it seemed

much happier and lay down next to the man who was put in charge of it. Next morning it followed us like a dog. A photograph of it was taken on the second day of his imprisonment while I was giving him his bottle. By that time he was so tame that tying him up for the night was an unnecessary precaution.

He never left his nurse, and when the men hid from him in fun he would call them in peculiar shrieking tones. It was great fun to watch him play, frisking about in a grotesque way. Every one of his movements had the same grotesque character as the movements of a grown rhinoceros. Every unfamiliar object roused his wrath and without deliberation he would attack it.

A week or two after I caught him I gave him a playfellow in the form of a young waterbuck, and they were soon inseparable friends.

But it is just as hard to bring up a pachyderm as to catch him. At first we gave him pure milk; later on oats in milk, feeding him with a spoon. And still later he was taught to eat alone out of a pot.

This little rhino was afterwards sent to India.

But catching rhino will not always have such lucky results as in the case here related. An older rhino will usually die from exhaustion and distress at having lost its freedom. Unfortunately I have had some experience of this. We had come upon the tracks of a rhino cow and calf in a dense thicket. The latter was already half-grown, but I thought that I should not have many more chances of getting one, so I followed up the tracks. I was accompanied by twelve brave boys, who believed in success. I don't know how they got it, but they had drunk rather too much "pombe" and were in a most joyful frame of mind. The rhino cow charged the moment she saw us, and nothing but a shot in the head could have saved me from being trampled upon. The calf did not leave its dead mother, and although he offered great resistance we made him a prisoner. True, none of us came out of this adventure unwounded. We caught him in the morning, but the necessary help for moving him only came late in the afternoon when half a village helped to convey him to camp. Every one was overjoyed when at last we succeeded in doing so, and I had an exceptional pleasure that same evening, for on my return to camp I met a fellow-countryman who stayed for a day or two.

The young rhino only lived one day. He died from over-exhaustion, while my wounds made me remember the difficulties of catching him for a long time afterwards. We had equally bitter experience in a third case, which I have told of in the chapter on "Tracking Buffaloes."

After my first lucky capture I made serious preparations for the systematic work of catching wild animals alive. We built paddocks round our camp and then I had to get milch cows. I had to buy a large herd of them, because the African zebu gives very little milk and stops having it altogether when their calves stop sucking. If the calf dies the native has a curious way of helping himself. He preserves its hide with salt and holds it under the cow while milking. But the cow will soon discover treachery, and then there is no more milk to be had from her until the next calving.

I got cows from the Wagayas in exchange for buffalo hides. Fortunately there was no competition and I was able to get very good young material for my herd, getting two pregnant cows for one buffalo hide. I could have bought cows with their calves, that is, cows which were already giving milk, but previous experience warned me of the unwisdom of doing so. Good herdsmen will only try to get rid of a milking cow if something is wrong with her, for they would not part with her under any circumstances if she was a good milker. Of course it was a long time before I had all the cattle I wanted for my zoological garden in the wilderness, and it was the lack of milk that made me sell the first baby rhino as soon as possible. The money I got for it came just in time and helped me greatly in improving my outfit.

The Ruvana Plains would have been an ideal site for catching game, for many varieties are plentiful, but on account of the tsetse-fly horses cannot be kept, and in the Sudan giraffes and antelopes are generally lassoed from horseback.

In German East Africa vast areas were scoured officially and the zebras and antelopes forced into huge enclosures; but such methods were always far beyond my means, for they necessitate great numbers of men and costly equipment.

My quick-footed and intrepid natives could run down a young or weak animal which had been left behind by the rest of the herd, but such specimens would not usually live long, because they were often already naturally feeble and were further over-exhausted by the chase.

During my collecting expedition I caught animals with loop-nets, a method which I had learned from the tribes living east of the Victoria Nyanza. These nets are made out of the strong fibres of a plant called sanseviera and consists of a row of loops hanging loose on a cord, which is then stretched out and hoisted up upon forked poles. About eight to ten parallel rows of these nets are put up in places where game is known to pass. When the trap is ready, the beaters divide into two parties and drive the game from a distance into the system of hanging loopnets.

Naturally many beaters are needed for this work, and it will really only be successful if a sufficient number of men can be obtained.

When the game comes close to the traps the excitement begins. Suspecting danger, they will try to turn back. The beaters, who until then have crept up slowly, will jump up with shrieks and yells, brandishing their spears, and pursue the escaping animals, which, scared to death, leap into the rows of nets. If they succeed in getting through the first few lines they will be caught in the subsequent nets almost to a certainty. This was the time when I had to be very quick and firm with my men, for the wild man's murderous instincts are aroused in times of excitement, and they might easily have stabbed the kicking animals with their spears.

It is dangerous to approach a grown animal caught in the net, nevertheless we always cut the loops open and let them escape. These grown animals would not live more than a few hours in captivity after such a chase.

The young ones were conveyed to camp and turned loose in paddocks as soon as possible. The new-comer in his boma would be received with great curiosity by his fellow-captives and soon all would be friends.

When an animal came of its own accord to take its bottle we could regard it as tamed. But we lost a good many even of our youngest captives, as they die from over-excitement or indigestion caused by the sudden change of diet.

When they were quite tame they had fraternized with the zebu cows to such an extent that we could drive them out together to graze, and even if herds of their own species were grazing 500 to 600 yards away, they never even tried to desert. In this way we were able to drive our mixed herd of zebus and antelopes to Victoria Nyanza.

When they came in from grazing every evening, the zebu calves would ask for their mothers with loud bellowings and the orphan antelopes in different languages demand their bottles. When we appeared in the paddock with our whisky bottles stoppered with rubber suckers, sixty to seventy antelope calves would formally charge us. Sometimes they upset us and sucked at our ears, hands and clothes, while the more practical ones would get hold of the bottles. The gnu calves were the most sharp-witted of all antelopes; they were humorous, funny creatures and the grotesqueness of their movements made them interesting to watch. Although they show the strongest resistance when caught, they will become docile and even attached to man, and they gave me many a moment of enjoyment when watching their frolics and games in the paddock.

Unfortunately I could only bring back one live wildebeest to Budapest; the others died of the rinderpest and sea-sickness. When this one arrived home he was two years old and powerful. He used to graze with the cattle on my farm and often had fights with the bull of the herd, and although the bull was much the heavier, he was always beaten by my wildebeest. It was interesting to see that he had a special dislike for one of my cows. She was dark grey, almost black, and when they saw each other they would engage in such furious combats that they could only be separated with the help of several men.

I noticed the curious fact that nearly every antelope calf made friends with one of a different species, and when this friendship was sealed they would never leave each other any more. For instance, once a jimela calf ran off and the only way to get it to come back was to drive its companion, a small wildebeest calf, up to it. When it heard the mumbled sounds of its chosen friend it came back at once. There was a remarkable friendship between a young Thomson's gazelle and a crested crane. They used to have sham fights together, and when the little buck charged with his head down, the crane flapped his wings and pecked at him in defence. When they got tired of this game the gazelle would lie down to rest while the crane began to search for vermin all over him and then squatted down near him to rest also.

Beasts of prey must of course be caught in a different way. Only once or twice did we get a jackal in these loopnets. We got most of the carnivora by taking them from their lairs when quite young and then brought them up with bottles. It is less difficult to bring these up than the ruminants.

For catching fully grown animals we used large spring gins, the jaws of which we covered with fibres of plants to avoid damaging the leg of the captured animal. The traps were set as near as possible to camp, so that we could hear when an animal was caught and free it as soon as possible. The hardest task was to take them out of the trap. We kept long forked poles at hand for this purpose, and with these we forced down the head of the beast until we could put a strong, chained collar on it and thus render it harmless for the moment. We could then open the trap and free the leg, and by the light of torches we took the prisoner to camp.

Small animals—jackals or wild cats—were easily dealt with in spite of their sharp teeth, but bigger beasts of prey, for instance a full-grown spotted hyena, gave no end of trouble, and to get such an animal out of a trap is most dangerous work.

The least clumsiness or lack of courage on the part of one of the assistants at the critical moment may involve fatal consequences, for a bite may mean a smashed arm or leg which no surgeon can mend again. Men who have experienced deadly peril and have often looked danger in the face know how quickly fear spreads, and it will not be necessary for me to tell those who know natives that in times of danger I had to set an example.

In 1912 I brought back two spotted hyenas for the Budapest Zoo, both of which had been caught when fully grown. They survived and lived on through years of war-time scarcity. The larger one was a very interesting member of my menagerie.

After I caught him I put a strong collar round his neck and fastened him to a tree and my boys jokingly called him our watch-dog, but later we made an enclosure for him.

The loss of freedom by no means influenced his appetite. A few minutes after we had fastened him to the tree he was devouring the big pieces of raw meat which we threw to him. But the best idea of the greediness of a hyena may be obtained from the fact that if one succeeds in freeing itself from a trap and regains its freedom, it will return the next day, even with a damaged leg. I have actually caught the same animal in the same trap but half an hour after it had escaped.

Our "camp-dog" was of a very ill-tempered disposition, and so I was all the more astonished when my "munyampara" told me that he had made friends with a hen. In fact, my most diligent hen always visited him, pecking at his meat and cleansing him from vermin. Later she even laid her eggs inside his cage, which was most distressing for us, as we could never get those eggs!

Later I had to move the hyena as I needed his cage for a porcupine and so he was put on a chain again, but next day he was gone. We noticed it at once. My men followed him up and we drove him into a thicket where the loopnets had been put up. He bit a few of them through with his terrible fangs, but in the end we got him and, amongst the shouts of triumph of my men, he was brought back to camp.

I retired to my tent but soon had to come out again on hearing peals of laughter accompanied by the pitiful yelling of the prisoner. I found my men were flogging the poor beast and when I asked why, they said twenty-five strokes of the "kiboko" was the punishment for a man in the case of desertion, so why should a hyena not get it as well, especially as he had given us much "matata" (disagreeableness).

In after years this hyena went on making "matatas," for, when he was in the Budapest Zoo, he bit off the hand of a little boy.

Lions—without exception—can only be captured as cubs. Usually the mother must be sacrificed, for she will defend her young ones to the last and must be killed when doing so. It should be unnecessary to mention that a fight with an enraged lioness is far the most dangerous of all.

CAPTURED ANTELOPE CALVES IN THEIR BOMA. ON THE LEFT TWO WATERBUCK CALVES

MY MEN LEADING ANTELOPE CALVES

CAPTURED AND TAMED ANTELOPE CALVES GRAZING WITH ZEBU CALVES NEAR MY
CAMP ON THE RUVANA PLAINS

A YOUNG GIRAFFE, ONE MONTH OLD IN MY RUVANA CAMP

A YOUNG GIRAFFE, FOUR DAYS OLD

WILDEBEEST CALVES WERE ALWAYS THE FIRST TO SEIZE THE BOTTLE

Lion cubs are exceedingly helpless little creatures which lie about all day long, and only hunger will induce them to move a little. Their development is very slow, but they soon became the pets of our camp. They were as playful as kittens and friendly to all other animals. During my stay near Victoria Nyanza a young lion made friends with two fox-terriers. They came to play with him every day, and the big cub only lost his temper when the fox-terriers were too rough at play. He also tried to mix with the young antelope calves, but was rejected. They would not have him at any price, so he was always left alone.

I got two cubs on the Ruvana Plains for our zoo. The tamer one was very young when we caught him. We brought him up with the bottle, and from the very beginning he was a very sweet-tempered, nice little animal, the pet of all, and he tried to play and make friends with everybody and everything round our camp. This is why my men called him "Simba ya Uleja" ("European lion"), and I always accepted the names my men gave.

The other "wicked" one was caught when older. Perhaps he never forgot the day when his strong mother fell in battle and when he, taking to flight, was run down by men and a coat and a black robe were thrown over his head and no resistance was of any more avail.

He was a very unkempt little fellow and his fur was full of thistles and ticks. It was hard to clean him, for we had to hold the angry little thing down. Surely his mother's rough tongue must have been less painful than this new way of brushing and combing. But probably he would have forgotten and forgiven all this, for he began to make friends with me, if, during my absence, he had not been ill-treated by one of the natives.

After that the poor "simba msenzi" (native lion) could not bear to see a native. If one approached him, he charged and probably would have been dangerous, had the chain given way, or if he could have broken through the bars of his cage. I could stroke him, but he made me feel that he did not like it. He seemed to resent the fact that his fellow-prisoner was allowed to go about all day, while he was confined in a narrow cage.

It was very interesting to watch the behaviour of the two

little prisoners, when the simbas of the wilderness held their concerts. Although the European simba listened, the interest he took was not more than the natural call of the wild, while the other one was in a state of the greatest excitement, jumping about in his cage and trying to roar as if asking for the help of his powerful free brothers.

Monkeys are also driven into traps, and not caught, as we are told, with boots dipped in pitch. In the territory of Victoria Nyanza there are no apes, and the small monkeys and baboons are worthless, so catching them would be but a useless occupation. A full-grown baboon would be well worth catching, but I never succeeded in doing so without wounding him gravely.

We also had the luck to catch specimens of that rare and curiously-shaped animal, the aardvark. The most notable tribe living to the east of Victoria Nyanza, the exclusive Wagayas, were of help to me in this adventure. Although the Wagaya warriors do not like work, when I promised them wildebeest tails and buffalo skins for their shields, they quickly threw away their war-like finery and dug up the underground passages of this solitary animal. Frightened by the noise of thudding pickaxes the aardvark would go on digging its way underground, so the work of several days often turned out to have been wasted. Nevertheless I succeeded in catching five, two of which lived eight months in the zoo of Budapest. It was difficult to feed them, for they live only on white ants. I minced up meat and made the tiny pieces easy to swallow by dipping them in the white of eggs.

It is not only mammals that are caught in Africa, for the finest birds of the zoological gardens come from that continent. Ostriches can be caught when young, and rearing them does not require much knowledge.

On one occasion we were watching an ostrich nest from a distance for two weeks, waiting for the eggs to hatch, but just before the time was up, a lion attacked the sitting bird, and although she escaped, as the spoor told us, the nest was entirely disturbed.

During the daytime I used the traps meant for smaller beasts of prey to catch eagles and marabous. It was easy enough to catch greedy vultures, but much harder to trap a shrewd marabou. A very old marabou was prisoner on my farm and then with a newly arrived comrade he was sent to the zoo, whence he escaped in the autumn of 1921 when they wanted to put him into his winter quarters. It would be very interesting to know if he ever arrived in Africa, or if he met his death somewhere on his way. He was last seen about Szabadszállás (a place in Hungary) a few days after his escape.

We usually took young birds from their nests and brought them up, but I caught some with nooses near their drinking-places, as, for instance, the pride of our zoo, the wonderful crested cranes and the cautious secretary birds.

It is not only hard work to catch and bring up animals, but also a big undertaking to transport them, and preparations for their transport will take months.

It would take too long to give all the details of how their transport is organized. I can only say that if 50 per cent. of the animals arrive in Europe alive, you can count yourself very lucky. I have had some bitter experiences in this connection. When I started with a large collection of rare and beautiful beasts from the Ruvana Plains, my cattle were attacked by rinderpest. This plague spread into the captured ruminants and the expensive, arduous and difficult work of years was annihilated in the short space of a few weeks. With the wrecks of my collection I marched six days, till I came to the south-eastern shore of the Victoria Nyanza and there I stayed for a few days because of a strong hurricane. I then embarked on dhows (sailing boats) and sailed to Shirati. On our way the wind was not favourable, so the voyage of sixteen hours took us fifty hours. This delay meant the loss of more of the animals in my collection. I stayed in Shirati for a few months so as to give the animals a good rest and to make all preparations for the sea-journey. Meanwhile those animals which were infected with rinderpest died; on the other hand, I collected some more. From Shirati I crossed to Port Florence (now Kisumu) on a steamer, whence my menagerie had to be taken by rail (three days express on the Uganda Railway) and then we arrived at Mombasa on the Indian Ocean. I had great difficulty in getting all the necessary forage and at last I embarked on an ocean liner which took twenty-two days to

Marseilles. Then travelling by rail I arrived at last at Budapest with my zoo which, in spite of all the hard luck, still consisted of more than 120 animals and birds.

My great admiration and love of nature's creations took me out to Africa in early youth and there, through the real contact with all these wonders, I got to admire and love it even more. I found out while bringing up animals that the most different species will form friendships and be inseparable friends, and that no animal can live without society, or without a true companion. The loss of its friend will break its heart, or the meeting with its friend after a long separation will make it wild with joy. In the world of animals I have experienced love, gratitude, fidelity, attachment—all beauties of the soul—and very often I felt inclined to think what wonderful examples were thus set to the lord of creation, man.

CHAPTER XXVI

Birds

A FRICA is probably even richer in varieties of birds than of mammals. Professor A. Reichenow wrote a book called *Die Vögel Afrikas,* in which he gives the description of 2,500 kinds of birds, and since the year when this book was published, many new kinds have been discovered, so I suppose there must be over 3,000 different species of birds known in Africa. On the whole they are less sumptuous in colour and less gaudy than the birds of the South Sea Islands or South America. But Africa has a few magnificent specimens too, as, for example, the turacos of the forests (*Musophaga*), the nectarinias somewhat resembling humming-birds, various starlings, weavers in the mating season, king-fishers, golden cuckoos, green pigeons, etc. I do not wish, however, to write of these, but only of game birds which are of interest to sportsmen, and that briefly.

THE OSTRICH

The largest bird on earth, the ostrich, naturally deserves the first mention.

In all the countries through which I travelled—with the exception of Uganda and Unyoro, where ostriches do not exist at all—we found the splendid Masai ostrich (*Struthio masaicus*). The ostrich is exclusively a dweller in the savannas and plains.

As one traverses the arid, burning plains, over which floats the trembling Fata Morgana, one will often notice large black or grey balls rising out of the herds of zebra and gazelles. Even the new-comer will recognize them to be ostriches, however far off they may be, because the vigilant bird will have noticed the stranger and with a flap of its rudimentary yet powerful wings, trimmed with white feathers, it will give warning to its peacefully resting or feeding companions.

The ostrich is a useful neighbour for antelopes and zebras, because its far-seeing eyes from their height of 9 feet will quickly detect danger. But these services are reciprocated, for the keen sense of smell of its hoofed friends can also be of help to the ostrich. So they warn and defend each other mutually against man and dangerous animals.

Ostrich shooting has been prohibited since 1903 in old German East Africa and a licence was only obtainable by the Governor's permission. I was granted licences on my first and third trips because I could show that I was collecting for a museum.

I cannot imagine how the story of the ostrich hiding his head in the sand in the event of danger originated. I often hoped that the old cock I was after would do me the service of stopping and hiding his head in the sand for a few moments only, but unfortunately none would give a representation of this peculiarity.

The shooting of ostriches was forbidden principally in the interest of the ostrich farms, and at one time these farms were very plentiful in East Africa. But they never could produce the same valuable feathers as the South African ostrich farms did. Most of the feathers never came to Europe at all, but were only sold to native warriors of the Masai, Wakavirondo and Wagaya tribes, who wear them as head ornaments and will spend incredibly high sums to secure them. When I laid out the prepared skin of a splendid cock I had shot in the mating season to dry in the sun in Shirati near the Ngare Dowash, Wagaya warriors appeared and made high offers in the form of cows. It would have been much more profitable to sell them on the spot than to send them to Europe, and I had to take good care that the fine long feathers did not disappear.

The most recent English game laws allow the shooting of one cock ostrich in the year.

Of course the cock ostrich has the most beautiful feathers in the mating season. In Masailand this arrives in April and the beginning of May, and then it is not rare to hear the deep roll of an old cock ostrich, which can easily be mistaken for the roar of a lion. Even natives have often been deceived. In the mating season the necks of the cocks swell to a considerable size and turn bright red and they then fight desperately among themselves. My men always found and collected a lot of feathers on the scenes of these encounters, which they sold to the Wagayas.

The cocks take their part in the brooding and hatching of eggs, and often sit on the eggs while the hen takes an outing. Young hens will sometimes brood together. Once when going through some high grass in Ndassekera, I was startled by two grey creatures which jumped up just ahead of me They were two hens so intent on brooding that they only noticed me at the last moment and left their common nest in a hurry.

Sometimes one can find an ostrich egg in the sand of the plains quite out of breeding season, but such eggs are sterile and have ripened in the ovary because of the rich nourishment of the hen. When fresh such eggs have often provided me with a delicious omelette.

Brooding ostrich hens will often fall victims to the big cats, and their nests are frequently robbed by the spotted hyena. The young ostrich chickens have many enemies, although the grown birds can defend them effectively against the smaller beasts of prey, while the kick of an old cock would keep even a leopard away.

On my first trip I had the opportunity to observe a very interesting episode in ostrich life. I was travelling from Arusha to Ufiomi and had to touch the Marti Hills on my way. When hardly a day and a half away from Arusha I found buffalo tracks in a ravine overgrown with nearly impenetrable bushes, and as buffaloes were still very rare in these regions in 1905, I thought it worth while to stop for some days and try to get one.

In the dense bush it was impossible to get within range, and in the early mornings they did not appear in the open plain, so my only hope was to see them in the evening, when they came out to drink. On the evening of November 7th I went out with one of the Masai servants to the spot from which the buffaloes would have to emerge and there I saw this interesting episode:

It was already dark when my Masai kirongozi whispered "olosogwan" (buffalo). I saw immediately that it was no buffalo, but ostriches. I had already given up hope of getting a buffalo and was glad of getting a chance at an ostrich, so I fired but missed.

At the shot the cock turned like lightning and ran up to us and collapsed a few steps before us. He tried to get up again, beating his short wings, but could only move one or two steps. I was very surprised because I knew well that I had missed, but I soon understood. He wanted to divert our attention from his chickens which were somewhere close by. My kirongozi thought that the bird was badly wounded and ran up to him with his spear to kill him. I was so interested to see what would happen that I let him go and followed behind. When the Masai was near enough, the bird jumped up and tottered along. This went on for quite a while. Every time the Masai came near enough, the ostrich cock staggered to his feet and went on farther again.

By this time both had disappeared from sight when suddenly, far behind me and close to where I had shot at the bird, I heard its deep, gurgling voice.

After he had lured on the Masai for about 200 yards he returned as quick as lightning to his chickens. It reminded me of a scene so often seen at home in Hungary during partridge shooting, when the old partridge will pretend to be wounded and flutter about before the nose of the pointer in order to save her young.

Next day I was again out after buffalo early in the morning. I took a good look at the place where this ostrich episode had taken place and found the wing of a slaughtered chicken. A serval had got hold of it while the cock was risking his life in trying to divert our attention. Next day I killed another old cock which can be seen now in the Hungarian National Museum.

THE SECRETARY BIRD

Another bird typical of the African plains is the fine Secretary bird (*Sagittarius serpentarius*). The sportsman will very often see the cock striding over the plain, usually accompanied by his mate and looking from right to left. They are said to live on snakes, and on this account they are protected by the international game laws. But the secretary bird knows nothing about his good reputation or the kindly feelings of men towards him and has a very untrusting disposition, never coming within shooting range.

I always loved to watch the long-tailed, finely adorned secretary's hunting trips, and have seen him snatch up a mouse or a

WAGAYAS DIGGING OUT AN AARD-WOLF

SULTANI OF WAGAYAS WITH WIVES AND ESCORT

THE ANTELOPE CALVES ALWAYS CHASED THE LITTLE LION CUB OUT OF THE
PADDOCK
The assailant is a Jimela ; two waterbuck calves are watching Simba's retreat

" SOME MILK, PLEASE ! "

SIESTA

LION-CUB TEARING AN AARDWOLF CARCASS

lizard with his long legs, but I never saw him engaged in a struggle for life and death with the largest African snake, the Naja-haja or hooded snake, such as some books on natural history describe.

My own opinion is that the secretary bird is not the snake-killer he is supposed to be. As a collector I have shot some with special permission and have examined the contents of their stomachs, but never found anything that made me think they had swallowed poisonous snakes, although I found plenty of egg-shells, remains of birds, mice, and lizards.

Later I kept five in captivity and in 1912 transported them to the zoo of Budapest. These did not touch poisonous snakes, even when they were dead. Non-poisonous ones they devoured willingly. On several occasions I demonstrated to the District Officer at Shirati that they did not touch poisonous snakes, and this thorough German official was quite upset because these naughty birds did not do their duty.

Surely the secretary bird does a lot of harm to small game, which is not nearly balanced by his usefulness in eating an occasional poisonous snake. But in Africa guinea-fowl, francolins, and other winged game are so plentiful, that it would be a pity to persecute the lovely secretary bird because of the damage he does to them.

Other very remarkable members of the family of eagles are the short-tailed Bateleur (*Helotarsus ecaudatus*), well known for its grace-ful flight, and the white-headed Sea-eagle (*Haliaetus vocifer*) which lives near rivers, swamps and lakes and is a near relative of our white-tailed sea-eagle.

The short-tailed bateleur is perhaps the most beautiful of eagles. Its head, neck, the hind part of its back and underparts are of a dull black, while the top of the back and wings is chestnut brown. The skin of feet, eyelids and bare face are coral-red; its beak orange-coloured with a black tip. The tips of the wing feathers are curled upwards during flight.

The bateleur is the champion flyer of all birds. With outspread motionless wings it will soar on and on, and then turning in a sudden assault it drops like a stone, but before touching ground it will mount again with one or two beats of its wings to great heights. At close quarters one can hear the powerful strokes of the wings, making a noise like a flag flapping in the wind. This sound and the piercing cry "shaor" will always betray the presence of this noble pirate.

The cautious bateleur is hard to shoot with small shot. Sometimes it feeds on carrion, but only before it is visited by marabous and vultures. This is the best opportunity for getting a shot. On its roosting tree, which it does not change often, it can also be easily surprised.

The white-headed sea-eagle is of a more confiding nature. For hours it will perch on the top of a river-side tree and will take no notice of an approaching canoe. Its head, neck, breast and tail are white and it lives chiefly on fish; consequently water-fowl are not alarmed by its approach and go on cleaning themselves without showing the slightest concern even if it drops down right amongst them.

The white-headed sea-eagle also feeds on carrion, before other carrion eaters have taken possession of it. Smaller vultures (*Neophron*) will rise and leave when one comes on the scene.

THE HONEY-GUIDE

In my childhood I read much about the honey-guide and its doings appealed to my imagination, although I never quite believed that a bird without being taught, and of its own free will and altruistic nature would enter human service and help man to find wild honey. I thought these were fairy tales, but I was not right.

The honey-guide is a bird well known by natives. It belongs to the family of cuckoos and is about the size of a starling. Its colour is greenish grey. Rising up before the traveller it flutters from tree to tree through the thinly timbered savanna forest, warbling all the time and indicating the way to the wild bees' hive. Its intention is probably to get the larvæ after men have emptied the honey-cells, as without such help it could hardly get its favourite nourishment. There are many known varieties of this bird in East Africa, but the *Indicator indicator* and the *Indicator variegatus* are the two which will act as guides to man.

I think there are no natives in East Africa who do not know and take advantage of the habits of this useful bird.

During my long wanderings through Africa I, too, have

profited by its help and the men of my safari got several buckets-ful of honey, thanks to its guidance.

But pleasant and as useful as the honey-guide can be in helping man to get honey, it can be equally unpleasant when the hunter is after big game and is fatal to the stalker. My men would throw things at them to stop their noisy chatter, but they only had all the more to say. Hunted game is very cautious and will listen to every sound. They know that for many thousands of years the honey-guide has usually been followed by man. When game hears its voice, it will get uneasy and leave the danger zone. I often had to kill the treacherous bird with my ·22 Winchester, which makes little noise and will not scare big game away.

Natives recognize yet another habit of this interesting bird. They declare that very often the honey-guide will lead man into danger and allure him into a thicket, where, instead of finding honey, he will be caught by a lion or leopard.

Sir F. Jackson, in a paper published by the "East Africa and Uganda Natural History Society," replies to the question whether honey-guides really take man into the claws of big beasts of prey. He refers to two bad experiences he had himself. Once he was led to a bush from which a leopard emerged suddenly and once he shot a serval in similar circumstances.

I also can give a curious experience with a honey-guide.

In January, 1914, I was hurrying to the carcase of a bull elephant I had shot on New Year's Day in the swamps of Lugogo. It was the one which had charged me and which I was forced to shoot. I intended to take some photographs of the vultures and marabous assembled on the carcase. Curiously enough no hyenas had appeared and so only a few birds came because they could not open the thick skin of the elephant. So I could not get any photographs. When crossing over the burnt savannas a honey-guide flew towards us very noisily. As we were in need of sugar and we had no means of getting it we followed the bird.

After we had covered a distance of about 2,500 yards it perched on a dry tree near an ant-hill covered with bushes, and from this tree it continued its "tak-tak." My men declared that the bees would be near, and I thought so too, because the bird did not fly farther. We examined the tree, but found no bees. We then searched on the ant-hill, but in vain. At last one of the porters cried out "Allah!" and the next moment he killed a puff-adder with his spear. When the bird saw that we had finished off the snake it stopped chattering, just as it does when the bees are found.

Of course my men were furious because the bird did not only deceive them, but had even lured them into danger, and wanted me to kill it, which of course I did not do.

Who could tell why the honey-guide had led us to one of the nastiest members of the family of vipers? It is just as unexplainable as the adventures of Sir F. Jackson with the leopard and serval. I believe that it recognizes these animals as enemies, and as it cannot harm them itself—as it can in the case of bees—it leads against them the age-old enemy of the wilderness, man.

GUINEA-FOWL

At break of day, when we leave our camping-place with our safari, or when the day is over and we pitch our tents for the night, we shall usually hear the cackle of guinea-fowl. It is a sound reminiscent of the poultry yards at home. One comes across the guinea-fowl in more open places, in bush and near cultivated land. These are mostly the crested guinea-fowls (*Numida*), but, of course, there are many sub-species.

The guinea-fowl is not a sporting bird, for it is an obstinate pedestrian, and it is almost impossible to make it rise out of the thorny bush in which it has taken refuge. It is rather easier to get it out of the high grass, and on such ground a good pointer would be of use, but in East Africa no pointers can be kept, as they are said to lose their noses, and I think tsetse-flies would soon kill them.

I have often noticed that the jackal-like native dogs will soon force guinea-fowl to perch on trees. These perched guinea-fowl scold their enemies with a terrible cackle. They will do this when any beast of prey approaches and have very often thus warned me of the presence of a leopard.

On my two last trips I used my ·22 Winchester on guinea-fowl. When they were settled on a branch and I knocked one down, the others would start a great noise, and stretching out their necks, looked like a row of champagne bottles. They only thought of leaving after seven or eight had tumbled off the tree. Of course this plan only succeeded when I shot from a good distance and was well hidden, although the report of a small ·22 Winchester-Automatic can hardly be heard even near at hand. Probably the reader will regard this form of shooting as unsporting, but circumstances in Africa excuse it. We wanted guinea-fowl badly, not only for museum purposes, but also for food. Young guinea-fowl are very tasty and old ones make excellent soup.

African hunters usually take no shotgun on a formal hunting trip and so most hunters shoot any guinea-fowl needed for the pot with a rifle. And in order to damage the meat as little as possible, they try to shoot the birds in the head or neck. To shoot them in any other part of the body is unsportsmanlike.

Natives, especially the men of the caravans, catch them with different traps and nooses, and use also light bows with blunt arrows. The rice-growing Swahilis, who have settled round the Jippe Lake, east of Kilimanjaro, have invented a curious way of catching guinea-fowl. They make a very strong "pombe" out of sugar-cane and in the dry season place a basin filled with it near water-holes. The guinea-fowl get tipsy after taking this alcoholic drink and can easily be caught by the men lying in wait.

In the dry season we found enormous flocks of guinea-fowl near any water. On the Balangeti, a tributary of the Ruvana River, which flows into the Victoria Nyanza, I was stalking buffalo and saw hundreds of guinea-fowl every day at dawn. It was the same on the Oliondo (near the Great Rift Valley), where I saw the troops of about 700 or 800 birds in a single flock.

In the waterless savannas round Kilimanjaro I met with the most elegant member of the guinea-fowl family, the *Acryllium vulturinum*. It earned this denomination because of its naked head and neck. The feathers of the neck are like bands, blue above, black below; the feathers near the quills are shaped like lancets with a long white stripe along their middle. The feathers on both sides of the breast are also blue. The most striking characteristic is that the two middle feathers of the tail end in a point and are much longer than the others.

This variety lives in the highlands of Masai and Somaliland, and the southern boundary of its habitat is Kilimanjaro.

I have always been surprised that no one has tried to acclimatize this richly coloured guinea-fowl in Europe; and the more as they are better fliers than the other kinds, i.e. the crested guinea-fowls.

On the highlands near the Daryama River, at the foot of Kilimanjaro, I saw numbers of these birds, which were sometimes very troublesome, as the noise they make when startled always threatens to spoil a hunt. There I was generally on the tracks of rhino or of buffalo. In dark forests and in the river-side jungles one may come across guinea-fowls of the genus Guttera, of which there are also several varieties. Instead of a horn casque on their heads they have got a kind of hood, or knot, of feathers. These birds are rarely seen because they dwell in the darkest forest amongst impenetrable creepers. I got one or two for my collection, but I had to follow them for hours before I could get a shot.

Near my Ngare Dowash camp I shot a couple of these guinea-fowl under very interesting circumstances. I went to inspect a trap and as I came up I heard the chatter of guinea-fowl. At first I thought that they had gone to the trap to eat worms and I hurried towards the sound with my small ·22 Winchester-Automatic. On coming up I saw five or six guinea-fowl with their backs to me scolding something in the thicket. I knew that there must be something hiding there, but the collecting ornithologist got the upper hand in me and I shot one out of the unsuspecting lot, and as they made off on foot I got a second. Then I heard the rattling of chains, puffing and growling, and a trapped leopard tried to come for me. It had dragged the trap along, and as it had caught in the thicket, it could go no farther and was crouching there. I knocked it over with the third bullet of the ·22 Winchester-Automatic, in its neck. The birds had been abusing their helpless enemy.

In the forests of Africa there must be many kinds of guinea-fowl, which are probably sub-species of the Guttera.

FRANCOLINS

Innumerable kinds of francolins are found everywhere over East Africa. Each district seems to have got its own variety.

Their size and colour differ greatly. The bigger ones are as big as our hens, while the smallest are not as large as a partridge.

I have not the space to give details of all the different kinds, and will only say that they are divided into two main classes: francolins with naked necks (*Pernistes*); and real francolins (*Francolinus*).

Those with naked necks prefer ground covered with high grass. In the early morning or before sunset one can hear them on the top of an ant-hill or on some stunted, thorny tree scorched by grass fires. They emit a very unpleasant coarse crow and surely the Swahili name "Quare" comes from this. Similarly the crested guinea-fowl is called "Kanga," the other species, the Guttera, is called "Kororo," recalling their characteristic voices. At dawn and before sunset it is most easy to get them, and there is much less difficulty in driving them and making them fly than is the case with guinea-fowl.

The *Pernistes* are rather large birds. The naked neck is of a bright yellow or red and this colour is the chief clue by which to distinguish the different kinds.

There are many more sub-species of the real francolin, more than thirty being known in East Africa and probably many more not yet classified. For most African hunters only preserve birds which are rich in colour; the francolins go to the kitchen.

I always wished for a good pointer when I was shooting francolins. It would be great sport and one could make wonderful bags.

During and after the rainy season one will often be startled by the sudden whir of the Harlequin quail. They are similar to the European quail, only darker, the breast and neck being black (*Coturnix delegorguei*). In many places, for instance at the foot of the Letema Mountains, they were so numerous that my men caught them with butterfly nets.

PIGEONS

East Africa is also very rich in pigeons. They are seldom real game birds, but the Swahili esteem them from another standpoint. They imitate the wild dove's cooing with these words: "Kuku mfupa . . . tupu, mimi niama . . . tupu." (Fowl is only bones, I am all meat.)

Although I collected all kinds of birds I never liked shooting turtle-doves, for the plumage of doves is so lightly set into the fat skin, which gets easily torn, so that my native skinners never succeeded in skinning them well, and I always had to do it myself.

At the very beginning of my first trip I was collecting birds at the foot of Kilimanjaro. Through a break in the dense foliage of a tree I saw a kind of starling and shot at it when, to my surprise, there fell not only the starling, but also a gorgeously green-coloured, red-legged and red-beaked pigeon, and quite a flock of them rose with a great flutter of wings. These green pigeons (*Vinago*) were feeding on ripe berries of the tree, but my inexperienced eye could not make them out among the green foliage, the less so as they became motionless at my approach. Later I saw many "ningas" (the Swahili name) and very often relished their dainty flesh.

These birds live only on berries and tasty fruits, and African "gourmands" declare that their flesh takes on the aroma of the berries they eat. All natives whose religious laws permit eating them, esteem them highly. They hang up nooses made out of the tail-hairs of the wildebeest on the trees on which the birds feed and sometimes they catch several dozen on one tree.

The masses of these pigeons which will flock to one tree when the fruit is ripening are inconceivable. Their curious piping, which is so different to the ordinary cooing of pigeons, is heard from afar, and if one can get unnoticed under the tree and fire at one of them, generally three or four will come down at once and the rest flutter up with a terrific noise.

After two or three days one will not find a single pigeon on the same tree, and none even in the neighbourhood. Having eaten up the berries, and perhaps having got tidings that the fruit of a ficus tree has ripened many miles away, they have travelled on.

SAND-GROUSE

On the sandy plains one will often put up the sand-grouse, a bird with the body of a partridge but the flight of a pigeon. If one examines a dead sand-grouse (*Pterocles*) one may notice that a very near relation of this bird is also to be found, though rarely, in Europe, namely the *Syrrhaptes paradoxus*. On the dry plains sand-grouse come to drink at a water-hole at sunset, and their wonderful flight is a pleasure to watch.

ZEBRA COLT CAUGHT IN A LOOP-NET
Animals as old as this were usually set free

A MARABOU IN MY RUVANA CAMP
This bird lived ten years in the Budapest Zoo, and escaped in 1921

No. 3. Cliff of the Weald. Male seen sitting on a large limb in some quite close...

MUSHROOM-SHAPED ANTHILL NEAR THE BUGOMA FOREST

A THREE-STORIED WHITE ANT BUILDING

COCK OSTRICH SHOT NEAR NGARE DOWASH

The young ones are quite good to eat, and on the Danakil Plains we lived on them for weeks because there was no other game to be had. The preservation of their skins is very difficult, and so we only tried to prepare those which were shot cleanly. If they were badly smashed it was better to hand them to the cook.

BUSTARD. STORKS. MARABOUS

Many varieties of bustard are to be found on the savannas and plains of East Africa. The dwarf bustards (*Eupodotis canicollis, Lophotis gindiana,* etc.) often rise from the high grass almost at one's feet, and if one has a shotgun in hand it is very easy to bag them.

It is harder to get within range of the giant bustard (*Choriotis kori*), which is even larger than the Hungarian type. The Boers call this bird "Gom-Paauw" (gum peacock), because they think that it eats the resin of acacia trees.

It can usually be seen, alone or with its mate, striding over the plains with dignity. Its gait is very peculiar, as it swings backwards and forwards, while it hurries from the danger zone of man crossing the savanna.

Flocks of bustards, or rather couples and several single birds in close proximity, are only to be seen during a grass fire or plague of locusts. Grass fires will always bring great flocks of birds along, and one will then see the most different of species side by side, searching for insects and reptiles on the half-burned ground.

Big locust raids will also cause great concentrations of all sorts of birds as well as the larger beasts of prey and bustards will then be plentiful. Many storks also will settle down, and I came across the European white stork on such occasions in the winter months.

In Africa the European storks were very confiding, and it almost seemed as if they had recognized their compatriots, of whom they knew they need not be afraid. I could usually watch them from very close quarters as they went along eating the grasshoppers and caterpillars, so that if any had been ringed I must have noticed it. (Sometimes the plain was covered in the true sense of the word with little black caterpillars.) We always found one or two marabous in the company of our storks, and it would seem that the former live on the best of terms with their smaller European relatives; and as they stride along amongst them they look as if they were guiding a group of tourists. My men called these marabous "kirongozi yao" (their leaders).

The marabou (*Leptoptilos crumeniferus*) follows the dietary habits of vultures rather than that of storks and feeds on carrion. Only in times of grass fires and locust plagues, or when rivers dry up and the beds are alive with fish, do they revert to their original habits.

The protection of marabous in English territory has made them extremely confiding, and they will perch on trees round the camp. In former times in German East Africa they did not trust the white man so completely and could judge the effective range of a gun with great accuracy.

The feathers covering the lower part of the tail are the so-called "marabou feathers." They are fine fluffy feathers and were once greatly in vogue, so everybody tried to get them. But many birds have rather worn and ragged feathers, and consequently more were killed than could be made use of. I have often heard it stated—of course, over whisky and soda—that the marabou which does not let you approach has good feathers, and the one you miss has the best of all!

WATER-FOWL

Near water there are always innumerable water-fowl. On deep and large rivers and lakes there will be comparatively few, and probably the snake-necked Cormorant (*Aningha rufa*) is still the most common in such localities.

Shallow waters and swamps are the true El Dorado of water-birds. Various kinds of snipe rise from the puddles and in flooded areas there will be many marsh snipe. In such places I stopped collecting for a time and enjoyed some excellent snipe shooting. The African marsh snipe has similar habits to the common snipe, and when the shooter slips in a puddle or sinks in a bog, they will then flash away from all sides.

They make a delicious dish and taste even better than do those at home—at least I found it so in Africa.

The ducks are also well represented and many European varieties can be recognized amongst them. I did not eat them because they all smelt of fish oil.

The beautiful Nile geese (*Chenalopex aegyptiacus*) can be seen wherever there is water. They very often perch on trees, and so in Africa geese can be shot off trees. They also have another curious trait. If you shoot one out of a gaggle the others do not make off, but crowd round it with loud cries of "ghe-ghe," so that you can shoot at least five or six at the same time. Young Nile geese are excellent when roasted, and my kitchen saw them regularly.

The big spur-winged goose (*Ploctropterus gambensis*) is also very common everywhere. On the eastern shores of the Victoria Nyanza they do considerable damage in the bean shambas of the natives, and women and children have to be constantly on guard to frighten them off.

The superb crested crane (*Balearica regulorum gibbericeps*) is also frequently found on the shores of Lake Victoria, and is now protected. The crested crane does not leave its dead mate, and even if on the wing it will fly to its falling comrade. I often have watched their stately nuptial dance, which is wonderfully imitated by the "crested crane dance" of some native tribes.

I must mention one curious fact. English settlers asked for permission to shoot a crested crane for Christmas, as this bird was regarded as a substitute for the Christmas turkey of an English home.

White herons are also protected, and the Queen of England is the patroness of these "virgin white birds." They have increased enormously everywhere, and in some places I found big settlements of herons on river banks, lake shores and swampy forests. Although protected everywhere they are very suspicious, whereas the lesser heron will usually let one approach within shotgun range.

Amongst herons we must give first place to the giant heron (*Ardea goliath*), a huge bird which is also very common near water in Africa. One can best appreciate its size when it stands amongst other members of the heron family.

Many thousands of pink flamingoes can be seen on the natron lakes of the Great Rift, filtering the mire with their curved bills, and catching crabs, shells and other tiny organisms. They do not mind being approached and go on fishing without the slightest concern, and so one can take good photographs of them. They also make a wonderful sight when they take to wing as they rise from the surface of the water like a pink cloud at dawn.

The protection of the English Government is extended over two other stork-like birds. One is the Saddle-billed stork (*Ephippiorchynchus senegalensis*), which derives its name from the yellow dent on the upper part of its red bill. We can see this beautiful bird alone or in pairs on the boundaries of great marshes; but I never saw many of them. It is the largest African bird after the ostrich and if wounded can defend itself very effectively.

The other protected bird is the Shoe-bill (*Balaeniceps rex*), the bird most characteristic of the Upper Nile. One or two decades ago it was the greatest ambition of every African bird collector to get one. This bird, which is larger than the marabou, was known long ago, but museums could only secure one or two specimens with great difficulty, because the revolt of the Mahdi made it impossible for travellers to enter the districts where they are found.

Werner, a German explorer, mentioned this bird for the first time in 1840. He had heard through his Berber elephant hunters that a bird like a pelican, but without the pelican's throat bag, existed in the swamps of the White Nile. An Italian slave merchant, Nicola Ulivi, brought the skins of two "Shoe-bills" to Khartoum eight years later, and a description of the bird was made from these skins.

The "Abu Markub" (Arabian for "father of slippers"—its beak closely resembles a big wooden slipper) was also discovered afterwards on the western shore of Victoria Nyanza. On my third trip I searched for them there in the papyrus swamps, but found none. The natives knew nothing about them, and when I showed them the coloured picture of the "abu markub" I was told that no such bird dwelt in their country. When I have promised big baksheesh, some came with tidings of a Shoe-bill, but I soon found out that what they had seen was either a giant heron or a lonely pelican.

On my fourth trip I succeeded at last in seeing and killing one on Lake Kioga. They were not rare there, and I used to see some every day in the marshland. It was hard to approach them, for even in the lightest canoe and with the best paddlers we could only get through the "sudd" with difficulty. But these are the favourite habitat of the *Balaeniceps,* and I very rarely saw them in open places when fishing from the edge of a floating papyrus island.

It was terribly hot there and alive with mosquitoes, so I left as soon as I had shot the four Shoe-bills on my licence.

After I had reached the nearest steamer station, whither sixteen natives paddled me in a large canoe, I put up my tent and laid out the skins to dry in the sun. A German trader who saw them bandaged with paper strips thought they were crocodiles, and really the large beak of this bird can quite easily be mistaken for a croc's head.

THE GREY PARROT

Now I will make a bold jump from the noblest bird of the African swamps to the most interesting and best known bird of the forest. The grey parrot is known to us from our zoos and also as a pet. I will not describe its appearance, and I fancy everybody knows that it has the greatest capacity for learning words.

I did not come across this bird until on my fourth trip, because it can only be found in the western parts of East Africa, where the western rain forest zone is beginning. They brood and hatch in Uganda in the forests on the borders of the great western rain forests and they fly in parties or in pairs to the wild date forests on the banks of brooks. At sunset they return to their roosting tree, generally the oldest tree of the forest.

I liked to listen to the whistling chatter of parrots on my way out or back from my daily work. The couples seemed to discuss the events of the day, and their language is rich in its diversity of tones.

They fly over at a considerable height, but sometimes fog brings them lower down. Once I shot the male out of a couple flying on a foggy morning in the Bugoma forest. The female did not leave the dead body of her mate and fluttered round it talking to him. Then I swore never to shoot another grey parrot.

In East Africa and still more in Uganda the "kasuku" (the name the natives of the safari give parrots) is a very common pet. Every Indian "duka" (shop) has one. They get them from the

Congo, where the dwarf inhabitants of the forest, the hunting tribe of Wambutis, trap them with nooses made of some animal's hair. The natives of Uganda do not catch them, probably because they will not venture to climb the giant roosting trees.

The greatest fault in their talking is that they seem to pick up easily the most forceful expressions. But this is quite natural as such expressions are pronounced by all nations with a specially emphatic accent.

I met the most original "kasuku" near Hoima in the home of an Armenian who lived near the bara-bara (road) leading into the Congo. He had also a little coffee plantation, but did everything else but work on this plantation. His house was covered with papyrus and was a kind of caravanserai for the elephant poachers going and coming from the Congo and the Lado Enclave. They called themselves "gentlemen poachers," and it cannot be denied that most of them were gentlemen, notwithstanding the fact that they had been elephant poaching in Belgian Congo.

This "kasuku" was like a phonograph. He repeated every word he heard from these elephant hunters and never forgot what he had learned. One could die of laughter when he recited what he had heard perched on the shaft of some broken rickshaw in the sunny courtyard. He used some selected expressions on the police inspector of Hoima in various languages, which gave a lively picture of his popularity amongst the poachers.

On my third visit I was surprised to hear my own voice calling my boy with some Hungarian imprecations.

As a collector I dealt with every class of animal, from the big mammals down to microscopic organisms. But I spent most of my time collecting birds and because of this I got the name of "Bwana Ndege" (Mr. Bird) during my first trip, and this nickname stuck to me throughout all my African expeditions.

This part of my work was despised by the hunting or warrior tribes. They were always joyfully ready to accompany me big game hunting, but were far less keen to come on my bird-collecting trips. When I tried to engage men for butterfly and insect collecting, they refused to come at all, and I could only get one or two children, or else men from other tribes.

For myself, I can say that the excitement of collecting birds in an untouched region was just as great as big game hunting, and if I got a bird which was described in Reichenow's book as very rare (Professor Reichenow, *Die Vögel Afrikas*), or better still, if I thought I had got a "species nova," I derived the same pleasure as from shooting some fine specimen of big game.

Successful bird collecting is no easy task and needs great knowledge of the life and habits of birds as well as of the country. The collector must know when and where berries of certain trees and bushes ripen; which flowers bloom and which birds visit them. Some giant trees bearing wild fruit will be the meeting-place for diverse sorts of birds, and the collector must take advantage of these few days, for they disappear after the fruits are consumed, without leaving tracks.

Bird collecting is most difficult in big forests. Here one may search for hours amongst the thick creepers and dense foliage before one can see the bird whose voice has enticed one for so long. And then seeing does not mean securing! And how many are lost in the thicket after being killed, for it is very hard to find a dead bird in the thick undergrowth. On some occasions I lost eight out of ten and my men, armed with bush-knives, could only bring out two after a long and tedious search.

It was a happy day when I got a specimen for which I had been hunting for days and weeks. Sometimes it was only an unknown voice which awoke my interest and I had to make sure of the owner. It was one word more of the mysterious language of the wilderness which I had learned to understand, for the bird collector will be mostly guided by the chatter of birds in the forests. Through the daytime the forest is silent, as birds chatter only in the morning and before sunset.

I never could lift the veil of mystery off some sounds which I heard very rarely, although I spent days in searching. Many birds which I wanted badly I sighted when I was after elephants and had no shotgun. I also missed some very good chances at big game when I was bird collecting. This only proves how impossible it is to do two things at a time!

CHAPTER XXVII

Hunting Equipment and the Management of Trophies

I will not describe my hunting outfit of former days, but will tell you what I would take along now if I had the chance of going to Africa again.

I would certainly take a very accurate, high-velocity magazine rifle. This could be either a 6·7 Mannlicher-Schönauer or a 7-mm. Mauser. But under no circumstances would I use Austrian ammunition for the Mannlicher-Schönauer. On my last Uganda excursion, as mentioned in a previous chapter, I was not satisfied with it. This, by the way, is not only my opinion. W. D. M. Bell, the famous elephant hunter, discarded the Mannlicher-Schönauer because of the Austrian ammunition and took to the 7-mm. Mauser.

Rifles regulated and sighted for "S" cartridges are no good for big African game such as the elephant and rhino, and I do not consider them suitable for African huntings.

It is advisable to take as well a big-bore double-barrelled cordite rifle. The most common bore is now the ·500/·465, which is especially convenient, as you can get the ammunition for it in Africa.

This large-bore double-barrelled rifle is especially useful in dense forest or elephant grass.

The old-fashioned big-bore Paradox guns (4-, 8-, and 10-bores) are hardly ever used now. On our last trip amongst the sportsmen travelling on our ship there was only one who had a 10-bore Paradox, and it is very likely that he never used it at all. In the days of high-velocity rifles these heavy pieces of artillery belong to the past, not only because the effect of the high-velocity small-bore rifle is so much greater, but also because of their greater accuracy.

HEN OSTRICH

AN OSTRICH NEST LAID WASTE BY LIONS

FLAMINGOES OVER LAKE NATRON

CRESTED CRANES IN THE MIMOSA FOREST NEAR VICTORIA NYANZA

Collecting eggs of the *Scopus Umbretta*, a member of the Stork family

The African Grey Owl

WILD DATE PALMS IN UGANDA

WATERBUCK BULL SHOT IN ELEPHANT GRASS BORDERING THE BUGOMA FOREST

In case I would not be able to secure a double-barrelled cordite Express (these modern elephant rifles are exceedingly expensive), a 9·3-mm. Mauser or a 9·5-mm. Mannlicher-Schönauer would do very well instead. The latter only in the event—as with the 6·7-mm. Mannlicher-Schönauer—of D.W.M.K. or cordite ammunition being obtainable for it.

I would use a telescope sight only on the 6·7-mm. I only began using one during my last trip, and to be honest, I am rather sorry that I got into the habit. If I had to tackle dangerous game, the telescope quickly came off the rifle.

Of course only the best telescope sight ought to be used. Such a rifle must always be carried by hand, because the great heat and the shaking it goes through during the caravaning can influence the delicate cross wires with disastrous effects.

If I could manage it I would take two magazine rifles and a miniature rifle taking the "·22 Long" cartridges. Automatics have recently been prohibited in English colonies.

I would complete my outfit with one or two shotguns. For sport a 12-bore, because the necessary ammunition would not have to be taken out from home; but for collecting purposes a 20- or 16-bore would be better, with sufficient half-charge cartridges. I found these more convenient for small birds because a half-charge cartridge will do less harm from the same distance than a small-bore shotgun does with full-charge cartridges. Sometimes one is compelled to shoot from very short range and then nothing would be left of a little bird.

For the long sea journey the rifles must be well oiled and wrapped in oilpaper and then laid into their cases. I always let my gunsmith prepare my battery before shipping it.

Tins of 25 to 50 cartridges ought to be carefully sealed. For a hunting trip which, not counting the journey out and back, would last three to four months, I would take 400 cartridges for each rifle. Of this number 300 would be soft-nosed and 100 solid bullets. For the big cordite rifle I would take 150 cartridges, half solid and half soft-nosed. If the trip was to be of longer duration, then, of course, proportionally more ammunition would be needed.

Shotgun and ·22 cartridges can be had in Africa, with the

exception of the special cartridges, such as the above-mentioned half- and quarter-charge cartridges. I would take a large stock of ·22, because it is the best and cheapest cartridge for practice.

A big game stalker needs a very good field-glass. It is all the more necessary in Africa, where the sportsman is surrounded by a completely new and strange country and by unknown animals which show themselves in the most surprising ways. An African hunter cannot be imagined without good field-glasses.

During my last trip my gunbearer knocked my field-glass against a rock and made it useless and so I had to undertake my Bugoma forest excursion without a field-glass. I missed it greatly and suffered considerable losses in consequence. This sad experience impressed me with the necessity for taking a reserve glass along.

Nothing can give a sportsman in Africa greater pleasure than sitting on a hill-top or an ant-hill and from there observing the lives of free, wild animals. I would not miss this chance for anything and therefore I would not grudge the cost and would take two field-glasses in my outfit. They ought to have powerful tropical lenses with a magnification of six or eight diameters.

The water-bottle is also a very important part of the outfit and must hold at least about 3 quarts. I prefer an aluminium water-bottle with a felt covering and provided with a patent lock. A large bottle is essential, especially when elephant hunting, for one may have to spend the night in a waterless country. Many hunters, myself included, have had to forgo the chance of a fine bull when threatened by the most terrible thirst. On arrival in Africa it is a good plan to get a few canvas water-bottles as well, because water keeps so cool in them, although a certain amount is lost through continual oozing and evaporation.

A reliable compass is also a necessity even should one be able to obtain very good guides. Of course I do not mean a toy suitable to hang on your watch-chain, but a serious implement.

Traps are only required by those who are collecting for scientific purposes, and even then I would not take any lion traps as I would never have the heart to trap lions.

For an ordinary expedition I would suggest taking the following implements and chemicals for preserving trophies: one or two dozens of large skinning knives for the big mammals, and three small ones for birds. Three scissors and tweezers of different sizes for the same purpose. Six to eight pounds of natrium arsenicum to preserve the skins, which I have personally found to be far better than arsenical soap. Besides, huge quantities of this would have to be taken, for one lion's skin alone absorbs about 5 lbs.

Salt and alum required for preservation can be procured in any African town.

I can give the following advice for the preservation of trophies. Before starting the hunter ought to take some lessons in skinning from a good workman. There are some clever native skinners, but their work is only of value if the sportsman has sufficient knowledge to be able to control their work.

When I had no very reliable skinner in my service I always cut the skin of a lion or a leopard open myself and helped with the more difficult parts such as the claws, ears, eyes and nose, or at least I kept my eye on the men. I can only advise every sportsman to do the same, if he seriously values his trophies.

If our time for skinning was limited, we cut the head and feet off and finished skinning them in camp.

One must be very careful to avoid doing any harm to the roots of the whiskers of lions and leopards, as then the trophy will lose one of its most attractive features. I would advise the hunter to count these whiskers in the presence of his men, for many native tribes believe in their magic power and take them as "dawas."

One should not forget to cut out the clavicles of lions and leopards, which are quite rudimentary, as these are the "lucky bones."

On reaching camp the scraping of the skin must be begun at once. I always established my men under a shed or the shadow of some large tree and they sat around the skin scraping off the flesh and fat with well-sharpened knives, the more experienced doing the head and feet. The ears must be carefully turned inside out and the smallest pieces of flesh cleaned off as otherwise the hair will slip.

If this work is not completed by sunset—big hides, such as

a giraffe's, need a week's work at them—the skin must be liberally covered with salt, folded up and put into some "hyena proof" place. Next day the work can be continued.

When the skins were scraped enough I made my men rub in a mixture of three-quarters of salt and one-quarter of alum, and in very damp weather I put in more alum. The parts round ears, nose and mouth must be very carefully salted. I used to prick these parts with a bunch of needles bound together so as to ensure the salt getting well into the thicker parts of the skin. When this was done I painted the skin with a 5 per cent. solution of natrium arsenicum. Skins thus prepared should be placed if possible under a shed or a shady tree to dry—and never under any circumstances in the sun. The skin should be well stretched on a stretcher and the edge pegged all round with pegs about 8 inches long.

The more slowly a skin dries the better.

Lions' skins especially must be treated very carefully and not pegged down on the ground in the sun after the natives' usual custom. The majority of lion skins which are brought to Europe need the taxidermist's greatest skill, for when these skins are unpacked they look as if they had been attacked by white ants.

Speaking of white ants, I should warn the inexperienced that they often give one very disagreeable surprises. For instance, it is quite possible to wake up in one's hut one morning to find that one's best pair of boots has been eaten up during the night. It may also happen that when one throws a mackintosh over one's shoulder, half of it is missing and only ribbons hemmed with clay left. Once when the weather was fine I did not use my mackintosh for some days and by then it was gone.

If the trophies have not had a sufficient treatment with poisonous solutions they will certainly be attacked by white ants and so must be kept in a place which is not only immune against hyenas, but against white ants.

If we only want to mount the head and neck of some animal, we should make our cuts very low down in the back and chest, as the taxidermist will only then be able to mount it artistically.

The scraping and drying is carried out in the same way as already described.

If no salt and alum are available, clean ashes make a good substitute for the mixture described. If the necessary poisons (natrium arsenicum or arsenic soap) are not available one must take special care to prevent termits from getting into the skin.

One should never cut the horns of buffaloes or antelopes off the skull, because the trophies would then lose much of their value and appearance. The best way of preserving them is to scrape off the flesh, scratch out the brains and dry them in the sun. It is not advisable to boil them. If they are overboiled the bones will get loose on some parts such as the nose and fall away from each other. It is better to do the boiling at home in Europe.

These skulls drying make a dreadful smell and ought to be kept far away from the tents, but again care must be taken to prevent hyenas getting hold of them, for these fine smelling trophies will attract hyenas from miles around.

The horns should also be smeared with natrium arsenicum after being dried, and if this is not available, paraffin will do almost as well. If this is not done some kind of insect will get into the horns and bore holes, in which case the trophy will be ruined after a few months.

The foot of an elephant or rhino can be mounted and makes an interesting trophy. To do this the leg must be cut off and the flesh and bones taken out. This is a very hard and tedious work, but native skinners are well suited for such monotonous work, and if closely watched, will prove very useful and able. The complete cleaning out of an elephant's foot will take two or three days.

When it has been properly cleaned out it must be treated with salt and alum; then with poison, and finally it must be filled with wood ashes to prevent it from losing its original shape. It dries slowly and I usually left them in the hut of some native acquaintance and fetched them weeks later whenever I could do so without having to make too big a detour.

If one wants to make sticks and whips (kibokos) out of rhino and hippo hides, the best method is as follows: The underneath parts of the rhino and the back skin of the hippo only ought to be used. The skin must be cut in strips three fingers thick, and these leather ribbons hung on a tree with heavy weights attached to the ends and left there to dry.

Should any sportsman wish to bring back some skins of birds he will be well advised to take a few lessons in their preparation from a competent taxidermist before starting. A few native skinners understand how to skin birds, but the work can easily be learned by any sportsman.

Bird skins must be treated only with natrium arsenicum, and salt and alum should be avoided.

For the skinning and drying of feathers after washing I used potato powder which I took out with me, although sawdust will do as well, and I frequently used this too.

The bills, eyelids, and feet of the prepared birds should be smeared with a solution of natrium arsenicum to preserve them against mice and insects, and I have lost many bird skins through neglecting to take sufficient precautions in this respect.

INDEX

343

SKETCH MAP
TO ILLUSTRATE
MR. KITTENBERGER'S EXPEDITIONS.

Scale of English Miles.
0   50   100

London : Edward Arnold & Co.